The World is Black and White

Other books by Christopher Knight:

St. Helena

Ferocity

The Laurentian Channel

Bestseller

Season of the Witch

Pandemia: A Novel of the Bird Flu
and the End of the World

**Visit audiocraftpublishing.com
to read free sample chapters
and order on-line**

This book contains the complete
unabridged text of the original work.

An AudioCraft Publishing, Inc. book
published by arrangement with the author.

Front cover design and layout © 2008 AudioCraft Publishing, Inc.

AudioCraft Publishing, Inc.
PO Box 281
Topinabee Island, MI 49791

ISBN: 978-1893699-97-7

PUBLISHER'S NOTE
This is a work of fiction from cover to cover. Names, characters,
places and incidents are the products of the author's imagination or
are used fictitiously. Any resemblance to any person
living or dead is purely coincidental.

Printed in the United States of America

First Printing - August, 2008

Author's Note

I am grateful to friends who offered insight and feedback with this book: Ann Rowland, Suzanne & Brent Chapman, Ken Wright, Teri and Sheri Kelley, Kristin Tant, Terah Peek, Mary Durston, Lynn DeGrande, along with all advance readers and reviewers. Your comments are appreciated.

My wife has always asked if I might ever write something other than 'that dark, spooky stuff.' All I can say is that I did the best I could. This one's for you.

Christopher Knight
July 4, 2008

The World is Black and White

Part One: First Step

The distance is nothing; it is only the first step that is difficult.

-Marquise du Deffand

1

Bay City, Michigan.

When I was ten years old, I found a quarter in the street. Someone had painted it black on one side and white on the other. I had no idea why it had been painted, but I was glad I found it. Instead of dropping it into the teeth of the nearest gum ball machine, I adopted it as my 'lucky' quarter. I took it everywhere. It worked, I guess. If I did well on a quiz at school, I credited my lucky black and white quarter. One time while fishing, I caught a thirty-inch northern pike, which could only have been possible with the little piece of extra black and white luck I had with me.

Over time, the paint faded and chipped. I was thirteen, I think, when I re-painted it. I used some paint that I'd had for one of my model airplanes. It worked great, and it must've been pretty good paint, because it never chipped again.

That was about the time I began thinking about how different the quarter was, being that one side was white and one side was black. They were the exact opposites of each other. And I would think a lot of the world was like that: black and

13

white. There were things that were right; there were things that were wrong. People got into trouble when they didn't do what was right, and that was the root of all the world's problems. Everything, really, was black and white. It was that simple. I knew this because I was a teenager.

And teenagers know *everything*.

o o o

About the time I found the quarter, I got another piece of dandy information: my parents weren't my parents. They were my aunt and uncle. Lacy and Bruce. My *real* parents had been killed in a car wreck when I was two; I had no memory of them. My baby sister and I had been schlepped off to live in Bay City with Lacy and Bruce. They didn't have kids of their own. When we found out our real parents had been killed, it didn't take too long to find out Bruce and Lacy hadn't been all that thrilled with becoming our legal guardians, regardless of whether we were flesh and blood. That's a pretty shitty thing to find out, no matter how old you are. Oh, they never came right out and told us they didn't want to take us on, but after we found out the truth about our real parents, things began to click. We figured it out.

I never called them 'Mom' and 'Dad' after I found out they weren't my real parents. I called them Lacy and Bruce. Not even Aunt Lacy or Uncle Bruce.

Just Lacy and Bruce.

2

I ran away from home three days after I turned sixteen. Stole Bruce's car. He and Lacy were sleeping off a bender, and I knew they wouldn't realize the car and I were gone until the following day.

Both Lacy and Bruce are raging—and I mean *raging*—alcoholics. No shit. I mean, they're drunk *all* the time. Not just at night or on the weekends. All day *long*. They drink screwdrivers for breakfast, and they're tuned to the max all day. Lacy smokes like a chimney, too (unfiltered Camels, if that tells you anything), and she's got this really thick hack. Sometimes she coughs up blood. Her doctor says she's going to kill herself with cigarettes, if the booze doesn't do it first. She doesn't care. She drinks all day. So does Bruce. He's been on disability for years, so he just sits around all day and gets hammered. Lacy comes back from the bowling alley where she holds down a stool in the lounge just about every afternoon, and they drink together. They fight a lot, too. Not like fistfights or anything. Lots of yelling. They scream at each other like cats in an alley. Then, they get all quiet for a while. Later, they'll sleep it off. Usually, after they sleep, they'll forget they even had a fight. It's pretty pathetic. No wonder my sister ran away.

Ellen took off last year, when she was barely fourteen. She says our other uncle—Bruce's half brother, Phil—tried to get frisky with her. She told Lacy and Bruce. Bruce was mad as hell . . . at *Ellen*. He said it was *her* fault. I mean . . . can you *believe* that shit? He told her she dressed real slutty-like half the time, showing off her belly-button ring, shaking her ass and things like that, and it would be only natural for a man to behave that way, being that she was trying to show it off so much. My sister is really pretty, too. All my friends wanted to come over a lot just to see her. She dressed in pretty skimpy clothing, I must admit, but she wasn't a sleaze at all. Guys thought she'd go all the way, and they try. All the time. But she won't let them. We got along okay and all that, but we weren't ever what I'd call 'close.' I think the only thing we had in common was the fact we had to deal with Lacy and Bruce's constant drinking.

o o o

Growing up, we just thought they were normal. I had no idea Lacy and Bruce were so fucked up until around the third grade. There was this kid who lived on our block. His name was Robbie Sinclair. He was an okay guy. We would catch turtles at the creek together. Both of us were great at catching anything like that: turtles, frogs, toads . . . anything that hopped, crawled, or tried to get away. Robbie, he would catch a dozen frogs and put them in the pockets of his sweatshirt. He could keep them there, too. He was *that* good. At school one day, I asked him if he wanted to come over for a game of checkers. He said his mom and dad told him not to go into our house, because my mom and dad (meaning Lacy and Bruce, of course) were elkies. I thought he was talking about the *animal*. Elks. I really did. Well, come on . . . I was in third grade. I thought that 'elkies' was, like, the plural form or something. I told him they weren't elkies, they were humans, just like his mom and dad. Robbie said his mom and dad told him they were elkies and they were dangerous, because elkies do things without thinking. Bad things, too. When I got home, Lacy was in the kitchen, smoking and doing a jigsaw puzzle. It was one of those mountain scenes with a billion pieces. She'd been working on it for a month. (Drunks should *not* do jigsaw puzzles, if you're wondering.) Bruce was in his chair, watching a rerun of a show called 'Sanford and Son.' I've never seen one episode, but I can pick out that one black guy's voice anywhere. He's funny, I suppose, in a funny-black-guy sort of way.

I told Lacy and Bruce that Robbie's parents told him they were elkies. I had to talk loud, because I had to speak up over the television.

"That kid's a fuckin' little shit," Bruce snarled. He never looked up from the TV. "I don't want you hangin' round with that little shit no more, ya hear?"

I didn't say anything. Even in third grade, I'd learned not to disagree with anything Lacy or Bruce said. Especially late in the day, when they'd had a few good hours to get oiled up. I still hung out with Robbie after that, but he never came over to our yard. And I certainly didn't invite him inside our house. God knows what Bruce would have done. Oh, he wouldn't have done anything to hurt him. Bruce wasn't like that. But he could scream up a storm, he could. Hell, yes. He would have scared Robbie half to death and probably called his parents a bunch of names. After fifth grade, I didn't hang out with Robbie anymore, and he never again set foot in our yard. Most of my friends were like that. Most of them didn't want to hang around our house if Lacy or Bruce were around.

3

When Ellen took off, she didn't say good-bye to anyone except me. She probably e-mailed a friend or two, but no one else. I remember the night she came into my bedroom. It was around midnight, but I was still wide awake. I'd been trying to sleep, but I was too worried about a damned test in biology class. I never really applied myself at school, and I hardly ever studied. I remember my guidance counselor calling me into the office in sixth grade, telling me I had tested well and had a higher than average IQ, that I was a pretty smart cat and could have a decent future, but I was blowing it by not paying attention or putting forth much effort. He went into the whole bit about how, if I put some elbow grease into my studies, I could get into any college I wanted. But I didn't have plans for that, and I still didn't see the point of studying something that was boring. He was a nice guy and all, and I knew he really was trying to help me. But, like I said: I knew everything. Black and white, just like my lucky quarter.

o o o

Ellen came in that night and closed my bedroom door behind her. She had just turned fourteen a couple of months before. All she was wearing were her U of M sweats and her bra; I could see pretty good in the moonlight. She was thin, but her boobs were starting to get bigger, I noticed. Of *course* I noticed. I mean, she's a girl, and all that. But she's also my *sister*. She was cute, yeah, but as far as being attracted to her? No way. They make jokes about shit like that in those backwoodsy hick towns. I suppose those kind of things, incest and all, go on everywhere. You just don't hear about it much. But my sister, she was sure getting sexy as hell, if a brother could notice in a brotherly sort of way without anyone thinking he was a pervert. I couldn't blame my friends for wanting to come over all the time (when Lacy and Bruce weren't around, of course) just to get a look at her. I was kind of proud like that. I know it might sound weird, but it's the truth.

o o o

Anyway, Ellen was sniffling and carrying on and all that, really quiet-like, and I sat up in bed. She sat down next to me and hugged me tight and cried really hard into my shoulder. I didn't say a thing. I just let her cry. I didn't know what was wrong. Earlier, I'd heard her arguing with Lacy and Bruce, which was something she didn't do very often. Neither of us did, really. It was pointless.

After she'd pretty much cried herself out, she told me about Uncle Phil trying to get at her. She said he came into her room the night before. See, Uncle Phil was as much of a drunk as Lacy and Bruce. Once in a while, the three would get together and play cards. Uncle Phil's got this scorpion-like way about him, though. He doesn't look like someone you'd trust, but up until then, I never had a problem with him. I don't know what it is about the guy. He's just got a greasy look, and his eyes don't

19

seem to work the way most people's eyes do. When he's drunk, he's about as predictable as a cheap bottle rocket. Sometimes he laughs and is funny; other times he gets so angry his eyebrows knit together. And when he's really tuned, he becomes catatonic, like an autistic scarecrow. Regardless whether he's toasted or not, when you're talking to Uncle Phil and he's looking at you, you can tell he isn't really paying attention, even though he is, in his Uncle Phil sort of way. It's like the binoculars are pointed at you, but the thing's out of focus. It's eerie.

o o o

Ellen told me Uncle Phil came to the house looking for Lacy and Bruce. She told him they weren't home, and he asked where I was. She didn't know. Then, Uncle Phil asks Ellen if he can come in and wait for Lacy and Bruce. She says sure, she's getting ready to go to a friend's, offers him a beer and all. Uncle Phil loafed around for about an hour, watching television, farting, and drinking beer. Drank eight beers! In an hour! Can you believe that? *Lacy and Bruce* couldn't drink eight beers in an hour. Oh, they probably could, if they were beer drinkers. Bruce's more into the hard stuff. Lacy, too. But they always have beer around.

So Ellen says she's in her room, trying to decide on a sweater: the red one, the yellow one that's cut low, or the fuzzy pink one with the fat turtleneck. Her door is open a crack, and she notices that Uncle Phil is peeking in on her. When she catches him, he knocks on the door and pushes it open a little. Starts telling Ellen what a pretty woman she was becoming. Takes a step into her bedroom. Ellen said she was a little nervous and all, but not too much. After all: it's Uncle Phil. Bruce's half-brother. A relative, of sorts. He says he's done waiting and is going to go home. Then (get this!), he reaches out and gives her a good-bye hug. He's *never* done that before, and

Ellen said it made her really nervous. Scared, even. Then, Uncle Phil put his hand on her rear end and held her even tighter. Then, he kissed her neck. Ellen pushed him away, but he copped a feel of her boob.

Ellen started to cry again, and I held her to me like an overprotective lion.

"He told me that he knew I liked it, Greg," she sobbed. "He was so *gross!* He told me he wanted to make me feel real good, like a real lady."

Ellen said at that moment the front door banged open, and in walked Kaylee Carmilly—one of her friends from down the street—who had a habit of not knocking before she came into your house, if she knew you well enough.

Well, Ellen said Uncle Phil backed right off really quick-like, and stepped out of her bedroom just as Kaylee started coming down the hall. That's what saved Ellen. She was sure something would have happened if Kaylee hadn't shown up at that moment. But the worst of it was when she told Lacy and Bruce, and Bruce gave her that line of shit about her deserving it, that she dressed like a slut, and she was probably teasing Uncle Phil, anyway, and he probably hadn't meant anything, he was just paying her a compliment.

o o o

So my sister tells me she's running away. She says she can't take it anymore, that she and a friend from school are splitting to Florida. This friend has a car, and they're going to go down there and get jobs. She said there were lots of jobs in Florida.

I tried to talk her out of it. I told her it would be dangerous, that there were all kinds of freakazoids out there.

"And they're a lot worse than Uncle Phil," I told her. "Jesus, Ellen . . . don't you read the news? Aren't you *scared?*"

"I'm scared staying *here* anymore," Ellen said quietly. "It's just getting worse. It'll never get better, Greg. You *know* that. Lacy and Bruce will never change. Not ever."

o o o

In a way, I kind of envied Ellen. She'd had enough, and she was going to do something about it. She had a plan. Sure, it might not be the *best* plan, might not be the *safest* plan, but it was a *plan,* sure as hell. Something to look forward to. For her, there was at least a *chance* of getting out of here. She'd finally had enough and wasn't going to take it any more. She was thinking of bigger and better things.

"But you don't have any money, do you?" I asked her. She shook her head. She was broke, like me. I had a little money—fifty bucks or so—but other than that, I was busted.

"No," she said. "But we have enough for gas money to get down there. We can sleep in the car. Lots of people do that. I read about it."

Wonderful, I thought. *She read about it. Now she's a travel expert.*

"Ellen, you're not going *camping.* You're running away. It's not going to be like Jellystone Park."

No matter what I said, I couldn't talk her out of it. And I tried. God, did I try. But Ellen had already made up her mind. I think, looking back, I probably wasn't all that convincing. I mean . . . I *tried* to tell her she was making a mistake, *tried* to tell her it was a bad move, that she should wait. Or, at the very least, go ahead and run away—but stay around town. That way, I could be around to help if she needed anything. But something told me Ellen's idea wasn't all that off-base. After all, what did she have to look forward to around here? Lacy and Bruce were pretty much broke, and they'd never help her with college . . . which is what she wanted. Ellen wanted to go to college and major in business. That's what she's always wanted to do. Own or manage a business. Even when we were little kids, when we played, she was always taking on the role of some store owner. When she was seven, her favorite activity was to pretend she owned an ice cream store, and she would give away free ice cream to everyone. I told her: "Ellie, if you *give* away ice cream, you're not going to make any money. You're going to go out of business." She just smiled and laughed. She didn't understand, and she didn't care. She owned a pretend ice cream shop, and she gave away free pretend ice cream. Everybody loved her. And she loved it.

o o o

I told her I would miss her, and I dug out all the money I'd stashed in my top drawer. She didn't want to take it, but I made her. I figured she'd need it a lot more than I would. She gave me a hug, a really good, long squeeze, and said she'd miss me, too. I tried once more to persuade her, but I could tell her mind was already made up. About an hour later, I heard the front door click quietly shut. Ellen was gone.

On top of all that: I failed that fucking biology exam the next day.

4

It was a phone call, one year later, that made me do the same thing my sister had done. I hadn't spoken to Ellen since she'd run away. I'd been worried, because she hadn't called or written or anything. No e-mails, nothing. She'd left a note for Lacy and Bruce, saying she was running away and why. They called the cops, of course, but even *they* said there wasn't really much they could do. Runaways are a dime a dozen. They said she'd probably come home on her own after things didn't work out. If anything, Lacy and Bruce drank more. It didn't take long for them to drop the whole issue. In their eyes, Ellen was gone, and that was that. It was *her* fault that she left, her decision. That's what *they* thought, anyway.

Me? I missed Ellen like hell. I was really worried. I kept hoping to hear from her, hoping for a phone call, for something. I had dreams where I saw her face on the side of a milk carton. In the dream, I was holding the milk carton, looking at her pretty, smiling face. Only, right behind her stood Uncle Phil, grinning like a viper, and his hand was reaching around to cup her breast.

But, if anything, Ellen is smart. She really is. I kept

telling myself she was probably working at a high-end clothing store during the day and waiting tables at night. Ellen was never afraid of hard work, no way.

And I kind of envied the fact that she would be in Florida, where it would be warm and sunny all winter, as opposed to the cold and snow of Michigan. Myself, I hate the cold weather. When winter's high tide comes in, the state gets shitloads and shitloads of snow. In the forest, it's probably really pretty, covering trees and all. But here in the city, it makes everything gray and nasty and stale. The buildings become cold and lifeless. The sky is drab and dreary. The wind is ill, and its chill is as caustic as bleach. I wouldn't go outside in the winter if I didn't have to. I sure could in Florida, if it was seventy degrees or something. I would go to the beach every day. I would love the warmth of the sun, the swaying palm trees, and the smell of the salty ocean. I'd love to spend some time there.

Turns out, I'd get my chance a lot sooner than I thought.

5

The phone call that made me decide to run away was from Ellen, of course. Lacy and Bruce weren't home, and I was reading some lame book—*Last of the Mohicans*—for school. Don't get me wrong: I like reading. I can't figure out why so many people don't read. But a lot of books I'm supposed to read for school I just can't get into. *Last of the Mohicans* was one of them. I couldn't get past the first three pages (sorry Mr. Cooper). I remember reading the first paragraph and thinking, *I've got to go through five hundred pages of this shit?* No way. On the other hand, my whole class read *Lord of the Flies* in sixth grade. Now, there's an awesome book. I've read that one twice.

o o o

I was in my bedroom reading when the phone rang. We don't have phones with caller I.D., so I had no clue who it was.

"Hello?" I said as I pressed the phone to my ear.

"Greg? It's *me*."

Ellen.

"Ellen? Jesus! Where are you? *How* are you?"

"I'm in Florida. I'm in West Palm Beach." She sounded tired, worn down and a bit frantic.

"But how're things? What are you doing?"

There was a pause. Then: "Things are . . . okay. I mean . . . they could be better. They could—"

And then she just lost it. Started crying, right there on the phone.

"Look, Ellen, what's wrong? What's the matter?"

"I . . . I need help," Ellen stammered. "I need—" I heard what sounded like a voice in the background, interrupting. Then, Ellen came back, her voice a hurried whisper. *"I'm at New World Peace Center. Be here on October 10th. You can't come any sooner than that. Or later. October 10th. It's a day for—"*

The line went dead.

"Ellen?!?! *Ellen?!?!*" I was almost screaming into the phone. I knew she was gone, but I was filled with an overwhelming helplessness. I hung up the phone. Then, I just stared at it. I stared at it for the longest time, watching it, waiting for it to ring again, ready to pounce like a fox hunting a mouse. I tried doing that star-69 thing, where you can call back the person who last called you. It didn't work.

Ellen is in Florida, in West Palm Beach. At New World Peace Center? *What the hell is that?* It sounded new-agey, like a place where people go to munch on herbs, do yoga, chant weird phrases, and channel the spirit of a village bread maker from ten thousand years ago.

Anyway, that was all I knew. Whatever had happened on the other end of the line, whatever was going on, she hadn't had time to tell me what was wrong. All she'd been able to give me was the name of some place and a date. October 10th. Nine days away.

o o o

My mind was spinning with hundreds of scenarios, none of them good. Ellen would be fifteen. She was fifteen and pretty, and a runaway in West Palm Beach, Florida. Prime target for a sleazy pack of wolves.

And what was *New World Peace Center*? Sounded churchy. Then again: maybe it was some place for runaways. Maybe she was safe there.

No, that's not it. There was too much fear in her voice.

o o o

So I really didn't have to think about it. I knew I would head to Florida and find Ellen. Crazy, I know . . . especially when I had no other information to go on. All I knew was that she sounded like she was in trouble, in West Palm Beach at *New World Peace Center,* whatever the hell that was. That's all I had. So what? I'd find her. Besides . . . I was doing nothing here anyway. Taking off had been in the back of my mind ever since Ellen left. Not a day went by when I didn't wonder about her. I always worried and wondered if things were better for her, if things were working out.

Apparently not.

o o o

I packed up everything I thought I'd need into a black duffle bag. I had an old, two-man pup tent I've had since I was in Cub Scouts. I brought that, along with a sleeping bag. A few shirts, shorts, jeans, a towel, toothpaste—shit like that. I had almost a hundred dollars in my drawer. I had a savings account, too, but there was only about twenty bucks in it. I kept my card tucked beneath a gel insert in my shoe, just in case I ever misplaced my wallet (which I've done before, on several occasions). If I needed to, I could withdraw some cash from an

ATM somewhere along the way. And, of course, I took my lucky black and white quarter.

o o o

It's funny. I never really thought twice about making off with Bruce's car. I just never considered any other alternative. I wasn't going to hitchhike, and I certainly wasn't going to steal someone *else's* car. Besides . . . stealing a car from a relative wasn't quite stealing, not really, when you think about it. Bruce's got a Pontiac Grand Prix that's only five years old. I still can't figure out how he afforded it. Maybe there was enough insurance money left over. When I was little, Bruce fell on some ice at a grocery store and sued. He wasn't even hurt, but he faked it really well. He settled out of court for about seventy-five thousand dollars; he and Lacy lost most of it gambling at Indian casinos.

o o o

While I packed, I couldn't get my mind off Ellen. She'd sounded so sad, so lost, so needy. It broke my heart. I worried more about her than Lacy and Bruce did. Oh, when she first ran away, Lacy and Bruce were pretty freaked. Lacy even stopped drinking for a couple of days. Didn't last long. She got the shakes really bad, but they went away when she started drinking again. Then, after a couple of weeks of not hearing anything from Ellen, Lacy and Bruce stopped talking about her. And you know what? Not once did they ask me if I knew where she was. Not *once*. I wouldn't have told them, of course. I would've just played the dumb-brother routine. The last thing I would do was rat on my sister. And besides: I really didn't know where she was. All she'd told me was she was heading to Florida with a friend. That doesn't tell anyone a lot. The cops, they asked me, of course. But I just played dumb. *Geez . . . I dunno. I got no idea where she went.*

o o o

My plan to make off with Bruce's car was pretty simple. Lacy and Bruce would be home around midnight, shitfaced. Probably have a few more drinks. Bruce might fall asleep in his ratty chair. He did that a lot. He'd make a drink and say he wanted to catch up on the news. Then, he'd plant himself in his chair and stare at the television like a catatonic clone. His eyes would be all glossy and glazed. Half the time I don't think he was even following what was going on. One night, he watched the Home Shopping Network for fifteen minutes before he figured out he wasn't watching the news.

o o o

Anyway, I knew Lacy and Bruce would be home soon. I put my duffle bag and the rolled up pup tent in my closet and climbed into bed. I could fake sleep. Hell, Lacy and Bruce wouldn't even check on me. Once in a while, Lacy would pop her head in my bedroom door before she hit the sack. But usually, if my door was shut, they knew I was home, probably sleeping.

I actually fell asleep before Lacy and Bruce got home. The electric garage door woke me up, and I was a little disoriented for a moment. I hadn't planned on sleeping, and I didn't think I'd even been that tired. My bedside clock said it was just after one in the morning, so Lacy and Bruce were a little later than usual. I heard the garage door close. Then, the door to the breezeway opened, and I heard them stumble into the house. Muffled voices. Turns out, Lacy *did* open my door and poke her head in, but I faked sleep and she closed the door. I figured I'd wait until they sacked out, then wait a little more so they were really zonked before taking off. The garage door would make noise, but I doubted it would wake them.

o o o

Two hours later, I picked up my duffle bag and pup tent and slipped into the hall. I felt funny, sort of, sneaking around like that. I'd done it before, of course. But before, I'd only been sneaking out for a few hours. Now, I was ripping off Bruce's car . . . and skating off for good. I even left him a note, telling him thanks for giving me permission to take the car camping, that I'd be back in a couple of days. I promised I'd take good care of his car and all that. See . . . I knew he'd find the note in the morning, and he could never remember what he'd done or said the night before. He was too shitfaced. I laughed out loud while I wrote the letter. I could almost see him standing in the kitchen in his white boxers and T-shirt, reading my note and scratching his head, wondering: *Did I really give the kid permission to take the car for a couple days?* He wouldn't figure it out for a while; at least until the next afternoon. By then, I'd be in Tennessee.

Shit just never works out the way you want it, though.

6

Swiping Bruce's car was even easier than I thought. I was quiet enough and all that, but the garage door was kind of clunky and loud. Still, I was pretty sure it wouldn't wake Lacy or Bruce. Just to be safe, however, I didn't start the car right away. Instead, I put it in neutral and pushed it out of the garage. Then, I ran to the driver's side door and leapt in. It rolled down the driveway to the road, and I had to fight to turn the damned thing. I forgot that since the engine wasn't running, the power steering didn't work.

o o o

I managed to get the car onto the road without smashing into anything. I started her up, put 'er in drive, and off I went. I looked back at my dark house, and all of a sudden I had a thought. I don't know why it popped into my head at just that moment. Once in a while, shit like that happens. You're going along, doing something, then all of a sudden you get a totally different thought that seems to come from out of nowhere. That's what happened. I was looking in the rearview mirror at our dark house, all sharp angles and mysterious shadows. The streetlight gave everything a dusty white glow. Suddenly, I saw my friend, Robbie, from years ago. Of course, he was only in my mind, he wasn't *really* there. But it was him, as a third grader. He said one word, and my God . . . it sounded so real I flinched. It was like he was right next to me. Then, he popped out of my head like a burst bubble.

I looked at the road ahead, then glanced in the mirror at the dark house, fading as I drove off.

Elkies, Robbie had said. *Elkies.*

I never saw Lacy and Bruce alive again.

7

It was just past three in the morning, and the city was pretty desolate. A cop watched as I cruised through an intersection, but he didn't pay me too much mind. I wasn't speeding or swerving, and that's probably what he was looking for.

I passed Tyrone Whiting's old home, and that brought an avalanche of memories. He and his family have been gone for years, and the house has been vacant ever since. Tyrone was a great friend, and everybody loved him. He was just so damned *kind*. If you were eating in the lunchroom with him and he caught you eyeing something in his lunch box, he would give it to you. No . . . not *give*. He would *insist*. He was just like that. Anyway, I'd go over to Tyrone's place, and his mom was a big, round lady. Two hundred pounds of love. Every time she saw me, she would light up like a neon sign. I mean, she would just *beam*. Looking back, I think she knew Lacy and Bruce were elkies, and she probably felt sorry for me. When she saw me, she would spread her arms wide. "Gregory Chappell, come give this momma a hug!" she would say, and she would squeeze me until my sides split. I really liked her. She was always pumping me full of cookies and lemonade. She always told me I was welcome in their home anytime, anytime. Mr. Whiting was really great, too. He worked at Delphi and had a Good Job. Tyrone said his dad liked the job because the money was good, and he got Good Bennies. I hadn't a clue at the time what 'Bennies' were. I asked Tyrone and he just shrugged. He thought they were some kind of shoe.

Then one week, they just up and left. Moved away. I never got a chance to say good-bye to Tyrone. A couple of years later, I found out they'd moved on account of Mrs. Whiting got sick really quick, and they had to go to another city where there was some special hospital. Mrs. Whiting died. I found out about it at school, in Mr. Keebler's class. I overheard a couple of other kids talking about it; apparently, someone's mom had kept in touch with the family. It was all I could do not to cry. I don't know how I held back the tears, but I did. Until lunch time, that is. Then I went out onto the playground and cried my eyes out. A teacher found me—Mrs. Beal—and she asked what was wrong. I told her. Well, she sat right down on the ground next to me and held my hand. She was really nice. She said everybody, no matter who you are, has problems to deal with. The trick is in how you deal with them. She said Tyrone had a good family, and what happened was tragic and all that, but good families know how to stick together to make the best of things. She said she knew it might not be too comforting to know, but maybe just the fact that I was crying was helping me. It's good to care about people, she told me. It's good to care about them and love them and be hurt when bad things happen. And it's good to help them when you can. Everybody, she said, even me, was going to have their share of problems. You just gotta stick it out and work through them.

o o o

That brought on a whole new slew of memories. Mainly,

Ellen and me, growing up. I remembered when she fell off her bike and I carried her—best I could for an eight-year-old—into the house. She didn't need to be carried, but she'd banged her head and was bleeding and screaming bloody murder. Another time I got stung by a yellow jacket—it was my fault, as I'd been tossing rocks at a large, gray, paper nest—and Ellen ran inside to get Lacy and Bruce. She was screaming at the top of her lungs. "Greg's dying! Greg's dying! He got bit by a bee, and he's *dying!*" She really did think it was all over for me. I did, too. That thing really hurt. It didn't stop me from throwing rocks at beehives, not in the least. But I sure as hell learned to be more careful about it. And how to aim better.

○ ○ ○

I started getting really depressed and all, thinking about Ellen, so I turned on the radio and spun across the dial until I found a rock station. Wheelz 104.5 was playing Nickelback, and I tapped my fingers on the steering wheel.   I headed for I-75, which is the interstate that runs north and south through Michigan. All the way to Florida for that fact, which was lucky for me. I've never been to Florida, and if I was going to drive there, I wanted the easiest possible route.

When I got on I-75, my whole attitude changed. I'd been wondering all along what I was *really* getting myself into. Wondering how this whole thing was *really* going to end up. Wondering if I really *was* doing the right thing, but, at the same time, knowing I had to do *some*thing. As I sped up to a smooth seventy-five miles an hour and flicked on the cruise control, I resolved to do one thing: stop thinking about Lacy and Bruce so much. I was leaving them behind. Whatever shit Ellen was dealing with, whatever problems I was going to face, I was going to do it without Lacy and Bruce. I wasn't going to blame them for anything, I wasn't going to think unkindly about them. I knew that would be hard, but I made a mental note that whenever I caught myself thinking badly about them, I would think of something else. I had nothing to gain and probably a lot to lose. Besides: I had other shit to worry about.

Like finding Ellen.

8

I drove a couple hours before I started to get tired. That's a crappy feeling. When you're really sleepy, it's not very smart to get behind the wheel of a car. I figured I could find some out of the way place not far from the highway and set up my tent. Or, at the very least, sleep in the car if the weather was shitty. So far, though, the weather was holding out. It was early October, the time of year when temperatures dropped in Michigan. So far, though, it was still pretty warm. Warmer than usual, anyway.

o o o

An hour after I'd crossed into Ohio I pulled into a rest stop. It was just after six. The sun was rising, and there was a smudge of dirty pink in the eastern sky. There were a few cars parked and about a dozen semi trucks. They were lined up like angled dominos. All of their running lights were on, lit up like yellow and red fireflies. Diesel engines chugged evenly.

o o o

I parked the car next to a big white semi truck.

Midwestern Logistics, Inc. was printed on the side of the trailer in big black letters. Its engine was revving, rolling high and low, flexing its iron muscle. I had no idea what Midwestern Logistics was, and I didn't care. I just knew I had to take a leak, and then I had to sleep. I would sleep for a couple of hours and take off again. I wasn't worried about being found out, as I was far enough away. Even if the cops were looking for Bruce's car at this very moment (which I was sure they weren't), they wouldn't be looking in Ohio. It would be a couple of days before Lacy and Bruce realized *by golly, that little bastard just ain't comin' back.*

o o o

I hopped out of the car, locked the door, and stretched. It felt good. I strode through the lot, weaving between semis. They were all running, and the smell of diesel fuel was nauseating. I held my breath until I made it across the lot.

Some guy was standing in front of a urinal, finishing up his business. He nodded as he walked past me, washed his hands, and left. While I had my turn, some other guy walked in, yapping on a cell phone. He made his way to a stall and banged the door shut. I heard his zipper and a ruffle of clothing, and all the while he chatted away on his phone. How can people do that? Can't they just hang up for a few minutes? What's wrong with telling someone, *'Hey, I'll give you a call back in five, after I take a healthy one?'* Nothing, that's what. But this guy, he kept right on chatting, and he was making some pretty loud body sounds. Thick, chunky ones, too. I had to believe whoever he was talking to *must* have heard. I almost started laughing right then and there. If one of my friends called me and I heard him making noises like that, I would hang up. Call me after the healthy one.

9

Sometimes when I'm really sleeping hard and I get woken up suddenly, I freak out a little bit. I think a lot of people do, especially if they're really sleeping deeply and find themselves suddenly jolted. I fell asleep on Matt Dunbar's couch one night, and he woke me in the morning by doing a belly flop on me. I'm talking one of those WWF bone-crunchers. Not only did it scare the hell out of me, it completely knocked the wind out of my lungs. Try waking up, confused, and not being able to breathe. It's not fun, trust me. When I finally caught my breath, I punched him so hard in the shoulder that it left a bruise for two weeks. Hell, no, I wasn't sorry. He deserved it.

o o o

But this time, I freaked because I woke up in the back seat of a car. There was a loud tapping sound—that's what woke me up. It took me a minute to remember I'd stolen Bruce's Pontiac, that I was at a rest area in Ohio. It took me another second to realize some girl was tapping on the passenger window.

"Hey, you wanna party?" the girl said.

I was still half asleep, and pissed off, too. I sat up. The clock on the dash glowed a blurry 7:14. I hadn't been sleeping long. The sky was lightening, but a mantle of steely, gray clouds hung like dirty drywall. And some girl—some lot lizard—is tapping on the window, asking if I want to party.

"No, get out of here," I said, and I laid back in the seat and closed my eyes.

"Come on," she urged, tapping on the window again. "You know you wanna. Fifty bucks."

I opened my eyes. "Just get out of here," I said.

"You got a smoke?" she asked.

"No," I snarled. "Leave me alone."

"Your loss," she said, slithering off without a sound.

It's seven in the morning and I get propositioned in a rest area, I thought.

I fell back to sleep.

10

I slept a lot longer than I'd wanted to, and it was the heat of the day that woke me, not any of the sounds from around the rest area. I seemed to have been dimly aware of the noises: trucks entering and leaving the rest stop, a stale horn here and there, splashes of voices spilling out. The sounds were very hazy in my crashing surf of sleep, and none of them woke me. It was the damned heat that did it. I awoke to the sun beating down, cooking the car. The interior of the Pontiac had become an oven, and I was its roast. I was drenched in sweat. My hair was sopping. I was clammy all over. Dizzy, even. I pushed the car door open and tumbled outside, holding the door open to keep my balance. It felt thirty degrees cooler, even in the sun. There was a nice breeze blowing, and that helped a lot. It felt good on my wet skin.

But my clothing was soaked, and I needed to get out of them. And I needed to get moving, too. I'd slept a lot longer than I thought I would, and I was behind schedule. It was past noon; no doubt Lacy and Bruce were awake and had discovered the Grand Prix missing. Bruce would be reading the note, quizzing Lacy, trying to remember. Now *that's* funny.

Still, I had to assume that maybe he *would* figure it out. Maybe he *would* call the cops. Maybe he was smarter than I thought. It would be best to get moving.

11

I wanted to get out of my sweat-soaked clothing, but I didn't want to put on anything clean until rinsed off. The rest stop didn't have any showers, but I supposed I could just wet a washcloth and wipe down. I've done it a few times, in a pinch. It sure doesn't give you that really clean, fresh-from-the-shower feel, and you don't want to do it if you're going out on a date or anything. But it works, if you've got no other options. Problem was, I'd heard all kinds of awful stories about rest stops on freeways. Guys looking for sex with other guys. That kind of stuff. I was a little nervous about stripping down in a rest stop, even if I was in a stall. I didn't want any part of some weirdo looking for a quickie.

o o o

So I said screw it. I got into the Prix and drove off. I figured I would stop at a convenience store, pick up a couple bottles of water, some food, and a map. Then, I could maybe find a lake or a pond or something. If I could find some place out of the way, where no one else was around, then I could just strip, take a dip, wash my hair, and dry in the sun. Just like a frog or a turtle. I was actually looking forward to it.

o o o

I'd gone about thirty miles when I saw someone walking on the side of the freeway, which I thought strange. People aren't supposed to walk or hitchhike on the freeway, and I hadn't seen any broken down cars anywhere.

Then I could see that it was a girl. As I passed, I recognized her as the lot lizard that had been tapping on my window earlier, trying to drum up some business. And it looked like she had a bruise on her cheek. She was carrying a purse, only it was bigger, almost the size of my duffle bag.

Yeah, you're right: I stopped. Of course I did. I should've just kept going, but I didn't. I figured the least I could do was give her a lift to the next off-ramp or something. People shouldn't be walking on the freeway like that. Especially women or girls. Too many freaks on the loose. I read somewhere that at any given moment, the FBI is tracking something like one hundred serial killers in America. No shit. Think about that: right now, there are at least one hundred people the FBI knows about, doing nothing but planning to rape and torture and murder someone. *That's* fucked up. Like I said: people shouldn't be walking on the freeway. Especially women.

o o o

Well, the lot lizard wasn't in a big rush to get to my car, so I backed up until I reached her. I rolled down the passenger window. She wasn't going to stop. She was going to just keep right on walking, ignoring me.

"Hey," I said, "what're you doing?"

She glanced over at me and continued walking. "What'ja

do, change your mind?" she sneered. Not real ladylike, but, then again, I didn't expect high social skills from a girl who was willing to blow for cash at a rest stop.

And man—did she look rough. I guess I didn't get a good look at her early in the morning and all, but she had a bruise on her cheek and a small cut on her neck. Her mascara had run, and she was sweating in the morning sun.

Then, she came over to the window and leaned down.

"You need a lift?" I asked.

"What's it gonna cost?"

"Nothin'," I said. "I mean . . . I don't want anything. I just thought you might need a ride and all."

Then she opened the door, climbed in, and stared straight ahead. "Go, then," she said, and I pulled onto the freeway.

o o o

We weren't even up to the speed limit before she had her shirt off. I'm not kidding. She wasn't wearing a bra, and I could see everything. Her boobs were small, as boobs go. Teacups with pink nubs, that's what they were. Not that I'm an expert on boobs; not by a long shot. But I was wise enough to know that these were a little less than average, and I wondered if it was bad for business, having small tits. I figured if you're selling your body, you'd better have some prime product.

She caught me staring. "Get your eyes back on the road before you kill us both," she snapped as she pawed through her oversized purse. A little embarrassed, I quickly looked up and fixed my gaze on the freeway and the cars ahead of us. But I was still conscious of the semi-naked woman in the passenger seat. Out of the corner of my eye, I watched her pull out a fresh T-shirt and slip it on, and I was immediately more comfortable. I mean . . . it's not every day a girl just takes off her shirt in front of you, especially when you don't know her name. But just the way she did it made me feel odd. No doubt she was used to it, taking her clothes off in front of a man, and I wondered how many times she'd done it. She didn't look like she was too old, maybe in her early twenties. Still, I had a strange feeling, a premonition of sorts, telling me I was getting into something over my head. Maybe I shouldn't have picked her up. Maybe I should have just kept going.

"Where you headed?" I asked, my eyes trained forward. But she had her shirt on by now, and I glanced over at her as she slipped her seatbelt across and snapped it into the buckle.

"Where are *you* headed?" was her reply.

"Florida," I said.

She paused, contemplating. "Sounds like as good a place as any," she said finally, and before I had a chance to say anything more, she'd fallen asleep, her head resting against the passenger window.

12

She slept until I stopped at a convenience store, where she only stirred slightly as I pulled the car into the lot, parked, and killed the engine. Her eyes flickered and I asked if she wanted anything, but she was asleep again before I even finished the sentence.

Inside the store, I made a beeline for the restroom before cruising up and down the aisles. I was hungry, but I didn't want to fill up on junk food. I bought some jerky and a couple of sandwiches, as I figured the hooker was probably hungry, too. That was funny, when I thought of it. The Hungry Hooker. It sounded like the title of a book or a movie.

o o o

I grabbed several bottles of water and found a big road atlas—a huge, hulking slab of book with detailed maps of every state—for only five bucks. I placed everything on the counter and dug into my pocket. The girl cashier looked me up and down, then turned her nose away in juvenile contempt. I'm sure I was smelling pretty ripe. Matter of fact, I was feeling pretty ripe, too, and I wondered if the girl in the car noticed. All of a sudden, I was really self-conscious about my body odor and what other people would think. Man. I couldn't get out of that store fast enough. When the girl behind the counter handed me the bag, I sort of leaned out and took it, trying to keep my distance from her. I probably smelled as gamey as a fish dead for two weeks in the sun.

o o o

The lot lizard was still asleep in the car. Before I got back in, I opened up the map on the trunk and found a small lake a couple miles away. Lucky me. On the map, there was a picture of one of those little tents next to the lake, indicating it was a campground or picnic area of some sort.

So, that's where I headed. I got back into the car and quietly shut the door, so I wouldn't wake the hooker. Then, I headed out to find the lake, which was easy enough to get to. It was only a mile or so off the main road. There was a small picnic area, and a big white sign with red letters warned: NO OVERNIGHT CAMPING. No problem. I just wanted to rinse off and be on my way.

There was only one other car there, and it was some guy chatting on a cell phone. The great part was that there was a small hill with a clump of trees that provided some cover. From there, you couldn't see the lake from the small dirt parking lot. And there were no houses on the lake, either, which was a good thing. I didn't want to get arrested for public nudity.

o o o

The hooker was still sleeping. I cracked the windows a little, took the keys from the ignition, snapped up my duffle bag from the back seat, and quietly closed the door. She never stirred, and I had a horrible thought: what if she's dead? I didn't know anything about her. She might be some drug addict, and she might have overdosed. Then, what would I do?

I'm like that, sometimes. I start thinking of the worst possible things that could go wrong, the scariest scenarios imaginable, no matter how outlandish or farfetched they might seem. I guess I get it from television or the movies.

With that train of thought, I started thinking about all of my favorite television shows when I was a kid. I loved a lot of different shows, but there was something about television that didn't seem real. Even the sitcoms that were supposed to be accurate representations of 'real life' didn't seem truthful. I picked up on this at an early age, too. Even when I was little, I could see through all the garbage they fed us on television. I noticed they only had pretty girls and handsome guys on the shows and in the advertisements. And I noticed there were no fat people on television, either. All around me, in school and everywhere, I saw a lot of fat people. But you didn't see them on television. Or in magazines, either. It's almost like fat people don't exist in the world of TV and magazines. All the television stars and models—especially in commercials—seemed so perfect they weren't even real, with slender bodies, silky hair, and a nine-mile smile of blistering white teeth. I couldn't figure that one out. I mean . . . I couldn't give a rat's ass if anyone was fat or not. No difference to me. People come in all shapes and sizes. But it was so obvious there weren't fat people on television that it seemed to me like someone had made a conscious decision to keep them off. Oh, sure, there were a few. But not very many, compared to the population as a whole. And remember: I was a little kid when I was thinking this. I was in fourth grade—Mrs. Handel's class—and we used to do this learning exercise. What we would do was raise our hands if we had a really perplexing question, something we really wanted to know about, something we were curious about. We would discuss the question with the rest of the class. After all, someone in the class might know the answer. One time a girl asked where her grandfather went when he died, and we all talked about that for an hour. Everybody had something to say about that one. Most, however, agreed the girl's grandfather had gone to heaven and was spending his time doing what he loved to do most while he was alive. The girl said he loved to hunt deer, so most classmates agreed her grandfather was probably hunting deer in heaven. This was all fine and dandy until a kid raised his hand and asked where deer go when they die. That threw everyone for a loop, because it wouldn't make sense for a deer to die on earth and go to heaven, only to be shot to shit by the girl's grandfather. That would suck if you were the deer. I raised my hand one time and asked why there were no fat people on television. Mrs. Handel looked really confused, and I told her to keep an eye on television, and she'd see there were hardly any fat people in the shows, and none in the advertisements. Mrs. Handel assured me that yes, there were *large* (she never once used the word 'fat') people on television. But a couple of days later, Tony Miller, a kid who sat right next to me, came up to me in the playground. "You know," he said, "you're right. There ain't a lot of fatsos on TV."

"I know," I said. "I told you."

13

When I came back from my swim, the other car was gone. The hooker was sitting on her butt, legs crossed, facing the lake and smoking a cigarette. I felt a ton better, fresh and clean. I'd washed my hair and changed into a pair of shorts and a fresh T-shirt. I felt like a million bucks. I hung my towel on a tree branch, then sat a few feet from the girl and tossed my dirty clothes aside. Now that I was out of them, I really could tell how bad they reeked.

"I thought you were dead for a while," I said. Dumb, I know. But it's not every day that I strike up a conversation with a hooker. Come to think of it, I don't strike up a lot of conversations with anyone, unless I already know them.

The lot lizard didn't say anything. She just kept puffing away on her cigarette. It was kind of annoying, really, and I don't know why. It was as if she had this superior attitude, like she didn't have to talk to me if she didn't want to. Like I was kind of beneath her, or something. (Of course, in her line of work, there were probably a lot of guys beneath her. On top of her, too.) It pissed me off. But I didn't let it show. Instead, I asked her another question.

"Do you have a name?"

She blew a plume of smoke, and it was ripped away by the breeze. Then, she stuffed the cigarette into the sand. "Everybody has a name," she spat.

"All right," I said tersely, "then what do they call you besides 'oh, God,' and 'oh, baby'?"

"Fuck you," she snapped.

"I thought that was your job." (I know it was kind of a nasty thing to say, but Jesus . . . all I was doing was asking a simple question. Besides . . . what was she going to do? Get pissed and storm off? So what?)

I fully expected her to get up and leave in a huff, but she didn't. Instead, she drew her knees to her breasts, hugged her legs, and looked away. "Dawn," she said.

"I'm Greg," I replied, feeling a little victorious. "Howdja get that bruise?"

"Boy, you're a nosy little shit, aren't you?" she sneered. She didn't look at me. All she did was stare out over the lake. That pissed me off, too.

"Yeah, well, I'm the one giving you a lift. I'm just curious, that's all. Excuse me for living." Then I got up, walked to the car, and came back with the sandwiches and bottles of water. I didn't say anything to her, either. I just dropped the food and the bottle on the ground in front of her, retrieved my towel and dirty clothes, and walked back to the car. I popped the trunk and tossed the bundle inside.

"I'm not staying here all day," I said. I closed the trunk. "I can give you a ride, but I wanna get moving."

Then she turned and looked at me. For the first time, I saw something in her eyes that was . . . different. Up until now, she'd seemed so rough and tough. She weakened somehow. Like she'd been wearing a mask and had let it slip a little bit. It was almost corny. I softened up a hooker with a ham sandwich and a bottle of water.

"Can you give me ten minutes?" she asked.

I just nodded. I was still pissed I guess, but it really wasn't worth the effort.

Dawn got up, walked to the car, and pulled her shirt over her head. I looked away. I heard her walk off, and when I turned back around, she was slipping over the hill topless, wearing only her jeans, carrying her large purse. I have to admit, even though she was a hooker and all, that was sort of a sexy look: slinking through the grass in her jeans, her bare back turned to me, her dark hair drifting down her shoulders. Here I was, sixteen, with only one sexual experience under my belt. Now I'm with a girl that slips in and out of her shirt like she's in a changing room at a department store, not the least bit self-conscious or shy about her body. I mean, when I finally did it with a girl a few months ago, it was her first time, too. We were nervous as hell. Lights off, and all that. And the condom was a pain in the ass. It took five minutes just to get the thing on, on account of it was so dark (and we'd never done it before). It was fun and exciting, sure, but I knew I'd need a bit of work in the sexual prowess department.

o o o

Ten minutes later, Dawn came back over the small hill. She was wearing shorts and yet another fresh T-shirt. Her hair was wet, clinging to her face. All of her makeup was off. She looked different, she looked her age. But she didn't look like a hooker anymore. She looked like she could be the girl next door.

"Ready?" she said, managing a midwestern, neighborhood-girl smile. More disarmament.

"Yeah," was all I said.

We got into the car and set off again.

14

We didn't speak until the car was back on I-75, headed south. I wasn't sure what I wanted to say to her. I was curious as hell, sure I was. I wanted to know a lot of things, but I wasn't sure if she'd be up for telling me. She seemed testy, but the sandwich and water seemed to have lightened her up a little, maybe nicked away at the chip on her shoulder. Finally, I just asked her where in Florida she was going.

"Depends," Dawn said. "Where are *you* going?"

That pissed me off.

"Look," I snapped, "why don't you just cut the shit, huh? What's your problem? Did you just wake up this morning and decide you'd just catch a ride and go wherever the driver was going?"

She smirked. "Something like that, yeah."

"Howdja get that bruise and that cut?" I asked, still not sounding very nice. I wasn't really thrilled with her holier-than-thou attitude.

"Some trucker got a little rough, that's all."

"That's *all?*"

"It happens," Dawn said, reaching into her purse and

pulling out a cigarette. "Not that often, though. I guess it goes with the territory."

"And you put up with it?" I asked.

"I'm here, aren't I?"

I was getting more and more pissed by the second. "Do you have to answer everything I ask with a question of your own?"

"I don't know, do I?" she said with a smirk that dimpled her cheeks.

I thought I was going to about drive right off the damned road. Then, Dawn laughed and slapped my leg. "Hey, lighten up, lighten up," she said. "Shit. Are you always this uptight? And why are you so nosy?"

"I'm not always uptight," I bristled. "And I'm not being nosy. I'm just curious, that's all. If you don't want to tell me anything, that's fine." Man, I was really steamed. I mean . . . I was just trying to be nice and all, giving her a ride. I didn't want anything from her. I didn't even care if she chipped in for gas or not. I was going to Florida, anyway. If she wanted to ride along, fine. Happy to have the company. But if she was going to be a salty bitch for the entire trip, well, I was going to dump her at the next off-ramp. I'd have more fun chatting with the dashboard and listening to the radio.

"So, do you want the spiel?" she asked. She inhaled from her cigarette and blew a plume of smoke out the window, which was open about an inch. I didn't really want her smoking in the car, but at that point, I guess I didn't really care that much.

"What's the 'spiel'?" I asked.

"You know. The *spiel*. The shit I tell everyone when they ask the same thing you do."

"How about you tell me the truth?" I asked. "I'm not a customer. You don't need to treat me like one."

Something about that struck a nerve with her or something, and her mask fell again. She seemed to freeze for a moment, but when she realized I'd caught her reaction, her mask came back on. Not all the way, though. It's funny. I'd seen her naked from the waist up—tiny nipples and everything—but I was catching these glimpses of the real girl, the *real* Dawn, that she seemed to guard more than her physical body. It was *that* that she seemed to hide, a part of her she didn't want anyone to see for whatever reason. Her body might be an open book with a lot of crinkled, dog-eared pages, but the real Dawn was fully clothed . . . and wore a mask.

"Okay," she said. "Not a customer." She took one last drag on her cigarette before rolling the window down and tossing the butt out. She really shouldn't do shit like that. Some idiot in Michigan did that a few years ago and started a fire that burned half the county.

Then, she turned in the seat so her back was against the passenger door. She stretched out both legs and placed them on my lap like she was on a sofa. She stretched her right arm onto the dash and draped her left over the back of the seat. Kicked back, relaxed, right at home. Her mask was still on, I could tell. But not all the way. I was getting a little peek at the real Dawn, whatever the hell her last name was. Then she smiled, and she really *did* look cute. She did. Just for an instant, she had this really sweet, innocent look to her. It faded in and out as she spoke. Sometimes more, sometimes less, but a little bit of the real Dawn poked through. She spoke, and she didn't stop for almost an hour.

15

Turns out, Dawn was nineteen and not in her early twenties as I'd guessed.

"I was born in Chicago," she said. "Well, not really *in* Chicago, but just outside. Arlington Heights, that's where I was born, but I just tell everyone Chicago, and they get the idea. Nobody knows where Arlington Heights is, unless you're from there. Pretty ritzy area." She lit another cigarette, then cocked her head to the side and exhaled a trumpet of smoke that quickly cycloned out the partially-open window. "My mom divorced my dad when I was three, so I never knew him. She said he was a real hosebag. Cheated on her a lot, I guess. She took me and we moved to Indianapolis. We didn't have a lot of money. She got a job, but the company went belly up, and we had to move again. This time, we moved to London."

I glanced at her, thinking that moving from Indianapolis to London was a hell of a move, which sparked a lot of questions I didn't ask, like, *How did your mom just up and decide to move to London?* and if she didn't have a lot of money, *How did she scrape together enough cash to move there?*

Seeing my questionable expression, Dawn laughed.

"London, *Ohio*," she said. "It's southwest of Columbus. Not a big town at all. Mom got a job there working at a furniture store. Sales, stuff like that. Plus, she worked part-time cleaning houses and offices. She didn't do too bad. Mom worked hard. It was just the two of us, so we didn't need a lot of money to get by. I really liked it there. The school wasn't very big, and I had a lot of friends. I've always made friends pretty easy."

She went on and on about certain friends at school and included lots of details, which got a little boring. But she seemed to enjoy carrying on, so I just let her spew it all out. She told me about her cat, Beanie, that she had for eight years, and how she almost committed suicide when the animal had been hit by a car and killed. Dawn said she was only thirteen at the time, but she said it was the worst thing that happened to her in her whole life. Even to this day. She also told me about a few of her boyfriends, what they did, where they went, how she broke up with them or they broke up with her. I remember thinking she's lived a lot in her nineteen years . . . certainly a lot more than my sixteen. We were only three years apart, but it felt like ten. It was fascinating to listen to her. She said in high school she was a prankster and was always getting into trouble with some of her practical jokes.

"One time, me and my friends found this mannequin in a dumpster behind this one store," she said. "They were chucking it out. Well, Tina Mitchell thought it would be fun to put some clothes on it and put it face-first on someone's front yard. This was right around Halloween, and we thought we might put a knife in its back. You know—make it look like a murder. We waited until after midnight this one night, then carried the thing to someone's yard—we didn't know who. But there was a car in the driveway, so we figured someone was home. Me and Tina and Jimmy poured three bottles of ketchup on the mannequin's back, all over the grass, on the knife. I mean—it looked gross! Well, the next morning, we found out there was an old guy that lived at the house, and when he went outside and saw what he thought was a dead body, he had a heart attack! I mean, a real *heart attack!* Holy shit, were we *scared!* And we felt awful, too. I pictured this guy, you know, going outside to get the morning paper and finding what he thought was a dead body on the lawn. Know what happened? He keeled over right there, on the grass, not five feet from where we'd put the dummy. One of the neighbors finally saw the two bodies and called 911. I guess it was quite a scene. At first, the cops thought they had a double homicide on their hands. Of course, once they found out one of the bodies was a mannequin, that confused the *shit* out of them. They didn't know *what* the hell was going on. It made the paper and the local television news. Good thing was, the old guy didn't die. I would've felt even worse than I had. I felt bad about the whole thing for a long time, but I think it's pretty funny, now."

I had to smile at that one. In my mind, I could see the old guy keeling over. Sad, yeah, but it would have been a lot worse if he'd died. And besides: Dawn said they hadn't meant any harm. They'd just wanted to freak someone out, being bored kids and all. Sometimes, shit just gets out of hand.

o o o

I pointed to a *Wendy's* sign up ahead. "You getting hungry yet?"

"A little bit," she said, and she lifted her legs and straightened up in her seat. She'd been seated like that for almost an hour. She was like my own personal storyteller, and I found myself enjoying her company. But she never got around to the thing I really wanted to know: *How did you start hooking?* It was on my mind the entire time, since the moment I'd picked her up on the freeway. I mean, nobody just wakes up one day and says 'gee . . . I think I'll be a prostitute when I grow up. I'm going to fuck and make money.' I guess I can see it if you're a drug addict. I can see that real easy. Habits like that cost money. *Lots* of money. But Dawn didn't fit the bill as a druggie. If she was a doper, she hid it well. I figured sometime I'd get around to asking her how she started tricking, but I'd have to be sort of diplomatic about it. I already knew she could be a little touchy. Still, while she was giving me her 'spiel,' I could sense moments of openness, moments she probably hadn't shared with anyone for a long time. And she seemed a little lighter, a bit more congenial, after she'd been talking my ear off for more than an hour. Maybe spilling your guts to a total stranger is good for you, after all. Dawn didn't know me from anyone, but she'd probably told me more about her life than she'd told anyone in a long time.

16

After we ate at *Wendy's,* I started thinking about Ellen again, and the trouble—whatever it was—she was in. I thought about Lacy and Bruce, too. I hoped they were still trying to figure out my note, wondering if they'd really given me permission to use the car for a couple days. There was a chance they hadn't even called the cops yet, which was good.

It was now the middle of the afternoon, and we were approaching Cincinnati, and, beyond that, Kentucky. With any luck, we'd be in Tennessee by nightfall. Where we'd stay, who knew. I had my pup tent. Or we could sleep in the car. Dawn still hadn't told me where she was going in Florida, or what she was going to do. But she was along for the ride, and I didn't care. Matter of fact, I was enjoying her company, now that she wasn't being a total bitch to me.

o o o

But like I said, I started thinking about Ellen again, and that got me worried. She was in some sort of trouble, I knew she was. Then, I started thinking about Dawn and how she earned her living, and my worry for Ellen grew to something of a slithering, sleazy horror. I couldn't picture my sister doing what Dawn did, not in a million years. It would kill me.

Then, I caught myself thinking about Lacy and Bruce and remembered my promise to myself and started thinking of something else. Dawn had once again fallen asleep in her seat, and her head was leaning against the window.

o o o

The miles flew by. Rural Ohio passed by in a flurry of beautiful postcards, all glossy and picture-perfect. Dawn slept through Cincinnati and never woke when I stopped at the Doorville exit to take a leak and fill up the tank. Now, I'm not prejudiced against anyone in Kentucky—I'm really not—but the wood tick at the filling station was the most homey, red-necky dude I have ever seen in my life. In the first place, the outside of the filling station was a dump. It looked like a junkyard: jacked-up, rusting cars and trucks, dismembered and left for dead. I was going to turn around and head on down to the next exit, but I was *really* getting low on gas, and I figured I might as well fill up now, being that I was already off the freeway. But man . . . what filth. What a pig-pen. I pulled up to the gas island and this big old country dude with filthy jeans and greasy flannel shirt came lumbering out of the station like a cement truck with a loose wheel. His hair was scraggly, and he had a beard like one of those guys from ZZ Top. But he was about 300 pounds if he was an ounce. Those guys in ZZ Top are good-sized southern boys, but they'd look like Texas runts next to this guy. And he didn't smile. His mouth sort of hung open, and his teeth (what was left of them) were yellow and brown, rusting away like some of the cars scattered about. He didn't ask me how much I wanted in the tank, didn't even acknowledge me being there. He just lifted the nozzle, unscrewed the gas cap, and started to fill.

And I really had to take a leak. A dirty white arrow painted on the side of the building pointed to *HIZ* and *HERZ*, but I was already sure I wouldn't be using their fine public facilities. I thought I was going to need a shot of penicillin or some other antibiotic just *thinking* about how dirty the *HIZ* room was. I'd get an infection just breathing in the air.

Instead, I made my way around to the back of the building, made sure there wasn't a Mrs. Redneck (or any brother/sister redneck, for that matter) watching, and took a leak in the bushes. When I came back around, the redneck dude was still pumping gas, but he was staring—no, *gaping*—through the driver's side window at Dawn. A funny thought struck me: I'd bet anything Dawn at least had standards of *some* sort, and there was no chance in hell—not for a billion dollars—she would do this guy. I mean, cash is cash, but already I was beginning to get a sense of Dawn and how she operated. This guy would have a better chance with some sideshow carnival freak. Maybe he could get it on with the bearded lady or someone like that.

When he saw me coming back, he snapped up really quick and finished pumping gas into the tank. The bill came to thirty-eight bucks. At three bucks a gallon, cash doesn't go very far. I dug two twenties out of my wallet and handed them to him. He mumbled something that I understood to mean 'be right back,' but I wasn't waiting. Hell no. Some of that redneck shit might wear off on me, and I wanted out of there, pronto. As I pulled back onto the freeway, I made a mental note that, if I ever came through this way, Doorville, Kentucky was now scratched off the list of places to refuel and take a leak.

17

Somewhere between Doorville and Lexington I began thinking really hard about my life. A lot about what I'd done, who I was, and where I was going. Not in a physical sense, obviously. I knew I was heading to Florida to find Ellen and help her. What kind of help she needed, I didn't know. But I was on my way.

But mostly, I started to think about the directions my life had taken, and where it *could* have taken. I mean, every time you make a decision, it's like there's this great cosmic boomerang you let fly. Sometimes you don't see it right away. Sometimes, you don't see it at all. Often, the boomerang comes back and hits you right in the face. Earlier in the summer, Matt Dunbar, Heidi Snipes, Roxanne Shields, and I were in Matt's mom's car, headed for the beach. It was a perfect, hot summer day. Well, there was this car in front of us, going really slow. I mean, tourist-slow. Geriatric-slow. I told Matt, "Hey . . . pass this idiot." And he was just about to. He'd had his foot on the gas and was going to fly past the idiot at ninety miles an hour. Well, he didn't. Later, he said he didn't know why. There were no cars coming, it was a legal passing lane. He just said at the last moment, it didn't feel right. Well, not a second later, this car comes whipping out of a driveway and makes a right-hand turn into the oncoming lane. He hadn't even looked in our direction. He just made sure no one was coming from the left, not thinking someone might be passing or something, coming the other way in his lane. We would have hit the guy head-on. None of us had been wearing our seat belts. In a word: we would've been *screwed*. We wouldn't have had a chance. That's how the cosmic boomerang worked. Only that time it had just whizzed by us, so close we could feel the sharp breeze. Every decision you make has some sort of boomerang reaction like that.

o o o

I wondered what the boomerang had in store for Ellen. Running off the way she did was bound to send that thing into orbit. It was bound to have some mighty force when it came back. Oh, sure, it doesn't always have to be a *bad* thing. Like that guy who won the Powerball Lottery jackpot. He won something like one-hundred million dollars. He'd been out walking his dog one morning, and he passed a small party store. He claimed he'd never played the lottery before in his life. Didn't even gamble with playing cards or bet on a ball team. Yet, something that morning whispered in his ear. *Go buy yourself a lottery ticket,* it said. And he did. A couple days later, all of his numbers came up. He went from a thirty-three thousand dollar a year job to being a multimillionaire overnight. That's the kind of boomerang I could handle. I wish that one would come and smack me upside the head. Knock me unconscious, even.

o o o

Dawn slept on, like she'd been up all night or something. (Duh. She *had* been up all night.) I wondered who she was with. What kind of a guy sleeps with a girl he meets at a rest stop? How often did they do it? I figured she slept mainly with truckers, long-haulers that knew they'd never see her again. Geez, I sure was curious. I guess the whole sexuality thing had something to do with it, of course, but I've always been really curious, anyway. My curiosity got me in trouble more than one time, that's for sure. That's why I didn't want to come right out and ask Dawn a bunch of stupid questions she probably wouldn't answer, anyway. If she wanted to tell me, she would. Otherwise, it would be best to just leave the issue alone. You can't blame a guy for being curious, that's all I'm saying. But we'd both done our share of chucking that boomerang up into the cosmos, and I kept wondering when that thing was going to come back and take a swipe at one of us.

18

Along both sides of the freeway, I was amazed at how many huge billboards there were, advertising various shops, restaurants, motels, stores, and the like. It really is like a lot of clutter along the highway. You can't drive five hundred feet without seeing a dozen huge signs. Some of them, they try to be quite clever, but most are just big, colorful rectangles advertising businesses and services. Others are just plain silly. I saw several big black billboards with white letters. They had these little cutesy sayings. One was: *Don't make me come down there—God.* It was supposed to be a message from God, right there on a black billboard. Another one read: *Loved the wedding. Invite me to the marriage—God.* Silly. I mean, the message was fine, but it just seemed silly to think God would go around and put notes up on freeway billboards. I wonder if there were people who actually *believed* it was the work of God or perhaps men who just believed God had told them it would be a good idea to advertise His Word. Maybe the Virgin Mary appeared to someone in a vision and said something like, *'Hey, Bob, why don't you put up a billboard with some messages from God. If you don't, you'll have only thirty days to live.'* Which got me thinking about that crackpot preacher a few years ago who claimed God told him if people didn't donate a total of a million dollars to his church, then God was going to strike him dead. I don't know if he got his million bucks, but I never heard anything about him getting taken out by God. Even old God had his own boomerang, it seemed. And I bet when ol' God clocked you with his boomerang, you sure as shit paid attention.

o o o

Twenty miles north of Lexington, I began wondering where we were going to spend the night. That felt weird. *We*. Where *we* would spend the night. I hadn't been away from home for twenty four hours, and already boomerangs were coming back around, changing things.

Dawn woke up and stretched in the seat, arcing her back like a gymnast. "Where are we?" she asked.

"Kentucky," I said, pointing to the clock. It was just past seven, and darkness was crawling in like a hushed secret. "We're almost to Lexington. Ever been there?"

She shook her head and yawned. "Nope," she said.

Then, a thought: before I'd picked up Dawn, I was alone . . . meaning I would have to stop for the night to sleep. Or, at the very least, get a few hours' sleep, then head out again. Now that I had someone with me, *that* someone could drive. We could just keep right on going until I woke up. Then, we could switch. Sometimes, I'm just brilliant. Just brilliant.

That plan sounded fine with Dawn, but she was hungry and needed to find a restroom, too. I needed the same.

"Lexington is about twenty miles from here," I said. "Can you wait that long?"

"Yeah."

o o o

When we got close to Lexington, there were a billion places to exit. I hopped off at the one that looked easy to get back on the freeway. Turns out, there were several fast food restaurants, a small strip mall, a couple of gas stations, and an enormous truck stop with a big Super 8 Motel across the street from it. I figured Lexington was probably a central hub for a lot of truckers.

The truck stop looked like it had the most amenities. A huge sign in the front listed all of the stores. There was a Subway, a McDonald's, and a Dairy Queen all under one roof. Plus a gift store, a clothing store, a jewelry store (at a truck stop?), and a grocery store. Other features included shower facilities, a FedEx shipping service, and a refueling center. There were dozens of semi trucks parked and more oozing in and out like big metal worms. Even before I pulled into the lot, I could smell the thick, phlegm-like odor of diesel fuel.

I parked at a space in front of the strip mall and got out of the car. Dawn scrambled out and we both stood for a moment, stretching in the final rays of daylight. Dark clouds were bunching up tight as knots, and it looked like it was going to rain. The air was humid and pasty, and it was a lot warmer here in Lexington than it was in Bay City.

It was sort of funny: I used to think I'd love to travel to different places and see all the sights and things like that. I'm not very well traveled, so any place that was different used to seem interesting to me. I've never been to Kentucky before, and there was a time when I would've loved to visit another state and just hang out for a while. Check out the different trees and animals, do some people watching, learn a little bit about the place. My own little real-life personal Discovery Channel. None of that interested me, now. I couldn't have cared less about Lexington, or any other city, for that matter. I guess maybe it was because I had a destination, and I just wanted to be there.

o o o

I locked the car, and Dawn and I walked across the parking lot toward the strip mall. It sure seemed busy for the middle of the week. Mostly, it looked like truckers. I mean, there weren't hardly any families out and about, and there were only a few little kids. There was one mom carrying a big, white bag in one hand. In the other, she was holding the hand of her son, and man, he was really giving her a time. He wasn't doing much walking, so his mom had to sort of drag him along. He had a sucker poking out of his mouth and the candy-ball portion of it created a molehill bulge in his cheek. He carried a balsa wood glider in his free hand. He was waving the small plane around in wide figure eights, totally immersed in his own playtime-world, completely oblivious to the fact that his stubby legs were just barely moving. It was really comical to watch, and I wondered how long mom was going to put up with it. Maybe she just was tired of dealing with his shenanigans and just found it easier to pull him along. At least he was in his own little world and not screaming and yelling. But with that kind of attitude, she would have trouble later on. Man . . . if you can't control your kid at that age, he's going to play you like a fiddle anywhere he goes. I could imagine the kid in a restaurant, turning his water glass over and screaming like a banshee because he couldn't have ice cream. Mom, of course, would finally give in because he was making a scene and all that, and hell . . . it was *embarrassing.* So, she'd let him have the damned ice cream. He'd be learning lessons like that every day, and by the time he was all grown up, he'd be worthless. No discipline at all.

o o o

There were restrooms at McDonald's, but Dawn said we should hike down to the other end of the mall to the Subway.

71

She said subs and salads are better for you. I almost laughed out loud. Here's a girl doing God-knows-what with total strangers and she was worried about the food she was putting into her body. But, then again, she was pretty trim, so maybe it was working.

o o o

We didn't say anything else as we walked. Dawn yawned a couple of times and raised her arms above her head to stretch. She fiddled with her oversized purse. And I thought about the fact that while we were both really quite different, there were a lot of things about us that were the same. For instance, we both had pretty much everything we owned in small carrying bags. I gave up on anything I had at home, which wasn't a lot. When I took off with Bruce's car, I just figured I would be leaving all of my shit behind for good. I had a nice mountain bike I would miss. I would miss my computer games. We didn't have a computer at the house, as Lacy and Bruce thought they were a waste of time and money. But I had a few games, and I would play them at school or on my friends' computers. And I would miss my books, too. I only had a few dozen, but some of them were good ones. No matter. No sense in looking back anymore. I was sure Dawn would agree.

19

After we finished eating, Dawn and I sat in the booth, finishing our Cokes. I was trying to think of something really witty and smart to say, something to impress her so we could get into some good conversation, but she beat me to it. Oh, she didn't say anything all that witty. In fact, it wasn't witty at all. She just took a sip from her straw, set the cup on the table, and asked me a question. She didn't look at me while she asked it, either. She was looking around, scanning the restaurant. Only after she'd spoken did she look at me. Her question was this:

"So, what's *your* story, Greg?"

Like I said: nothing witty, but man . . . that's a question I could take all night answering. We could be on *that* topic until the sun came up. When I thought about it, I realized she knew hardly anything at all about me. I hadn't told her I was on my way to find my sister in Florida, hadn't told her about swiping Bruce's car. Nothing. Of course, she hadn't asked, either. Up until then, it had been me doing the asking.

o o o

I laid out all the highlights for her. The Cliff's Notes version. I told her I needed to find my kid sister, that she'd run away, and I was worried about her. I said I didn't know exactly where she was, but I knew she was somewhere in West Palm Beach. And you know what was funny? When I told her I was sixteen, she was stunned. Literally. She said she thought I was closer to her age. Well, three years' difference isn't all that far apart, and I wondered if maybe now she would treat me differently, like a kid or something. Maybe I should have lied and told her I was eighteen or nineteen. I wasn't looking forward to being treated like a kid brother for the rest of the trip.

And I didn't go into too many details about Lacy and Bruce. I didn't think it was all that important. Nor did I tell her I'd taken Bruce's car. That wasn't important, either. I just kept it to the nitty-gritty, as they say. After all—she'd done the same. I knew a lot about her life, but only up to a point. The whole business of how she became a hooker was still a mystery. And I wasn't going to ask her about her work schedule. So, she pretty much knew the basic facts about my life. I tossed a few tidbits in there about some of my friends, some of the parties and concerts I'd gone to. Not much else seemed important. Then, after we'd finished our Cokes, I dumped the tray's contents into the trash, set it on top of the garbage can, and we headed back to the car . . . only to find the great cosmic boomerang had made one of its high-velocity, high-impact come-arounds.

20

When we got back to where I'd parked the Grand Prix, this was the problem:

The car wasn't there.

We stopped and looked around, and it took a moment to really sink in for both of us. The realization didn't hit me all at once, but sort of pulled me down, down, down . . . until Dawn spoke.

"Somebody stole your fucking car."

o o o

I just stood there like an idiot, like some frozen dummy. I wondered if there was someone filming us at that very moment, like those practical joke shows on television. That's what I felt like: like we had been set up. At any second someone was going to come walking over with a microphone, laughing, and a smiling camera crew would follow. We would all have a good laugh, and I would be on television in a few weeks.

But those thoughts vanished really quick-like as I began to realize not only was the car stolen, but everything in it: my duffle bag filled with clothing, my sleeping bag, my pup tent. And my money. I had ten dollars on me, but the rest of what I had—about fifty dollars—was in my wallet in my duffle bag. I was in Lexington, Kentucky, and the only things I owned were the clothes I had on and the ten bucks in my pocket.

o o o

"Shit," I said, which was the understatement of the year, considering the mess I was now in. There was nothing I could do. I couldn't call the cops, because I'd stolen the car from Bruce. I looked around in desperation, hoping to catch a glimpse of someone pulling away in the Prix. Which was silly, I know. What was I going to do . . . run after it? Chase it down? Nope. I was shit out of luck.

I tilted my head back and stared up into the dark sky. This whole thing was so messed up. I closed my eyes, wondering what to do. It was that 'rock bottom' feeling that everyone gets from time to time. Sometimes, it's not all that bad of a feeling. Other times, like now, it's *terrible*. You try to realize you're at that point, rock bottom, and know things can only get better, you can only go up. But I wasn't so sure. Maybe things could get worse. Maybe they could get a *lot* worse. I hadn't a clue.

Dawn, however, took the whole thing in stride. She didn't seem the least bit surprised, and it made me mad. I don't know why. I guess I don't know how I expected her to react. Maybe say some nasty things about the crooks or something. Or get all frustrated and pissed and all. She didn't. She just looked around, placed her hands on her hips, and nonchalantly said: "Man, that really *sucks*."

Then I was *pissed*. "Sucks?!?! *Sucks?!?!* What are you talking about?!?! Somebody stole my uncle's car! They stole it, and it had all my shit in it! I don't have *shit* anymore! How am I going to get to Florida without a car?!?! How am I going to get *anywhere?!?!*" I reached into my pocket, pulled out the ten dollar bill, and threw it into the air. Then, I dug into my left pocket, pulled out my black and white quarter, and threw it violently to the pavement. It made several harsh tinging sounds, like a bullet ricocheting off a pan. Then, it finally came to rest, white-side up. I pointed at it the way an accuser points at a felon. "That's all I've got to my *name!*" I shouted. "Ten lousy, stinking bucks and my not-so-lucky quarter! It won't buy me *shit!*"

I stopped when I saw the expression on Dawn's face. Or, rather, the *lack* of expression. Actually, she looked bored, like she was only being polite, waiting for me to finish. That pissed me off even more, and I knew she wouldn't have treated me that way if I was older, closer to her age. She was giving me the younger kid treatment, like she was better than me. I think I hated her a little bit at that moment.

"Are you done with your little tantrum?" she asked. She waited for me to reply, but I didn't say anything. I just stood there, steaming like a locomotive. Pissed as all hell.

She shook her head. "You've got a lot to learn about being on your own," she said. Then she laughed. "You've got to learn to relax and take things a little easier. Just standing there whining about how bad things are isn't going to get you anywhere."

"But somebody stole the car," I said. I was still whining, and I knew it. I just couldn't help it. I was at a truck stop in Lexington. All I had was ten bucks, my black and white quarter, and a hooker that didn't seem to understand the predicament I was in.

"So, the car's gone," she said with a careless shrug. She could have replaced the word 'car' with 'candy bar.' She sounded like she didn't give a shit one way or the other. Then, she opened up her oversized purse and dug out a wad of money. It wasn't a lot—it looked like she had maybe eight or nine twenties—but it was a hell of a lot more than what I had. "I've got a little money. We aren't going to starve. And there's a Super 8 right over there. I have enough for a room. We'll figure out what we're going to do in the morning."

"But we don't have a *car*," I whined. Oh, sure. I knew I was still whining, but I was still at that point where I was feeling sorry for myself. I do that a lot. I feel sorry for myself about something, up until the point I realize I *want* to feel sorry for myself. Like everyone is going to pay attention, that everyone is going to take pity on me or something. You know: 'oh, woe is me.' Like I'm the only one in the world with troubles. I don't know if it's just a bad habit or what. Usually, though, I snap out of it. Like now. The more I rehashed what Dawn was saying, the more I realized things weren't all that bad. She had some cash, and we wouldn't starve. And she had enough for a motel room, so we'd have a roof over our heads.

We. *We.*

I didn't like thinking in those terms. I was in another state, about to spend the night in a motel with a prostitute. Imagine what *that* would look like in the headlines of the High School Hallways. Oh, guys like Matt Dunbar would think it was cool. He'd ask all kinds of questions, looking for juicy details. *Did she blow ya? How many times didja do it? How much did she charge?* Crap like that. He wouldn't understand.

o o o

On the other hand, I was grateful Dawn was with me. She could have just left me there, alone. She wasn't tied to me in the least, now that I didn't have a car. That was the only reason we were together, anyway. We were both headed to Florida. And she could just as well change her mind. Find someone else to pick her up, and when they asked her where she was headed, she'd ask *them* where *they* were headed, and decide to go there. By tomorrow, she might be on her way to Nevada . . . and I'd be alone in Lexington, Kentucky, with ten bucks to my name. But then I remembered I still had my ATM card in my shoe, and there was twenty bucks in my savings account. There were ATMs on every street corner, for crying out loud. So, I had *that* going for me.

o o o

Thunder rumbled in the distance, and I looked up. The truck stop had become a phosphorescent garden of shimmering, lily-white lights, blooming in wide arcs and curves and domes. There were the familiar bells and chimes from the fuel pumps, a few distant honks. Voices chattered, and a radio played somewhere. Engines idled—dozens, in fact—and they all meshed into one giant, diesel orchestra. A tinny, distorted voice droned from an overhead speaker near one of the islands, calling out deals like a midway hawker. A dog barked somewhere. The sights and sounds were hypnotic. I had a really strange feeling of being inside some sort of great provincial pinball machine. I could even see the big steel ball coming at me, bantering off a fuel pump—

Ding! A thousand points!

—careening into a truck's wheel—

Ding! Ding! Five hundred points!

—across the lot and into the wall of the strip mall—

Bing! A hundred bonus points!

—and now it was heading for me, and I'd have to duck out of the way before—

"Are you just going to stand there?"

It was Dawn, bringing me back to whatever reality I was in. A few raindrops started to fall. My ten dollar bill was still on the ground at my feet, but a breeze tumbled it over. I reached down, picked it up, and stuffed it into my pocket. Then, I picked up my black and white quarter, flipped it into the air, caught it on the back of my wrist, and covered it with my opposite hand.

Black side up.

Dawn had already started walking. I dropped the quarter into my pocket and followed her across the lot to the other side of the street . . . wondering what that damned boomerang had in store, and when it would make another trip around.

21

I awoke confused as hell. My bed felt different, and everything was dark. The clock radio in my bedroom had letters that glow green at night, and it's bright enough to cast dim shadows. The clock numbers I was now looking at glowed red. And I usually sleep with my radio on really low, but now I couldn't hear a thing. Slowly, the haze of reality drifted back to me. I wasn't home. I was in a motel room at the Super 8 with a hooker named Dawn. She'd checked in and paid cash. Where was she? Next to me, in bed? I couldn't remember. I remembered showering, and that felt wonderful. I'd dried off and climbed into bed. I remembered being a little self-conscious because I was in my underwear and a real, live hooker was in the room with me. But I was suddenly so sleepy that I didn't care. The last thing I heard was the door close.

o o o

Gradually, I could see the outline of the drawn curtain. A faint light created a thin, rectangular corona around it. I felt good. Refreshed. I sat up slowly, listening. Gently felt around the bed. No Dawn. She was probably sleeping in the chair. I felt guilty about that, as she'd paid for the room. Sleeping in the chair probably wasn't all that comfortable. I reached over, found the light, and clicked it on. I winced and squinted in the bright, off-yellow flood. But the room was empty. Dawn wasn't in the chair. Nor was she in the room. Her purse was gone.

I was sure I'd seen the last of her. Now that I didn't have a car, she had no use for me. I wondered why she went as far as to pay for a motel room for me, though. She didn't have much more than I did. But, then again, she at least had a means to earn money. I didn't. Well, I guess I *did* . . . but not in a million years. Maybe she was just doing her good deed for the day, giving the kid a place to stay, and she'd hit the road. Things could be worse.

o o o

So, I had to plan what to do next. I swung my legs off the edge of the bed and rubbed my eyes with my palms. I had ten bucks with me. Twenty in the bank. A pair of shoes, shorts, underwear, and a T-shirt. And I had to get to Florida. Now, I've done some stupid things, but I've always managed to get myself out of the messes I get into. I was sure there was a way out of this one, but I didn't know what it was. My best idea was to maybe hitch a ride with a trucker who was heading south. I was sure I would be able to find one. Maybe I could give one of them my sob story about my sister in West Palm Beach. Or, even better: my dear granny, dying of some illness, alone. Yeah, that would do it. I'd probably be able to hork a few bucks from whoever gave me a lift. I know it was as shady as hell, making up a story like that, using people's emotions to get what you want. I felt bad about it already, just for even *planning* something like that . . . but not so bad that I wouldn't do it. Besides . . . I didn't *have* to use the story. I could try the truth, first. Then, if *that* didn't work, I'd ratchet up the sympathy meter a little higher with the sick granny story. Who could turn down a kid trying to make it to see his poor old granny before she kicked off? And when I got to Florida, I would be able to do what a lot of people do: sleep on the beach. Where would I get food? I'd worry about that when the time came. One thing was certain: there was a free breakfast in the lobby. I was going to load up like a squirrel gathering nuts for a hard winter.

o o o

It was just past six in the morning. I'd slept a fair amount, as it was almost nine when I took my shower the night before. If I could find someone headed to Florida within the next hour or so, I'd be a good ways along by tonight. Maybe not in West Palm Beach, but maybe Florida.

I had just put my clothes on and slipped into my shoes when I heard a soft click, followed by a buzzing sound. The door opened, startling me, and in walked Dawn. It was Dawn . . . but it wasn't Dawn. She was dressed in the same shorts and shirt she'd had on yesterday, but she looked like . . . well, she looked like *shit*. Exhausted, like she hadn't slept all—

Yeah, yeah. Of *course* she hadn't slept all night. She'd slept all *day*. She'd *worked* all night. That's what she *does*.

o o o

Looking at her, my heart knotted. I hadn't realized it, but during the day yesterday when she was telling me about her life, she'd changed. Her mask had fallen a little bit, and for a while she had been Dawn the Travel Companion and not Dawn the Hooker. Now, she was in shambles. Trashy and used. Thrown away.

She caught me staring. "What?" she snapped in her

Dawn the Hooker voice. She dropped her bag on the chair as she strode toward me. "What did you think I was going to do?" She put her hands on her hips. "What the fuck do you care, anyway? We've got a motel room. Money for food. Stop looking at me like that."

"Like what?"

"Like I'm less than a person," she snapped. "That's how they *all* look at me. Oh, sure, it's all fine when we're getting it on. I'm a princess, I'm a queen. Hell. Half of them, I could be their *daughter*. They have families, wives, children. Do you think they treat *them* like shit? Do you think they treat their wives the way they treat me after *I* fuck them?"

I don't know how I get myself into these conversations. I hadn't said anything to her. She'd just looked at me and knew. She *knew* what I was thinking. She could *see* it, she could *feel* it. When it came to reading people, not much was going to get by Dawn.

Then, I did something without even thinking about it. I took two steps forward, got right in her face, and hugged her. I just reached out, wrapped my arms around her, and hugged her. I didn't mean anything with it, nothing sexual, certainly. I just felt it was the right thing to do. I didn't know how she would react, but I hadn't given myself any time to think about it, either. I just . . . hugged her.

At first, she stiffened up. She didn't hug back. Then, she loosened a little. I didn't move, I didn't squeeze harder, I didn't say any comforting words. She didn't hug back, and that was okay. Maybe I thought she just needed to be hugged. Maybe she didn't have it in her to hug back. After all, she'd probably been hugged and groped a lot over the course of the night. God. That just made me sick. I felt bad for her, yes. I know she was a hooker and all, and it was her decision to do what she did, but she didn't deserve to be treated that way. I know. I was treated that way—sort of—for a long time.

o o o

When I drew back, her face met mine. There were no tears in her eyes, just a wary, cynical edge to her countenance. As if I was expecting something in return. Ten seconds went by, and then I spoke.

"Did you get some food?"

"No."

"The card on the table says they got some free breakfast shit down in the lobby," I said. "I'll go get some." I stepped around her and walked out.

22

The food in the lobby wasn't a spread fit for a king, but it was free. There were apples and oranges, some dry cereal, skim milk, orange juice, and coffee. Normally, if faced with those choices, I would have gone hungry . . . but I think survival mode was starting to kick into gear. I was quickly coming to grips with reality: I had *nothing*. If it hadn't been for Dawn paying for the motel room last night, I would've been sleeping under a tree or an awning somewhere. So, in light of that cosmic boomerang effect, a free breakfast was like hitting the jackpot. I carried away as many eats as I could and resolved to come back for more. The chick behind the desk shot me a nasty glance when she saw me all loaded up like I was, with apples and oranges and small boxes of dry cereal in my arms, but I ignored her. I didn't know what Dawn had paid for the room—fifty or sixty bucks, I guessed—so I figured we deserved a couple extra helpings of breakfast.

o o o

When I got back to the room, the bathroom door was

closed. I could hear the shower running. I sat down on the bed and dropped the food next to me. I peeled an orange, placed it on the dresser for Dawn, then I peeled another one and began eating it. And I tried—I really did try—not to wonder about Dawn, but I just couldn't do it. I wondered how many Johns she'd scored last night, and the night before that. How many had she slept with since she started? When *did* she start hooking, anyway? I know it was none of my business, and I would never ask her questions like that. But come on—I think anyone would have the same thoughts. Everybody's curious to a point. Up until then, I'd never even *met* a prostitute . . . none that I knew of, anyway. I'd see them on the streets of Bay City once in a while, but I didn't pay them any attention. They were mostly women dressed real gaudy-like, with flashy clothing and high heels. And I guess I didn't really wonder what they were like, either. It wasn't any of my business.

o o o

The shower ran for a long time. I turned the television on and flipped through the channels, but there wasn't much on. Infomercials, mostly. Some dude was selling this weird contraption that was supposed to work every muscle in your body. You could have a body like he had in only six weeks for four easy payments of just $29.99, plus shipping and handling. I'd seen this one on the air for years, so I figured they must be selling a buttload of them. There's never been a shortage of gullible people in America, that's for sure. Another channel had a hot-looking blonde with a hot-looking redhead. They were pitching jewelry that, according to them, you couldn't buy anywhere else. In fact, the blonde said as she showed off the ring on her finger, this was a limited time offer, and if you ordered right now, you'd also get the matching earrings and pendant, free. But wait, there's more, she told me. If I called within the next ten minutes, I'd get a free bottle of jewelry cleaner. Such a deal. P.T. Barnum was wrong: it's more like every second.

o o o

I killed the television just as the shower shut off. Dawn had been in there for at least twenty minutes. That's a long shower. It takes me something like three minutes, tops. I don't want to spend any more time getting spiffed up than I have to. Yeah, once in a while it's just nice to relax and soak up the hot water. Maybe that's what Dawn was doing. Maybe she was trying to get totally cleaned up from her night of work. Maybe twenty minutes was what it took. I didn't like thinking about that.

o o o

The bathroom door opened and white light spilled into the room. Steam rolled out, and there was Dawn, her hair wet and tangly. She was nude, except for a towel draped on her hips. She sure wasn't shy about her body. Yeah, it made me a little nervous. I looked away, but I didn't want it to seem all that obvious, like I had been trying to cop a free peek or something.

"I peeled an orange for you," I said, as nonchalantly as I could. "They're not bad."

"Thanks," Dawn replied, but she said it without much interest. Maybe she wasn't much of an orange eater. She'd told me a lot about herself yesterday, but there was much more I'd never know. Didn't *want* to know, in fact. No, that's not necessarily true. I wanted to know where she lived. She'd explained a lot yesterday, but she never got around to saying where she lived. Was there a place she called 'home'? An apartment? If so, wasn't there someone who might be worried about her? Her mother? Those were questions that were a bit too close to the *why-did-you-start-screwing-for-money* question. Most of what I knew about Dawn was a mystery, and it would stay that way.

o o o

So there I was, sitting on the bed, ready to bite into an apple, and Dawn pulls the towel from her waist as she steps out of the bathroom. Next thing I know, she's got it over her head, scrubbing back and forth, drying herself. I can see everything now. It was odd. She wasn't doing it to shock or show off, I knew. That's just who she was. Her body wasn't a secret. I'm sure at one time it was, but not anymore. I had a clear view of thin pink folds between her legs. Not a speck of pubic hair in sight. She turned, pulled out a pair of black lace panties from her bag, and slipped into them. Then, she continued drying her hair as she returned to the bathroom, her pushpin nipples at full attention. She had the towel over her head, scrubbing her hair dry and facing the mirror. I mean . . . there was no way she could see I was watching her. Still—

"You're staring," she said flatly. She never even glanced in my direction.

"Sorry," I said, before I could even think of anything else to say. I almost went into this lengthy defense about how I wasn't staring, no, not at all—but it wasn't worth going into. Besides . . . she was right. I *had* been staring. But only a little. I'd never seen a shaved beaver before. Not in person.

"Don't worry about it," she said. "Most guys do."

She didn't mean it in a conceited way, I could tell. Not at all. It was just a fact. I mean, if a guy is paying her, it's his time as much as hers. If he's been married to the same person for twenty years and goes out and hires a young hooker, you'd think he'd stare. After all . . . the hour would probably go by pretty quickly if that's how the hooker charged. Might as well get all your money's worth.

I looked toward the other side of the room, but there was a framed picture on the wall, and I could see Dawn's reflection in the glass. I looked away from it, too . . . and bit into my apple.

23

Downstairs, Dawn grabbed a coffee from the breakfast nook. I waited in the lobby, then we left.

The pavement was slick from the overnight rain, but the clouds were moving away. Stilettos of sunshine were slicing through, spearing bright hot spots onto trees and buildings, reflecting off car hoods and windows. The air was damp. Warm, too: probably around seventy degrees or so. It felt nice.

"So, now what?" I asked, for lack of something better to say. It probably came across sort of stupid, as if I were giving her the reins and letting her take control. Hell, she'd probably want to split on her own. She didn't need me. I'd be a hindrance. Bad for biz.

"Well, we figure out which one of these truckers is heading for Florida," she said. "And we see if we can hitch."

It was gratifying to hear her say that. If anything, it reassured me that my idea to find a semi headed for Florida had been a good one. Not that I needed reassurance, but I was glad to know Dawn had come to the same conclusion. And I was glad she and I were traveling together. She was strange and all, with a completely different lifestyle. But I didn't mind. Maybe the more I hung around her, the more I realized there was a wider reality in the world. I had no right to criticize what she did, when she did it, how she did it, whatever. Sure, prostitution is illegal. But there's an old Indian saying I heard a few years back—something about not criticizing someone until you've walked a mile in their shoes. I had a feeling I'd done a little walking in Dawn's shoes, and maybe she'd walked a little in mine. It gave me a different perspective, I guess.

o o o

"All right," Dawn said as we crossed the street to the truck stop. "Here's what we're going to do. I've got to make some phone calls. You go hang out in that Starbucks over there. Have a coffee or something." She reached into her bag and pulled out a twenty. I refused with a single raised palm.

"I've got money," I said, but I knew I wasn't going to spend it. Number one, I don't drink coffee, and number two, ten bucks was all the cash I had. A Starbucks coffee would wipe out a good chunk of all the money I owned in the world.

"Fine," Dawn said. "Just wait for me at Starbucks. I'll be back in a while."

I wanted to ask her who she was going to call. She'd never said anything about any friends. No current ones, at least. Maybe she was working for someone or something like that and had to check in. Maybe she had a pimp lining up jobs for her or something. She didn't carry a cell phone, and I thought in her line of work, that would be pretty handy. Mandatory, in fact. You could give your number to your customers, and they could call you up when they were coming back through town. But, for whatever reason, she didn't have a cell phone. Not that I knew of, anyway.

She walked toward a line of pay phones not far from Dairy Queen, which was dark and closed. I turned and walked into Starbucks. There were a half-dozen people in line and about the same number seated at various tables. I took a seat by the window and just stared outside. I couldn't see Dawn, and I began to get this gnawing feeling she'd given me the slip. Maybe that was her way of saying *See ya later, alligator.* Sometimes, I always think the worst shit, and I have to keep telling myself I have to look for solutions, not problems. If Dawn *had* given me the slip, so what? What would that change? Ellen would still be in Florida, and I was still in Lexington. With or without Dawn, I was heading to Florida. If she was with me, fine. And what would she do once we made it to the old Sunshine State? Who knows. She'd be on her way, I'd be on mine. People are like that. Some are meant to be a part of your life for a long time. Others, they just show up for a short period of time, until you no longer have use for each other. Yeah, that sounds cold. But you don't hang around people you don't want to hang around. It's not being unkind or anything. But your priorities change. I don't hang around Robbie Sinclair for the same reasons he doesn't hang around me anymore: we both have better things to do.

o o o

There *are* friends, though, those very few, that will never leave you. Oh, they might move away to a different state, maybe even out of the country. But they're so much a part of you that you know that when you see them again, it'll be like old times. Those are the friends you'd do anything for, at any time, for any reason. Friends you'd lie for, friends you'd die for. I started looking around the coffee shop, wondering about the people, how many friends each one of them had, where they were. Then I started getting all sad and bummed out. I realized that, at sixteen, I really didn't have anyone like that. None. My friends from school were great. But it all of a sudden hit me that I had

93

no one I would lie for, no one I would die for . . . except Ellen. And I wasn't sure why I was all of a sudden realizing this. Growing up, we never hung out together, we didn't share the things that typical brothers and sisters share. There would be days we wouldn't talk to each other. Oh, we weren't mad at each other, nothing like that. It was just that we didn't have anything to say to each other. Or, we were too busy keeping out of Lacy's and Bruce's way. And I was sitting there in that coffee shop and tears started to creep up. I guess maybe Ellen and I had more in common than I thought. Maybe I was wrong all those years. Maybe we really were close . . . in ways other brothers and sisters weren't. Maybe, because of our screwed up family life, we had to deal with shit that no one else did. Maybe I was just now realizing it, and it made me hurt and feel bad that much more. I was suddenly overwhelmed with worry for my sister—more so than ever before. I didn't want to wait for Dawn, I didn't want to wait to hitch a ride. I wanted to run, right from there, take off on my own two feet, and just get started. At least in the *direction* of Florida. I wanted to do anything—*anything*—that would give me momentum, to be able to tell myself I was on my way, I was doing something, that I would be there soon. I wanted right now to tell Ellen that no matter what was wrong, it could be fixed. I was on my way, and she was going to be all right. Big brother to the rescue. Cheesy. But it hurt thinking about it. It hurt like a bitch.

24

More and more time passed. People came and went, and I really began to wonder again if Dawn had split. No matter, I guess, but I didn't want to be wasting my time, hanging around Starbucks when I could be looking for a ride south. I was just about to get up and go look for Dawn when, lo and behold, there she was, walking across the parking lot. She was wearing sunglasses and applying some lipstick or lip balm as she walked, looking down at the pavement. Then, she looked up and saw me looking at her. She smiled weakly, and hiked her thumb in the air. I immediately knew we had a ride. Whoever she'd called, whoever she'd talked to, we were on our way to Florida. Rock and Roll.

o o o

I got up, walked outside, and met her on the sidewalk. "Good news?" I asked.

"There's a guy over there that's headed for Miami. He's leaving in about an hour. He says we can catch a ride with him. I told him you were my brother, and we're heading south to visit relatives. So, we've got some time to kill." Dawn reached into her bag, pulled out a magazine, and handed it to me. It was *Newsweek*, and it had a picture of North Korean dictator Kim Jong Il on the front. "To pass the time," she said, handing it to me. Then, she pulled out another magazine, *Cosmopolitan,* and held it under her arm. "I need another coffee," she said, and we marched into Starbucks.

I went over and sat at the same spot where I'd spent the last hour. Dawn caught my eye and made a motion, pointing to the menu board on the back wall, wondering if I wanted anything. I shook my head, and she turned back to the counter to place her order.

o o o

I absently flopped open *Newsweek*. I don't think I've ever thumbed through a copy. I never was big into magazines.

Dawn got her coffee and came over. She set the cup down, placed her magazine on the table, and sat. She didn't say anything, didn't even look at me. She just opened *Cosmopolitan* and flipped through the pages. I thumbed through *Newsweek,* but there wasn't much that interested me. I never really paid too much attention to what was going on around the world. I used to read the *Bay City Times* on occasion, just to see who killed who, who robbed what, shit like that. But the stuff in *Newsweek* just didn't interest me. I knew I should be more aware of what was going on in the world, that I should pay attention to world events, but I always thought that was what adults were for. Me? I was sixteen. I paid attention to my favorite bands, my friends, and girls that looked halfway decent. I paid attention to hot cars. Magazines like *Newsweek* bored the hell out of me.

o o o

I poked my hand into my pocket and pulled out my black and white quarter. It's funny: I'd had the thing for years, and I'd always expected to lose it somewhere along the line. I'd misplaced it on occasion, but I always found it. But I figured if I ever *did* lose it, I would just make another one.

I flipped it up in the air, caught it in my hand. Heads. Black. Flipped it up again: black. Again: tails. White.

Dawn glanced up from her magazine. She didn't say anything, but I could see the question in her eyes.

"My lucky quarter," I said.

"Why is it black on one side and white on the other?" she asked.

I shrugged. "That's how I found it. I guess I look at it and think about how the world is."

She frowned, confused. "How's that?"

I flipped the quarter over in my hand. "You know: black and white. Right versus wrong. Good versus evil."

Dawn raised her eyebrows. "That simple, huh?"

I nodded. "Pretty much." I flipped the coin and caught it in my hand. Black.

Dawn held out her hand, and I gave her the quarter. She held it up and looked at it. "Black and white?" she said. "Right and wrong?"

"Yeah," I said. "That's why people get into trouble. They do the wrong things."

"What if they don't know if it's the wrong thing?"

"Everyone knows the difference between right and wrong," I said. "It's black and white . . . just like my quarter."

Then, she stood the quarter on its edge on the table, holding it in place with her left index finger. She flicked it with a finger on her left hand and the coin spun frantically, only the rapid spinning blurred the colors of the coin. No longer did it look black and white . . . but gray. A little gray world, whirling in circles like a planet revolving around a sun.

"So, what's black and white now?" she asked.

I watched the gray ball swirling on the table for a moment, then I snapped it up and returned it to my pocket. Dawn returned to her magazine.

o o o

I kept looking at the clock on the wall, watching the second hand move at the speed of a glacier. Out of the corner of my eye, I'd watch Dawn, and I'd wait for her to look at the clock and say something to the effect of it being time to go. I hadn't asked her about the ride, where the truck was, nothing. She'd handled it, and we were going to Florida. But before she looked up at the clock, before she said anything about heading out to meet our ride, she closed the magazine and looked at me really serious-like, and spoke.

"Have you ever noticed there aren't any overweight people in these magazines?" she asked.

25

All clouds had drifted off, and the sky was a beautiful, butane shade of autumn blue that you only see during the fall, almost always before ten or so, before the midday haze kicks into gear. It seemed perfect and innocent, and the sun felt great. In Michigan, it had been getting cooler and cooler as fall drew near. I knew the farther south we got, the warmer it would be. Florida, no doubt, would probably be in the eighty-degree range for the next month or two. Fine with me. I was glad to be away from the cold and snow. If I liked Florida, I might just hang out for a while. Of course, that all depended on Ellen, and what was going on with her.

o o o

"He's over here," Dawn said, and I walked beside her as we made our way across the parking lot and beneath a service island. An invisible fog of oily diesel fumes hit me, and I about puked. So many trucks in one area had a way of stinking up the place.

On the far side of the lot, a semi with a white cab and a

silver trailer was parked. I could make out the silhouette of a man behind the wheel, smoking and chatting on a cell phone. When he saw us, he ended his conversation, opened the door, and slid out. He had a shit-grin from ear to ear, which struck me as odd.

Dawn spoke as we approached the man. "This is my brother, Tony," she said, and it caught me off guard. *Tony?* Okay. Now I'm Tony. I held out my hand and the man took it, but his wolfish eyes never left Dawn. He was probably in his forties, with thinning, brown hair. He had a bit of a paunch going, maybe a bit too much driving and eating Cheetos and not enough walking. Or a couple too many beers. But he seemed normal enough.

o o o

The man never gave his name. He just said something to the effect of 'gotcha, all set here,' or something like that. He opened up the passenger door and motioned me to climb in. Well, I've never been in a semi before, so I didn't know what to expect. I knew a lot of cabs had beds for the driver to sleep, and this one did. But it was pretty messy. Behind the seat (where the man motioned for me to go) was a cot with some clothes piled in one corner. A few candy bar wrappers were strewn about, some with blotches of melted chocolate. A coffee-stained foam cup was flattened on the floor. All in all, there was quite a bit of room, and I figured the ride to Florida wasn't going to be all that bad. I slid over to make room for Dawn . . . which proved to be unnecessary. The man had already picked out Dawn's place . . . in the passenger seat. With his help, she climbed up and sat. She shot me a quick glance, then looked away. The man closed the passenger door and went around to the front of the cab and climbed inside. He closed the door, threw the truck into gear, and began to pull away. Then, he reached over and gave

Dawn's thigh a squeeze. "Florida, here we come," he said, but he held onto Dawn's leg for a moment longer before he let go. Dawn stared straight ahead.

26

Thirty minutes of silence went by. Every once in a while, the driver (I'd learned his name was Joe) would reach over and slap or squeeze Dawn's thigh. Well, like I've already said, sometimes it takes me a while to catch on. I didn't know if I should be pissed, grateful, what. I didn't know. No, I didn't have feelings for her . . . not in *that* way. But there was just something about doing *that* to get what you want. I was now certain that while I was in Starbucks, Dawn wasn't making a phone call. She'd found some guy headed for Florida and had made a proper payment arrangement. Man, that's just messed up. Then again: Dawn knew her business. I would just keep my mouth shut. But it still pissed me off.

o o o

Anyway, we were on our way to Florida, and I tried to concentrate on what I would do when I got there. I didn't have a lot to go on to find Ellen. I didn't know anything about how big West Palm Beach was, and it was kind of overwhelming just to think about it.

Dawn refused to look at me, and I didn't know why. It was like she went out of her way to avoid my eyes, even when she made casual glances over at Joe when he'd say something to her. She'd try to smile, but it was easy to see her smile was strained and forced. I looked at her, but she never looked back at me. Never. It was really weird. I'd known her for about twenty four hours, but it felt like a lot longer than that. So, I decided that, when I got the chance, I would ask her the question I'd been wondering since last night.

27

The ride was boring as hell, but I still had my copy of *Newsweek* Dawn had bought me. Joe had a few old copies of *Sports Illustrated* tumbling around in the back, but those seemed even less interesting than *Newsweek*. I've never really been much of a sports fan. Growing up, I used to play softball, baseball, pond hockey, basketball—games like that—with my friends. But *playing* a sport is a whole lot different than *reading* about a sport or watching it on television. Of course, I never was really good at any of the sports I played, except dodgeball. Man, I could hurl a ball and knock the shit out of anyone. In fifth grade, I was playing dodgeball in the school gym during recess (it was raining that day, and we couldn't go outside), and I hit some kid in the head so hard he was knocked out cold. Unconscious before he hit the floor. I didn't *mean* to knock him out, but dodgeball is a dog-eat-dog game. Last year, the school board voted to ban dodgeball altogether, saying it promoted violent behavior. Think about that: you can play *Grand Theft Auto* and other video games where murder is simulated . . . but dodgeball is too violent. *There's* some logic.

o o o

Joe was busy trying to say shit to impress Dawn, and I wasn't remotely interested in *that,* so I opened up *Newsweek* just for something to do. I opened it to an article that just blew me away. It was about these gangs in Saudi Arabia that use kids to make money. During the Holy Month of Ramadan, these gangs would come in from different countries. They took kids that had been healthy and they would amputate their arms and legs, or give them some sort of wound—anything to draw the sympathy of the thousands of Muslim pilgrims who traveled many miles to pray and worship at some famous mosque. The kids would beg for money and had to give it to the gang members. I couldn't believe it. They even had a picture of this little girl who couldn't have been more than seven or eight. Her left arm had been amputated above the elbow. In the other hand, she had a small canister for collecting money. I felt like I had been punched. Here was this little girl, this little, precious thing, and she had gone through horrible disfigurement . . . for what? Money? If this is what the human race was about, I wanted no part of it. In no way could I remotely be a part of a race who could do this to an innocent little kid. I wanted to turn the page, to go on to something else, but I couldn't help but stare. The look in that little girl's eyes was *haunting.* It said 'Why me?' and 'Please help' and 'Why me?' and 'Why me?' and 'Why me?' over and over again. But that's what she was supposed to do. Her life wasn't hers anymore, it belonged to someone else. She was *owned.* She was owned until she wasn't good for anything anymore. In a few years, she wouldn't be so cute. She wouldn't be so pathetic. The article said when the kids reached that age, they didn't draw as much sympathy, so the gangs wouldn't use them. They would find more kids, *younger* kids . . . kids who could do a better job begging after they'd had their leg or arm chopped off. In a few years, those children, too, would be discarded. But the cycle would continue.

o o o

Joe said something and laughed. He reached over and gave Dawn's leg a squeeze. She didn't laugh, she didn't say anything. But she cringed a little. Oh, it was hidden well. She'd learned to do that. She was good at hiding shit, good at the masquerade game. But I saw it. Dawn cringed.

I looked away.

28

Corbin, Kentucky, is about eighty miles south of Lexington, and that's where we stopped to stretch and get a bite to eat. Dawn said she wasn't hungry, and I wasn't either. Seeing that little girl with her arm amputated was enough to curb my appetite for the day. It was hard to shake her picture from my head. What a sick, cruel world.

o o o

We pulled into a gas station that had a big parking lot. Dawn said she wasn't all that hungry, but Joe wanted to grab a snack and check something on his rig. He hopped out and closed the door. Dawn said nothing, and she didn't look at me, either. I crawled forward until I was only a few inches from her.

"Happy Halloween," I said.

She turned and looked at me with puzzled annoyance. "What?"

"How is it that you celebrate Halloween every single day?" I asked.

She glared at me. Dawn didn't know what I was talking

about, but she was sure the remark was intended as an insult. It wasn't, but I was going to get to my point soon enough. "What are you talking about?" she flared.

"Your mask," I said. "You keep it on all the time. Once in a while you take it off, but not often. Isn't it hard to keep it on all day long? Doesn't it get uncomfortable?"

"I still don't know what the fuck you're talking about," Dawn snapped.

"Dawn . . . I can see it. You hide behind your mask until you think it's okay to drop it. You drop it a little bit, not all the way, because you *have* to. You *have* to, because it's too much work to keep it on all the time. Masks are hot and sweaty and uncomfortable. You've kept your mask on since we left Lexington. You've got it on now. It's wearing you out, I can tell. I can see it in your face. Or, wait—*is* that your face? Or, is it your mask?"

I don't know why I went into it like that. I really shouldn't have said anything, or, if I did, I should have worded it differently. I didn't intend for the ensuing results.

Tears welled up in her eyes. She looked down. Then, she looked up at me. For the first time, her mask was gone. Completely. Don't ask me how I could tell. I just knew. Her eyes were sad, her cheeks were sunken. I was immediately sorry I'd said those things, and I mentally cursed myself for once again being senseless and stupid and moronic.

A tear dribbled down her cheek. "Halloween," she said, softly, looking away. She wiped the tear away, but another one quickly took its place. "I remember trick or treating, how fun it was." She was talking slowly, softly. Again, she wiped a tear from her cheek. "It was my favorite holiday. Even over Christmas. See, at Christmas, I didn't get many gifts, anyway, on account of Mom didn't have much money. But Halloween—"

She paused here, and her face brightened a little. She looked at me. "Halloween was great, because my mom bought me a witch costume when I was only four. It was pretty cheap—I think she got it at the dollar store—but I loved it." She looked away. "The mask was my favorite. It was thin plastic, with a rubber band that went around the back of my head. And I had a pointy hat. But what I liked best about it was I was able to hide, and no one knew who was behind that mask. Behind that mask, it was like the real Dawn was invisible. No one knew it was me, and I liked that feeling, pretending I was someone else. Stepping out of my shoes, stepping out of my life. My mom never knew it, but sometimes, I would wear my mask when I was in my bedroom. Once in a while, I would wear it to bed. I used to put it on just after Mom tucked me in for the night, and I would dream I really *was* a witch. A good witch, of course, one that could talk to the animals and help them. I would cast spells to help people. I know it probably sounds stupid."

Another tear spilled onto her cheek, and man, did I feel like a schmuck. I hadn't meant to drudge up all of this shit. Not by a long shot. I thought she might snap at me or something, but not go into all of this. But I did it. I cracked her mask.

"I outgrew the costume long ago, but I kept the mask up until a couple of years ago. I really did. There were times—God, I think I was sixteen—I still wore the mask to bed on occasion. I remember being more comfortable behind my mask, more *myself,* than at any other time. Sometimes, I wished I never had to take the mask off. I could just be someone else, someone no one knew. Someone who—"

She stopped speaking and dried her eyes. She was about to speak, but I spoke first. Really quiet-like.

"Someone who could hide the real you," I said softly.

She responded by raising her chin and sighing. Then, she looked at the floor. "A mask," she said. "I never knew how handy it would be. With a mask, it's easy to hide from the real world . . . but that means locking yourself in your own world. And that gets pretty lonely sometimes."

And when she looked at me, I had to fight not to cry myself. Her tears were gone, but her *eyes.* God . . . her *eyes.* Where had I seen them before? What pain could have possibly caused such a crestfallen bewildered look? Why, all of a sudden, were her eyes so familiar? I looked down, averting her stare, saw the copy of *Newsweek* still open to the picture of the girl with the amputated arm—

Then, I *did* cry.

29

Joe came back with another guy. He popped the hood, and the two men poked around like a couple of prairie dogs. After a few minutes, the hood clunked closed, and they walked away.

Dawn and I hadn't spoken for a long time. She saw me cry and reached out to touch my face, or pull me to her or something, but I drew away. I probably shouldn't have, and I don't know why I did. But she pulled her hand back and said nothing. I wiped my tears on my shirt sleeve, closed the copy of *Newsweek,* and tossed it onto the pile of Joe's *Sports Illustrated.*

"I'm sorry about bringing it up like that," I said. "I didn't mean for you to—"

"Forget it," Dawn said flatly. "It's no big deal." Her mask was back on. Not all the way, but it was creeping back up to that comfortable, protective spot. She wore her mask like a baby held a blanket, like an infant clutching a favorite toy, and for the same reasons. I think she actually believed she could take it on and off at will, whenever she wanted, changing color like a chameleon, acquiring a new identity like an undercover cop. The truth, I think, was she'd worn her mask for so long that she forgot how to take it off. In effect, she'd done what she'd always wanted: she became a different person. She became the woman behind the mask. I wondered if she really knew who she was anymore.

Sometimes, I wondered that about myself.

o o o

Joe came back with a deli sandwich, a bag of sour cream 'n' onion Doritos, a box of Little Debbie Star Crunches, a Moon Pie, and a Diet Pepsi. Go figure that one out. He's got more sugar and fat than a person needs for a month . . . and then he buys a *Diet* Pepsi.

But he also had one more thing: bad news.

"Got sump'n funky goin' on with the starter," he said.

"What's the 'sump'n funky'?" I asked.

He stashed the food on the floor by the console, took a bite of his sandwich, and talked while he chewed. "Don't know," he said, shaking his head, "but I gotta get 'er checked out."

"Where do we get it checked out?" Dawn asked, and I was blown away. Her mask was on, complete and total. The real Dawn was so different (from the *fake* Dawn?), and I could now easily see who was who. She was a magician: now you see her, now you don't. I wondered if she had a split personality, like some of those people you see on trashy talk shows. I saw one lady on some show claim she had six or seven complete and separate personalities. One of her personalities was a nymphomaniac. Another was a little boy. But she claimed it wasn't her fault, she just couldn't help herself, being that she had this disorder and all. Of course, this was on television, so you *know* how believable *that* was. But the people in the audience looked like they were believing it.

Still, I wondered about Dawn. She had two personalities, each as different as night and day. Question was: did she separate them? Or had she literally been able to squelch the 'real' Dawn, as some sort of survival mode? There was still a lot I didn't know about her. But I'd figured out a lot of the puzzle in the last twenty minutes.

o o o

"Well," Joe said, "we'll try Williamsburg, which is just up th' road a spell. If the news ain't good there, we'll try to make it to Knoxville. I know we can get 'er fixed there, but prob'ly not 'till t'marra. We can stay the night in Knoxville." He gave Dawn's thigh a squeeze. "Head out again t'marra, after we get 'er fixed."

When he said it, Dawn never moved, never wavered, but—and I swear to God—I *felt* her skin crawl. From the back of the cab, I *felt* it.

30

In Williamsburg, it was more bad news.

Joe pulled into a diesel garage, and the mechanic there confirmed the problem. The starter was going bad and needed to be replaced. They would have to order one. It would be better, like Joe had speculated, to travel on to Knoxville and get it repaired there, where any one of numerous shops would have the part in stock.

Joe returned to the cab and climbed in. He seemed in remarkably high spirits for a guy who was losing valuable road time. He reached over and gave Dawn's thigh yet another squeeze, a gesture he was growing quite fond of. "Just a slight detour," he said, and his hand slid a little farther up her thigh. If there was ever a moment I could have strangled someone, it was then. His idea of affection was a knife carving at the soul of—

Who?

The *real* Dawn. The Good Witch—the masked Dawn—couldn't have cared less. But to the real Dawn, this intrusive hand was a stiletto. Sharp, cutting. Killing. I wanted to reach out and smash my fist down onto his arm, shattering the bones into a million pieces. I wanted to snap his arm off, make him hurt, make him feel all the pain he was causing. Sure, what he was causing wasn't *physical* pain. But maybe it was worse. Maybe it was worse because it couldn't be felt all at once. It was a pain experienced over a long period of time, building and growing, festering. It starts with a gentle prodding, almost unnoticeable coming and going. Then, it's a gnawing. The gnawing turns into a chewing, which turns into—

I suddenly felt a wetness beneath my fingers, and I looked down. There was blood oozing from my palms on both hands. I'd been squeezing my hands so tightly my fingernails had dug into the skin. My hands were bleeding, and I felt like killing a trucker named Joe for a hooker named Dawn.

And I didn't know either of their last names. If it wasn't so real, wasn't so serious, I could have laughed. Maybe I should have.

31

We pulled into Knoxville around five. Joe knew right where he was going, as he explained he'd been over the road since he was eighteen and claimed to know Knoxville and numerous other cities like the 'back of his hand.'

Not far off I-75, we pulled into the greasiest, dirtiest roadside garage I have ever seen in my life. Disintegrating semi cabs and trailers littered the grounds for acres. There was shit *everywhere,* piled high. It was like a post-apocalyptic scene from a movie. Metal, steel, fiberglass, aluminum siding, tires, old axles, trucks on blocks—you name it. It looked more like a junkyard than a service garage.

"Hang tight," Joe said, giving Dawn another randy slap on the thigh. "Be right back." He opened the door and spilled out of the cab, leaving the engine idling.

Dawn turned and managed a weak smile. "Hey, at least we know we're on our way to Florida," she said. She was trying really hard to look on the bright side.

I wasn't buying it. I could tell she wasn't enjoying being around Joe. Maybe because of the nature of what she did. Maybe, as a hooker, you do your thing and move on. You take the cash and scram. You don't have to see the guy again. For an hour, or however long he's paying for, the girl pretended to care, pretended to show affection, pretended to enjoy it . . . no matter how much she hated it. And Joe. Jesus, he was by no means a looker. Not filthy-dirty, nothing like that. But he wasn't going to be gracing the cover of *GQ* anytime soon. And he had something we needed: a ride.

"What are you thinking?" Dawn asked. She was looking out the windshield, watching Joe and two other men approach the cab.

"I think it's an awfully expensive trip to Florida," I replied coolly. Dawn turned to look at me. Her mask was off for a brief moment, then it was back on again. She turned away, said nothing. I picked up a copy of *Sports Illustrated* and thumbed through it, totally uninterested, but not wanting to say anything. Hell, I didn't *have* anything to say. I told myself I should just shut up and be thankful I had a ride to Florida.

○ ○ ○

The hood popped up with a loud *clunk*. Joe and the two men did some fiddling around. I could hear muted conversation and a few chuckles over the idling diesel. After a few minutes, the hood closed, and Joe climbed back into the cab. "We'll git 'er fixed up in the morning," Joe said as he grasped the wheel. He checked his mirrors, backed up several feet, then pulled forward. "No big deal at all. They'll get to it first thing in the morning, and we'll be on our way." He didn't seem at all upset about having to spend the night or pay for repairs. I guess when you get to screw a girl like Dawn in trade for a ride, life's little speed bumps are put into perspective.

My guess was this: I was going to sleep in the cab, while Dawn and Joe would stay at the Days Inn that was near the I-75 off ramp. Just a hunch.

117

And how about that? Joe steered the truck across the overpass and right into the parking lot of the Days Inn. I hate being right all the time. Sometimes, I just can't stand myself.

o o o

There were quite a few restaurants, shops, and stores around. Several fast food joints, a Logan's Steakhouse, and a Red Robin were within walking distance from the motel. A short distance away was a Home Depot, a Best Buy, and a few other big box stores. All in all, a lot like Bay City—only the weather was a bit more palatable for early October.

Joe dug into his pocket and pulled out a wad of cash. He gave four twenties to Dawn. "Why don'cha see what ya can do 'bout a room," he said and gave her a serpentine wink. "I've got a coupl'a things to 'tend to here for a minute."

Dawn took the money, opened the door, and slid out. When she was halfway across the parking lot, Joe turned to me. "Say, you, ah, wouldn't mind baggin' it in here for the night, would'ja?" I think he had a hard-on already, just thinking about his upcoming night with Dawn.

I glared at him. I tried not to, but I couldn't help it. Then, I remembered the game I was playing wasn't mine. I was the freeloader, along for the ride. I wasn't much more than a parasite at this point, a flea on a dog's ass. My goal was to get to Florida. I had the clothes on my back, ten bucks in my pocket, two oranges, two mini-size boxes of Cheerios, a roof over my head for the night. I even had a current issue of *Newsweek* to thumb through, in case I got bored. In fact, I could probably bum Dawn's copy of *Cosmopolitan* and get my rocks off looking at the skinny chicks in skimpy clothing. Life was peachy.

"No problem," I said, and I looked away.

o o o

118

Joe slid out of the cab and vanished. I climbed over the passenger seat, pushed the door open, and slipped out. The evening was warm, and the heat from the pavement rose. It felt nice, actually. In Bay City, it was probably a little chilly. I thought again about Florida, and the prospect of staying there seemed better and better. There were probably more jobs, I was sure, and I could probably find work anywhere. It was funny. Three days ago, I was more worried about a stupid test at school. Now I was in Knoxville, Tennessee, with a slimeball named Joe and a hooker named Dawn.

But it was getting harder and harder to think of Dawn that way. I didn't like associating her name with terms like hooker, prostitute, slut, whore, lot lizard—whatever. That's not what she was, not really. I wonder if she even knew that herself.

o o o

Joe was farting around with something at the back of the trailer. Nature was calling me, so I walked across the parking lot to a gas station/convenience store. They had restrooms inside, and they were clean. Bonus. On the wall in front of the urinal was a page-size billboard, advertising the Days Inn right across the street. I've seen these before, these ads in bathrooms, and I always have a laugh. You'd be standing there with your pecker out, whizzing away, reading about how you could own a Suzuki motorcycle for only sixty bucks a month, or whatever they were advertising. There was just something funny about that. You couldn't even take a leak anymore without someone trying to sell you something. Used to be, the owner of the joint would put up the sports page or the front page of the local news. Now, they were selling shit. And the little billboard wasn't the only opportunity someone saw to make a buck. On the wall next to it was a condom dispenser. For seventy five cents, you could get a glow in the dark condom, a studded condom, or a ribbed *(for her pleasure!)* condom. I once saw a kid of about ten in a restroom, fumbling with the knob of the machine as I walked in. When the condom popped out of the dispenser, he looked at it like he'd been ripped off. He had no idea what it was. He must've thought he was getting bubble gum or a removable tattoo or a rubber ball or something. He flipped the small packet over in his hands, shoved it into his pocket, and left in a huff of disgust. I had laughed as I stood at the urinal, thinking about what would happen if he forgot it was there when he went home. I could see his mother finding the condom in the pocket of his pants and holding it up with a shocked, dumbfounded look. I'd laughed so hard I nearly peed on myself.

o o o

I went back outside. On the other side of the lot, Joe was still dinking around with something at the back of the trailer. Dawn had emerged from the Days Inn, and she was walking back toward the cab. She gave me a nod, like she wanted to talk to me, so I walked over to her. Her mask was off. At the front of the semi, she looked to make sure Joe was at the back of the trailer. Then, she pulled a plastic card out of her pocket and handed it to me. "Room 134," she said. "It's yours."

I took the card. On one side was the Days Inn logo, and the other side had an advertisement for Logan's Steakhouse. *(Show this card and receive 10% off your meal purchase! Alcoholic beverages not included.)* "But what about—" I started to say, but Dawn cut me off.

"We've got another room," she said. "You'll be more comfortable sleeping on a bed than you will in the cab." Then, she pulled out a twenty dollar bill. "Go get something to eat."

"Whatever," I said. This time I took the money. Man, did I ever feel like a third wheel. Seems like all I was doing was mooching off someone else. Hey, fine. In fact, I thought I might as well make myself scarce. Besides . . . I had just tripled my net worth. Now I had thirty bucks, not including the twenty I had in the bank. I was damned close to wealthy.

o o o

Joe walked up, carrying a laptop computer case and another bag. Dawn's mask was already back on, and she shot him a look that said *I am going to screw your brains out tonight, big boy.* That fast. And she did it well, too. Really sexy-like. She was smooth and cool, I gave her that. She could turn her charm on and off like a lamp.

"I, uh . . . I'm going to go grab a bite to eat," I said, and Joe looked at me like I was his son and I'd just graduated top of the class.

"Oh, hey, sure," he said, and he dug a twenty dollar bill from his pocket and handed it to me. "Make sure you lock the cab before you call it a night," he said. "See you in the morning." In Joe's eyes, he just bought me out of the picture for the rest of the night for twenty bucks. Now I had fifty bucks, cash, on hand. You couldn't do better on Wall Street. Forty bucks in thirty seconds? I doubted even *Dawn* could do that.

32

I left Dawn and Joe, not even glancing back as I walked across the parking lot toward Logan's Steakhouse. But when I got there, I saw a factory outlet mall on the far side of the lot. It was long and had about a billion stores. From where Joe had parked the semi, the mall was hidden. Now, it opened up like a city in a valley. There must have been four dozen stores: Publisher's Warehouse, Izod, J. Crew, Nike, Bass, Victoria's Secret, Paper Factory, Columbia, and more. But right smack dab in the middle of the parking lot was a Chinese buffet called the Mystic Panda. Hot dog. If there's one thing I love, it's Chinese buffets. Besides the fact I love the food, I love the fact that it's all-you-can-eat, and it's *cheap*. I was still feeling pretty rich, but that didn't mean I could afford to blow a bunch of cash on dinner. For about eight bucks (including tip) I could walk out of there packed to the gills. I probably wouldn't have to eat again until I was in Florida.

o o o

The inside of the Mystic Panda was like most other

Chinese restaurants. Red walls with yellow trim around the windows. There was a big aquarium against one wall. Four enormously fat goldfish, damned near the size of volleyballs, drifted among plastic seaweed. The fish moved in a dream, like they'd been pumped with Oxycotin.

And the place wasn't very crowded, either. Maybe a dozen people or so. There was one lady seated in a wheelchair who looked like she was trying to accompany the goldfish in the bloat department. Rolls of fat splayed out over the seat, and when she raised her fork, a curtain of fat dripped from her arm. I had to look away, it was so disgusting. People that size have no business being at a Chinese buffet. They should be at home, eating celery and walking on the treadmill until they shed the pounds. No doubt she was in the wheelchair because her legs wouldn't support her. It was sad. Really, really sad. What was worse: the woman couldn't be more than thirty years old. And to go one more, she had a daughter who looked to be about eight or nine, and she was shaping up to be a living bowling ball herself. I looked away, hoping I hadn't already spoiled my appetite.

The girl at the counter—a skinny, dark haired Asian girl—motioned me to follow her, and she led me to a booth by the window, where I had a great view of the parking lot and the outlet mall.

"Anyteeng doo trink?" she asked. Very choppy English.

"Hot tea and water," I replied, not sitting down. I was heading right for the buffet island. The girl nodded and skirted off. It was a scene played out a hundred times at every Chinese buffet I'd eaten at.

o o o

So, I was sitting at my booth eating my Kung Pao Chicken and fried rice, when I looked across the parking lot and saw Joe and Dawn coming out of one of the stores. He'd latched onto her arm like a lamprey on a trout. She was carrying a white bag. Full of clothes, no doubt. It was funny, and I laughed out loud. I felt like shouting 'get everything you can!' but I thought it would probably scare the fat lady and her daughter. Probably everyone else in the restaurant, too. I took a bite of food and watched as Joe and Dawn walked past a few stores, then vanished inside Victoria's Secret. Joe was getting ready for a hot time in the ol' town tonight.

Good for Dawn, I thought. *If she's going to screw him, she might as well get some freebies out of the deal.* I was feeling good. Oh, I knew that boomerang could come swinging out of the sky at any moment (it was about to, in fact . . . I just didn't know it yet). But right now, I was eating good, I had fifty bucks in my pocket, and I was halfway to Florida. Things were working out all right.

o o o

I made a couple of trips to the buffet table, and so did the fat lady. Just before I looked away in disgust, wham! That damned boomerang clocked me upside the head so hard it made me dizzy. See, what I saw at that moment was the fat lady had no legs. She literally had *no legs.* She wasn't in a wheelchair because she was too heavy—she was in a wheelchair because that's the only way she could get around.

Well, I went from ten feet tall to about two inches in a split-second. Fact was, my stupid brain went wild and formed another silly-ass opinion. I'd mentally berated the woman. Sure, she was overweight. But I still felt bad. I thought about that old Indian line again, about walking in someone else's shoes. Truth was, the fat lady wasn't ever going to walk in her *own* shoes, let alone someone else's. Maybe she ate too much, maybe not. So what? I had every right to judge her if I wanted to, had every right to have my own opinion about her. But I still felt pretty embarrassed. If there was one good thing, one saving grace, it was this: I hadn't opened up my mouth. Oh, I would never chastise someone like that to their face. Not to their face, I wouldn't. But in my mind, behind their back, maybe to my friends when the victim was out of earshot. I'd say something like, 'Did you see that chick (or dude) over there? Jesus . . . they've got no business in a buffet.' Sorry, it's cruel, I know. But I do shit like that. You know . . . think things or say things without thinking them through. Now, I felt bad for every time I'd done or said something like that. Sometimes, I wish my brain had a rewind, where I could back up the tape and erase over the stupid stuff.

o o o

I walked up to the cashier where an older Asian lady stood. She had graying hair and a bright, shiny smile. All she did was nod, as I figured she probably knew very little, if any, English. I turned around and glanced back. The lady in the wheelchair and her daughter were at the buffet again, on the other side of the room. The Asian girl who'd seated me walked past their table and set down the bill tray. I hustled over, picked it up, and returned to the cashier. My bill and theirs totaled just under sixteen dollars, so I just gave the older Asian lady a twenty and walked out. I know it's not much of a gesture of atonement, but it made me feel a little better. Of course, if I went around buying people their meals every time I felt guilty about thinking something stupid, I was going to be broke forever.

o o o

I walked outside. As I made my way across the parking lot, I saw Dawn and Joe emerge from Victoria's Secret. He was still clutching her arm like she was an escaped convict. Joe was now carrying one bag, and Dawn had another. Even from far away, she saw me—I was sure she did—but Joe didn't. I turned and walked across the parking lot to find my motel room.

33

The room was clean and the bed felt great. I had cable television, a hot shower. Awesome. Dawn didn't have to do it, but I was glad she did.

It was only eight o'clock, so I killed some more time rummaging through the stations. There wasn't much on. News, a few game shows. Animal Planet was showing some reruns of Steve Irwin, the Crocodile Hunter. He'd been killed earlier in the summer by a stingray. Harpooned through the heart. I wondered what Ellen thought about that. The Crocodile Hunter had been sort of a hero to her. Lots of people thought he was an idiot and all, catching poisonous snakes with his bare hands and wrestling crocodiles. I thought he was cool, though. He seemed like he really, genuinely cared about wildlife and the environment. His show brought the natural world right into the living rooms of millions of people. It just blew me away how he'd grab a snake and start talking about how poisonous it was, how it could kill him with a single bite. He'd even said on several occasions that, sooner or later, his job would kill him. It was sad it had been sooner.

o o o

After watching the rest of Crocodile Hunter, I killed the television, showered, and crawled into bed. I know it might sound trite, but I thought it was cool that I would actually be able to take *two* showers—one that night and one in the morning. If I'd spent the night in the semi cab, I'd be shower-less. I closed my eyes and mentally thanked Dawn. And I wondered what, at that very moment, she was doing. With Joe. I wondered why it bothered me.

I fell asleep, sort of. I was only dozing, in that half-space of not-quite-awake, not-quite asleep. At some point, I heard a soft buzzing and a click—and my motel room door opened.

I sat up instantly when light from the hall poured into the room. I could see Dawn's silhouette and the shadow of a couple of big bags. Then, the door closed behind her. The room was murky, but I could make out her form and shadowy features as she walked toward the bed. Paper bags crinkled.

"What hap—" I began to say, but she shook her head, stopping me in mid-sentence.

"Nothing," she said. "Nothing happened tonight. I'll explain in the morning. Just don't leave the room until I say. Until I explain."

"Can't you explain now?" I asked. I really was wondering what the hell was going on.

"I'm really tired right now," she said, and with that, she pulled the covers down. She kicked her shoes off, slipped out of her jeans, and climbed into bed next to me. It was an awkward moment, sort of. She caught me completely off guard, unprepared, as she snuggled next to me. Slowly, I raised my arm around her until my hand was on her waist. She draped her arm over my chest, and we fell asleep.

34

Morning came. I awoke just after five. Dawn was still next to me, in the same place she was when she came to bed. She hadn't moved an inch. I could hear her soft breathing and could feel her body pressed to mine.

I lay there for a long time—at least an hour—not wanting to disturb her. And talk about a confused head. On one hand, I was a bit repulsed at the thought of having a prostitute next to me. Obviously, many men don't feel that way. But I did. There was just something about the whole thing that seemed unclean, unhealthy. I guess one of the reasons I felt this way was because the hookers I was used to seeing walking the street were not at all what I found attractive, to say the least. Dawn didn't look anything like the hookers I was accustomed to seeing, but it didn't change the fact that she screwed for money.

Then, there was the other side. The Dawn without the mask. There was a part of me that cared about her a lot, and I didn't know why. For the life of me, I didn't. Sure, I've had girlfriends before. Sort of, anyway. I mean, I've had girls I've cared about. And golly-gee . . . I've even had sex. One whole time. But that's not how I felt about Dawn. I was trying to get it straight in my head: how was it that I liked her? I fully admitted once I saw the *real* Dawn, the woman behind the mask, she was suddenly attractive. Maybe even beautiful. Was that it? But if it was, how could someone learn to like someone who could so easily slip away into someone else's shoes . . . a someone else wholly different, yet the same? Someone who wore a Halloween mask as a permanent disguise?

These thoughts ping-ponged around my head for an hour. Finally, I settled on the things I knew: Dawn was a hooker. She was confused. Oh, she didn't come right out and say it, but I knew, especially after our Halloween conversation in the semi. And she had been kind to me. She'd paid for my room (twice) and gave me money for food last night. There was something about her that wasn't so tough as she let on to believe.

o o o

How did she get a key to my room? And what had happened between her and Joe? That was driving me nuts. I didn't think I'd see Dawn until morning. Hell, I thought she'd be spending at least until midnight just modeling all of the shit he'd bought her at Victoria's Secret. Maybe they had some fight or argument. Who knows. All I knew was that I was glad. Oh, we probably lost our ride to Florida. Big deal. We'd find another one.

We. We. There it was again.

o o o

Dawn yawned and drew her arm back. I turned my head as she opened her eyes. She said nothing. Instead, she pulled the covers back and stood. She was wearing a a pair of black panties and a black lace bra as she stumbled sleepily into the bathroom and closed the door. She emerged a few minutes later and walked to the window, where she pulled back the drape a tiny bit and peered outside. It was still dark, but the glow of the lights in the parking lot streamed in. I figured she was looking for Joe's semi, wondering if he'd left or not.

"What happened last night?" I asked.

She let the curtain fall back into place, and the room darkened again. Then, she sat down at the edge of the bed. "Do you want the juicy version with all the details?" she asked, and I could hear the smile on her lips.

"Do you think I need to hear it?" I asked, wondering if I actually wanted to hear it at all.

Dawn laughed. "Oh, I think you do. It's pretty funny. See . . . Joe had this idea he was going to record us having sex with his webcam and his laptop computer. But it wasn't just sex. He's into other things. Bondage, shit like that. He said I'd like it rough. I told him I wasn't interested in all that, and I really didn't want to be recorded. He said 'tough,' that he had paid for the room and my new clothes, and he was going to get his money's worth. Then, he pulled some ropes from his bag. He got this really weird look, and . . . I don't know. He changed. I could see it in his face and eyes. He looked crazy. I guess I realized I was going to have to play his game. I don't think, at that point, I had any other choice. I got a little scared, even. I knew he wasn't going to let me leave. And I knew if he tied me up, something was going to happen. Something that wasn't good. I could feel it. If I knew he was just going to tie me up and have his fun without hurting me, it wouldn't be so bad. But I got a really bad vibe. Really bad.

"So, I played along, sweet talked him, told him I wanted to have my fun first. As it turns out, old Joe enjoys spankings. So, after he hooked the camera up to his computer and began recording, I said I wanted to tie him to the bed first. He'd been a bad, bad boy, and he needed his punishment."

She was making this up. She *had* to be making this up. But I let her continue. Even if she was making it up, things were getting really interesting. It was like I had my own, live version of *Penthouse Letters* right in front of me.

"And he let me," Dawn said. "I undressed him and ordered him on the bed. I tied his wrists to the bedframe corners, all the while telling him what a bad boy he was. He loved it. I gave him a couple of slaps with his belt, too. Drove him nuts. He really thought he was in for a good time. Then, I went over to his computer and stopped recording. I deleted the file and booted up his e-mail. He had no password protection or anything, so it was easy."

"What was easy?" I asked.

"There were a bunch of e-mails from his wife. It was easy to set up a link to the live webcam and send it to her. When she clicks on it, she's going to see a live video feed of her husband, tied to the bed in room 255 at the Days Inn in Knoxville, Tennessee. I'm sure he's still there, right now."

My jaw dropped and hung open. "What was he doing the whole time you were fiddling with his computer?" I asked.

"Oh, not much, at first," Dawn replied. "But when he realized what was going on, he went crazy. First, he started calling me names. He kicked and flailed, trying to get free. When he realized the predicament he was in, he got awfully sweet awfully fast. He basically begged and pleaded. It got so pathetic I almost called it off. *Almost.* But the thought of his wife seeing him like that . . . plus the fact that he's stuck there for the maid to find him . . . well, I couldn't just pull the plug early."

"Remind me never to really piss you off," I said.

Dawn laughed. "Better not," she said playfully. She stood. "Come on. Let's get on the road before Matilda the Maid discovers loverboy."

35

We ate the fruit and cereal I had taken from the Super 8 the morning before. There was another truck stop about a half mile back; we figured we could head there and try to find another ride. Nice guy that I was, I carried Dawn's bags of clothes Joe so graciously bought her the night before. Dawn said he spent something like a hundred bucks at Victoria's Secret alone . . . including ten bucks for an edible thong he insisted on buying for her, saying he might be interested in a late-night snack. Puke.

"How did you get a key to my room?" I asked.

"I just went to the front desk and told them my room key didn't work," Dawn replied. "She asked me what room I was in and made me another key. Simple as that."

As we walked, all I could think about was Joe tied to the bed, and what his wife would think when she opened up her e-mail, clicked on the link, and saw a real-time video of her husband naked and tied to a bed, flopping around like a walleye on a stringer. And I would have loved to be a fly on the wall when the room attendant came in to make the place up. That's something that would be great to have a video of, something you could e-mail your friends and post on the web. I started laughing out loud as we walked.

"What?" Dawn asked as she found her cigarettes in her bag.

"I keep thinking of what you did to Joe," I said.

Dawn lit her cigarette. "He's a pig. He's got a wife and three kids. One of his daughters is my age."

"I imagine you can't be too picky when you do what you do," I said. It just slipped out like the wind, and it was (of course) the wrong thing to say at the wrong time. I certainly didn't mean it to sound the way it did. I just thought that, in her line of work, she couldn't be too choosy if she wanted to make money. I mean . . . why do you go into that line of work unless you're desperate for cash? (See? I really gotta get some sort of filter between my brain and my mouth, until they come up with that rewind button.)

Dawn stopped walking, and I immediately began verbally backpedaling. "Uh, what I meant was, was, I guess that you—"

"—would fuck anybody," she finished. "And you know what? You're right. Almost. I *would* fuck just about anybody. But that doesn't mean I have to *like* it. I don't—"

"—I didn't mean it the way—"

"I know *exactly* how you meant it," Dawn interjected, taking a drag from her cigarette. Then, she went off like a hand grenade, and all I could do was hold the pin and take the shrapnel like a man.

"You know . . . you've got a *lot* to learn. What I do, number one, is *my* business. Number two, my business can be with whoever I want to do business with. Do you think just because people don't take their clothes off that they're not screwing people every second of the day? If you decide you're not going to do business with someone just because you don't like them, you're going to find out how quickly you won't *have* any business. And it doesn't matter if you sell cars, real estate, whatever. The fact is, Greg, we are *all* prostitutes, whether you like it or not. That includes *you*. But we *can* choose whose bed we sleep in."

"I *didn't* mean it the way it sounded," I repeated, glad to be able to get it out in a complete sentence. "What I meant was . . . was that . . . ."

Shit. What in the hell did *I mean?* I knew what I thought, or, I *thought* I did, anyway. But the more I *did* think about it, the more I realized I'd pretty much dug a hole for myself.

She started walking again, and I was glad. And I just figured the best thing to do was apologize.

"I shouldn't have said that," I said. "I'm sorry. I wasn't thinking. The longer you know me, you'll realize sometimes my brain has no tourniquet while my mouth is on full-throttle."

"No shit?" Dawn spat, staring straight ahead. "I would've never known."

○ ○ ○

I started thinking I would be a lot better off once we reached Florida. When we did, Dawn would be off on her own little trip, wherever that was. She still hadn't told me where she was going. I think the idea sounded good to her, being that she had a free ride. Hell, she could make money anywhere. Why not Florida?

Regardless, I didn't care. She'd be gone and out of my life. She was a confusing person, and it made me tired trying to figure her out. She was a prostitute, and prostitutes use people. Sooner or later, I would get used, and I didn't even have to sleep with her. It would probably be best to keep my distance and not to be so nosy. What she did was her own business. Maybe she was interesting to me because of the whole sexual aspect. I don't know. I kind of liked her. The *real* Dawn, that is. The one without the mask. But it would probably be best to just leave it alone.

o o o

We weren't a hundred yards from the truck stop when I started to feel really bad. Not emotionally, in my head or anything. Physically. My stomach was really upset. At first I just blew it off, figuring it would just go away. But my stomach began to ache, and pretty soon it felt like a hot knife in my gut. I stopped walking, dropped Dawn's shopping bags, and stooped over. Just as Dawn asked me what was wrong, I blew my cookies on the shoulder of the road. It was bad, and the vomit burned my throat like drain cleaner.

"Shit, Greg," Dawn said, rushing to my side as I dropped to my knees. "Are you *all right?*"

I answered her by puking again, violently. My whole body shook. And not only that, I all of a sudden felt like shit all over. I was sweating, but I felt cold. I was nauseous and dizzy. My stomach felt like I'd swallowed a bowl of lava.

"What's the matter?" Dawn asked. She sounded really worried.

"I don't know," I wheezed. "All of a sudden I just felt sick. I just felt—"

I puked again, but it was mostly dry heaves that burned my throat and nostrils like napalm. I did, however, feel a little bit better after a moment, and I was able to stand up.

Dawn was looking at me like I had just landed from another planet. "You're as white as a ghost," she said. "When did you start feeling like this?"

"Just now," I said. "God, I feel like *shit* all of a sudden. Tired."

"Do you want to sit down?" she asked.

I motioned forward with my hand. "Let's go to the truck

stop," I said. My voice was barely a whisper.

Dawn grabbed me by the arm. "You look like you're about to pass out."

"I think I'll be okay," I said.

"Do you take anything? Like, medication or anything?"

I shook my head. "No," I said. "Nothing."

Dawn picked up one of the shopping bags I'd dropped, and I picked up the other. We started walking, and I was taking small steps because I was exhausted. Something was up, that was for sure. And I was certain it wasn't a cold. Colds don't come on like that. Not that fast. The flu? Maybe. But it still seemed like it came on really quick. I wondered if it had anything to do with the dinner I ate.

o o o

By the time we reached the truck stop, I was completely spent. I made it to a bench near the convenience store and collapsed onto it, dropping Dawn's shopping bag next to me.

"You're freaking me out," Dawn said as she sat down. "Like, has this ever happened to you before?"

I shook my head. Sweat covered my face, my arms, all over. My clothing felt damp and clammy. "No," I replied. "It must be some sort of stomach flu."

"There is a park over there," Dawn said, turning briefly and pointing. "Do you want to go lay down in the grass? There are some trees and shade."

Laying down sounded good, but the park, although it was only about a hundred yards away, seemed like miles. I wasn't sure I'd make it that far. But I'd give it a shot.

"Yeah, let's do that," I said.

Dawn helped me to my feet. I was dimly aware of my surroundings: trucks; cars; the cool, morning air. A kid was squawking like a seagull about not getting any candy, and there was someone not far away talking obnoxiously loud on a cell phone. There were several stores, but I didn't bother to look at what they were. A Fairfield Inn loomed beyond the park.

"Come on," Dawn urged. "I can get the bags." Which was a good thing. At that point, my arms were beginning to feel like lead pipes. I don't think I could have carried anything. Even my hands felt like they were pulling at my arms, like I was carrying cinder blocks.

And I was getting worried. I'd never had anything quite like this happen to me before. Sure, I'd had the flu a few times and chicken pox when I was little. *That* sucked. But the feeling I had right then was right up on the list. I felt worse than shitty.

o o o

Well, we made it to the park okay. Dawn dropped her bags and helped me to the ground. I laid down beneath a tree, and Dawn placed one of her bags of clothing beneath my head.

"Like . . . do you need to go to the hospital?" she asked.

"Just give me a few minutes," I replied.

That was the last I remembered of the park.

36

I woke up in bed to the very faint sound of a television. I was in a motel room. Talk about confusing. I was sure that we'd left the motel room already, unless I'd only dreamed that Dawn had come to my motel room, slept beside me, and then told me what she'd done to Joe. Was that it? Had it been a dream? Must've been.

I opened my eyes. I was feverish and, although I'd obviously been sleeping, I was tired. My skin felt hot and clammy.

Dawn was sitting in a sofa chair. Beyond her was a window. The curtain was partway open, and the sun was setting. *Setting.*

When Dawn saw me move, she stood, then sat down on the bed. Now, I was *really* confused. "You're alive," she said.

"That's debatable," I replied.

"Are you feeling any better?" she asked.

"I don't know," I said. "Where are we?"

"Room 312 of the Fairfield Inn," she said. "You don't remember coming here?"

I shook my head. "No. I don't."

"You were pretty out of it. I let you sleep in the park until noon, but it was getting hot. You were sweating bad. Drenched. I came over here and got a room—I didn't want to go back to the Days Inn—then came back and got you. You don't remember walking over?"

I tried, but damned if I could. It was an eerie feeling.

"You were, like, in a stupor," Dawn said. "You had a really high fever." She placed her hand on my head. "You still do. Not as bad, though. I have a sneaking suspicion you ate at the Mystic Panda last night."

I glared at her. "Yeah, I did. Why?"

Dawn hiked her thumb toward the television. "It's all over the news. Food poisoning. Lots of people that ate there yesterday are sick. Somebody died. Health department came in today and closed it down. When I saw that on the news, I almost called the hospital. I still will, if you want."

"No, no," I said, shaking my head. "I'll be fine."

"Can I get you anything?" she asked. I hadn't realized it at first, but her mask was off. She was just plain, sweet Dawn.

"No, I'm . . . actually, a glass of water would be great."

o o o

Dawn went to the bathroom and drew a glass of water while I propped myself up on my elbows. She brought the glass of water and held it to my lips. I drank, but I looked at her. Dawn unmasked.

Later, when the local news came on, the lead story was about the Mystic Panda and the cases of food poisoning. They had a picture of the person who had died. It was the fat woman in the wheelchair.

37

I fell into a broken, fragmented sleep, consisting of strange dreams. Dreams of Ellen, of Lacy and Bruce, Dawn, Joe. In one particularly weird one, Matt Dunbar and Dawn were a couple, and I was actually jealous. Stupid, I know, but I woke up sort of pissed off about that. In my dream they had been making out in Matt's car, and I came up to them. They never even stopped kissing. I never said anything to them. I just walked away, hurt and angry. Dawn was mine. That's the way it seemed in the dream, anyway.

o o o

While I drifted in a feverish daze, I was barely conscious of Dawn moving around. She'd placed a cool washcloth on my head, refreshing it every so often with a new, cooler one. A few times she brought me water, and I vaguely remember sitting up just enough to drink.

The alarm clock/radio provided a waning, green light. It was three forty-five. Dawn lay on the bed a foot away, clothed, breathing softly. I had been fortunate she was around, that's for sure. If I would've been alone, I might've passed out somewhere. No doubt someone would find me. Then, I would've been taken to the hospital, and they'd probably have found out who I was, find out I stole a car and ran away. They'd probably ship me home. I'd go to jail for stealing Bruce's car.

But I felt a lot better. My fever had broken, and I didn't feel queasy and nauseous. I still felt tired, but, all in all, it was a huge improvement. I was hungry, too. That was a good sign.

I climbed out of bed slowly, not wanting to disturb Dawn. I walked quietly through the darkness, to the bathroom, closing the door before turning on the light.

Did I ever look like *hell*. My face was gaunt and my cheeks were sunken. My skin looked sallow and pasty. I looked and felt like a corpse. Night of the living Greg.

I showered, and that made me feel a little better. There was also a small razor with a few other complimentary toiletry items near the sink. I was having to shave more and more, and it was getting to be a pain in the ass. I used to look forward to the day I would start to shave. Although I only had to do it a couple times a week, I was already bored with it. And I wasn't looking forward to the prospect of having to shave every day for the rest of my life. In seventh grade, there was a kid—I can't remember his name—who had to shave every day. I mean, if he didn't shave every day, he would've had a beard within a week. In eighth grade, he grew a mustache. He looked quite a bit older than he was, and he was well-known for being able to buy liquor and beer at the store. He looked old enough that clerks didn't bother asking for his I.D. when he bought beer. Not usually, anyway.

o o o

The shower and shave were refreshing. I was still tired, but not exhausted and drained like I had been. I wondered what it had been at the Mystic Panda that had caused the food poisoning. I don't remember anything tasting bad. Matter of fact, everything had tasted pretty good. By the time I'd left, I was pretty filled up.

But the lady in the wheelchair had died. She hadn't been so lucky, and I felt bad. Her daughter no longer had a mother. There was something wrong about that, having your mother taken away from you when you were so young, when you still depended on her for so much. At least, when my parents were killed, Ellen and I were too young; we had no memory of them. It was going to be worse for the girl, being that she was eight or nine And I had paid for their dinner. I paid for the woman's very last meal.

Thinking about that made me feel like shit again, so I let it go, and started thinking about how lucky I was I hadn't gotten sicker . . . or worse. And lucky that Dawn had been there to help. She'd paid for not one, not two, but three hotel rooms now. I was really grateful, and I wanted to do something nice for her. Flowers, or something. I just wanted to let her know I was thankful for everything she'd done. Chances of finding flowers at three in the morning were slim and none, but I resolved in my mind to do something like that for her. At least before we made it to Florida and went our separate ways.

o o o

I turned off the bathroom light and opened the door. I had to wait for my eyes to get used to the dark again.

From the darkness came Dawn's soft voice. "How are you feeling?"

I had hoped not to wake her. "Better, a lot better," I replied quietly, a bit self-conscious that I was completely naked. Then, I shrugged it off. It was really dark in the room. And besides: it's not like she hasn't seen a naked dude before.

"I washed your clothes. They're on the chair."

"No shit?" *Ah, that's me. Master of the English language, a charmer with every word.* What an idiot. "Thank you. Really. Thanks a lot."

"No problem." She sounded sleepy.

I found my clothes and pulled my T-shirt over my head, then slipped into my underwear and jeans.

"I'll check the lobby and see if they have any snacks," I said.

"They do," Dawn said. "Not much. A fruit basket and a juice machine. Some cookies. But the night attendant would probably pull out some cereal if you ask. Don't forget the room key. It's on the desk by the lamp."

"Cool. You want anything?"

"No. I'm going to sleep for a while."

"All right."

o o o

I found my socks and shoes, slipped into them, and left the room. When I opened the door, light from the hall spilled in. I turned around. In the dull shadows, Dawn lay on the bed, eyes open, watching me. She looked sleepy.

"Thanks again," I said. "I really mean it."

She smiled sweetly and closed her eyes.

38

The lobby was tomb-silent. There was no sign of the attendant anywhere. I probably could have swiped half the furniture and all of the magazines if I wanted.

There was a basket of fruit on the breakfast bar, and next to it was a tray of cookies that looked like they had M&Ms mixed in. I've had those before. Tasty. A juice machine—apple juice and orange juice—bubbled softly. Next to it were two air pots with coffee.

The night attendant—a chick who looked half black, half Hispanic—came out from the back office. She saw me and jumped. I'd scared the shit out of her.

"Sorry," I said. She smiled and said something in Spanish, then made an attempt at asking me if she could help me with anything. Only, it took a moment for me to figure out what she was saying. She must've just gotten off the boat yesterday or something. I asked her if she had any cereal, and she gave me this really strange look.

"Cereal?" I asked, making a cup with my left hand and a spooning, dipping motion with the other. I felt stupid. Here I was in the United States of America, and I had to use sign language to try to get a mini box of corn flakes.

She kept looking at me, and I could tell she was really trying to figure out what I wanted, but she shook her head.

"Never mind," I said, and I walked over to the breakfast bar. Fruit and cookies didn't sound all that bad. I grabbed a banana, an apple, three cookies, and then drew a cup of orange juice. There was a small eating area with several shadowy tables, but the lights were off. No problem. I found the switch on the wall, and the room bloomed into a brilliant white. I sat at a table . . . and then noticed the computer monitor on the other side of the room. A tiny green light on the side of the monitor was blinking. I walked over to it and moved the mouse, and the screen came to life. Rock and roll. I could check my e-mail.

I returned to the table and grabbed my food, then sat down in front of the monitor. I logged into my Yahoo account. Thirty-three new messages. Junk. Junk. Spam. Spam. One from Matt. It was from before I'd taken off. He'd forwarded a joke and a link that had some funny videos. There was more spam, more junk. I'd started getting a lot lately. But the very last message made me freeze. I had half of a cookie in my mouth, but stopped eating altogether. The subject header read: *Please Come.* It was sent from *SillyKitty123*.

That was Ellen's e-mail address.

39

I quickly popped out of my comatose state and clicked on the message. Blank. Ellen had written nothing. It was just a blank e-mail. It was sent at nine forty-four last night.

I quickly tapped out a reply, keeping it simple, but asking for more information.

Ellen:

On my way. Where are you? Directions? I'm in Knoxville, Tennessee. Hope to be in Florida in a day or so. Hope you're all right. Send me another note if you can. Don't know when I'll be able to check next, but I'll try. See you soon. G.

Her note was really confounding. Usually she tapped out short messages, if she sent me anything at all. Mostly, though, all she did was forward me crap that had been sent to her. Half of it I deleted without opening. But she was trying to get a message to me. Had she tried calling home? No, probably not. If Lacy or Bruce had answered, she probably would have hung up. Unless, of course, she really was in a *lot* of trouble. But, if I knew Ellen, she wouldn't be asking Lacy or Bruce for anything, ever again. And if she *did* happen to talk to them, they would, no doubt, tell her I'd stolen Bruce's car and run away . . . in which case, she would know I was on my way to Florida. Either way, I hoped she would get my message so she would know I was on my way.

o o o

I minimized the window and opened another one. I Googled *New World Peace Center*. Nothing came up of any relevance. I tried several other search engines, all with no luck. Strange. In this day and age, virtually every group or organization has a web site. Even if it's just a simple one. Odd.

I tapped off a note to Matt. I wrote that I 'borrowed' Bruce's car and was taking a little vacation. (No mention that the car was no longer in my hands.) I was careful not to give him too many details, just in case someone started asking him about me. No doubt the police would quiz my friends, and probably had already.

I finished eating and sat for a few moments, staring at the screen, thinking about Ellen's e-mail. The more I thought about it, the more worried I became. I hadn't seen her in a year. The phone call—and now her e-mail—had been the only communication I'd had from her. *In a year.* That's not Ellen. I kept thinking that after a month had gone by, she'd contact me. E-mail or something. I didn't have a cell phone and neither did she. Oh, I kept talking about getting one of those prepaid deals, but they were a lot of money when you're between jobs. I had other shit to spend my cash on besides cell phone minutes.

I got up, intending to head back to the room. Instead, I walked outside. The parking lot was lit by bright, sugar-blue lamps. There were only a couple dozen cars; not a busy night for the Fairfield Inn. The air was warm and fresh. A few cars hummed along I-75. On the other side of the park, the truck stop seemed rather lively for the early hour.

I tried to make out the place where I'd slept in the grass beneath the tree, but it was too dark. I was still amazed (and a bit stunned) I couldn't remember walking from the park to the hotel room. Couldn't recall a thing, no matter how hard I tried. But I sure was glad Dawn had been there.

o o o

To the east, a barren, dark road stretched into a sea of ink. I was still a bit tired, but I thought a slow walk—just a short stroll—would be good. Besides: I was bored. And I didn't want to go back to the hotel room and wake up Dawn just yet. She'd been taking care of me all day and probably hadn't had much sleep. The very least I could do was give her a little bit of time to snooze.

There were no lights on the road, and the further I got from the glow of the lights in the parking lot, the better I felt. And I could see stars, too. It was cool. There was no moon, but a billion stars glittered overhead. I started wondering about intelligent life on other planets. I wondered if, somewhere, maybe near one of the stars I was looking at, there was a planet that was similar to ours. Full of idiots running around, buying stupid motion sensor toys that sing and do stupid stuff like that dumb Billy Bass wall mount that was so popular a couple of years ago. Would they really have shit like that on other planets? Probably. But, then again, you never know. As I looked up into a field of countless, endless stars, I found it hard to believe that, out of all those suns, there wouldn't be at least a few dozen planets that could support intelligent life. Maybe the strongest evidence supporting intelligent life on other planets was the fact they haven't tried to make contact with us. (Leaving all of the redneck farmers who had been abducted and had their assholes probed out of the equation, of course.)

o o o

I didn't walk too far. I was still weak; I didn't want to get a half mile away, only to have to crawl back to the hotel. So, I turned around and headed back. When I got to the hotel, I sat on the curb for a while, listening to the sounds of the freeway, the sounds of the night. Far away, a siren screamed.

I looked at the bright lights of the truck stop in the distance, and that gave me an idea.

40

The night attendant was behind the front desk when I returned to the Fairfield Inn. She gave me a bored glance, but managed a smile and said something in her native Martian tongue, or whatever language they spoke on the planet she was from. I smiled, nodded, walked through the lobby, and turned into the hallway. The pool room was dark, the water still and glossy with jagged reflections. I stopped in front of the elevator and pressed the button. A bell chimed immediately, and the steel doors opened. I stepped inside and pressed the third floor button. The doors closed and the elevator rose.

At the door to our room (it felt strange just *thinking* that: *our* room), I fumbled with the plastic key until I finally got the thing inserted. I was trying to do it quietly without waking Dawn up. There was a buzz and a click as the electronic locking mechanism engaged. I pulled the key out and slowly pushed the door open. I heard the shower running, which I hadn't expected. Dawn was awake and up. But then, I thought, it would be even better.

I flipped on the light and walked into the room. The bathroom door was closed, and a thin blade of light splayed from the bottom of the door. There was a small desk lamp on the table near the television; I turned it on and placed the small vase of flowers and the card beneath it. Then, I left the room and went back down to the lobby.

41

I felt pretty good about the whole flower thing and was actually surprised to find them. They weren't very fresh, being that I bought them from a truck stop. No matter, really. Like they say: it's the thought that counts. I think everyone likes to get gifts, but they forget that *giving* makes you feel pretty good, too. Makes *me* feel good, anyway. That whole adage that says it's better to 'give than to receive' is true, although for different reasons. A couple of years ago, I gave my sister a compact disc by her favorite band, Green Day. It wasn't even her birthday or anything. The CD had just been released, but she didn't have the money for it. I had some money saved from mowing lawns around the neighborhood, and I started thinking about how happy she would be if, right out of the blue, I just up and bought the CD for her. And I started thinking about how good it would make *me* feel if I bought it for her. I could see Ellen jumping up and down and dancing all around. She'd freak. But see, here's the deal: there *was* a reason. The more I thought about it, the more I wondered just how happy it would make *me*. I figured I'd feel pretty happy to give her something that would make *her* happy. I know some people might think that's a selfish thing to do, but it's really not. After all, if you give a gift and expect something in return, that's not a very noble reason to give the gift in the first place. But this was different. I decided I would buy the Green Day CD with my money, and no matter how Ellen reacted, I was going to be happy knowing I'd spent my money on the gift and gave it to her just because I thought she'd liked it. I bought the CD and put it on her dresser with a note that said: *I just thought you might like this. Have fun listening.* - *Greg.*

When she came home from school, I waited patiently in my bedroom, pretending to do my homework, until she discovered it. Oh, you can bet I knew the exact moment she found it. She let out a gasp and a squeal and came running into my room. At first, she was shocked and wanted to know why I did it. I told her there was no reason in particular, that I knew she'd wanted the CD but didn't have the money. Well, she just about clean knocked me right off my chair. She literally *leapt* into my lap and squeezed me so hard I thought she was going to crack my ribs. Then, she ran off and she had this sort of lilt, like she was floating on air. And if I had to rate how I felt, I would say a flat out perfect ten. Maybe even eleven. I felt pretty good about what I had done. Hell, I probably felt as good as Ellen. So, if there's something wrong about giving a gift because you want to feel good, I'm guilty as hell. Sue me.

o o o

It was almost six in the morning, and the night attendant was joined by a black lady, maybe in her early twenties. And she was really good-looking, too. You could tell she put a lot of time into looking nice and getting ready for her job. She and the night attendant got busy setting up the breakfast buffet. They weren't even open yet, but the black lady told me to go ahead, dig in if I was hungry. Well, I guess I wasn't all that hungry after filling up on fruit and cookies earlier, but I helped myself to a small box of cereal. They had other stuff they were putting out, too: yogurt, hard-boiled eggs, muffins, donuts. Waffles, even. I decided I'd wait a few minutes, and then put together a little tray for Dawn and take it up to her. That would knock her out. Flowers, a card, and breakfast in her room. I'd be a hero. Captain Considerate, that's me.

o o o

I hung around the lobby, sitting on a couch and reading *Golf Magazine.* I guess I wasn't really reading it as much as I was *laughing* at it. Oh, I have nothing against golf, or any sport, for that matter. Golfers, it seemed, always took the game too seriously. When you think about it, the whole concept is silly. You hit a little ball, chase after it, hit it again, then repeat. It's a bit comical. And they call this 'exercise.' I've always heard golfers say that: how golf is good exercise. Well, I've golfed before, and I can truthfully attest that *that* ain't exercise. Not in the slightest. Exercise is when you get your heart pounding and you work up a sweat, and you do it for maybe a half hour or so. Take those people that compete in those triathlons. They swim across Lake Michigan, run to Manitoba, then bike to Bolivia. Yeah, I'm exaggerating a little, but you get the picture. Now *there's* some serious exercise. Or tennis, even. I've seen tennis players on television get pretty worked up at their game. But golf? That's just a lazy person's way of getting out of real exercise. What gets me is half the people that tell you it's good exercise will flop their ass down in a golf cart and chase their ball down with it. That's so funny that it's almost sad. I'm only sixteen and I don't claim to know a lot, but I'm old enough to know that golfing is not exercise. All it gets you is a nice walk in the grass, and if you can keep from getting pissed off at yourself when you hit that little white ball into the pond or the sand or the woods, well, that's probably not all that bad.

Another magazine on the table was called *Parenting*, and in big block letters in the upper left: *Latest Burping Techniques!* I about laughed out loud. *Latest burping techniques?* Someone wrote an article about this?

The smells coming from the breakfast bar were pretty enticing. French toast and waffles had been added to the buffet, and it was a pretty good spread. I put together a mixture of a little of everything: a yogurt, a hard-boiled egg, a small box of *Froot Loops,* French toast, a muffin, a cup of juice, and a coffee. I was on the elevator headed up when I realized I'd forgotten the milk and had to go back.

When I finally made it back to the room, I opened the door and could hear the hair dryer in the bathroom. She'd found the flowers and the card, as the envelope had been opened and the card was laying next to it. The bathroom door was partway open, and the air in the room was warm and steamy from Dawn's shower. I knew she probably hadn't heard me come in, and I didn't want to surprise her and all, so I called out to her.

"I brought you some breakfast," I said. The hair dryer clicked off, and the door opened farther. And there's Dawn, in this really sexy, slinky white teddy that must have been one of the items from Victoria's Secret. And it didn't cover much, I'll tell you that right now. It didn't cover much at all, and I'm not the least bit ashamed to say she looked good. Better than good.

She smiled weakly. "Thanks," she said. "And thanks for the flowers and the card."

"Hey, no problem," I said. "Thanks for taking care of me. I thought I was going to die a couple of times."

She went back to drying her hair, and I guess I was disappointed. I didn't know what reaction I was expecting for giving her the flowers and the card. I thought that girls loved to get things like that. Maybe Dawn did, but she sure didn't show it. It was just a simple card with a cartoon duck on the front. On

the inside was printed: *You're everything you're QUACKED up to be!*
Yeah, corny as hell, I know. But the card rack at the truck stop
was pretty picked over, and all the other cards were even worse.
I'd written, very simply:

> *Thanks for being my nurse. —Greg.*

That was all.

Then, I started thinking about the time I bought that CD
for Ellen, and how I told myself I was going to be happy about
it, no matter what her reaction was. And, I had to admit, if Ellen
would have just picked up the CD and said something like,
'*Thanks, Greg,*' and hadn't let out with all the whoops and hollers
and wiggly dance, well, I guess I would have been disappointed.
So, I decided right then and there that I did the right thing. I
really *was* appreciative of Dawn taking care of me when I was
sick, and if I didn't get the reaction I was hoping for when I
gave her the flowers and the card, well, it wasn't her fault. It was
mine. I was expecting something in return for the gift, and if
that something was supposed to come from Dawn, well, then,
I'd given her the flowers and card for the wrong reasons.

o o o

Dawn finished drying her hair. She came out of the
bathroom, picked up her tray of food I'd brought her, and sat
on the sofa.

"Thanks for breakfast," she said, but she didn't look at
me. I blew it off and turned the television on. It was six, and I
found the local news. They were still talking about the food
poisoning at the Mystic Panda and how charges against the
owners might be brought. Apparently, the place had been cited
several times by the health department for violations. And there
was going to be a fundraiser for the fat lady in the wheelchair
who'd died. Actually, the fundraiser was going to be for her
daughter, as the woman was a single mom. No job, no

insurance, no nothing. How she got along like that without legs—a single mom, raising a daughter—was beyond me. It was really sad. And now this poor girl would probably wind up in some home somewhere, or sent to live with a relative, like Ellen and me. Regardless, her mom was gone forever. The whole thing made me sad all over again, so I changed the channel. But I was getting sort of tired, and my eyes were heavy.

"I think I'm going to take a nap," I said.

Dawn looked up. "I got the room for two days, because I didn't know if you'd be up for leaving today," she said.

"I'll sleep for a while, then see how I feel. I'm pretty tired. Not quite back up to speed."

Then, I climbed onto the bed and fell asleep right there, without climbing under the covers, without even taking my clothes off.

I woke up three hours later, and Dawn—and all of her things—were gone.

42

That's a hell of a thing to wake up to, let me tell you. I guess I didn't know what to expect, but I didn't expect *that.*

The curtain was drawn and the room was dark, except for the thin light banding around the drape. It was bright enough to see a little, and the first thing I noticed was that her two shopping bags were gone. Dawn's oversized purse that had been on the desk was gone. The flowers and the card were still there. Other than that, it was like Dawn had never existed. I was sure she was gone for good, too, otherwise, she would have left her shopping bags. If she'd just gone out to go for a walk or to go shopping—or to make a few bucks, even—she would have left them. Nope. She was good as gone, that's for sure. She'd even cleaned up after herself. The tray of food was gone.

Well, I felt like shit. I was pissed, sad—everything. And I didn't know why. It wasn't like she was my girlfriend. Far from it. But, maybe, in the course of a short couple of days, we'd become friends, if only out of necessity. I guess I was finding out just how little of a necessity I really was to Dawn. She didn't need me, and I knew it. She never had. I hadn't needed her, no way. I mean . . . I sure was glad she was there when I got sick, but I probably would have survived without her. We'd gotten together over a matter of convenience, that's all. For whatever reason, Dawn had decided that it wasn't so convenient anymore. I'd become her beast of burden. She'd let go of the leash and got the hell out of there.

o o o

I looked for a note, but there was none. Nothing in the bathroom. No Dear John letter on the pillow.

Screw it, I thought. *She's a hooker. That's her job. She uses people like they use her. After all . . . what was that she'd said? 'We're all prostitutes, but we could choose whose bed we slept in.'*

Still, I felt sort of empty, and I didn't know why. Dawn was different, for sure, but I'd enjoyed her company. I had been looking forward to her company on the rest of the trip to Florida, as a matter of fact. I knew she'd be gone after that, but it was something certain, something sure. Dawn's companionship had at least been *something* that was dependable, if only for a short period of time.

So, I decided to go for another walk and get some air. No doubt it would be nice outside, with the sun and all. This was one of those things that you do to hide something else, one of those things you do to trick yourself into doing something you really want. And for me, what I was really hoping was to find Dawn. I thought I might find her wandering the truck stop. Maybe she was looking for customers, maybe she was looking for a ride. Maybe she was already gone. Of these, the last idea seemed most plausible. After all . . . she'd taken all of her shit with her. She was off on her own.

o o o

I took the elevator down. The lobby was a little busier,

now. It was almost ten, and there were a few breakfast stragglers picking over what was left at the buffet, which, according to the sign, had ended at nine-thirty. Most notably, there was a tall, thin, older woman picking over the remaining fruit like a vulture tearing at highway road kill. If I got within three feet of her, I bet she'd spread her wings and try to peck my eyes out.

The pretty black lady was behind the motel desk, as smiling and chipper as a chickadee. There was some guy dressed in a snazzy suit with a snazzy briefcase. He had a copy of the *Wall Street Journal* under his arm, and he looked important. Maybe he was, but, if there was one thing I was learning, it was that appearances are *always* deceiving. Things are *never* what they seem, despite what they look like or what you think you know. He might be the perfect family man with 2.1 kids, a white Chevy SUV, a wife that modeled underwear for *Newport News* (when she wasn't busy doing her dutiful work for the PTA and running her kids to and from soccer practice), and a golden retriever named Buddy or Snickers. Then again, he might be a serial killer. You can't judge a book by its cover—but that's what I'd done with Dawn. I think everybody does, to some extent. After all, when you walk into a bookstore, what is it that draws your attention? The cover, that's what. In fact, that's what people say all the time, and they don't even *think* about it. They pick up a book and say, *'Gee, this looks like a good one'* . . . not realizing that they've just judged it by its cover.

But Dawn was different. She was different in the fact that the cover of her book gave absolutely no indication as to what her story was *really* about. Her cover might have been *Penthouse Letters,* but her text was as perplexing as a trigonometry textbook.

o o o

I strode through the lobby and outside. The day was

warm, sunny, and a little humid, even. The air was robust, full of the thickness of fall. I wondered what my friends were doing in Bay City. It was nearly ten; that meant Matt Dunbar would be stopping by the vending machine in the cafeteria between classes to get two *Kit Kats* and a *Milky Way* bar. Maybe a bag of chips, if they had any left. Potato chips were the first to sell out after the guy came and stocked up the machine once a week. Mrs. Gilooly would be bitching up a storm about how no one studied for their test, and half the class was going to fail if they didn't get their act together. Lacy and Bruce, I was sure, were probably still sleeping. Or they were already awake and shitfaced; one of the two.

And me? I was in Knoxville, Tennessee, walking around in the sunshine, pretending I wasn't looking for a hooker I'd met only two days ago.

43

I walked through the park to the truck stop. It was a lot busier than it had been earlier. Trucks were everywhere. There were several dozen parked in rows and just as many pulling in and out. The air was thick with diesel fumes, and the rumble of engines sounded like a steady drone of various instruments, all meshed and knitted together.

And no, I told myself as I weaved in and around, no, I was *not* looking for her. The trucks, they were fascinating. Yes, that's what I was interested in. And look: there's a girl right up there carrying—nope. That was someone else I wasn't looking for.

Thirty minutes later, after I'd wandered through the truck stop inside and out, I succeeded in not finding the girl I hadn't been looking for in the first place.

This is pretty pathetic, I thought as I stood just outside the doors of the truck stop. *She's gone.* People were coming and going—men, mostly—with looks of stern consternation, like they were on a mission, like they knew where they were going. Everyone was in a hurry. Some carried coffee, snacks, things like that. Ten hours from now, they might be halfway across the country. Just like Dawn.

So, I mentally said, *To hell with it.* Time to make my own plan. I needed to be in Florida by October 10th. Sure, I had a week, but I still didn't know where in the hell I was going, other than the name of the place where Ellen was. *New World Peace Center* in West Palm Beach. But I figured once I actually got to West Palm, someone somewhere would know something. I could probably find a listing in the Yellow Pages, for that matter.

o o o

I walked into the convenience store and bought a folding map of the United States, as the one I'd had was gone with the stolen car. I still had thirty bucks left, not counting the twenty in my savings account. I'd still have to watch my expenses. Thirty dollars wasn't a lot to live on for a couple of days, let alone a week.

I went outside and headed back to the hotel. On the way, I passed a big, green dumpster overflowing with trash. There was stuff piled two feet on top of it, and garbage had spilled over onto the ground. It was like the Mt. Everest of refuse. I was downwind, and the odor coming from it was rank: a mixture of rotting paper and piss. But something small caught my eye. It was a book. A paperback. I walked over to it and picked it up. It was brand new, except for the fact that the front cover had been torn off. It was called *His Heart's Desire,* by Margaret Stamos. Some sappy romance book, no doubt. But I looked around and discovered a few dozen more paperbacks, all new, all without covers.

And it occurred to me: having no covers gave all the books a level playing field. There was no way you could pre-judge the book by looking at a bare-chested, long-haired stud holding a hot chick with big hooters. You couldn't be attracted to the book by a dazzling sunset or a mysterious, foggy city. No fancy colors, no embossed foil etching to catch your eye. There was no way you could judge a book by its cover. You had to go on the title alone.

o o o

I tossed *His Heart's Desire* into the dumpster and found several more books. One happened to be a science fiction book called *Galaxy Quest,* by Raymond L. Marshall. Never heard of him, and the title sounded kind of cheesy, but I figured it might help pass the time when I found a ride to Florida. The back cover depicted a short summary of what the book was about, and a small picture of a futuristic space-warrior clad with a silver and purple suit. Next to him was a well-endowed woman with the same outfit. Both were blasting away at something with their super ray guns. Zap! Zap! I stuffed the book into my back pocket, walked back through the park, and into the hotel.

44

The maid was servicing the room when I returned, so I went back down to the lobby to hang out for a while. I sat down in a big recliner and pulled out the paperback I'd pilfered from the dumpster.

Galaxy Quest turned out to be pretty good. It was about this guy named Robert 342 (I imagined the numbers were supposed to be his last name) who was 'frozen' and sent out into deep space at light speed. His mission was to look for a previous craft that had been sent out, but never heard from again. To make things more interesting, they also froze and sent along a mate for him (of course!), Lora 447, who was actually not a real woman at all, but some sort of cyborg-type thing that looked, felt, and acted like a real human. I only read about forty pages or so, right up to the point where Robert 342's ship was slowing and he was waking up from his ten billion mile journey. The story wasn't all that original, but so far, it was interesting and the writing was pretty good. The author didn't go on for paragraph after paragraph, describing the character's *jutting, masculine jaw* and his *chiseled, muscular body*. Nor did he go on about the female cyborg's *voluptuous, heaving breasts* (fake as they were) or her *soft, supple, lips.* I hate that in books. I mean, sometimes its okay, especially if you're looking for a lot of detail. But mostly, if you're just reading for pleasure, wanting to get into the story, I don't give a rat's ass about all the extemporaneous bullshit. Give me the story, pronto, or I'll go find something else.

о о о

Thirty minutes passed, and I figured the maid was probably finished cleaning my room. As I rode the elevator up, I thought about the maid at the Days Inn discovering Joe, naked on the bed, tied up, with his wanker flopping around like a sausage link as he tried to get free . . . and all the while, the webcam broadcasting all the hot action in real time. You gotta love technology.

My room smelled like peaches and vanilla. It was clean, and I actually felt spoiled. I'd spent the last three nights in hotels, which was more than I had in the entire past five years. I'd never had to make the bed or clean up after myself. Having invisible little elves do all the work was pretty cool.

о о о

I spread the map of the United States on the bed, trying to estimate the distance from where I was in relation to West Palm Beach, which was way down on the southeastern coast of the state. I-75 went down the other side of the state, through Tampa, Port Charlotte, and Fort Meyers, until it turned east and went across the everglades to Fort Lauderdale, which was a ways south of West Palm Beach. Of course, I wouldn't be the one doing the driving, so any route I took to West Palm Beach was fine with me . . . as long as I was there by October 10th.

○ ○ ○

I looked at the clock. 11 a. m. I could do one of two things: I could try and find a ride that afternoon, or I could wait another day. The room was paid for. If I stayed on, I would at least have a roof over my head tonight, for sure. The more I thought about it, the better it sounded. I was still a little weak from the food poisoning, and I'd been up early. It wouldn't be long before I was tired, and I didn't want to be traveling all weak and sleepy. I might just get sick again, and that was the *last* thing I wanted. I'd feel even better the following morning, if I'd be able to get a good night's sleep.

And then I suddenly remembered something else: Ellen's e-mail. I'd e-mailed her back; maybe she had time to reply. I got up and hurried down to the lobby. There was only the one computer, and there was some hotshot guy in a business suit on it. *Galaxy Quest* was still in my back pocket, so I pulled it out and got back into the story. Our hero, Robert 342, had just awakened. He was billions of miles from earth, and he was in the process of waking up his companion, Lora 447. Together, they brought the ship out of its semi-hibernation state, going through all sorts of routine tests. Suddenly, there was a blip on the radar, and they recognized it as the ship they were in search of. They were only several thousand miles from it, and soon it was within sight. I was really getting into the story, so much so that I almost forgot about the hotshot at the computer until he stood up, slipped on his sport coat, picked up his briefcase, and walked off.

○ ○ ○

I closed the book. I'd have to wait to see what old Robert 342 and Lora 447 discovered about the old spacecraft. At the moment, I was much more interested in finding out if

Ellen had sent me an e-mail.

I logged into my account. The first few e-mails were just junk shit: offers for credit cards, cheap Viagra, and hot stock tips. One e-mail from Matt. Nothing from Ellen. I opened up Matt's e-mail. His note was short.

Hey, man! Everybody's looking for you! Where in the hell are you???????

That was it. I sent him a quick reply, simply saying I'd fill him in as soon as I could. I told him not to worry, that I was fine. Then, I opened up another window and tried some more searches for the *New World Peace Center.* Nothing came up at all. That just seemed so strange. Even if it was a new place, almost *everybody* has a web site. *Everybody.*

The computer made a strange *bing!* sound. Some sort of alarm or something. I closed the window and looked at my e-mail. There was a new message—from Ellen. She'd sent me an e-mail just seconds ago . . . which meant she might still be at a computer. I grabbed the mouse and clicked on her message.

45

Her e-mail didn't contain anything on a personal note, but it *did* contain an address. 4586 Montoya Dr., West Palm Beach, FL 33480. That was all. There was no message, no phone number, nothing. Just the address. I jotted it down quickly, then I opened up another window and went to a mapping web site. I typed in the address . . . and there it was. Awesome. Now, at least I knew where I was going. I had a concrete destination of where the *New World Peace Center* was. Where Ellen was.

o o o

An ink-jet printer was attached to the computer, so I printed the directions. The color ink was getting low and the map turned out a few funky shades of yellow and pink, but that didn't matter. It was readable, and that's what counted.

I felt refreshed and renewed. I knew where I was going, knew where I was headed. I'd make it to West Palm Beach by the 10th, for sure. I'd find the *New World Peace Center*. I'd find Ellen. I swear, I wanted to leave right then. Get started finding a ride, and get on the road. But I talked myself out of it. As much as I wanted to be on my way, I knew I should probably rest another day. No need to waste a perfectly good hotel room and all. I could kill some time and read *Galaxy Quest*. I *really* wanted to find out just what Robert 342 and Lora 447 found when they reached that old spaceship. There were several scenarios I predicted: 1) the old crew had been killed by some space virus; 2) the old crew was gone completely; or 3) the old crew had been taken over by some alien life form. There were other possibilities, of course. It was just up to good old Raymond L. Marshall to surprise me.

o o o

Back in my room, I closed the drapes, took off my clothes, climbed into bed, and opened *Galaxy Quest*. My second scenario quickly unfolded: the old crew was missing . . . but, while Robert 342 and Lora 447 investigated the old ship, they had no idea that other alien crafts were approaching. Yeah, it was predictable. Sometimes, books are, but it doesn't make them any less fun to read. I forgot about everything, at least for a while. I forgot about Lacy and Bruce, Ellen, stealing Bruce's car (and having it stolen from me). I even forgot I was in a hotel room. In fact, I was so wrapped up in my book I didn't even think about Dawn again . . . until I awoke in a gloomy darkness, and she was standing at the side of my bed.

46

After, when we lay in bed together, I was thinking about Raymond L. Marshall's book and how predictable it had been. Like I said: I'm pretty good at figuring out where a book is heading and what's going to happen to the main characters. But I would never have predicted Dawn would come back. I was sure she was gone for good. More than sure. I had been *positive*.

o o o

I don't know if she had awakened me or not, as I didn't remember hearing any noise at all. Matter of fact, I was really zonked out. In the afternoon, I had been nodding off while reading. Things weren't looking good for Robert 342 and Lora 447, as they'd been taken prisoner by a powerful alien race known as Drioleans. They'd escaped, but they were still on some planet, trying to evade their captors. I started nodding off right when they were attempting to steal an alien craft and escape into space. I was almost three quarters of the way through the book, and it was really good, but I was tired. I marked the page with a piece of Fairfield Inn notepaper and put it on the night stand. I turned off the light, and the last thing I remembered was looking at the clock. It was just after five in the afternoon.

Next thing I know, it's dark. Stale mercury light bled around the outline of the window curtain, giving the room a haunting, surreal glow. Dawn was standing beside my bed, ghost-like. Shocked? Hell, yeah, I was. I didn't jump or anything. Didn't even flinch. Maybe I thought I was dreaming, or I maybe I was really sleepy. It's a good thing it wasn't an axe murderer standing there, though. I'd be dead.

I spoke. "When did you—"

She silenced me with a single finger placed to my lips, where it rested for what seemed like a long time. Then, she pulled her shirt up over her head, revealing a red lace bra . . . no doubt, another one of Joe's gifts. Then she slipped out of her shorts, and her panties went with them. She pulled back the sheets, got on her knees on the bed, leaned forward, and kissed my lips gently. I started to speak again, but she stopped me.

"No," she said. "Not now. I'm so glad you're here. I was afraid you'd already left."

○ ○ ○

Her kisses were exquisite, like nothing I'd ever known. I tried to push aside the fact that she was, of course, much more experienced at this than I was. Dawn was, in fact, a professional. This was her *job*.

That was another thought I pushed away. I didn't want to think she was just doing her job, that I was just another customer. Hell . . . I didn't even have money to pay her, and she *had* to have known that. So I just pushed the thought away, gently, and Dawn made it easy. We kissed for a long time, and our lips never parted. Her tongue was warm, with a bitter taste of nicotine that I was familiar with. My last girlfriend smoked on occasion, and the taste of cigarette on her lips didn't bother me any which way. I was happy just to have a pair of lips and a tongue to play with.

o o o

Later:

Dawn collapsed forward and slowly curled her arms around the back of my head and buried her face in my neck. Every few moments she would give a gentle little twitch with her hips, and the effect was intoxicating. If one can be sexually drunk, I was legally there.

We lay together for a while, breathing heavily, our sweaty, hot skin pressed together. Finally, she drew up and climbed off the bed. She gently tugged the condom from my softening penis (she'd had one in her purse; there were more, I was sure) and vanished into the bathroom. The door closed and a thin bar of light escaped from the bottom. Then, I heard a flush, the light went off, and the door opened. Dawn came back to bed. She crawled up next to me, and I slipped my arm around her. I felt incredible. Wonderful. Satisfied. I felt powerful and unstoppable. King of the Universe, even. I pulled the covers up to my chest.

We slept.

47

I sat in the park, cross-legged, eyes closed, letting the sun dry my tears. Dawn's note was in my pocket. I'd thrown it out, but then, just before I checked out of the room, I went back up and got it. I don't know why. There were a lot of things I didn't know at that point.

o o o

I'd awakened several times during the night, always to Dawn's warm body next to mine. Mostly, I cupped her with my left arm, holding her close. I didn't want to move, I didn't want her to move. Once, I awoke to find that we'd turned, and we were spooning, with my right arm around her. I could feel her soft breasts press against my arm as she breathed. The feeling was wonderful, beautiful. I'm not one who uses the word 'exquisite,' but I could now officially add it into my mental vocabulary, being that I now not only knew what it meant, but had experienced it firsthand. Something inside me had changed. Dawn had changed everything. For the first time since we'd met, I felt I really knew the *real* Dawn, finally. The mask wasn't just *off:* it was completely discarded. Oh, I'm sure she could easily slip it back on, and probably would from time to time. But I *knew.* She couldn't fool me. I could see right through the mask, could see right through to her, right to her soul. The wonderful, beautiful woman she was. She wasn't just street trash, as so many of her customers probably thought her to be. She wasn't a filthy slut. I felt ashamed that I could have ever imagined her like that. She was real, she was genuine, she was pure. Crazy, I know. But I knew the *real* Dawn. I knew her perhaps better than anyone, and I was certainly qualified to make an assessment. It's funny how everybody just offers up their convictions when they know so very little of the facts. And I'm including myself in that lot, too. Like judging a book by its cover. Sure, it's hard not to. In most cases, maybe our first impressions are correct. But we certainly don't know the entire story of someone's life by looking at a photograph or shaking a hand or nodding a hello. Not hardly. And right there, in the middle of the night, holding Dawn in my arms, I decided that I would try—the best I could—not to be so judgmental. Opinions are opinions, of course; there *is* a difference. Opinions are fine. But I put a note in my mental day planner. I would really think twice about judging anyone unless I really had the knowledge to back it up. Like my knowledge of Dawn. The headline back home would read: *Greg Chappell Sleeps With Prostitute.* Would it be true? Yes. Would it be accurate? Yes. Would it be a fair assessment? Would it be just? Hardly. You just can't judge a book by its cover.

o o o

I hadn't known why she came back, but I was so, *so* glad she did. I was more complete, I thought, than I have ever been in my whole life. I had never felt like that before. And it wasn't just the sex part of it, either. (Although, admittedly, it *did* play its own, perfect, blissful part. No shame in that.) But I sure felt more for Dawn than I had ever felt for anyone. I'd dated Annette Deering for nearly three months, and our relationship had been consummated with an awkward attempt at sex. It was the first time for both of us, and, while it was exciting and all that, we both knew we had a lot to learn. It just turned out that she was going to be learning it with someone else. Oh, we liked each other, but we didn't have any really deep feelings for one another. Annette was fun to be around, and I'd known her for a few years. We hooked up at a party, and, somehow or another, we wound up making out in a back room. We dated from then on, but we didn't do a lot. Neither of us had a lot of money. Mostly, we would go to movies or hang out with friends. We broke up only a few weeks after our tryst. She was the one who did, actually. She'd met some guy and wanted to go out with him. I was hurt, sure. But I didn't feel that pain in the gut, that horrible knife in my stomach, the feeling I was about to throw up. The feeling I had as I sat in the sun in the park, knowing Dawn was out of my life forever.

o o o

I'd awakened alone in the motel room. The morning sun was burning sulfur seams around the edges of the curtains. Dawn wasn't at my side, but it never occurred to me she might be gone again. Certainly not after last night. She was probably getting some breakfast down in the lobby.

But when I sat up and looked around, I had a horrible deja-vu feeling sweep over me, pressing me down. Her large purse was gone, and there was no sign of her bag of new clothing. The bathroom door was open; the light was off. The flowers and card were gone, replaced by two sheets of hotel stationery.

A note.

48

Dear Greg:

I don't even know where to begin, but I've been sitting here for an hour without writing a single thing. So, I'm just going to write, and see what comes out. Maybe the words will come if I just start somewhere.

First of all: thank you. I don't think you'll ever know what you've done, how much you've helped me. There's so much you still don't know about me, but you know more than probably most people. I don't know how you came up with that Halloween mask analogy, but it really was right on. You made me see something, all of a sudden. It hit me when we were talking about it in Joe's truck. It hit me so hard I thought I was going to have a nervous breakdown or something. But Joe came back, and I was able to get my 'mask' back on. You're right: I've been wearing that thing for so long, sometimes I don't even know myself. Even now I wonder if I know who I am, really. I like to think I do. I don't know for sure. But, most importantly, I think I can find out who I am. I think I can get back to the person I am. Maybe it's not too late.

I never set out to be a hooker. (I know you are wondering how I got started; everybody does.) I was at a party one night, and I met a guy that was really forward. He just came up and asked me if I wanted to fuck, and I laughed and said no. He kept pestering me, in a nice sort of way. A little

178

later on, he said he had a hundred bucks, and I could have it all. Well, I don't think I have to go into all the details, but I really needed the money. A couple of days later, a guy called me and said he was a friend of the guy that I'd slept with after the party. He had money, too. I needed money. Mom and I weren't getting along real well, and I was thinking of moving out. Anyway, that's how it started. When Mom found out, she completely freaked. She threatened to call the cops, so I took off. I lived with a friend for a while, and I still have some of my shit at her place. But mostly, I went from truck stop to truck stop. The money was really, really good. I'm sorry, but it's true. It's hard to even write about it now, as I feel so ashamed and embarrassed. But it's the truth, and I can't change it. I can only change the future.

o o o

I liked how she put that: *The money was really, really good.*
Was. *Was.*

o o o

No one—not ever—has ever given me flowers before. Never. None of my boyfriends, in school, not a secret admirer, no one. When I saw the flowers on the desk and read the card, I couldn't take it. Everything just came down on me. I was so confused. I couldn't believe someone would do that. For **me**. I know you did it 'just because,' and that was what made it worse. Does that make sense? You've shown me . . . I don't know. I don't know how to write it or say it. I don't know exactly what it is that you've shown me, but I know I'll figure it out, in time. The important thing right now is that I have a clear idea of what I need to do. I certainly don't have all the answers, but I know I need to make some changes. And I don't think it's too late. Hopping from truck stop to truck stop, from guy to guy, well, I'm lucky I'm still alive. There were times when I'd be with a guy and wonder. There were times I was so afraid I was going to be killed. Oh, my mask (as you call it) hid it just fine. But most of those guys don't care about

179

me in the least. In fact, they'd much rather see me dead than have their wives or girlfriends or bosses find out about me. To them, I'm a toy. I'm a liability. I'm disposable. And maybe that's how I've thought of myself, for a long time. Oh, I don't blame anyone. Not Mom, not anyone. It's easy to get confused when you don't even know who you are.

Greg, you showed me differently. I'm not going to get all corny on you, but I think, in some strange way, you saved my life. You really did. I believe it with all my heart. Some things really are black and white, like you said. Not everything, of course. But it's hard to recognize those things, sometimes. Maybe things get mixed. There's too much gray, and you don't always see what's black and what's white.

I'm going back to Ohio. Home. I'm going to try to fix things between Mom and me. That's a start. From there? Who knows? It'll be a clean slate, I hope. A new beginning. It will take some time, I know. I can't fix things overnight.

I've already written more than I thought I would, so I'd better wrap it up. Just know this, Greg: there is a part of me that will always be grateful for what you've done. Always, always. I will think of you often, and I hope that you will think of me in a good way. I won't blame you if you don't, but there will always be a part of me that loves you, I promise you that. Of course, you might hate me. But I hope you don't. I hope you understand. Please, please understand, Greg.

I hope you find your sister, and I hope she's okay. With you as her brother, I know she'll be safe.

Now, I'd really better stop writing, because I'm crying so hard that I can't even see the paper.

Thank you, Greg. I love you for who you are. Always.

—Dawn

P.S.: There is a Bible in the lower right hand drawer of the desk. Look inside it before you go.

o o o

I was sobbing and shaking as I finished her letter. I felt

light headed. I kept thinking *no, no, no, no,* again and again. *She can't be gone! Not after last night! Not after—*

I dropped the note and it fell to the floor in leafy arcs. I continued sobbing, my face in my hands. Dawn was gone. I had no picture of her, nothing to remember her by, except for her letter. And memories.

Finally, after I'd stopped crying, I knelt down on the carpet and pulled the lower right-hand drawer open. There was a black, faux-leather covered book with gold embossed letters: *HOLY BIBLE.*

Inside it were twenty-five twenty dollar bills.

Five hundred dollars.

49

I sat in the grass in the park until around noon. The world spun in dull circles, but I wasn't aware of it. Time could have stopped, or twenty years could've gone by. I couldn't tell, and I didn't care. In bed, laying next to Dawn, I had been sure something wonderful and great had happened. I was sure we'd be together. There was a certain symmetry, a rare magic I'd felt, holding Dawn as we fell asleep together. I was sure the boomerang had come back on a good swing, like that guy that won the Powerball lottery. Only this was *better*. I wouldn't have traded that feeling for all the money in the world.

Now, Dawn was gone. We had one night together, one night of enchantment. I didn't hate her for leaving, like she thought I might. Not in the least. I knew she hadn't used me. Quite the contrary. It hadn't been a one-night stand. She'd given me a part of herself that I would take with me everywhere, forever. And maybe she'd taken the same from me.

But maybe that wasn't true. Maybe I just told myself that so I wouldn't go crazy. It's the only way I could come to terms with it. Dawn wasn't mine, she never was, and she never would be. Fact is, no one *ever* would be. You can't own people, you can't control them, and it doesn't matter if you're married to them or whatnot. If you do, that's not a relationship: that's *slavery.* Dawn had been a slave to something she'd created—and now she was free. She said I'd helped her, but I certainly didn't feel like I'd done anything. I guess you just never know who's going to come into your life, or when they will. Or what you will learn. Or maybe what *you'll* teach *them.*

o o o

I stood. I needed to do something—anything—otherwise, I was just going to sit there and go crazy. I had to stop thinking about Dawn, or, at the very least, come to grips with the reality of the situation. Dawn was gone. She was gone for good this time, and she wasn't coming back. Her letter was safely in my back pocket. The money she gave me was packed into my right front pocket.

So, I decided I'd walk to the outlet mall and buy a new duffle bag. Then, I'd get some clothing. Nothing extravagant—maybe just a pair of shorts and a couple of shirts. Something clean to change into. I'd buy some jerky, some water. I'd find a trucker headed to Florida. And when I thought of Dawn, I would try not to hurt.

o o o

Even in the park, I could smell the strong scent of diesel fuel from the truck stop. I walked through the lot, around numerous trucks, nodding to a few men who bustled about. Then, I walked along the road that led back to the Super 8 Motel. The parking lot around the Mystic Panda was suspiciously empty, and I remembered how sick I'd been, how Dawn had taken care of me. I thought about the fat lady with no legs in the wheelchair. I thought about her chunky daughter, and how she had lost her mother. In the scheme of things, I really didn't have any problems.

o o o

The outlet mall was swarming with people. I looked for a men's clothing store and found an L.L. Bean that looked like it would fit the bill. And they had good prices, too. Sure, I knew the clothing was defective with slight variations and imperfections—but that's the nature of outlet malls. Get rid of all the shit they can't sell at full price. I found a pair of shorts that fit, and, try as I did, I couldn't find anything wrong with them. Same thing went for the shirts I looked at. Nothing. They looked fine to me, and I got out of the store with two shirts, three pairs of underwear, three pairs of socks, and a pair of khaki shorts all for under fifty bucks, which was great. I was going to make Dawn's five hundred dollars go as far as I could. The only thing I didn't find was a duffle bag. The ones I found were for kids. They were small and colorful, with cartoons all over them. I've got nothing against cartoons, but I'm not traveling across the country with *Scooby-Doo* or *Teenage Mutant Ninja Turtles* or a *Hello Kitty* plastered on my duffle bag. I figured I could pick up something else along the way.

After browsing around aimlessly for about twenty minutes, I crossed the parking lot and walked to the truck stop. Like the one near the Fairfield Inn, it was buzzing with activity. There were trucks coming and going, trucks parked. Engines idled. Guys—and a couple of women, but not very many—scurried around the lot, some of them chatting with one another, others yapping away on cell phones. Everyone seemed busy, focused. And I was sure that out of all of the trucks around, someone *had* to be headed for Florida. Which was another thing to think about: how was I to go about it? Walk around and ask? I was pretty new at this. Dawn, of course, had

184

an advantage. Not me. I didn't have anything to offer, except maybe some cash to chip in for gas.

Thinking of Dawn and the fact that she was gone made me feel sad all over again. It really, really sucked. And I couldn't stop thinking about her, even though I knew I had to. I *had* to. She was gone, and she wasn't coming back. It was final.

So, here's what I did: I went into the convenience store. The place was big, too. There was a small deli with some tables and booths. I went over to the deli and decided that, even though I wasn't all that hungry, I had to have *something* in my stomach. Maybe that would help take away a little of the ache I felt. I doubted it, but you never know.

I bought a cold turkey sandwich and a Mountain Dew and sat at a booth by the window. Someplace where I could see outside and just think of other things: Ellen, and how she was doing. How this whole thing was a mystery. While I ate, I again wondered just what in the hell the *New World Peace Center* was, and why she was there. Maybe it was one of those shelters for runaways, or something like that. But what was the significance of October 10th? What was so special about that day? Why couldn't I come on the 9th, or the 11th? Ellen had been very specific about the date, that much was certain. But why? I guess I wouldn't know until I got there.

o o o

Several people mulled about, and I was vaguely aware of conversation, chatter, occasional laughter. But it all seemed like it came from behind a wall, like I was in my own glass room, my own world. It was impossible to believe that, all around me, things just continued on as normal. But they did. Nobody in the world gave a rat's ass how I felt, and that's just the way it was. I know it's shallow to think the whole world should stop for poor old me, but like I've said: I do that from time to time. I just wallow around in my own sorrow, feeling sorry for poor, pitiful me, no one understands, no one knows. The only good thing about it is that sooner or later, it gets really old. Tiring, in fact. It takes a lot of energy to feel sorry for yourself all the time. When you finally get worn down, you realize the lonely, self-induced pity-party you're having is pointless. Nobody is going to bring you back up except yourself. Friends and family? They can be there to help you, sure. But you have to let them. If you don't let them, you just keep wallowing in the same, stinky shit until you're finally ready to come around.

Apparently, I looked as bad as I felt, because a guy stopped at my table. He was a big dude, too, with a red flannel shirt, untucked, billowed out by a good-sized gut. He had a thick handlebar mustache that reminded me of steer horns, and he was wearing a blue baseball cap with the logo of some lumbering company. He was probably about my height, but probably two, maybe three times my weight. Bright, blue eyes. Kind eyes. He was carrying a coffee and a bag of pretzels.

"Boy . . . ya'll look like the whole world just took a big crap on you," he said in a thick, southern drawl.

I smiled. I liked him instantly. The man was disarming, harmless. Actually, I was surprised he even noticed me sitting there. I thought I was oblivious to the world, and vice-versa.

But what do you say to someone—a stranger, no less—when they say something like that to you? Walk away? Smile and leave it at that? I mean . . . it's kind of an awkward position, when you think about it. I didn't feel like going into the whole story with anyone, let alone a trucker at a truck stop/convenience store in Knoxville, Tennessee.

So, I just nodded, and the big old dude sat at my table. "Whelp," he said as he set his coffee down, "sometimes, luck just don't work the way ya always want it to." He tore open the bag of pretzels and offered me some. I declined simply by shaking my head.

"I'm not worried about luck," I said quietly, almost beneath my breath. "It's the boomerang that keeps coming around."

He smiled like he knew just what I was talking about. Started talking to me like we'd been good friends for years. "Boomerangs," he said. "You know, when I was a kid, I saw an ad for a boomerang in a comic book. It was three or four dollars, I don't remember. But see, not long before that, I'd seen a TV program that had this black dude in Australia—Aborigine, I think—wearin' nothin' but a loincloth. He had a boomerang, and I'll be damned if he didn't throw that thing and clunk a kangaroo right in the head and knock that sunnuvagun out cold! And you know what? That boomerang bounced offa that critter's noggin, went up into the air, turned, and came back to the black guy. Oh, it didn't come *right* back to him. He had to sorta anticipate where it was coming back. He ran a few feet and snapped that boomerang right out of the air. Then, he and a few of his Aborigine friends walked over to the kangaroo. That thing was dead 'er 'n a doornail, he was. They tied him to a big old stick and carried him off.

"When I saw the ad for a boomerang in that comic book, well, I just knew I had to have it. Had to. I saved up all my nickels until I had enough. Gave the change to my mom, and she wrote a check, bein' that nickels and dimes and pennies, they don't go all that well through the mail. I went to that mailbox every single day. The wait just drove me crazy! Every day I dreamed about what I would do with that boomerang. I even thought about making my own loin cloth, like that Aborigine guy, so I could be just like him, huntin' in the woods with my trusty boomerang. 'Course, I was a little skinnier back then, you know." He laughed and shook his head. "I just thought it was that simple, you know? Chuck that thing out and watch it soar up into the air and come back around."

He laughed again and sipped his coffee, then dipped his

hand into the bag of pretzels. Then he looked away, like he was momentarily distracted. When he turned to look back at me, he was smiling, chewing on a pretzel. He pulled another one out of the bag and popped it into his mouth. He gave no indication he was going to continue his story.

"So, what happened?" I prompted.

He brightened, as if he was glad he'd been able to goad me into continuing. "Well, it finally came in the mail," he said. "I think I about peed my pants. I couldn't believe it when I got home from school one day and saw that brown box on the porch, addressed to me. Damned near fainted.

"So's anyways, I tore into that thing like a mad dog. Pulled 'er out, and there she was, in my hands. I felt just like that old Aborigine dude I seen on television. I ran right out into the yard, I chucked that thing as hard as I could. It sailed!" He shook his head and sipped his coffee. "I couldn't *believe* how that thing flew! Way up into the air, spinning and spinning, twisting and turning. Up and up, higher and higher. But really quick, I realized something was wrong. That boomerang wasn't coming back. It kept right on going, going, going . . . then it was gone. It disappeared behind the trees on the other side of the field."

Just as he finished his sentence, a cell phone chirped. The man shifted, stuffed his hand into his left breast pocket, and pulled out his phone. He eyeballed the caller ID, then flipped the unit open. "Rucker, here," he said. There was silence as he listened. Then: "Gotcha. Thanks. I'll be in Boston by tonight. See ya then." He closed his phone and stuffed it back into his pocket. I almost laughed out loud. *Rucker?* I thought. *Rucker the trucker? He probably had it on his business card.*

And he'd said he was headed for Boston. So much for asking him for a ride.

"Truck's ready," the man said, sliding out of the seat. "Hey, look, kid. I don't know what's eatin' at you, but it prob'ly

188

ain't worth worryin' about. I look back at all the worryin' I done about dumb things and recollect it was all a waste of time. Yer better off puttin' stuff behind ya and lookin' ahead. You take 'er easy." He winked and began to walk off. But I admit it: I was dying to find out what happened to the boomerang, so I asked him.

He shook his head. "I couldn't find that damned thing. Ja ever lose somethin' like that? Something really important?"

My blood iced. A lump formed in my throat. "Yes," I said.

"Well, I searched and searched, up 'till dark. I hunted for it the next day. Got some of my friends involved, too. We didn't find it. Then, about a week later, I heard that some kid not far away had found it. I marched right over there to his house, ready to reclaim what was rightly mine. Funny thing, though. The kid that found it, he was only maybe five or six. He was in his front yard, playing with the boomerang, swinging it around like it was an airplane. Well, I knew who the family was. The old man, he was kilt in a factory accident. Family was real bad off, even worse than we were, and we didn't have it so good. But this family, they didn't have *nothin'*. And this kid . . . the only clothes he had were handed down from his brothers. I don't think he never had any new clothes in his life. And I knew for sure he didn't have no toys.

"Well, it was hard to do, but I just walked away. I let the kid have the boomerang. I just couldn't see marching up and taking the thing away from him, even though it was rightly mine. Some things are like that. You think they're yours, and, maybe they are, maybe they aren't. My daddy always useta tell us kids: you ain't rich because you learnt how to git lots of stuff. You get rich by learnin' when and how to give it away. Sometimes, things are only s'posed to be yours for a short time."

Without another word, Rucker the Trucker turned and ambled off. He never looked back, and I never saw him again.

50

I sat at the table for a long time, and my thoughts jumped from topic to topic like a football. When I was little, one of our neighbors had one of those nylon, multi-colored footballs. As it spiraled through the air, it became a blur of colors. But for me, the most exciting part was when the football hit the ground. Because of its egg shape, you never could tell where the crazy thing was going to bounce. I used to borrow the football and entertain myself by tossing the thing into the air and letting it hit the ground. I tried to anticipate where it would bounce, so I could catch it in the air before it bounced again. Sometimes I was successful; mostly, though, I wasn't. One time, the thing bounced up and hit me in the face, giving me a bloody lip. I remember being mad at the football, and I picked it up and slammed it down onto the ground, like I was punishing it. It bounced right back up, and the narrow end hit me in the eye. I wailed like a siren.

That's what my thoughts were doing: bouncing in one direction, then another. Then another. I went from Ellen to Dawn, to Lacy and Bruce, to my bag of new clothing, to the wad of twenties in my pocket. Then, I bounced from Rucker the

Trucker to Joe tied to the bed in the motel room. Back to Ellen, then Dawn, then the lady in the wheelchair that was now dead. I must've sat there for an hour, just letting my thoughts bounce around. Nobody asked me to leave; no one else paid attention to me.

o o o

Gradually, I refocused my thoughts on what I was doing, where I was going, and how I was going to get there. As I looked around, I had to believe *someone* was headed to Florida. From Knoxville, I-75 shot straight south into the panhandle, so I was certain there were a number of truckers who would be heading in that direction. Maybe not to West Palm Beach, but at least to Florida.

But how would I go about finding a ride? I was a little uncomfortable just walking around, asking dudes if they were headed to Florida, and, if they were, asking for a lift. Sure, most of them were probably nice enough and all that, but I'm sure there were some weirdos, too. I read a book about a serial killer who escaped detection for years because he was always on the go with his truck. He'd pick up prostitutes—men and women—and murder them, dumping their bodies hundreds of miles from where he'd picked them up. When their bodies were found, they were often so decomposed that they weren't identified for a long time. Some of them were never identified at all. It took ten years before they caught the guy, and only because one of his victims escaped and wrote some sort of message on a bathroom mirror in a truck stop. The guy was convicted of killing dozens of people, but he claimed there were far more than that. Maybe there were, maybe there weren't. Anybody crazy enough to kill people like that is crazy enough to lie about it, too.

o o o

I started scoping out some of the trucks, looking for insignias on their cab doors or on the trailers themselves, some kind of indication they were from Florida. That way, I'd at least have a point on which to strike up a conversation. I could point to the decal and say something really witty like, 'You from Florida?' In which case, I could begin my series of 'where you headed?' questions, in hopes of hitching a ride.

Problem was, I couldn't get myself motivated to do shit. I just sat there, knowing I *should* be pounding the pavement, looking for a ride, talking to people. But I wasn't doing anything about it. I think I would have done anything at that point, as long as it got me out of looking for a ride. I hadn't anticipated I'd be without a car. That's the sucky thing about life: you make your plans, and the world might just go along with you and let you do your business. In most cases, the world is pretty agreeable to your ideas. But then there's the other times, the times when the world gets this big, shit-eating grin, looks down, and says, *'How can we mess with Greg Chappell today?'* The world had been doing enough of that the past couple of days. Oh, I'm sure the world has been messing with lots of people. I'm not the only one. Sometimes, it sure felt like I was, though.

o o o

So there I was, feeling like hell, waiting for that tired-of-feeling-sorry-for-myself feeling to come over me, so I would get up off my ass and do something, when a guy walked right by my booth, chatting on a cell phone, telling someone about how he's headed for Chattanooga, Tennessee, that afternoon . . . and then on to Florida. I about crapped my pants. I snapped up my plastic shopping bag and nearly fell out of the booth. I dashed after the guy, not wanting to seem too rushed, not wanting him to know I was following. I figured I'd keep a distance until he hung up the phone, then I'd tell him I overheard him talking about going to Florida. I contemplated what to say and decided against the ailing grandmother bit. While it might garner some sympathy, the guy would probably see through me like gin. So, I opted to just tell him the truth: I was on my way to Florida to find my sister.

He tucked away his phone just as he reached a big, dirty, white semi. The cab and trailer were white, but there was a layer of gray dirt, thicker near the lower portions of the truck. It looked like he'd been on too many dirt roads.

"Sir?" I said as I approached him. He turned. "I overheard you talking about going to Florida," I said. I stopped a few feet from him. "I really need a ride there. I mean, if it's not too much trouble." I was going to keep speaking, pleading my case, but I decided to shut up. I'd already laid it out: anything else I said might blow it. He could make his decision based on what I asked and what he saw.

He looked me up and down. If I were in his position, would I give me a ride? I wasn't dirty, and I didn't look at all like a hitchhiking scragglemuffin. But I was a little young, and he probably thought I was a runaway. I tried to read his mind, tried to anticipate what his answer would be. He appeared nice enough. A thin build, maybe forty years old or so. Dark hair. He had a scar on the right side of his forehead, probably from an accident of some sort long ago.

"Where ya headed?" he asked. He seemed a bit unsure. Obviously, I wasn't any threat to him. But you never know. He had to be cautious of who he gave rides to, just as I had to be careful who I hitched with. You never know people, not really. That's how John Wayne Gacy got away with killing all those kids. He was an upstanding guy in the community, going around to children's hospitals performing as a clown. His construction business was making something like three-hundred grand a year.

He did a lot of community work and was well-liked by everyone. But he killed something like thirty-three kids over a few short years. Buried most of them in the crawlspace beneath his house. And he had a wife and kids, too. How do you get away with murder for so long, burying the bodies beneath your house, and not have your own *family* know about it?

"West Palm Beach," I replied.

"You a runaway?" he asked, his voice heavy with vigilance.

"No," I said, shaking my head. "Just headed to see my sister. That's where she is."

The man looked me up and down again. "You ain't carrying much."

I managed a smile. "I figured I wouldn't need much. Coupla changes of clothes. Toothbrush and stuff." Jeez, was I sounding *stupid*. And the guy knew it, too, because he shook his head.

"I don't think so," he said as he turned away. "It's not my policy to pick up riders."

"I can chip in for gas," I said. "I mean . . . I don't have a lot, but I can help out."

Still, he shook his head. "Sorry, kid. But the times bein' what they are. It's a shame. When I was your age, I hitchhiked from Los Angeles all the way home to Pittsburgh. Didn't have to worry about much. Nowadays . . . well, it's just not a good thing. Sorry." He opened the cab door and climbed in.

And I wasn't going to press him. After all, if I was in his shoes, I'd have the same concerns. I'd be wondering if the kid was a drug addict. Or a murderer, or a rapist. Who knows. I couldn't blame him one bit.

o o o

I walked back to the convenience store and sat down on

a bench next to the wall. Trucks came and went, people scurried by.

And the man came back. The one I'd asked for a ride.

"I suppose I can give you a lift, if you want," he said. "Prob'ly could use the company."

I about shot off the bench. "Really?!?!" I exclaimed. "Oh, man, that's great. Thanks. Thanks a lot." I picked up my bag of clothing. I don't know what changed his mind, but I was glad he did.

"I gotta stop in Chattanooga, though," the man said. "We'll be there later today, then we'll head on down to Florida. I can take ya as far as Daytona Beach. You can probably find someone headed the rest of the way down ninety-five to West Palm."

"Thanks," I repeated. "How much cash do you need?"

The man waved it off. "Forget it," he said. "I'm headed that way."

A jolt of energy rushed though my system. Wow. All the way to Florida. Not quite to West Palm Beach where Ellen was, but it was great to know that by this time tomorrow, I'd be in the sunshine state.

And I would've been there, too . . . if the world hadn't decide to have another go around of fun with one Greg Chappell from Bay City, Michigan.

Part
Two:
Black
and
White

The truth is rarely pure and never simple.

-Oscar Wilde

51

His name was Arnold Mulhousen, and he turned out to be a non-stop chatterbox. He talked and talked and talked and *talked!* I heard about his sister's divorce ('her husband was a' cheatin' on 'er, he wuz') and about how his mom was killed ten years ago in a car-deer accident. Turns out his 'maw' (that's how he pronounced it, anyway) was drunk, and she didn't see the deer until it was too late, probably due to the fact that she was: A) shitfaced, B) it was after dark, and C) she'd been driving without headlights. It was funny: here he was, talking about his mother being killed in a car wreck, and he was joking about it.

"She had a blood-alcohol level of 1.6," Arnold said. "But ol' Maw, she could hold her liquor. Fact, if she'da seen th' deer, she'd probably still be here today."

"But she didn't have her headlights on?" I asked.

Arnold shook his head. "No. But you gotta understand the moon was out something bright that night. I know, 'cause I was out fishing with a couple friends, and we didn't even need flashlights. That's the night I caught that huge old catfish . . . ."

And that's the way it went, I swear to God, all the way to Chattanooga. Arnold laid out his Kentucky Fried Monologue, and I chewed and swallowed every word. His stories were pretty humourous, too, like the time he'd set fire to his old man's hardware store while smoking his first cigarette at the age of ten. The building burned right to the ground, but old Arnold got out of it on account of he'd run off and pretended he was working in the field. He told me about the time he and his friends went hunting, only to discover a big plot of marijuana growing . . . just as the harvesters arrived.

"That was 'bout the only time I really thought I was gonna leave this world," Arnold said. "I really didn't think we were gonna get outta there with our lives. Those guys had machine guns, everything. And they used 'em. It was like a little mini-war, or something. They were there defendin' their field of pot, and all we were doin' was huntin' some birds. But we made it out alive, surprised to say. We ran into the forest with those guys after us. We were able to split up and lose 'em. When we finally *did* get away, mum was the word. We were all maybe eighteen, nineteen years old. If we went to the cops, we were sure those guys would be comin' after us. Fact, ol' Johnny Beerman's dad was a cop, and one time . . . ."

He had story after story after story, and he didn't seem the least bit apprehensive about having a stranger riding in his cab. In fact, I couldn't imagine the guy traveling across the country without a companion to talk to. He just seemed like he had to talk to someone all the time. Or, maybe it had been so long since he'd had someone to talk to that it all spilled out in one long, gigantic gush, with only a few pauses here and there to sip from a bottle of water. And the more he talked, the more I liked him. He seemed like an everyday sort of guy that had a lot of really interesting things happen to him. Either that, or he was just really good at making his stories interesting. Some people are like that. They can take an otherwise boring story and make it seem exciting, and keep you hanging on the edge of your seat. Other people, well, if they can't relate a good story, it doesn't matter what they're trying to tell you. They're just plain *boring*. Not Arnold, though. He could probably tell a story about a tree in his yard and make you hang on every word.

One thing was certain: Arnold's stories sure helped me forget about Dawn, at least for a while. And the time flew by. When I saw a sign that read *Chattanooga 10 miles,* I couldn't believe it. It seemed liked we'd only been on the road for a few minutes. I hoped Arnold had a bunch more stories . . . at least enough to get us to Daytona.

"I got a coupla errands in Chattanooga," Arnold said as we approached an off-ramp. "Take me 'bout an hour. There's a place up here, not far from the freeway. Big mall, restaurants. I'll dropyawf there. Be back to grab a bite to eat at Taco Bell, so meet me there, say—"

He glanced at his watch.

"—four o'clock?"

"Sure," I said, and I was actually looking forward to getting out and stretching. I still needed a backpack or duffle bag for my clothing, too. I was sure I'd be able to find something inexpensive in the mall.

o o o

Arnold dropped me off at the far side of the parking lot of Hamilton Place Mall, which was right off I-75. He didn't tell me what his errands were, and I didn't ask. Maybe he had a hottie waiting for him somewhere, but I doubted it. He really didn't seem the type. And besides: an hour wasn't going to give him a lot of time.

"Taco Bell is right over there," he pointed as I slid out of the cab. A wave of warm air washed over me. "Meet you there in an hour."

"Got it," I said. "You need anything from the mall?"

Arnold shook his head. "I'm all set. But I won't be

hanging around for ya. If you're not at Taco Bell in an hour, I'm heading out."

"Got it," I repeated, and I closed the door. The big truck roared off.

o o o

Hamilton Place Mall was pretty big, as far as malls go. It wasn't enormous, but it was better than average. Bigger than any of the malls we had in Bay City. I've never been a big fan of hanging out at a mall, unless I'm bored or just want to people-watch. Ellen, though, could *live* at the mall. She didn't even have to buy anything. She could spend the entire day—the entire *day*—at the mall, just browsing, trying on clothes. One of her favorite things was to go into FYE and go to listening stations, where you could listen to actual music from a CD that you swiped under a bar code reader. I did that once in a while. It was a great way to preview a CD before you bought it. Some bands—even the popular ones—put out some pretty shitty stuff. I didn't want to buy a CD that had only one or two good songs on it. Another good thing was that the listening stations allowed you to check out some of the new bands that you had never heard of, without spending a dime. I did a lot more listening than buying, but it was a lot of fun just the same.

The mall parking lot was half-full; I was surprised to see so many cars. More than you'd expect on a weekday afternoon, anyway. I imagined the place probably turned into a regular zoo on the weekends.

o o o

I half-jogged across the parking lot, carrying my paper bag. A car drove past with four black guys in it. Actually, I could hear them coming before I saw them. The thumping bass sounded like someone beating a mallet on a drum. They rolled on past, eyeing me, the lone cracker, on my way to the mall. Then, they were gone. The next time I saw them, I had a gun jammed in my ribs.

52

I strode through the entrance and was greeted with the familiar sights, sounds, and scents of a mall. There was an arcade somewhere close by, and I could hear muted blips and bloops and zips and zaps. I smelled hot pretzels, caramel, and hot dogs. Muzak music drifted from everywhere, competing over the soft rushing sound of a water fountain. People chatted, and some kid was crying hysterically in front of KB Toys. Apparently, he wasn't getting something he wanted, and he was showing the universal signs of displeasure most toddlers learn as soon as they're capable of walking. This kid was really going at it, too, laying on his belly, slapping his palms on the floor, kicking his feet. And his mom wasn't doing jack-shit about it. She was too busy looking at something she'd bought at some other store, completely oblivious to the horizontal tyrant at her feet.

o o o

I stopped walking when I reached the convergence of the mall. There was a big, glass-enclosed sign—a mall directory—right in the middle where four halls met. Off to the side was an information/help desk, where a very happy looking older woman chatted with a young couple pushing a baby stroller. The guy had a road map of tattoos over his right arm and shoulder, and he looked bored out of his skull. His wife or girlfriend or whatever was wearing a pink tank-top, and she had a tattoo of a butterfly on her left shoulder. The kid in the stroller, for his part, was quiet. His eyes were open, and he was in an placid haze, looking all around like he was a spaceman who'd just landed on some strange and wonderful planet. At least he didn't have any tattoos, yet.

That got me to thinking about the book I had in my bag. *Galaxy Quest*. Robert 342 and Lora 447 sure had their hands full with those Drioleans, and I thought if I could find a shop and get some sort of bag, then I might find a bench outside and have some time to get back into the book. I only had about seventy pages or so to go, and I could probably finish it before I had to meet Arnold at Taco Bell. In fact, that's what I would do. I would buy a bag or a backpack and hike over to Taco Bell.

o o o

I went over the list of stores in the mall. There were over 200 stores in all. Lots of specialty stores like Banana Republic, The Bombay Company, Rocky Mountain Chocolate Factory, stuff like that. There were also some department stores, and that's where I decided to go. If I bought a bag at Banana Republic, I'd sure be stylin' . . . but it would probably cost me a hundred bucks. I just needed something to carry my stuff, not make a fashion statement. There was a JC Penney store just a few stores down, so that's where I headed.

Sure enough, I was able to find a black nylon backpack for fifteen bucks. While waiting in line, I also saw a phone card, which was sure to come in handy. I picked up one and placed it on the counter with my backpack.

"Ya'll can get an instant ten-percent rebate and a free umbrella if ya sign up for a JC Penney credit card," the lady cashier said.

"No, thanks," I said. I guess an umbrella might come in handy, but if I started collecting everything that came in handy, I'd need a truck to carry it all in. But the cashier, she was a persistent bitch about the whole thing.

"You're sure you don't want to sign up? It'll only take a moment, and ya'll will save ten percent. And ya'll get an umbrella."

I shook my head (again), and (again) said "No, thanks," and handed her two twenties. She took the bills and tapped at the register, then she shrugged and shook her head, like I was a fool for passing up the deal of the century. I thought she was done, that the sales pitch was over, but she opened her mouth again as she put my backpack into a paper bag. "I just don't know why some people don't want to save money when they can."

I rarely get to the point where I *really* tell someone how I feel. Usually, I *think* it, but I don't say it. Now, however, something inside of me had had enough. I'd politely told her no, I wasn't interested . . . *twice*. She had to get that last, condescending, belittling comment in there, and that's what sent me over the edge. I put her in the sights of my mental 12-gauge and unloaded on her with both barrels.

"First of all," I snapped, "I ran away from home a few days ago by stealing my drunk uncle's car. I picked up a hooker named Dawn. Someone stole the car, I got food poisoning and nearly died, wound up sleeping with Dawn—fell in love with her, I think—then she left me. I have no job, no wallet, no fucking identification whatsoever, and I'm hitching rides to Florida to find my sister at some place that has a name that sounds like some new-fucking-fangled new age center where they chant in another language and don't eat meat. So, you can bet I've got other things on my mind than a fucking JC Penney credit card and saving ten percent. And I won't even begin to tell you what you can do with your umbrella."

The cashier was speechless. Her jaw went slack and her mouth hung open in a dumbfounded, shocked look, like I'd slapped her or something. I literally had to take my change out of her hand because she forgot to give it to me.

"Have a nice fucking day," I said and stormed off.

I heard the man who was in line behind me chuckle and say, "I don't want no credit card or umbrella, just like that guy."

o o o

I shook my head as I hustled off. I know it wasn't very nice to do that to the cashier, but sometimes people just don't take *no* for an answer. You try to be nice, try to tell them you're not interested, but they press and press to the point where you really get pissed off. But I didn't want to sign up for their credit card, I didn't want to save ten percent, and I didn't want a damned umbrella. I wanted a Nachos Grande with extra cheese at Taco Bell. I wanted to finish reading *Galaxy Quest*. I wanted to listen to more of Arnold's crazy stories all the way to Daytona. I wanted to find Ellen.

And, as I glanced up to see a Victoria's Secret store and the mannequins dressed in skimpy, sexy lingerie, I realized with a twinge of pain that I wanted Dawn . . . but that wasn't going to happen. I had to get used to that fact, whether I liked it or not.

53

As I made my way back to the middle of the mall, I saw one of the funniest things I think I'd seen in a long time. The little kid that had been throwing a tantrum was standing *in* the fountain! He was actually *in* the fountain, in the water, soaked from head to toe. The water in the fountain came up to just below the kid's knees, so he wasn't really in any danger of drowning or anything. His mother was oblivious, reading the store directory while chatting on her cell phone. Even the lady at the information desk hadn't seen the kid, as she was busy talking to a couple of old people. And the little kid was having the time of his life, scooping up change people had tossed in. While I watched, he must've picked up a dozen pennies and put them in his pocket. And the look on this kid's face said it all. He was in heaven . . . and he looked cuter than hell.

o o o

I kept walking, turning the corner to head out of the mall. Then, I realized I was carrying two bags, which was kind of silly. I'd bought the backpack to hold my stuff, so I found a bench, sat down, and re-packed, throwing the plastic bags away. The backpack would prove useful, I was sure, as I could either carry it or wear it on my back. It wasn't really high-quality, and I sure wouldn't be making any fashion statements with it, but it was inexpensive and would serve its purpose nicely.

Only about ten minutes had passed since Arnold had dropped me off, so I still had a fair amount of time to kill. I wasn't all that hungry just yet, so I thought I'd just find a place out of the way, pull out my cover-less novel, and see if I couldn't finish it before it was time to meet Arnold at Taco Bell. I walked out the front doors of the mall and into the warm sun. Again, I wondered what the weather was like in Michigan. No doubt cold and cloudy, and probably rainy. I was digging the warm temperatures, that was for sure. I thought about Arnold's job, about being a trucker. He'd probably seen the extremest of the extreme when it came to weather. I thought it might be fun to sort of tour around the country like that. I mean . . . you'd probably get a real feel for the land that way, like you'd really get to know your home. The wide screen, full-version. I don't think most people get a chance to do that. They pretty much hang around their home state for most of their life. I was a good example. This was the farthest I'd ever been from Michigan, and I'd never been in another state. Sure, my reasons for travel could be considered something other than 'vacation,' but I did sort of enjoy being out of my home state, even under the circumstances. It was new: refreshing, exciting, adventurous, alluring. At the same time, I was still a little worried about what was going to happen. No, maybe *worried* isn't the proper word. Maybe *uncertain* was the best way to describe it. I'd never been on my own before, not really. But, then again, I realized I'd pretty much been on my own my entire life. Same with Ellen. She'd been on her own, and we'd been on our own together. None of what I was going through was all that different, really. It was just coming at me a little faster . . . and the climate and terrain were unfamiliar.

o o o

I was glad I'd bought the backpack. Everything fit perfectly inside of it, and there was even a side pocket that was the right size for my paperback book. While I walked along the sidewalk in the monstrous shadow of the hulking mall, I unzipped the pocket and pulled out the book. Up ahead, where the mall ended, was a grove of sparse trees. It looked like it might be a picnic area of some sort, although I didn't see any tables or benches. From there, I figured I could sit beneath a tree facing the parking lot, read, and watch for Arnold's big white truck to roll in. When he did, I'd hightail it over there and we could eat together, then be on our way. And he'd pump me full of stories all the way to Daytona, I was sure.

I pulled out *Galaxy Quest* and slipped my backpack over my shoulder. I was really looking forward to finding out what happened with Robert 342 and Lora 447. Oh, I'm sure they'd escape from the Drioleans. That's just how books are. They always have a happy ending, even though that's not how life always is. Sometimes, the whole book is spoiled because the ending is just too unbelievable, too perfect. Sure, I think everyone wants to see the hero win and wind up on top, but sometimes, the author has worked really hard to get his character into so much trouble that it takes an impossible miracle for him or her to get out of it. That's when the author throws in something silly and completely out of left field, knowing they'd better wrap up the story and finish it, no matter how ridiculous the ending seemed. I was really hoping *Galaxy Quest* wasn't going to end up that way. I was sorta liking the main characters, and I was rooting for them to get away from the Drioleans. I was sure they would, but I was hoping Raymond L. Marshall didn't go for the cheap cop-out and have some sort of stupid, ridiculous ending.

o o o

I started reading while I walked, and once again I heard the distant thundering of rap music, muffled within a car. I vaguely remember it getting closer before it died off. I must've really been into my book, because I didn't even know a car had pulled up alongside me. And I didn't know there was anyone around until it was already too late.

The car stopped suddenly and the rear door flew open. At the exact same time, two black guys were at my side. One of them jabbed a gun into my ribs so hard it took my breath away.

"Git in th' car, motherfucker!" the black guy with the gun ordered, pushing me off the sidewalk. The black guy on the other side of me had already picked up my backpack and had me by my arm. Before I knew it, I was in the back seat of the Rapmobile. There were two more guys in the front seat, and now I recognized them as the ones I'd seen while walking through the parking lot just a little while ago. The guy with the gun slipped in next to me, while the other guy ran around to the other side and got in.

My car had been stolen, I'd nearly died from food poisoning, and now I was being kidnapped at gunpoint by four nasty-looking black guys—and I wasn't even halfway to Florida.

This sure was turning into one fucked-up trip.

54

It was probably the rain that woke me up, or maybe my aching head. Maybe a combination of both. Talk about being disoriented. For a moment, I didn't even know who I was. If that's never happened to you, it's a pretty scary feeling. And when you happen to be face-down in the weeds, wet and clammy, it's even worse.

I rolled onto my side and I thought my brain was going to spill out of my head. My shoulder and ribs hurt, too. Sharp branches were poking at me. I somehow managed to roll onto my back. A light rain drizzled from a dull gray sky. There were a few trees looming over me, but I couldn't seem to focus on them. Maybe it was the rain in my eyes, I don't know.

And talk about confused! Where in the hell was I? How did I get there? It was a really freaky feeling, not knowing anything about where I was. I started to go over things in my mind, right from the start: stealing Bruce's car, Dawn, riding with Joe and Dawn in the semi—

Then, I had to pause and really work to think of other things. They gradually came back to me, but it was hard, as if they were memories that had been stored away for a long time, and now were dusty and old. And I had no concept of time, or how old the memories were. I was having sort of a Rip Van Winkle moment: I might have slept twenty years. That's how ancient the memories seemed.

And my *head.* Good God . . . why did it hurt so bad? And why was I laying here in weeds and brush, in the rain? What state was I in? Had I only dreamed everything?

I sat up, and another jolt of pain stabbed the side of my head. I reached up and felt something caked near my temple. When I pulled my hand away, there were flecks of dried blood and mud on my fingers. That *really* freaked me out. What had happened? An accident of some sort? I kept going through the files of my hazy memory as best I could, remembering the bout of food poisoning, Dawn taking care of me. Then, I was on my own, and I remembered Arnold chatting my ear off in the semi, getting dropped off at the mall; the kid throwing the tantrum; the bitch cashier trying to get me to sign up for a credit card by bribing me with an umbrella; Taco Bell—

Wait a minute. I never made it to Taco Bell. I had planned on having a Nachos Grande with extra cheese, but first, I was going to read my book and—

The black dudes.

Then it came back to me. I had been walking along the sidewalk near the end of the mall, when the black guy poked me in the ribs with the gun. Then I was in the car, and the guy put the gun to my head. The guy on the other side of me was rifling through my backpack.

"Gimme yo' fuckin' wallet, cracker!" the guy with the gun said.

"I . . . I don't . . . I—"

"Gimme yo' fuckin' wallet, white trash! I'll blow yo' muthafuckin' head off!"

"I don't have one!" I managed to blurt out. Holy shit. It was the real deal. I was getting robbed. Maybe worse.

"Waz in yo' fuckin' pockets?!?!" he yelled, poking the gun harder into my temple.

"I've . . . I've got money . . . in my . . . my right front pocket."

I felt a hand dig into my pocket, and the guy with the gun suddenly raised his fist, displaying the wad of twenties. "What else you got, muthafucka?!?!"

"That's it, I swear," I said. "I don't have anything else."

"Yo one fuckin' dumb-ass whitey," he said. "Keepin' money in yo' pocket like that. Dis' a dangerous neighbo'hood, what, wid all us niggas 'round."

This brought a round of laughter from the other three black guys.

"Where you from, white-ass?" the other guy in the back seat asked. He'd finished sifting through my new backpack and tossed it to the floor.

When I didn't immediately reply, I felt the gun poke my temple again. Hard.

"Mi . . . Michigan," I managed to reply.

"You a long-ass ways from home, boy," the guy with the gun said. He was flipping through the twenties. "Man, you got over fo' hunna dollas here, white boy. Wassa muthafucka like you doin' with dis kinda cash?"

"I'm . . . on my way to Florida," I said.

"Florida, huh," he said. "Well, we might be able ta hep ya 'long, right, niggas?" More laughter from around the car, which by now had pulled out of the parking lot. We were speeding down a busy street, fast, and I remember hoping the cops would see the car and pull us over.

Then—

I couldn't remember anything more. I tried to, but I couldn't. That was the last memory I had, hoping that a cop would see the car and pull it over for speeding. There was a big gap between then and now, and I couldn't dredge it up.

I heard a noise. It was a gritty drone, the sound of tires on gravel. The sound grew louder and louder, until I realized that's exactly what it was: a car approaching. I looked around, but I didn't see a road or highway or anything. Then, I realized I was in a ditch as the car suddenly roared by, unseen. It couldn't have been more than thirty feet away. But, laying in the ditch like I was, no one passing by on the road would be able to see me.

I got to my knees and noticed my backpack in the grass. I picked it up and stood. The pain in my ribs came back, but I didn't think anything was broken. My head was far worse, and it throbbed more than ever as I got to my feet. I was dizzy, and I nearly fell over. There was nothing to steady myself, and it was tricky standing, let me tell you. Somehow, I managed to remain vertical and not tumble over onto the ground.

I felt my head with my hand and found a nasty, sore lump. I was sure there was a pretty bad gash there, too, as I felt more dried blood matted in my scalp and on the side of my forehead. But I was alive. I had *that* going for me. The black guy had held the gun to my head the whole time, and let me tell you, it's nothing you want to go through. It's so scary you can't even think, but you have to. They could have killed me and tossed me into a ditch, just as easily as they had tossed me out alive. My best guess was the guy clocked me with the gun, knocking me unconscious. Then, they dumped me—

Where? Where in the hell was I?

It took some effort, but I gathered up my backpack and walked up the short embankment, emerging on a muddy, dirt road. Behind me was a thick stand of trees; the other side of the road was a simple field of tall, auburn-colored grass. Beyond the field, in the distance, tree-covered mountains rose, mostly obscured by fog and mist. The landscape was panoramic and colorless, like an Ansel Adams photo. Potholes in the road were now turbid puddles, distorted by the falling drizzle. To my left, the road stretched out for a few hundred yards until it crested and disappeared. To my right, it turned and vanished in the trees.

And I had absolutely no idea where I was. There were no buildings, no signs. I could've been a mile from the city, I could have been a hundred. Judging by my surroundings, it was most likely a hundred.

"At least they didn't kill me," I said out loud. The words came out muddled. My voice sounded strange in my head, booming, and I wondered if I had a concussion.

I opened up my backpack and was surprised to find all my clothing was still there. Even my book and the phone card. The backpack was water resistant and my new clothes were damp, as was *Galaxy Quest,* but it was all there.

Suddenly, a thought hit me like a bee sting: if only I'd signed up for that JC Penney credit card, I'd have an umbrella to keep the rain off.

And then I started laughing. It began with just a giggle, then erupted into all-out gut-laughter, so hard my ribs ached where the black dude had poked me with the gun barrel. With each outburst, it felt like my brain was banging against my skull. It hurt, but I couldn't stop laughing. Suddenly, everything just seemed so damned *funny.* Don't ask me why; I don't know. Maybe it had something to do with the fact I'd been knocked silly. The only thing I knew was that I was standing in the rain, bloodied and dirty. I had a backpack with my clothing, my book, and the clothes I was wearing. I dug in my left pocket and found I still had my black and white quarter. Those black guys took all the money Dawn gave me, but they didn't kill me. Oh, they gave me a giant egg on my head, but they could've just as easily blown me away. I was glad they didn't, and right then I felt like one very lucky son of a gun. Very lucky, indeed. And even luckier: I heard road noise again. It grew louder and louder, until I could tell the sound was coming from the right. I turned in time to see an old green truck ambling toward me, bouncing in ruts, tires splashing through puddles.

55

As the truck approached, I saw four people crammed next to one another inside the cab. It slowed, and the people stared at me. Then, the vehicle stopped right in front of me. A single windshield wiper on the driver's side batted back and forth.

Pock. Pock. Pock.

Oh my God, I thought. *Hillbillies. They really do exist. The really do.*

Now, I'm not being mean or anything, and I remembered my mental note about being judgmental, about forming opinions without all the facts, about judging books by their covers. But the four people in the cab of the old truck looked to be the homeliest, most backwoodsy people I have ever seen in my life. I could hear the banjos twanging in my head, that's how hillbilly they were.

Ba-nah-neer-ner-ner-ner-ner-ner-ner . . . .

o o o

The driver and head hillbilly was large. He wore a dark blue shirt and a dirty white baseball cap with some sort of insignia on it, but it was so smeared with grease that it was unreadable. His hair beneath it was brown with streaks of gray mixed in, unkempt, and sort of twirly. His beard and mustache seemed to be slowly overtaking his entire face, like some strange, brown moss. The man's teeth were large and yellow, and I had to stop myself from recoiling at the sight. And the man's age was unidentifiable. He could have been forty, he could have been sixty. I just couldn't tell. One thing for sure: he looked liked he'd seen a lot of tough years.

Next to him was a young girl, maybe ten or so. She had dishwater blonde hair, straight as wire. Her eyes were wide, like giant, blue marbles with white rims. She was looking at me like I was a ghost.

The girl next to her was older, maybe eighteen, and obviously the younger girl's sister. She, too, had long, stringy, dishwater blonde hair and the same wide-eyed look in her eyes. Her mouth was open a little, and, like her father, her teeth were yellowed and unhealthy looking. Her skin had a sort of sallow appearance and her eyes seemed a little sunken.

And on the other side: Mother. Whoa. Her hair was blonde-gray, frazzled, shoulder-length. She was a carbon-copy of Dad Hillbilly, her age impossible to guess. Her mouth was closed, which was probably a good thing, as I don't think I wanted to see what those teeth looked like.

Seconds passed, and I realized no one had said a word. Finally, the driver spoke. I was expecting hillbilly language, a southern, backwoods drawl so thick I'd have to mull it over a few times before I understood. I was surprised when he spoke clearly, with only a hint of southern accent.

"Son, what in the world happened to *you?*"

I'd forgotten that I had a head wound, and I didn't even know what I looked like. I imagine I was a pretty sorry sight, all dirty and wet, with God knows how much blood caked to my head.

I thought quick. "I, uh . . . I had an accident," I said, raising my hand to my head.

Mom Hillibilly spoke, and her words came slowly, carefully. But she, too, spoke clearly.

"Are ya'll okay?"

"I think so."

A strange pause followed. Rain continued to fall. The wipers batted back and forth.

Pock. Pock. Pock.

"Where ya'll from?" Mom Hillbilly asked, obviously knowing full-well I couldn't be from around there. They probably knew everyone for miles.

"Michigan," I replied. Then: "I had an accident." I repeated this to sort of reiterate that I needed help. Maybe they could give me a lift somewhere. I didn't think I needed to go to a hospital, but it would be nice to get to a restroom or something and get cleaned up as best I could.

"You got a pretty good bump goin' there," Dad Hillibilly said. "We're headin' home, and I guess if you want, you can come get cleaned up. Take care of that cut you got there."

"That would be great," I said with relief. Home meant out of the rain. And, I didn't want to be too presumptuous, but maybe it meant some food and water, which I was badly in need of.

Dad Hillbilly hiked his thumb to the back of the truck. "Climb in. It'll be a little bumpy, but we don't have far to go."

"Thanks," I said, and I stumbled to the back of the truck while Jethro and the Clampetts looked on. There was no tailgate, so I just sort of rolled onto the bed and crawled up closer to the cab. Dad Hillbilly was watching me in the rearview; Mom Hillbilly and the two girls were rubbernecking like cranes, their heads rotating around like three owls, staring at me like they'd never seen another human being in their life. But maybe it was the blood. It probably wasn't too often they came across some kid on the side of the road, all beat up and dirty and wet.

I turned around, facing the road behind us. The truck started moving, and its exhaust was loud. And in my mind?

Ba-nah-neer-ner-ner-ner-ner-ner-ner . . . .

56

Dad Hillbilly wasn't kidding: the road was bumpy. The truck wasn't going very fast, but I was bouncing all over the place. My head throbbed every time we hit a rut or pothole. There really wasn't anything I could hold onto except for the side of the bed, but I managed. At least the guy wasn't driving like a maniac.

When I glanced around and looked into the cab, the two sisters had their heads turned, watching me with curious fascination. When they saw me looking at them, they turned and faced the front. No doubt Dad Hillbilly didn't make a habit of picking up people on the side of the road.

o o o

It started to rain harder. It wasn't too cold, either, for which I was thankful. This time of year in Michigan, a rain like this would freeze the marrow in your bones. But here—wherever the hell I was—the rain was warm and, despite my harrowing condition, actually pleasant in its own way. The drizzle got me thinking about Ellen and how she never had any sense to come in out of the rain. It could be pouring outside and she'd stay out in it, getting soaked. Not only did it not *bother* her, but she actually enjoyed it. Often, when it started to rain, she'd go outside, raise her arms out and look upward, eyes closed, letting the rain wash over her as she spun around in pixie circles. She was always doing that, except, of course, during a thunderstorm when bolts of lightning ripped open the sky. One night she even snuck outside, just so she could walk around in the rain. I asked her about it once, why she liked to walk around in the rain, and all she said was that it seemed so pure and natural and clean, like the rain became a part of her, and she became a part of the rain. I used to think it was silly, but Ellen enjoyed it so much, I couldn't help but just shake my head and smile whenever she did it. It drove Lacy nuts. She was always hollering at Ellen for staying out in the rain, telling her she was going to catch pneumonia or something, that it was going to make her sick, and if she had to go to the hospital, just who in the hell was going to pay the doctor bills, being that we didn't have any insurance and all? Ellen didn't care and kept right on enjoying the rain whenever she wanted.

o o o

The road began to narrow as we wound through dingles and dells. The trees grew thicker, tighter. I'd been aware we were heading uphill quite a bit, like we were climbing the foothills of a mountain. The road became even bumpier, and twice I smacked my head on the back window. We passed a small barn on the left, and I saw several chickens dawdling aimlessly, strutting about, pecking at the wet ground. Next to the barn was the hulking, decomposing remains of an old truck—and I mean *old.* I don't know much about old vehicles, but I figured the thing had to be from the twenties or thirties. It had no tires and was completely rusted, the color of chocolate caramel. Small trees and long grass grew up and around it. Several thin saplings had grown up through the floorboards and the nonexistent windshield.

The truck lurched to the side, then stopped. A German Shepard loped up. I like dogs, but when I see a big one coming at me like that, I'm always nervous. But this Shepard was nothing but a big ol' happy mutt. Wet and dirty, but his tail was wagging and he had that *oh-golly-it's-great-to-see-you* look as he approached. He ran to the back of the truck and placed his front paws on the bed. He gave a single bark that was as husky and solid as a shotgun blast. This was my greeter, my Welcome Wagon, at Hillbilly Home in the Woods.

o o o

I scrambled out of the back of the truck and if a guy could have been licked to death, I would have been. That happy dog was all over me, jumping, dirty paws on my wet shirt and pants. Dad Hillbilly opened up the door and hollered, "Bo! That's enough!" and I'll be damned if that dog didn't stop what he was doing. He calmed right down, still wagging his tail like crazy, but at least he wasn't bouncing all over the place and getting his muddy paws all over me. Not that it mattered: I was already muddy and soaked.

About twenty feet away was a house—sort of. It was a wood structure, made of the same wood as the barn, or so it appeared. The lumber was old and weathered, as gray and rough as elephant skin. The porch leaned to one side. Even the house itself seemed to have a bit of the leans. Water dripped from the roof, as there were no gutters. Banjo music twanged again, if only in my mind.

"Come on inside," Dad Hillbilly said. Mom and the two daughters had climbed out of the truck, and they were still giving me that same alien look.

"What happened to *you?*" the youngest girl asked.

226

"Eve, hush," Mom Hillbilly said. "He's our guest." The younger girl looked away shyly. Then, the three women followed Dad Hillbilly. I walked behind them with the happy Shepard at my heels, sniffing my butt as I dodged puddles and traipsed over the wet ground. When we reached the porch, it sounded like it was going to break. There were creaks and moans beneath our weight, and I thought for sure it was going to give way. But it didn't. And the front door wasn't even closed all the way. Dad Hillbilly just gave it a shove, and it squeaked open. I followed the four into their house. Bo, the happy German Shepard, scampered off into the rain, heading for the barn.

o o o

The house was clean. Spotless, in fact. All of the furnishings were old, but well taken care of. There wasn't a speck of dust anywhere.

"You two go to your room," Mom Hillbilly ordered her daughters in that slow, methodical voice. The girls obeyed wordlessly.

"There's a washroom right here," the big man said as he walked through the kitchen. I followed instinctively and stopped at the door of a small bathroom. The room was tiny, but it had a small sink, a toilet, and an old bathtub with a shower head on the wall. The tub had one of those curtain-like things that went around it for privacy.

Dad Hillbilly turned and looked me up and down. "You look to be about Isaiah's size, so I'll see if I can rummage up some dry clothes for you. How's that head?"

"It's okay, I think," I said. "Sore. I think I'll live."

"Well, go on, get yourself cleaned up. I'll have Sarah put some food on."

"Thanks," I said, and I stepped into the bathroom, turned on the light, and closed the door. I felt a little bad for thinking of the family as 'hillbillies,' but man . . . that's what they were. Sure, they were nice enough and all, but they looked just like what you'd expect a hillbilly to look like. But they were showing me some pretty good hospitality as far as I was concerned, and the very least I could do was be thankful and respectful while I was in their home.

I turned and looked in the mirror—and gasped. A root system of dried blood had caked down the side of my head, around my ear, and down my neck in jagged lightning bolt patterns. I looked like an extra in a zombie-horror flick. Worse, actually, because my blood was *real.* My face was dirty with streaks and patches of mud, my hair was matted with dirt and blood. There was blood on my shirt, mostly on my shoulders. No wonder the family had stared at me like they did. If I had been laying on the ground when they came by, they probably would have thought I was dead.

My head was feeling a little better, but I sure had a big bump. The gash was packed with blood and dirt, and I'd have to do some scrubbing to get it clean. I decided to press my luck and ask if I could take a shower.

I opened the door. Mom Hillbilly was in the kitchen, busily preparing a meal. "I, uh, I was wondering, I mean, if, if it isn't too much trouble, if I could take a shower, maybe?"

Mom Hillbilly nodded. "Oh, no trouble," she replied, very calmly. "Towels are in the cabinet."

Hot dog. A shower would really feel great. I closed the bathroom door, found a towel in the cabinet, and turned the water in the bathtub on. It took about a minute to warm up. Then, I stripped, carefully placing my grimy, wet clothing on the toilet so I wouldn't get anything dirty. I stepped into the tub, pulled the curtain around, and lifted the shower lever. The water shocked me for a moment, and it stung a little when it hit my wound. But it felt awesome. Dirt and dried blood flecked off me, and the water in the bathtub turned shades of cinnamon and cayenne pepper. There was a bar of soap in a tray on the side of the tub and a bottle of something that appeared to be homemade shampoo. I picked up the bar of soap and realized it was homemade, too. It had a different texture than most soaps. Smoother. Hardly any scent to it, but it lathered up just fine. I was right about the shampoo, too. It felt great in my hair, except for when it got in the wound. It stung like a hornet, for a moment.

All in all, I had been really fortunate. Yeah, the black guys had stolen my money. And I was pretty banged up and dirty. But I still had my new clothes, even if they were wet. The map I'd printed at the Super 8 was ruined, but I was sure I'd be able to get another one. And *Galaxy Quest?* That would dry, and I'd be able to finish it.

I couldn't report the incident to the police, either. There was a good chance the cops were looking for me, at least in Michigan, if Bruce had reported his car stolen and me missing, which I was sure he had. Somewhere, someone might put two-and-two together. Then I'd be screwed.

I got to thinking about something else, too. I've been around blacks all my life. Went to school with them, had lots of black friends. I don't have a racist bone in my body. Not even a racist hair follicle. But I've always wondered why black guys can get away with calling each other 'nigger,' like the guys in the car had. When they say it, it's fine. But a white guy? If a white guy called a black guy a nigger, he'd get the living shit beat out of him. If you were a celebrity and used the N-bomb in public? Your career would be in the toilet, unless you took a bunch of stupid 'racial sensitivity' classes. But the scar would still be there and nobody would care, because you'd used the dreaded 'n' word. Personally, I didn't give a rat's ass either way about the word. Nigger was nigger. There could be black niggers, there could be white niggers. Actually, I thought it was kind of a boring word, anyway, and I never used it. Not because I thought it was offensive, I just thought it was a word that didn't mean all that much anymore. I heard it all the time. And I never got offended when my black friends called me 'cracker,' 'whitey,' or anything else. Made no difference to me. It was all in jest, part of social culture. But those four black dudes that kidnapped me? Didn't matter what you called them. Guys like that gave their race a bad name.

o o o

I realized I should probably finish up my shower and get dried off, but the hot water just felt so *good*. I hadn't even thought about what I was going to change into, but it turned out I didn't have to worry about it. When I pulled the curtain back, my dirty clothes were gone, and there was a clean shirt and a clean pair of faded denims folded on the vanity, near the sink, compliments of my hosts. A pair of black shoes sat near the door, shiny as onyx. My lucky quarter was on the vanity, white side up.

I dried off, stepped out of the tub, and dressed. I was surprised to find the pants and shoes fit perfectly. The shirt was a little big, but I could easily live with it. I dried my hair, found a comb in the drawer of the vanity, and did my best to look presentable. My hair covered up the gash, but if you looked, you could easily see where I had been struck. My head damned near looked lopsided. But I felt ten times better than I had ten minutes ago. A thousand times better. It's amazing what a little shower and some fresh clothes can do for you.

o o o

I plucked my black and white quarter off the vanity, dropped it into my pocket, and opened the bathroom door. In the kitchen, the family was seated around a round table made of solid oak. The only thing on it was a small vase filled with a couple of flowers. Everyone's head was bowed, and Dad Hillbilly rested his elbows on the table, hands clasped. His hat was off, and a comb had been dragged through his scraggly hair.

They were praying, and I felt awkward. We never prayed at our house, not once. There was a kid in school who was always praying, and I mean *always*. He prayed before classes, he prayed before he took a test. He prayed before and after lunch. It got to the point he couldn't even make a simple decision without stopping to pray about it. I once saw him in front of a vending machine in the lunchroom. He was actually asking God whether he should choose the Skittles or the Cheese Doodles. I thought that was a bit too much, stopping your life to consult God every time you wanted to do something, no matter how trivial. Didn't he understand the creator of the universe probably had a lot better things to do than give nutritional guidance to a pimply-faced teenager? He probably prayed before he brushed his teeth, wanting God to help him get rid of all the plaque, keep his teeth cavity-free, and make them extra-special white so he could maybe bang the head cheerleader after the big game Friday. Of course, God wasn't going to allow that to happen, and the kid would probably spend Friday night at home, spanking his monkey.

But I was in someone else's home. They had been nice to me. More than that. I tiptoed out of the bathroom, down the hall, and slowly sat in the only open chair at the table. I bowed my head. I didn't pray or anything, nothing like that. But being respectful was the right thing to do, and besides: I really was thankful. I was clean, dry, and alive. I could smell food in the oven, and I knew I would be fed. There was a *lot* I had to be thankful for . . . and I knew it.

So, I guess, in my own way, I must have at least *thought* some sort of prayer.

57

Dinner was an interesting affair, to say the least. I couldn't put my finger on it, at first. But then, it became apparent: nobody did any talking but Dad Hillbilly, whose name, I found out, was Mr. Hollister. That's how he introduced himself. Mr. Hollister. And during the entire dinner, the girls—Eve, the youngest, and Ester, the oldest—didn't utter a sound. Neither did Mrs. Hollister. When Mr. Hollister spoke, he spoke to me and me alone. Oh, he was in no way disrespectful to his family, not in the least. But I got the distinct impression that the women in the family, especially during dinner, should be seen and not heard. Still, he was very polite and treated me like a guest. Better than that. I felt elevated, important. And he never asked me about my 'accident.' If I wanted to share what happened, they would allow me to do so in my own good time.

"You said you're from Michigan," Mr. Hollister said as he took a bite of meat. I'm not sure what it was—some sort of beef—but it was delicious. So was everything, really. Potatoes, corn, green beans, bread (homemade, I was sure), cranberries, and some other goop I couldn't identify. It didn't look very appealing, but I was going to eat everything on my plate.

Whatever the goop was, it turned out to be pretty good.

"Yes," I said. "Bay City." Then, I did the thing everyone in Michigan is famous for: I raised my right hand, like I was taking an oath. See, the state of Michigan is shaped like a mitten. (The Lower Peninsula, anyway. The Upper Peninsula is a whole different ball of wax, as they say. It's like a different country altogether, once you get across the Mackinac Bridge.) Anyway, it's easy to use the index finger on your left hand and point to where you live on your right hand. Bay City is in the middle of the Lower Peninsula, on the eastern side of the state, on Lake Huron. Of course, it probably didn't mean anything to the Hollisters, but at least it gave them a visual, something they could *see,* even if they didn't know the shape of Michigan. I was able to point to a spot on my hand, a point of reference, and it somehow made it more real, more tangible. And the daughters hung on every word. It was addicting. When I spoke, I felt I was on a stage or something. That's really how I felt. I don't know if it was because maybe they didn't get many guests, or what. But they sure seemed interested in everything I had to say.

"I live right about there," I said, at the crook between my thumb and index finger. "See how that place kind of looks like a bay? That's where I live. Bay City is right on Lake Huron." I told them a little bit about my city, but there really wasn't a lot to tell. As far as cities go, it's a lot like most. "Madonna's from Bay City, too," I said. I was met with blank stares, and it occurred to me they had no idea who Madonna was. Then, I finally got around to telling them about my 'accident.' I skipped the whole runaway/stealing Bruce's car bit, and instead explained I was hitchhiking my way to Florida to be with my sister. I told them about the four black guys that had ambushed me, stolen my money, and hit me on the head, I guessed, because I had no recollection of the actual assault. "I don't even know where I am," I admitted. "Those guys forced me into their car at the mall in Chattanooga, and I woke up in the ditch, soaking wet. My head is feeling a lot better than what it was, though."

"Chattanooga is about forty miles west of here," Mr. Hollister said. "You're in Georgia, now. Nearest town is Bolton Hills, 'bout three miles southa here."

"Seems like a pretty out-of-the-way sorta place," I said as I scooped up some green beans with my fork.

"Well, we like it here," Mr. Hollister said, glancing at his wife. "Quiet, peaceful. We get by, by the grace of God."

Mrs. Hollister uttered something under her breath. Her lips barely moved. I started to get a weird feeling, like these people might just be some of those religious fanatics, the kind that come around to our house once or twice a year on Saturday mornings. I remember being out in the yard one of those times. This was a long time ago, and I must've only been seven or eight. A big, blue mini van with fake wood paneling on the side pulled up to the curb in front of our house. There were four or five people inside. I was in the yard, playing with my trucks or something, I don't remember for sure. Anyway, two of the people in the car—a woman and a man—get out of the car. They're dressed really nice, too: the man is in a suit, and the lady, she's in a dress. I remember her being very pretty, too. She said something to the driver of the vehicle, then closed the door. They were both carrying books and some papers, and they walked right up to me.

"Why, hello there, young fella," the man said. "And how are you today?"

"Good," I said.

"Tell me," the man said, kneeling down. "Is your mom or dad home?"

I nodded. (This was before we found out our real parents had been killed in a car wreck.) "Yes," I replied, "but they're sleeping." It was around eleven o'clock, and it wasn't uncommon for Lacy and Bruce to sleep until early afternoon on

234

Saturdays. In fact, Ellen and I had a standing order not to wake them up on Saturday mornings. It made it our favorite day of the week. We could do pretty much anything we wanted, and we didn't even have to ask.

"Well, I'll tell you what," the man said with genuine smile. "I'm going to give you a few things. Can you see to it your mom and dad get them?"

I nodded again, and the woman handed me a couple of pamphlets. Then, the man patted me on my head and ruffled my hair. They were nice people. "See you later, buddy," the man said, and they walked over to the McKinley's house and knocked on the door. The mini van rolled down the street and stopped in front of the house. I remember thinking something to the effect that it was sort of a reverse Halloween, going door-to-door like that. Only, they weren't trick-or-treating; they were giving stuff away. And they weren't wearing costumes.

I looked at one of the pamphlets they gave me. Inside were colorful drawings of people, all smiling and happy. An Asian lady was working in a garden. A black man was fixing a flat tire on a car, and he looked like he was having a great time doing it. A white guy with an all-American smile was hugging his two children. There was printing on the paper, but I didn't read any of it. I turned the page, and there was a drawing of what appeared to be a huge bomb going off. People were watching it, too, with expressions of shock and horror. Some were running. I remember thinking: *They should have been on the other page with the other people who were smiling and happy.*

I took the pamphlets into the house and put them on the table. Later, when Lacy and Bruce woke up, Bruce saw the papers on the table. He was furious.

"You didn't talk to them, didja?" he fumed, his voice raspy from sleep.

"No," I said, shaking my head.

"That's a goddamned good thing," Bruce said, and he

picked up the pamphlets and threw them into the trash. "All you gotta do is say two words to them people, and they'll be coming back every fuckin' weekend. Like fuckin' feedin' stray cats. If they come back, you run and hide, ya hear?"

I nodded, not really understanding why Bruce was so mad. But even at that age, I think I'd given up trying to understand everything Bruce told me. The man and woman had been sorta nice, but if Bruce said not to talk to them, well, I'd better listen. Next time Ellen and I saw the mini van, we ran inside. They came to the door and knocked, but we pretended no one was home. We stifled giggles as we hid in the kitchen. It was kind of fun, in a little kid sort of way.

o o o

After dinner, Eve, Ester, and Mrs. Hollister cleaned up the dishes and the kitchen. Mr. Hollister invited me into what he called the 'parlor,' which was what I would have called the 'living room.' It was almost like I'd stepped back in time, back into the 1800s. The room had a couch (old and worn), two rocking chairs (equally as old, I was sure), a coffee table, and a desk near a window. There were a few potted plants about, and a big bible sat on the coffee table. It was one of those leather bound ones—not fake leather, like the ones in motels—with faded white letters on the cover, and it looked like it was a hundred years old. Mr. Hollister saw me looking at it.

"Belonged to my father's father," he said. He was proud, most obviously, and sincere. "He was in service to the Lord all his life. Church pastor for over fifty years. Have a seat," and he pointed to one of the rocking chairs. "You've had a rough day. You sure you're all right? You want Sarah to take a look at that?"

"I'm fine, thanks," I said, sitting in the chair, which looked to be handmade, maybe even by Mr. Hollister himself.

"We don't get many people passing through," he said. "We're sort of 'out of the way.' We like it like that."

Mrs. Hollister came into the living room carrying a tray; Eve and Ester followed. The tray was placed on the coffee table. It contained a steel pitcher and two ceramic mugs. "Coffee?" she asked.

Not wanting to be impolite, I nodded. Coffee never appealed to me, but I could drink it if I had to. Mrs. Hollister poured me a cup, and I was again struck by her gentle nature. They were simple folks, I gathered that much. And they were certainly hospitable toward their guests . . . which, according to Mr. Hollister, they didn't receive all that often.

o o o

We talked—or, I should say, Mr. Hollister and I talked—and I was happy he didn't ask me too many questions. If he found it strange that a teenage kid was on his own, headed for Florida, he didn't say anything. Mostly, if I wasn't saying anything or asking any questions (which I didn't), he told me about how his family had been in Bolton Hills for years and years, and how they'd been blessed over and over. He told me about his son, Isaiah, who had gone off to college to be a 'learned' man, but he was hoping his son would come back to the 'homestead' someday. He looked a little sad when he told me about it. Eve and Ester did, too. Mrs. Hollister looked away.

o o o

And I'd figured out what had struck me as odd: there was no television in the room and no radio. Not a computer in sight. Come to think of it, there wasn't a phone around, either, which was really strange for this day and age. I read somewhere that the average house in America has like two or three televisions and four radios. And phones? Hell . . . *everyone* has a phone in their home. How do you get by without one of those?

o o o

I had no idea what time it was. Early evening, but I didn't know exactly. We hadn't talked about me staying the night or where I was going to go. Or how I was going to get there. And I was getting a little stressed about it. I didn't want to impose, and I certainly didn't want to come right out and ask if I could spend the night. The Hollisters had already been quite gracious, allowing me to shower; giving me some clean, dry clothing; having me stay for dinner. Mrs. Hollister had even gone as far as washing my dirty clothes, I found out later, including the new clothing in my backpack that had been soiled by the rain.

I needn't have worried about accommodations. Mr. Hollister must've already made plans, or perhaps he read my mind.

"Well, it's gettin' on in the day," he said. "You're welcome to spend the night tonight, in Isaiah's room," he offered. "Course, you're welcome to join us for evening church service."

Well, what was I going to do, refuse? Say something like 'Sorry, but that's not my bag? I think I'll stay here and chat with the chickens.' Right. I did the same thing anyone else would have done if they'd been shown that kind of hospitality.

"Oh, that'd be fine," I said, not knowing what in the hell I'd just gotten myself into.

58

The Bolton Hills Church of God with Signs Following (no shit—that's what it was called) looked every bit as old as the Hollister's house. The only difference was that it had a relatively fresh coat of white paint, but even that didn't do much to spruce it up. We'd walked there, along a grassy two-track that wound through the forest, up and down and around. The rain had stopped, and the sky had cleared. The air was damp and punky with the acrid scent of aspen and pine. We'd walked about a half mile in silence, until Mr. Hollister spoke.

"There we are, right up there," he said, pointing ahead through the trees. I could barely make out the church. "My great grandfather helped build that church when he was a boy," Hollister explained. "It burned once, right to the ground. But they had 'er re-built in less than a week, praise God."

I was feeling a little uncomfortable. I didn't know much about religion and had never read the bible. I knew the basic stuff: Jesus walked on water, turned water into wine, did a bunch of miracles, fed a shitload of people with only a fish and a muffin, things like that. Then, they thanked him by nailing him to a cross. But he outsmarted them and lived. I knew about the ark and the guy that built it, Noah. But that was about it. If you were to give me a Bible quiz, I'd probably score below five percent. I was clueless. I guess I believed in God and all that, but religion, for the most part, confused the hell out of me, if you pardon the pun. I guess I couldn't understand why there were so many of them. Religions, that is. There were thousands of religions, all over the world, and every one of them says they're right, and that all the others are wrong. In fact, that's what the whole war on terror was all about: religion. But it's more than that. Here in America, religions can't even agree. Oh, they all might have the same basic beliefs, but then, people start forming their own opinion about what God wants them to do and how they should do it. And none of them get along, not really. If they did, they would all come together and not have so many different types of churches. This had been pointed out to me by a kid back home in Bay City, Martin Khul, who was a grade ahead of me. He was in my gym class. I don't know how we got on the topic, but one day, we started talking about religion. He said he was an atheist. I knew what an atheist was, but I'd never met anyone who claimed to be one.

"You are?" I asked.

"Yeah," he replied. "I don't believe there is a god."

Growing up, Lacy and Bruce weren't religious, but I'd heard about religion all the time. It was on television, the radio, in the newspapers. Lots of my friends went to church, and once in a while, they'd invite me. While I might not have known much about religion, the very fact that so many other people were religious led me to believe *of course* there was a God. At least, that's what I assumed, and I never gave the matter much thought. Just because my family didn't go to church didn't mean we didn't believe in God. I guess I just never thought much about it, being a kid and all.

"How can you say there is no God?" I asked. "Everybody believes in God."

"Which one?" Martin asked me.

"What do you mean?" I replied.

"Which 'god' are you talking about?"

"There's more than one?" I asked.

Martin nodded. "Every religion has their own god or gods," he said, "and they all say they're right. So, which god is the real one?"

I was getting pretty confused. I really hadn't given much thought that there might be other gods that people worshiped. I thought God was God.

"Think about it," Martin continued. "Take the biggest religions in the world—Islam, Christianity, Bhuddism, Hinduism—and compare them. Not to mention each group has their own splinter groups that don't even agree on what they should agree on. But just take the big ones. If there is a One True God, then all the other religions must be wrong. In fact, Hindus worship thousands of different gods. Doesn't that seem weird to you?"

I nodded. It *did* seem a bit strange. But I didn't know all that much about Hinduism, either. Still, I found it hard to believe there wasn't a God, and I wasn't following Martin's argument.

"But how do you *know?*" I asked. "If God is invisible, how do you *know* there is no God?"

"Think about it, Greg. It's just this big huge mass deception that began a long time ago, when people wanted answers for something. Science didn't exist, not like it does today. People had to come up with other reasons why their crops dried up, why a plague killed millions of people, why a volcano erupted. What better way than passing that shit off on an angry God?"

"But that doesn't prove God doesn't exist," I said, knowing full-well I was in a little over my head. But the whole notion of there not being a God was ludicrous.

"Let me put it this way," Martin said. "You believe in God, right?"

"Yeah, sure," I said.

"The Christian God?"

I shrugged. "I guess so."

"Why?"

I was growing increasingly uncomfortable with where this conversation was going. I wanted to be able to speak with conviction, but, truth be told, I guess I didn't have much. "I . . . I guess because everyone else does," I said. A weak argument, sure. But it was the truth. I think a lot of people believe in God because they've been around the concept all their lives.

"Fine," Martin said. "You believe in the Christian God. But if you were born in, say, Saudi Arabia, which is mostly Islamic, which god would you believe in? Theirs, or yours? Would you be a Christian . . . or a Muslim?"

I was totally confused by now. Martin had obviously thought about this whole issue a lot. It didn't make him right, not by a long shot. But he did have a point, and he knew it.

"You'd probably be a Muslim, just like ninety-eight percent of all other Saudis," Martin continued. "The fact is, everybody believes in the god they were raised with. People worship the god their parents worshiped, and their parents before them. Nobody hardly ever questions it. You believe in something not because it's *there*, not because of the evidence. You believe it because you were *raised* that way. It doesn't make it *true.*"

I didn't say anything. It had been the most I'd ever thought about God or religion or spirituality. And I'd certainly never had any conversations about it. Not like this, anyway.

Finally, Martin flashed a disarming smile. "I think you're a lot like me," he said. "You believe in your God. That means you've discarded all of the other gods in the world. I've done that, too. I've just discarded one more god than you have."

I thought about that for a long time. In fact, I still think about it once in a while, and I thought about it again as I made my way with the Hollisters to the front doors of the old church in the woods.

59

Other people were gathering, emerging through the dark forest, seeping out of the oily shadows like mysterious gnomes. And they all looked like they could have been related to the Hollisters. They pretty much dressed the same: lots of black pants and white shirts. A few suits, but not many. Most of the men had beards. Not all of them, sure. But most. The women and girls wore long dresses, like Mrs. Hollister and her daughters. And nobody seemed to pay me any mind. I guess, wearing Isaiah Hollister's clothing, I must have looked like I fit right in. There was something comforting about that, but equally disturbing, too. I wasn't sure if I *wanted* to fit in.

A man—the church pastor, I presumed—greeted us at the door. He was wearing gray polyester pants and a white shirt with a gray bow tie. His beard was long and gray, but he had no mustache. He shook Mr. Hollister's hand, then mine. "Welcome, friend," he drawled. Then, we went inside the Bolton Hills Church of God with Signs Following.

○ ○ ○

There wasn't much inside the church. It looked pretty much like any other church I'd seen. The pews were solid wood: old, dark, and shiny. At the front of the church was a single podium. Behind it, a big, bare crucifix was mounted to the wall. The floor was wood: clean and glossy. Six stained glass windows were on each wall; their colors were dark and drab in the early night. A few dim sconce lights adorned the side walls, casting a dusky, yellow glow.

Mr. Hollister led the way, and we took our places at the very front row on the left. That was unnerving, too. I was really new to all this religion stuff, and I wasn't sure I wanted a front row seat. I always figured the front row was usually reserved for the real hardcore fans, and I certainly didn't fit in that category. Not by a long shot. But I was right on the inside end, at least. An aisle seat. The podium was only a couple feet away. Mr. Hollister was next to me, then his wife, then Eve and Ester.

Other people arrived, and I could hear broken fragments of greeting and a little laughter here and there. I turned around to look. That's one of the problems with sitting in the front row. You never know who's coming or going, unless you turn around. I tried to do it as nonchalantly as I could, not wanting to be nosy and all that. But I was curious.

Soon, the little church was about a quarter full. Maybe thirty people in all, and it looked to be families. In fact, it looked like each family had their own pew. In a setting this small, I'm sure everyone knew each other, and they probably had their own seating that they'd grown accustomed to over the years. Maybe it was like a pecking order or something. Maybe, the longer you go to church, the farther you move up. Like tenure. If so, we were at the top of the heap. Important worshipers, us in the front row.

o o o

A door closed, and I heard footsteps approach the front of the church. The man I'd shaken hands with walked past me, his shoes clicking on the hard wood floor. He walked around the podium, placed his hands on each corner, and looked around. He remained that way for nearly a minute, holding the podium, looking around at each one of us. When he looked at me, he gave me a subtle nod and a smile. Then, he bowed his head and began praying. I noticed everyone else had bowed their heads, so I followed along. The shift made blood run to my temple and forehead, and the throbbing drove me nuts. I don't remember what was said, something about the Lord being with us, guiding us that evening, amen, and all that. When he was done, organ music began, lofty and full. I hadn't even seen an organ when I came in, but now that I looked, I could see it over on the far wall. There was a woman seated at it, playing, her back to us. She was wearing a white dress and her brown hair was spun in a tight bun, a perfect, inverted bowl.

Then, everybody was standing. I snapped to my feet, trying to look like I knew what I was doing, like I'd done this before. People started clapping hands, then began singing. I hadn't a clue what they were singing, and nobody had any books. Man, did I feel like a fish out of water. Pick me up and put me back in the bowl, because all I'm doin' is floppin' around. Mr. Hollister must have sensed my unease. He leaned over and spoke softly into my ear.

"Don't you be worried about not knowin' the songs," he said. His breath was husky and smelled of old tea. "Nobody's gonna care. You're welcome here."

Well, that made me feel a little more at ease. Took the pressure off, sort of. So, I just clapped my hands and let everyone else sing the song. I tried not to move my head very much, on account of the throbbing. Then the song ended, and everyone sat down.

The preacher started talking, referencing something out

of the Bible. He went on about some dude who had a couple of hundred wives or something like that. I thought that was illegal, but if it was in the Bible, then, I guessed it was probably all right. Besides: it had been a long time ago. People knew better nowadays, especially with all sorts of funky diseases going around. You sure didn't want to be dipping your wick into two hundred different women, regardless of whether they were your wives or not.

The preacher went on and on about the mighty Lord and His swift sword, and how glorious it'll be when He comes back to get His faithful. This brought a few 'amens' from around the church. The preacher said the righteous will be saved, but all sinners will burn in a lake of fire. He picked up a Bible and quoted several passages, but he never had to look at the words as he spoke. Hell, he never even opened it. The guy was good, I'll say that much. And the more he spoke, the more people got worked up. One lady stood up, stretched her arms wide, palms up, and closed her eyes. She started praying in a whisper, even while the preacher spoke. Nobody seemed to care that she was in her own world, doing her own thing. They just let her carry on. Someone else stood and was now doing the same thing. Organ music started playing (which was a good thing, as the banjo in my head had started again, and I needed something to drown it out), and people started clapping. Some stood, but Mr. Hollister remained in the pew. I figured if he stood up, I would . . . but until then, I wasn't going anywhere.

Then came another sound: gibberish. I mean, that's really what it was. Someone was speaking—loudly, at that—in the pew behind me. But it was some weird language I'd never heard before. It was just plain *bizarre*. I noticed most people had stopped clapping and were listening to the guy and his blubber.

Suddenly, I figured it out. (I'm not *completely* clueless, I just play one in real life once in while.) The guy was speaking in tongues. I'd heard about it, but I didn't know much about the whole thing. Apparently, if you're a really big fan, God will do something to you to make you speak in a weird language nobody can understand, unless He allows you to. Well, God wasn't allowing me to do shit, because the guy behind me sounded like he was spewing out a blue streak of garbled psychobabble. I couldn't understand a single word of it.

Then, the preacher joined in, speaking plain English, acting as translator. It was a message from the Lord, he said, and the Lord was apparently telling everyone (through some funky language, translated through the preacher) that He was coming, and soon, and nobody will know the day or the hour, but it was going to be soon, brother, and you best be prepared, because ol' Jesus was pissed, and He was going to kick the shit out of a lot of people. (I'm paraphrasing, of course. He didn't really use the word 'shit.' But you get the picture.) I heard some other noises, some footsteps, and I didn't pay any mind until a guy walked right past me up to the altar. He was carrying a big wooden box, and he placed it on the floor. I wasn't sure, with all the other sounds and noises going on (and that guy behind me and his gibberish), but it sounded like there were sounds coming from the wooden box. A buzzing sound, maybe. It had a lid with hinges, but it was closed. I wondered what was in it.

Then, the man behind me stopped speaking. I turned a little and saw him with his hands raised up, chin tilted back, eyes closed. Silent. The preacher spoke.

"Brothers and sisters in the Lord, we have been faithful." There was a smattering of amens, and the preacher raised his hands and continued. "We have been faithful, and as Mark tells us in chapter sixteen, verse seventeen: He tells us, brothers and sisters. What is it that He sayeth?"

Without missing a bit, Mr. Gibberish spoke up, speaking in plain southern English. *"And these signs shall follow them that believe; in my name shall they cast out devils; they shall speak with new tongues; they shall take up serpents; and if they drink any deadly thing, it shall not hurt them; they shall lay hands on the sick, and they shall recover."*

This was followed with a few more amens. More people stood, and Mr. Gibberish began to move toward the front of the church, his hands in the air. He was mumbling something. Probably more gibberish.

"And Luke tells us, very clearly, in chapter ten, verse nineteen. Brother Samuel, what does Luke tell us?"

From the back of the church, a deep voice boomed.

"Behold, I give unto you the power to tread on serpents and scorpions, and over all the power of the enemy: and nothing by any means shall hurt you."

There were more amens, and more people stood. The organ began again. Brother Gibberish, standing next to the box on the floor near the alter, began to shake. His eyes remained closed, tightly, and his brow knotted into a washboard. He looked in deep concentration, focused. Then, he reached down and pulled the lid off the box. It didn't take me two seconds to see what was inside.

Rattlesnakes.

Maybe six, maybe eight. I couldn't tell.

Now, remember: that box was only a few feet away from me. I could see those crazy snakes as plain as day. I could see their dragon-fire eyes glistening, and I could see their tongues flicking. And the snakes were big, too, as far as rattlesnakes go. There's only one kind of rattlesnake we have in Michigan—the Massasauga rattler—and they don't get very big. These things, though—holy shit. Each one must have been at least three feet long and as big around as my wrist.

About this time, people started praying on their own. In soft voices, mostly, and to themselves. I couldn't understand what anyone was saying. In the pew next to me, Mr. Hollister gazed forward, real serious-like. Next to him, Mrs. Hollister's head was bent. Her eyes were closed, and her lips were moving.

Eve and Ester were watching Mr. Gibberish and the box of writhing, hissing rattlesnakes.

The whole episode became surreal. I felt like I was in a movie theater, watching some odd documentary. But the droning organ, the chanting prayers, the buzzing rattlesnakes—they were an all-too real reminder that what was happening around me wasn't something on television.

Then, Brother Gibberish—I swear to God this happened—reached down with both hands and picked up three rattlesnakes! He stood up, holding the snakes in his arms as their tails vibrated and wrapped around his wrists. All the while, he spoke quietly, repeating something over and over, trance-like. From around the church, prayers grew louder. There were more amens, more words of encouragement.

And I was so damned close to those snakes I could make out each scale on their heads. One of them had his mouth open, and I could see his two fangs, like curved, poisonous needles. I thought he was going to bite Brother Gibberish right then and there.

This is as fucked up as fucked up can be, I thought. *It doesn't get any more fucked up than this.* I know it's probably not something I should be thinking in a church, but it was the truth. It's what I was thinking. And I was thinking how in the hell I could get away from Brother Gibberish and those snakes. I mean, they were literally close enough to bite me if they wanted. One strike, and *wham!* It'd be over.

I was pressed back in the pew as far as I could go. The only thing I could do was get up and run, which had its own consequences. It would show everyone I didn't have faith, that I was scared. Next to me, Mr. Hollister didn't look the least bit concerned. Of course, he was a foot farther from the snakes than I was. If anyone was going to get bit, it was going to be Brother Gibberish, or me. Maybe both. Through Isaiah's pants, I felt my lucky black and white quarter in my pocket, and, of all times, I really hoped it wouldn't fail me now.

So, I didn't do a thing. I'm not what you'd call an outdoorsy-type person, but I'd heard if you ever came across a coiled rattlesnake, the best thing you could do was freeze and hope it would go away on its own. And you certainly don't try to pick up the thing.

But Brother Gibberish! Talk about taking his own life in his hands! He raised those snakes up high, all the while speaking in a voice just above a whisper. Then, I'll be damned if he didn't start dancing around like a possessed puppet! He was tapping his feet to the organ music, moving around, raising the snakes up, then down, then up again, jigging like a circus monkey.

And the rattlesnakes? They looked none too happy about these shenanigans. I watched the buttons on the their tails blur as they shook, louder and louder, and I couldn't help but wonder what the snakes were thinking. *Look, buddy, we're going to bite your ass, and we're going to bite your ass something hard if you don't can the chanting and the jitterbugging and put us back in the motherfucking box.*

Just when I thought things couldn't get any weirder, a woman walked past me. Before I knew it, she'd reached into the box and had a rattlesnake in each hand, holding them up for the congregation to see. Her eyes were closed, and, just like Brother Gibberish, she began praying and tapping her feet to the music. There were shouts of more encouragement, amens . . . it just went on and on. At one point, one of the snakes struck out at the woman, missing her face by only an inch or so. A few in the congregation gasped, but the woman handling the snakes had her eyes closed and never saw how close she'd come to being bitten. The flock, however, probably thought it was a testament to her belief, on account of God must've seen how devoted she was and wouldn't allow the reptile to bite someone with that much faith.

It was the craziest experience I think I've ever had. The

whole thing took on a carnival-like atmosphere, and I could almost see the preacher, carrying a big bullhorn, enticing the crowd while calliope music piped. *Step right up, step right up, ladies and gentlemen! See the amazing snake man and snake woman, without fear, handling poisonous, man-killing snakes! Step right up and see for yourself, before one of the snakes bites their ass and they fall dead to the ground! Step right up . . . .*

The organ music died. Brother Gibberish and Sister Almost-Got-Bit-In-The-Face stopped dancing. The woman bent over and placed the snakes back in the box. Then she stood up, stretched her arms out like a swan, and smiled up to heaven. She had faith; she had proven it. Brother Gibberish, too. Now, it was his turn to return the snakes to the crate. He lowered the three he held in his arms and dropped them into the box.

Evidently, Brother Gibberish's faith wasn't quite as strong as Sister Almost-Got-Bit-In-The-Face, because one of those rattlers turned right back around and *bam!* Nailed Brother Gibberish right on the forearm just below the elbow. The snake was a blur, but ol' Gibberish knew he'd been bitten, all right. He grabbed his arm and fell to his knees. His eyes bulged like white cysts, his mouth open in a silent scream.

The preacher sprang, and he closed the lid of the wooden box. There were gasps and cries from the congregation, and I could hear all sorts of different prayers being recited. Several other men rushed toward the front and knelt down around Brother Gibberish. I was thinking maybe someone had a snakebite kit handy, and they were coming to his rescue. Nope. The men placed their hands on him and started chanting prayers like monks in a monastery.

The organ began again, and I started looking around for the flying saucer that had obviously dropped me off on this whacked-out planet. I wanted to find that thing and get the hell out, pronto.

Well, a couple of men finally wound up helping Brother

Gibberish, ushering him out of the church. The service continued, just like nothing had happened. The preacher gave a sermon about not putting thy God to thy test, and I thought: *Isn't that what you just did?*

Crazy.

60

Not a word was spoken as we weaved through the dark forest back to the Hollister's home. Man, was I glad to be out of that church. There was just something *wrong* with what they were doing, I knew that much. Pulling live rattlesnakes from a box and boogieing around with them? Thinking that if you have enough faith, you're not going to be bitten? *Hello? Anybody home in there?*

o o o

I didn't ask Mr. Hollister what happened to Brother Gibberish. I knew rattlesnake bites aren't *always* fatal, but they were *always* serious. I wondered if they took the guy to the hospital or maybe just took him to his house and prayed. And I wondered if they did that at *every* church service. If they did, how many people got bit? Sooner or later, you're not going to have much of a congregation if somebody gets bit by a venomous snake each week.

o o o

When we arrived back at the house, Bo the German Shepard came out of nowhere and scared the living shit out of me. No bark, no warning. He just ran right up to me and jumped up. I yelled bloody murder. I thought I was being attacked by a wolf until I started getting licked in the face. Then, I laughed and pushed the dog down.

"Bo! Barn!" a thin voice piped. I was Eve. I heard paws in the dirt and saw the dark form of the dog trot obediently away.

Inside the house, the girls vanished. Mrs. Hollister scurried about the kitchen, and Mr. Hollister asked me to have a seat in the parlor. He had a formal way of doing things, this man. Very rigid and self-disciplined. It was sort of odd. Here they were, in the middle of the hills of Georgia. They seemed to have an okay life. I didn't know what Mr. Hollister did for a living—farming, maybe—and they seemed to get by all right. But they seemed to shun all the benefits of modern technology. No computers, no phones, no radios, no TVs. I wondered if they even knew what they were. I actually felt sorry for Eve and Ester, growing up that way, not being able to take advantage of the things most Americans simply took for granted.

o o o

I joined Mr. Hollister in the parlor, in the same rocking chair I'd sat in earlier. Mrs. Hollister brought in a tray of tea, poured each of us a cup, and then whisked off down the hall. I heard a bedroom door close.

No lights were on in the parlor. A light over the stove glowed in the kitchen, casting dark shadows around the room. I could see Mr. Hollister's silhouette in the rocker on the other side of the room. He raised his cup and took a sip of tea.

"What you saw," he began, "upta' church. I didn't think

they'd be doing that tonight. Otherwise . . . well, I probably wouldn't have asked you to go. See, most folks, they tend to get a little bit, oh, I don't know—*scared*—by what they see. I admit, I've been a little scared myself from time to time."

Scared? I thought. *How about completely freaked out?*

"See, folks around here, we're different."

No shit?

"We tend to keep to ourselves, tend to keep away from all the evil in the world around us. Some things—like what you saw tonight—people just don't understand. But to us, well, most of us growed up like this. It's our way of life. Nobody has to understand it, nobody has to like it. But we think we got it pretty good. We take care of each other, here. We look after one another. Our family is as big and old as the hills. We don't have any crime, nothin' to worry about like the rest of the world. Now, I know some people call us crazy, especially when you see something like tonight. Oh, there's other things we do, too. Not me, not my family. Others. Others, they drink poison. Strychnine. I've seen it. I've seen people guzzle that stuff by the gallon. I've seen 'em live. I've watched some die. I've probably seen four dozen people die in that church since I was a little boy. They'll tell you it's a matter of faith, and, for the most part, it is. How about you? You got faith?"

I thought about it for a moment, before saying "Yeah . . . but not enough to pick up a live rattlesnake."

Mr. Hollister laughed good, and I mean *good*. He let out a deep belly laugh before catching himself. "Whoop," he said, "gotta keep 'er down. Ladies'll be trying to sleep. But that's a good policy. Just because you got faith doesn't mean you need to go around tuggin' on rattlesnakes, you know what I mean?"

"Yeah," I replied.

"My son, Isaiah," Hollister said, "he's offta school. College. New York. He's a good boy. Hard worker. Respectful. He used to handle serpents. Lots of 'em, matter of fact. Nearly every time they brought 'em out. Got bit last year, though. Got real sick. That changed him. I think, up 'til that point, he thought he was bulletproof, as a lot of young people do. I did, when I was young. He pulled through, but he did a lot of thinking. Wanted to see the other side of life, the more worldly side. That's fine. He's a young man, and a good one. If he decides to come back, he'll be more'an welcome. Old Albert Pike's kid did the same, a few years back. Went to Chicago, of all places. Thought he'd like it better. Came back in about a year. He was at the service tonight, as a matter of fact. I asked him why he came back. Said he got 'lonely.' I asked him how he could be lonely in a city of four million people. He said I wouldn't understand unless I was there. I told him I thought I had a pretty good idea what he meant. The world, it's lonely. Family fills that up. We got everything we need here. Oh, I'm sure you noticed we don't have much. We've got electricity, but not much else. Simple as can be.

"But, I'm ramblin' on, and you're probably tired. Come on. I'll show you to your room. You can decide what you want to do in the morning. I can give you a lift somewhere, get you on your way again."

o o o

He stood, and I followed him down a short hallway to a small bedroom. He flicked on a light. The room contained a single bed and a dresser. My backpack was on the bed. On the dresser was a black and white framed picture I knew must be Isaiah Hollister. He looked to be about twenty. Rugged and good looking. Clean shaven.

"This is great," I said quietly as I glanced around the small bedroom. "I can't thank you enough."

"You get some sleep. Head doin' better?"

I nodded. "Lots, yeah. Thanks."

With that, Mr. Hollister turned and walked off, closing the bedroom door behind him.

o o o

I didn't waste any time getting out of my clothes and getting into bed. Any other day, it might've felt a little stiff. Tonight, however, the bed felt like I was floating on a dream. The pillow was soft as a cloud, and I heaved a satisfied sigh as I settled in for the night. And I was just about asleep when I heard a wooden *clunk* on the floor, right next to my bed. Something had fallen.

I reached over and turned on the lamp, squinting in the piercing brightness. I looked down.

On the floor was a knot. An actual knot, from a piece of wood, was on the floor. It was oblong, smooth on two sides. Big and round as a ping pong ball. Without getting out of bed, I reached down and picked it up. Then, I turned and looked at the wall behind me. There was a dark hole where the knot had fallen from. But in the darkness of that small knothole, an eye was staring back at me.

61

The eyeball was suddenly replaced by a pair of lips. Ester's lips.

"Turn the light off," she whispered, and I obeyed by clicking off the lamp. Then, I was in total darkness. Ester's soft voice came again: *"Were you sleeping?"*

"Sort of," I replied. But I wasn't angry or anything. Curious, but not angry. I heard other whispering, and I realized Eve was on the other side of the wall, too. The wall was more than just a board, though. It had appeared, in the brief moment I'd seen Ester's eye, that the wall was probably studded with two-by-fours, packed with newspaper for insulation. It was a fire trap, for sure, but that's what people used before spun fiberglass and foam board.

"I'm sorry we woke you up," Ester said, and I leaned forward with my ear close to the knothole, straining to hear her. It was obvious she didn't want to be overheard.

"It's no problem," I said, in my own hushed whisper. *"Is something wrong?"*

"No, nothing is wrong," Ester replied. *"We just don't get to talk to many people from out there."*

"From out where?" I asked.

259

Eve spoke, and her whisper carried a slight lisp. *"You know,"* she said. *"From out there. Anywhere. Different places."*

"Well, I guess I never thought of it that way," I said, and I suddenly realized these girls had probably never been to the city, or anywhere that was populated. When Mr. Hollister was telling me about living here, removed from society, he meant it.

"What are malls like?" Ester asked. *"You said you were at the mall when those bad guys grabbed you."*

I couldn't believe what I was hearing. Ester had to be my age. Was it really possible she knew nothing about shopping malls? Could she really have been kept away from the city her entire life? Yes, I was sure it was possible. In Michigan, there is a popular island called Mackinac. It's not very big, but it's a popular tourist destination because of its historical significance over a few hundred years. I saw a story on television about a woman who had lived on the island her entire life, without once taking the twenty-minute ferry ride to the mainland. She claimed it was because she couldn't swim, and if something happened to the ferry, she feared she would drown. It was pointed out to her that there had never been a ferry accident where people drowned, but that didn't matter. Water was water, and she was afraid. Her fear held her prisoner on that small island for all of her seventy-nine years, and she never experienced anything beyond the island.

"How old are you, Ester?" I asked.

"Fifteen," was her soft reply. So I was only a little off. *"How old are you?"* she asked.

"I'm sixteen," I said. *"You mean to tell me you've never been to the mall? You've never been to a city? At all?"*

"No," Ester replied. I could hear the sadness in her voice, and it made *me* sad. I couldn't imagine what it would be like, cooped up in the mountains, not seeing anything new or different. Mr. Hollister had made a valid point about how it was great that everyone in the hills looked out for one another, like

they were all family. (Maybe they were.) That's great and all, but there wouldn't be any harm in checking out the city once in a while, just for some culture, maybe to see and learn something new. Check out a flick and grab a tub of buttered popcorn once in a while. Couldn't hurt.

"Father forbids us to go to the city," Ester replied, *"until we're old enough to go on our own."*

"Go on your own? What's that *supposed to mean?"* I asked.

"Father says there are things that draw us to the city, things that aren't good. He says we're not mature enough to understand and won't know how to deal with them."

Banjo music sifted through my head again. I couldn't believe I was hearing this. The sisters really didn't have any clue what it was like beyond the safety and comfort of their family and the woods around them. Clearly, it was driving them mad.

"But how do you know anything about the city if you've never been there?" I asked.

It was Eve's turn to speak. *"Isaiah tells us,"* she whispered in that cute little lisp of hers. *"When Isaiah visits, he tells us all about the city. The people, the buildings, everything. We talk through the wall, just like we're talking to you. But it's been a long time since he's been back. Ester says she thinks he's not coming back, but I hope he does. I miss him."*

"He brought us an MP3 player," Ester said, to my amazement. I figured these girls probably wouldn't have known what a cassette player was, let alone an MP3 player. *"Put your ear up to the hole."*

I did as Ester asked, and I could faintly hear what sounded like country music, very faint and very tinny. Ester must've been holding one of the earpieces up to the hole. Then it faded out, and Ester's voice returned.

"It has hundreds of songs," she said proudly, *"and if it stops working, Isaiah gave me an extra battery to put in it. Then, it'll work again."*

"Have you ever eaten in a restaurant?" Eve asked.

Man, if these girls ever *did* go to the city, they'd never survive. It would be information overload in the first sixty seconds.

"Yes," I replied. *"Lots of times. There are restaurants all over the place."*

"Father says Mother's cooking is better than any restaurant," Ester stated.

"Well, you're father's probably right about that," I said. *"And your mom's cooking is probably a lot safer, too,"* I added, remembering my episode at the Mystic Panda.

o o o

We talked for what seemed like hours. Eve and Ester were starving, in an intellectual sense. Oh, I'm all for innocence and all that. Kids grow up way too fast these days. I saw girls in Bay City that couldn't have been more than twelve, wearing makeup, stuffing their shirts to make it look like they had boobs. In some cases, they looked a hell of a lot older than what they actually were. Sad thing was, by the time they were my age, most of them were going to be knocked up or on drugs, or both. Their life would, for the most part, be over. It's too bad there wasn't a happy medium, somewhere between Bolton Hills and New York, where the two worlds could come together with the best each had to offer.

Obviously, that would never happen. But I kept wondering what kind of life the girls would have, either way. If they stayed here in the hills, they'd be naive all of their lives, never realizing the benefits and wonders of the modern world. Sure, they'd probably be safe, probably get married to a good old Bolton Hills boy, pop out a few kids, and keep them away from the city, too. They'd be safe and happy, for the most part . . . as long as they didn't pick up any rattlesnakes.

But if they *did* go to the city, let's say, *tomorrow*—man, would they be in trouble. They would be eaten alive. Outside of Bolton Hills, these girls would have the social skills of a waffle maker. They would have no idea how to act, how to react, what to do. In short: they would be lost. Their father and mother, in the hopes of shielding them from the world, would have done nothing to prepare them for what most people consider day-to-day reality. And I wondered how Isaiah got along. Somehow, he'd managed, or so it seemed. But—and this is only my prediction—I think Isaiah would become more and more scarce around Bolton Hills, and, when he did come back, he wouldn't be hanging around for very long.

I stayed up and chatted with the girls as long as they wanted, even though I was tired. I really did feel sorry for them. I mean . . . they had a good life, and all . . . but they were missing out on so much. Sure, the world can be a shitty place. You can get screwed royally sometimes. Maybe even lots of times. But it's not so bad that you have to hide from it. If there was any message I tried to get across to the girls, that was it. It was ironic, now that I thought about it. Ester and Eve would be completely defenseless in the city. They hadn't learned how to

(wear a mask)

protect themselves. They hadn't learned street-smart skills. Whereas, Dawn had taken her protective measures to the extreme, these girls were literal babes in the woods. In the real world, Eve and Ester would be ripped apart, chewed up, spit back out, and left to waste away in the burning sun of reality. In fact, it was just like Dawn had told me, while we were discussing Halloween in Joe's cab: *It's easy to hide from the real world . . . but that means locking yourself in your own world. And that gets pretty lonely sometimes.* And I think Eve and Ester were probably two of the loneliest girls I'd ever met in my life.

62

I awoke to the smells of heaven: eggs, bacon, toast. It was incredible. Even in the bedroom, I could hear bacon sizzling and spitting. Lacy never made breakfasts like that. Ellen tried, and she did pretty okay sometimes. But *this*—this was altogether different. Maybe it was because I was hungry again, maybe it was because I hadn't had eggs and bacon in a long time. Whatever the reason, my taste buds were dancing the locomotion from the moment I awoke. There was no way I could lay in bed for another instant with smells like that drifting around the room.

o o o

I slipped out of bed, dressed in my new clothes that Mrs. Hollister had been kind enough to wash, and opened the door. The smells of breakfast all came rushing at me, intense and full, cloud-like, and I had to keep myself from charging into the kitchen and ripping into the food like a grizzly. Somehow, I managed to trundle casually down the hall and into the kitchen where Mrs. Hollister and the girls were busy at work.

"Good morning," I said. They nodded and smiled. Through the kitchen window, I could see Mr. Hollister outside, emerging from the barn.

"Would you like coffee?" Mrs. Hollister asked.

I wanted to tell her that if I didn't get some of that food in about three seconds, I was going to rip it right out of the skillet. Man, I was hungry. The smell of breakfast made me ravenous.

"Yeah, that would be great," I said. The coffee hadn't been too bad yesterday, so I figured I'd give it another try. Mrs. Hollister motioned for me to take a seat at the table, where five places were set. Immediately, Ester came to the table with a mug and a pitcher. She smiled warmly. Even with her slightly misaligned teeth and her homely appearance, it was hard not to like her. She seemed brighter this morning or, at least, more alive than she had previously been. Her face seemed more animated. Eve, too, seemed cheery, and I recalled our conversation during the night, through the wall. Could it be, perhaps, that just *that* simple stimulation had been enough to brighten their attitudes? I was sure they rarely had contact with others, except for those in and around Bolton Hills. I felt bad for them. I wondered again, if they were ever exposed to the modern world, would they be able to adjust? Apparently their brother had. But it was different for women. Oh, I know that probably seems like a sexist thing to say and all, but it's true. Especially here, where Mr. Hollister seemed very overprotective of his daughters. I don't think they'd ever have the chance to see what it is *really* like in the real world. They'd either be scared shitless, or go completely opposite. That seemed funny. I tried to picture what Eve and Ester would do if they ever got into the real world and turned into hellion rebels. Go goth? Would they get tattoos and dye their hair purple? Nose rings and eyebrow piercings? The thought was comical.

o o o

Mr. Hollister came inside. He gave his wife a brief hug, then looked at me. "Mornin' Mr. Chappell," he said, which sounded strange. The only people who ever called me 'Mr. Chappell' were my school teachers, and usually it was when I was in trouble.

"Good morning, sir," I replied. I don't know why I tacked the 'sir' on, but it seemed like it fit at the time.

"Sleep well?"

"Yes, I did. Great. Thank you again."

Breakfast was served. Somehow, I managed not to tear into anything until Mr. Hollister had said the morning prayer. I was actually proud of the fact I didn't make a pig out of myself, being careful to take my time as the plates of food were passed. I was *that* hungry.

o o o

We ate in silence, for the most part. It gave me time to think about what to do, where to go. I didn't want Mr. Hollister to go through any more trouble than he already had, but I needed, at the very least, to get to a main road. I didn't have a problem hitchhiking, or walking for that matter. If I could get back to I-75 or some other main freeway, I was sure I could once again find someone headed south and continue on my way. Actually, I should have already been in Florida . . . but things just don't always work out the way you want them to.

o o o

While Mrs. Hollister and her daughters cleaned up the morning dishes, Mr. Hollister asked about my plans. I told him if I could get a ride to any major road or freeway, that would be great. I told him I was sorry, but I didn't have any money to pay him for gas. He didn't seem to mind.

"Well, let's be on our way, then," and he stood. I remember the look in his daughters' eyes as we walked out the door. After thanking Mrs. Hollister for breakfast and their hospitality, I glanced at Eve and Ester, who were drying and putting away the dishes. Maybe it was just my imagination, but it seemed like they were the ones who wanted to be taken away, anywhere. Somewhere different, somewhere exciting and new. It made me sad. Isaiah, no doubt, had put that taste in their mouth. I'd given them another taste, a bit more to chew on, last night.

o o o

I turned and walked outside. Bo, that silly German Shepard, came up to me and poked me playfully in the crotch. I petted him on the head. That seemed to be all he wanted, and the dog raced off. Chickens scattered in terror. I followed Mr. Hollister to the truck.

The vehicle ambled along the dirt road. Mr. Hollister told me he'd take me as far as Dalton, which was about twenty miles south of Chattanooga, and close to I-75. I told him I couldn't thank him enough.

"Well, I hope the rest of your journey is a safe one," he said, as the truck bobbled along ruts and bumps. "It's tough enough as it is. Seems like you got it a bit harder than most, at your age. When I was young, we didn't have all the things you fellas have. Life was pretty simple. It still is, for us, as much as we can keep it. We just got electricity and running water a couple years ago. Mostly, we try to keep to ourselves, take care of each other.

"Still, every year, I can feel the world closin' in on us. The girls, they're itchin' to know more about the world. Oh,

Isaiah, he gives them little ideas here and there about what things are like. Once in a while, they run into someone like yourself who gives 'em a little more information. They sure do like that little radio thing that Isaiah brought them. Oh, I know all about it. They don't think I do, but I do. When we have guests like yourself, which isn't often, they always make it a point to show 'em."

He glanced at me, but I looked directly forward. Had he overheard me talking with Eve and Ester the night before? I wasn't sure. But it was his house, and he'd said that he grew up there. I hadn't thought about it before, but he probably knew every little nook and cranny around that old place. Hell, he might've been the one, years ago, who popped that knot out of the wall. But if he *did* know I had been talking to his daughters last night, he didn't seem too upset about it. That was some good news, right there. The last thing I needed was a pissed off hillbilly coming after me with a shotgun.

It was odd. He seemed sort of sad, maybe a little resigned. Like he knew that times were changing, that they wouldn't always be able to live the way they had for God knew how many decades, shielded from the rest of the world.

o o o

We drove the rest of the way in silence. Gradually, the road smoothed, and we turned onto a paved road. Soon, we were passing houses. More and more street signs appeared, and we passed a convenience store that looked so dilapidated I was sure it was closed. Yet, I saw people inside and a few beat up old cars parked in front. Farther on, the town of Dalton came into view. He pulled into a Sunoco station.

"How's this?" he said.

"This'll do great," I said.

He stopped the truck, leaned to the side, and stuffed his

huge hand into a back pocket. He pulled out a scuffed and scarred wallet that was so old it could've been made from dinosaur skin. A ten and a five appeared in his hand.

"It's not much," he said, "but I think you got even less."

I shook my head. "I can't take that," I said. "Not after everything you've done for me."

He nodded and motioned with the bills in his hand. "Gowan, now, take it. You're gonna be needin' it."

"No, really, I—"

He made another motion with his hand. "Take it."

I reached out and took the two bills, holding them like fine China.

"I can pay you back," I said. "If I have your address—"

"You just take care of yourself," he said and stuck his hand out. I shook it.

"Thank you," I said. "For everything. You don't know how much I appreciate it."

"Oh, I know you do," Mr. Hollister said. "It was no trouble. I hope you get where you're goin' without any more bumps on the noggin." He smiled, and I laughed.

"I'm hoping for the same," I said, and I opened the passenger door. "Thanks again. I really mean it. And be sure to tell your family thanks again, too."

He nodded and closed the door. The old green truck chugged away, and Mr. Hollister never looked back as he drove off.

I stood where he'd left me, holding my backpack and the fifteen dollars, looking around, taking everything in, watching Mr. Hollister's vehicle become smaller and smaller, until it vanished over the crest of a hill.

I looked around, smiled, then laughed out loud. You could argue all you want against living the hillbilly, backwoods life, but something right then and there struck me, and I thought that maybe—just maybe—Mr. Hollister and his family had a pretty good thing going. For all of their backwoods, unworldly ways, maybe there was something inside of them—and other folks who lived that way—that was awfully damned smart, indeed.

63

I made a mental inventory of what I had. Everything I owned I was either wearing or carrying in my backpack. I had a phone card, too, but I wanted to save that for Florida, so I could use it to contact Ellen, if possible. I also had the fifteen bucks Mr. Hollister gave me. I was going to make that go as far as I could.

Then, I had a panicky thought: what if I'd lost my ATM card? I hadn't taken it out of my shoe since I'd taken off.

I stood on my left foot, slipped off my right sneaker, and peeled back the gel insert, breathing a sigh of relief. I pulled out my ATM card, stuffed it into my pocket with the bills Mr. Hollister had given me, and slipped my shoe back on. Rock and roll. So, I had fifteen in cash and twenty in the bank. I could live frugally and be okay . . . as long as I didn't get kidnapped and beat over the head again.

o o o

The sun was shining, and the morning was pleasant and warm. A sign indicated that I-75 was a mile up the road, so I started walking. I was in pretty good spirits, all things considered. My head didn't bother me, although it was still tender. I had a full stomach, a good night's sleep, and fifteen bucks in my pocket. I wasn't king of the world by a long shot, but I was feeling pretty good. That old boomerang had come around in a nasty way, but I'd bounced back pretty well, thanks to the kindness of some hillbillies.

I thought more about the Hollisters as I walked. In America (and a lot of other countries, I was sure) there are so many different people with so many different ideologies. From religion to ethnicity, people have their own way about things. I've heard America referred to as a 'melting pot,' but that didn't seem like the way it was. I mean, take the Hollisters and others around Bolton Hills. They were trying to stay in their own bowl, trying to keep from mixing in, trying to strong-arm the future—a future that was rapidly closing in. They were trying as hard as they could to keep their lives simple, to keep the big, bad world at bay. I guess it's their right, if they want to do that. But Eve and Esther? These girls wouldn't be equipped to order a burger at McDonald's. I'm not saying they were stupid, not at all. But naive? Hell, yes.

I guess it just seemed strange to me, in this day and age of computers and razor phones and PDAs and MP3 players, that anyone would want to *stay away* from technology. I could probably list a few hundred good reasons why technology has been so important and beneficial. Think about all of the medicines discovered and created, the diseases cured, all the good that has been done just in the last ten years. It just seemed like things would be a lot more convenient for the Hollisters. I mean, come *on:* no television? I wondered how they found out about the 9/11 hijackers. How many days went by before they heard about it? What if a tornado was coming? Without a radio or television, how would they know? And why did Mr. Hollister drive a truck? There were Amish people who wouldn't even go that far, choosing instead to use a horse and buggy. Maybe it was just personal preference. Or, maybe it was fear. I think many people that don't use computers are afraid of them. Before they even use one, they're overwhelmed and intimidated. Lacy and Bruce are like that. Bruce always said computers were stupid and a waste of time. Lacy was the same way. I think they were just afraid.

Anyway, I was thinking all of these thoughts about technology and all, when I remembered the real reason I was in the situation I was in: Ellen. I should have been in Florida by now. But how was I supposed to know my car was going to be stolen? And how was I to know I'd get food poisoning and get beat up and robbed by four black guys? It had been one hell of a trip so far, that was for sure. Now, I was in north Georgia. What the hell else was going to happen before I got to West Palm Beach?

64

The only problem with Dalton was there was no truck stop. I'd been hoping to find one. Counting on it, in fact, and I figured I'd be able to find someone else like Arnold heading somewhere in Florida. No dice. The only thing I found was yet another convenience store, and there wasn't a single semi in sight. They were flying by on I-75, sure, but I wasn't going to risk hitchhiking on the freeway.

Instead, I found a large piece of cardboard behind the convenience store near the dumpster. Inside, I borrowed a big, fat, Sharpie marker from the guy behind the counter and wrote FLORIDA in block letters on the cardboard. I gave him his marker back, thanked him, and left. I figured that, while it wasn't a good idea to hitch on the freeway, I *could* stand along the on-ramp, where people were moving at a reasonably slow speed, and hold up my sign. Oh, I knew I was breaking my own rule about hitchhiking, but I had no other option. Besides: I at least looked halfway decent. Clean cut, sort of respectable, I like to think. Still, I knew my chances of getting a ride were slim, but at least I *had* a chance. I just hoped I didn't get picked up by any one of the one hundred serial killers the FBI was tracking.

Someone like that would make those black dudes look like a church youth group.

o o o

I was in luck. I was picked up by some sales guy after waiting with my sign for about fifteen minutes. He was nice and all, and I forgot his name. He was only going as far as Atlanta, but that was fine with me. It was in the right direction. I didn't care if it took me ten different rides to get where I was going . . . as long as I got there.

Unlike Arnold, this guy didn't say much. He had the radio on, but his phone rang constantly. No sooner would he hang up than it would ring again. It got to be kind of annoying. On the radio, Sean Hannity was sparring with what he called 'liberal lunatics' that were calling in. I was kind of getting into it, sort of, just because people were getting so nasty. And I mean *nasty*. This one guy called up and was calling Sean all sorts of names. They were arguing back and forth about something, some foreign policy. Hardly anything worth shouting about, I was sure. But this guy was *pissed*. It was funny. But the driver's cell phone would ring, and he would reach over and turn the radio down and I couldn't hear it. He'd answer his phone and be on it for ten minutes. He didn't say much on the phone, either. He mostly just listened and grunted 'uh-huh' and 'yep' and 'okay' once in while. Then, he'd hang up the phone and turn the radio back up. By then, there was some other caller on the line, arguing with Sean.

Well, this went on the entire trip. I guess it didn't bother me too much, being that I had a ride. At least to Atlanta, Georgia. When we started getting close to the city, traffic started to back up. There was lots of road construction going on, too, contributing to the congestion.

"I'm headed for a hotel downtown," my cell-phone-addicted driver said. "If you're going on through, that's probably not the place to let you off. You'd prob'ly have a better chance finding a ride somewhere close to the freeway."

"Are there any truck stops close by?" I asked.

"I think there's a big one coming up in about three miles, where 575 merges in. You want off there?"

"That'll be great," I said. "Thanks again for the ride."

"No problem," he said as his cell phone rang. He was still on it when we came up on the truck stop a few minutes later, and he still had it to his ear when he pulled into the parking lot near a bank of pay phones. I got out, waved, and he hiked his thumb in the air with his free arm as I closed the door. He drove off with his left hand pressing his phone to his ear, and I got busy looking for another ride.

65

The truck stop was called Barbara's Roadside Rodeo, and it lived up to its name. It was easily ten times bigger than any of the truck stops I'd seen. There were trucks *everywhere*. I immediately began walking around, holding up my sign for people to see. Mostly, though, they just ignored me. I couldn't blame them. But I was sure that sooner or later, I'd find someone who would take a chance and give me a lift.

Unfortunately, no one really seemed all that interested in offering a ride. I think they probably saw how old I was and knew I was either a runaway or in some sort of trouble. Or likely to *cause* trouble. I mean, I think I look pretty respectable and all that, but respectable people don't necessarily hang around truck stops carrying a sign, looking for a ride somewhere.

o o o

After about an hour, I was frustrated. I began confronting people, asking them if they were headed to Florida. Some guys just shook their heads, others just ignored me. I didn't want to piss anybody off, so if they weren't conversational, I didn't say anything more. I just walked off to find someone else.

And I was getting hungry. I still had Mr. Hollister's fifteen dollars, and I figured I'd use a little of it for some food. Inside the truck stop, they had refrigerated subs on special for a dollar forty-nine. They were pretty big, too, although they didn't look like they'd be very tasty. No matter. I needed something to fill me up at the lowest possible price.

o o o

While I was eating the sub, I wondered if maybe my chances would be better if I hitched from the on-ramp, like I'd done back in Dalton. I'd had pretty good luck doing that, and the truck stop was turning out to be a bust. I knew there *had* to be trucks headed for Florida, but sure as hell nobody wanted to pick up a teenage hitchhiker.

o o o

The on-ramp was on the other side of the parking lot, so I hiked over there, winding around parked semis, watching for others either moving in or moving out. I had to walk across a narrow overpass to get to it, which was pretty unnerving, since there wasn't much room to walk. Cars and trucks literally passed by within two feet, and not a single one slowed down. But it looked like a lot of people were turning south onto the I-75 on-ramp, so I had that going for me.

I reached the ramp and walked backwards along the thin shoulder, carrying my sign in one hand, hiking my right thumb out with the other. My pack was slung over my shoulder.

And my luck changed, all right. It wasn't long before a car pulled right up alongside of me.

Trouble was, it was a Georgia State Trooper.

66

The cop turned his bubble-strobe light on and pulled off to the side of the on-ramp, right in front of me. I stopped walking. He got out of the car, eyeing me suspiciously, striding that *I've-got-a-shitload-more-power-than-you* stride that some cops have. Not all, sure. But a lot of them walk like that, and they do it really well. And he had what appeared to be the contents of an entire tool box strapped to his belt, all contained in small leather cases. I could tell this guy wasn't going to take any shit, and I was going to have a tough time weaseling out of this one. Hitchhiking on the freeway was illegal, but I thought on and off-ramps were okay. Maybe not.

Well, this cop, he turned out to be one helluva bulldog, that's for sure. He wanted my name and some identification. I told him I'd lost my wallet and didn't have a driver's license anymore. He wanted to know where I lived, where I was going, all that crap. I didn't lie to him, no way. If I lied to him and he found out, well, that would be just doing the salt to the wound thing. Turns out, though, he was just into the lecturing deal, telling me how dangerous hitch-hiking was, especially near the freeway. It became pretty obvious that he wasn't worried about *me* causing any trouble, but he was sure going to make sure I didn't do any more hitching in his county. He pointed, ordering me to turn around and get off the on-ramp, and said if he caught me out here again, he was going to arrest me. And I didn't doubt it.

So, I didn't have much choice but to head back. I started walking one way, and he got back into his car, killed the flashing bubble, and took off. I turned and saw him glance up into his rearview, making sure I was still moving, following his orders, and I was. I wasn't sure where I was headed, but I sure as hell didn't want any trouble with any Georgia cops. When I turned around again, he was gone, merging into the thick stream of vehicles speeding along southbound I-75.

And wouldn't you know it? My luck changed again, before I'd even gotten off the on-ramp. I was walking and carrying my Florida sign in front of me, and a blue van went by. Then, I heard a squealing of brakes. I stopped and turned around. The van was backing up. A car went by, horn blaring. The side door of the van opened, and I about shit my pants. There were several people in the van, but the first person I saw was someone that went to my high school! I didn't know him by name, but I recognized him, and he recognized me. He was a couple grades ahead of me. He had been a teacher's aid in my freshman chemistry class.

There were three other guys in the van and one girl. I didn't recognize any of them.

"Hey, you go to Bay City Central High," the guy said. I kept thinking his name was Ron or Rob or something like that. I wanted to call him by name, but I couldn't remember exactly what it was. So I nodded.

"Yeah," I said. "You were a teacher's aid in Mr. Ferndale's chemistry class."

"Yeah," he replied. "Two years ago. I graduated. Whattya doin' down here?"

I held up my sign. "On my way to Florida," I said.

"Hop in, man! That's where we're headed! Partyin' for a whole week!"

Hot damn, I thought. *I hit the jackpot. Not only do I have a ride all the way to Florida, but it's with someone I'm familiar with, from my own school.*

Another car roared by, its horn honking.

"Come on, man," the driver said, and I quickly scrambled inside the van. The door slid shut behind me, and we were on our way. I looked at the guy who had been the teacher's aid.

"Sorry, but I can't remember your name," I said.

"Todd Moore," he replied. (Not Rob or Ron . . . but close.) "And up there drivin' is Lucas. That's Shannon, Lucas's sister, and this is Eric." Shannon was in the passenger seat; Todd and Eric sat on upended milk crates, as there were no other seats in the van.

"I'm Greg Chappell," I replied.

Shannon turned to me and spoke as the van glided onto the freeway and merged into traffic. "Like, aren't you supposed to be in school or something?" she asked.

"Well, sort of," I said, and I gave them the infamous Cliff's Notes version, leaving out the details I didn't think were necessary.

"So, you're going to find your sister?" Todd asked.

"Yeah," I replied. "Something weird's goin' on. Don't know what. But I couldn't *not* come."

"Big brother to the rescue," Eric said. He smiled. Eric had long, blonde hair. He was rugged looking and muscular like a rugby player or a rock climber. He seemed cool.

"I don't know about any 'rescue,'" I replied. "But if she's in trouble, I wanna be able to help."

"Well, we're headed all the way to Fort Lauderdale," Lucas said. "We'll be passing right through West Palm."

It was perfect, and I started feeling really optimistic again. This whole trip had been so up and down, up and down, and I just wished things would smooth out. I really wanted the rest of the journey to be mellow and uneventful. Todd and his friends (they were also from Bay City, I learned) were talkative and fun. They had saved up enough money to head to Florida for a week. They had a tent, and their plans were thin as Saran wrap. They didn't know where they would camp, and that seemed fine with them. All they had was a map, some food, a van, and cash. A whirlwind week of fun. Caution to the wind, and all that. If I hadn't had other plans, it would have been my kind of vacation.

o o o

We drove and drove. When Lucas got tired, Eric took the wheel. They changed drivers without even pulling over. The van was on cruise control, so Lucas just slipped out of the driver's seat while holding the wheel. Eric slipped in and took the wheel, and the miles spilled out behind us as we drove on, past Macon, Berry, and dozens of smaller towns: Unadilla, Cordele, Wenona, Tifton, and many more. We celebrated nightfall by passing the Georgia/Florida state line, and the five of us clapped and cheered. Todd took his turn at the wheel. I offered to drive, too, but I wanted to get a few hours' sleep. In the back of the van was a mattress, and I stretched out. It was actually quite comfortable, and I had no problem falling asleep, listening to the faint chatter of my four new companions and tunes from the radio. Soon, all sounds faded completely. I fell asleep in darkness; I woke up in a hospital.

67

Everything was dark, and I could hear the chatter of voices echoing. They sounded weird, too, like they were being filtered through Jell-O. I couldn't understand what was being said because the voices sounded all garbled and mixed.

I opened my eyes slowly and was greeted by white, intrusive light. It was so bright I had to close my eyes again. The voices became clearer, and I soon came to the realization I must be in a hospital.

Talk about confused. My mind was fuzzy, and I wasn't thinking straight. It was like I had been drugged or something.

Duh, I thought. I probably *had* been drugged, if I'd been hurt. But how? Why? What hospital was I in? How did I get hurt? Who brought me here? What day is it? Where were Lacy and Bruce and Ellen? Were they hurt, too? There wasn't much I could remember beyond my own name, and it was maddening. I saw a guy in the news once who had a case of amnesia. It was a month before his fiancee recognized him on television. How freaky would *that* be? To be engaged to marry someone and not even know who they were? I hoped something like that hadn't happened to me.

My eyes were completely open now, and I looked around. I was in a bed with my back propped up a little. There was a curtain on my left, separating me from another customer. (Years ago, when Lacy, Bruce, Ellen, and I visited one of Lacy's sick friends at the hospital, that's how Ellen had referred to the patients. She was only six or so and had never been in a hospital. Walking down the stark white hallways, she would peer into rooms and steal curious glimpses of people in their beds. Finally, in her perfect little, innocent way, she asked "How many customers are here?" This caused Lacy and Bruce to laugh. I did, too, and that moment has been scratched into my memory. To this day, I refer to hospital patients as 'customers.' And to this day, it's still seems funny, if only to me.) Hanging on the wall, close to the ceiling, hung a television. It was angled slightly down, and the sound was off. A news program was on, and I could see a scrolling marquee at the bottom of the screen. It used to be they put those marquees up only when there was something urgent. After 9/11, they became standard. Now you could listen to the announcer tell us how some congressman in Maryland was caught doinking the babysitter and read about a plane crash in Istanbul . . . all at the same time.

o o o

To the right of me was something that resembled an electronic coat rack . . . only there weren't any coats on it. It had blinking lights and switches and dials. An IV dangled and a tube snaked down to my wrist where a bandage was wrapped. Hah. I *was* being drugged. There were a couple of small, electrical units on the rack, displaying digital numbers and things I hadn't a clue about. Great. I'm hooked up to R2D2.

I tried to remember just what in the hell had happened, but there was nothing that stuck out in particular. I couldn't establish any anchor, no reference point to begin piecing together a sequence of events that would have landed me as a customer in a hospital. There were things I could remember, of course, but there seemed to be no time line, nothing to link any memory together. It was frustrating.

And I got tired, just trying to remember. My eyes grew heavy, and I fell asleep.

68

Voices. Closer this time. I was awake, and I was once again aware I was in a hospital. I blinked a couple of times, wincing as the bleach-white light stung my eyes. I strained to keep them open, and tears immediately welled up. I could see motion—two people—hovering over me like gray clouds. A dream within a dream.

"You're awake," a woman said. I managed a nod and blinked a few times. One of the tears rolled down the side of my face, and my vision cleared. Two nurses—male and female—stared down at me.

"You were pretty lucky," the man said. "Do you remember what happened?"

I shook my head. "I don't even know where I am, other than a hospital," I replied. My throat was dry, and my voice cracked like static on the radio.

"You were in a car accident," the woman said. "We'll let the doctor know you're awake." And with that they left, leaving me alone in the room. (At least, I thought I was alone. Earlier, I realized there was another customer on the other side of the curtain: an old man recovering from some sort of surgery.)

A car accident? I wondered. *How? When? Am I all right?* I did a physical inventory of myself, wiggling my fingers, toes, moving my arms. My head ached and—

Black guys. They took my money and—

It wasn't much, but pieces of memories began dancing around my head. A rattlesnake. (Huh?) Rain. Walking on a dirt road. Cop. Semi trucks. Sitting in the cab of a semi, listening to someone talking. Food poisoning. Flowers. Robert 342. (Who?) Dawn.

It took a while, but I was finally able to piece everything together, from the moment I'd received Ellen's pleading phone call. I remembered everything . . . except, of course, how I came to wind up being a customer at a hospital. The van I was riding in must've crashed. I remember crawling to the back onto the mattress to sleep. That's probably when the accident had occurred.

So, I was in a Florida hospital. I didn't know much beyond that, and I tried to remember anything that would have given me a clue as to what had happened. Nothing came.

A doctor lumbered in, and I mean *lumbered.* He was huge. He was as big around as he was tall. Bald, with a very neatly trimmed beard and mustache. A stethoscope hung partway down his enormous chest—a chest that seemed to have been swallowed up by the top of his protruding stomach. He made a few adjustments to R2D2, then looked at me.

"So, you're awake," the doctor said, in a very cheery, pleasant tone. "How do you feel?"

"Pretty good, I guess," I said.

"You are one lucky young man," the doctor said, and he pulled up a cushioned chair that had been placed out of sight at the foot of my bed. To my left, on the other side of the drape, I heard a soft moan.

"What happened?" I asked.

"I was going to ask you the same thing," the doctor

replied in that smooth, mellow tone. I found myself taking a liking to him right away. I felt at ease, despite the condition I'd awakened to.

"I don't know," I replied. "I think I was sleeping in the van. I guess we got into an accident."

The doctor nodded, and he looked grim. "Your driver, I'm afraid, fell asleep. The van hit a viaduct, then rolled down a hill. For not being belted in, you are in miraculous shape. You've got several bumps on your head, one quite serious. But it almost appears that particular injury was a day or two old, and you re-injured it."

"Yeah, I, uh, I . . . hit my head," I said. "A couple days ago."

"You've got a few other bruises as well, but, all things considered, you were pretty lucky. You're going to be fine. What's your name?"

Think quick, I told myself. I didn't want to give him my real name, but if I lied, I'd start a whole slew of lies. No doubt he would want to call Lacy and Bruce, and I didn't want that happening. But once my real name got into the system, there was no doubt they'd find out I was a runaway. The police can figure that shit out in five seconds with computers and all.

Think. Think. Think.

"Matt Dunbar," I replied. My thought was this: I knew the Dunbar's had caller ID. Matt told me neither he, nor anyone else in his family, answer the phone when it's a number they don't recognize . . . especially if it's out-of-state.

The doctor picked up a clipboard that was hanging on the wall. "Got a number? I'll need to call your parents."

I gave him Matt's number, fairly confident that when the doctor called, no one would answer. At the very least, that would give me a chance to figure out what to do. I guess I was just paranoid they'd figure out I was a runaway, that I'd stolen Bruce's car, and then I'd be up Shit's Creek with No Paddle.

"What about . . . um—" I was struggling to remember my new friends' names. However, the look on the doctor's face told me a lot. Too much.

"The girl—Shannon, I think her name is—she has quite a few broken bones, but she'll pull through. Lucas and Eric—they were fortunate, like you. Lucas has a broken arm. Eric has a collapsed lung and a very severe laceration to his thigh. He's lost a lot of blood and is in intensive care, but I think he's going to be all right."

"How about—"

The doctor shook his head. "I'm afraid one of your friends didn't make it," he interrupted. He was very somber, very sincere. "I'm sorry."

I felt like I'd been sacked by a linebacker. Sure, I hadn't known Todd very well. But he was the one who'd recognized me walking along the on-ramp after the cop chased me off. He'd greeted me like an old friend when he opened the van door and insisted I ride with them. I talked to him more in the van than I ever had in Bay City, and I really liked the guy.

Life is not fucking fair. Not for me, not for anybody. All I wanted to do was go to Florida to help my sister. That's all. In the beginning, it seemed so simple. In fact, I should already *be* in West Palm Beach, right now, with Bruce's Grand Prix. I should have a good idea where Ellen is and what sort of trouble she's in. She was counting on me, after all. Hell, I can't even get to the *state* in one piece, let alone help her out. Some brother *I* am.

Like I said: life is just not fucking fair.

69

I fell asleep after the doctor left, and when I awoke, it was dark—sort of. The overhead lights were off, the television was off. The door was cracked open, and sterile white light slopped in. There wasn't much to hear as far as voices go. I could hear the faint hum of electrical units nearby; I hadn't a clue if I was hooked up to anything. The old man to the left of me was wheezing softly in his sleep. I heard a PA system summoning this person or that nurse or some doctor. Just the normal stuff, I guess. I had no clue what time it was, but I figured most of the hospital was asleep.

And I had to piss something *fierce,* but it's pretty freaky to be hooked up to a robot and not know what to do. I know there was supposed to be some nurse's call button or something, but I wasn't about to call one and have him or her help me to the bathroom. No way. This was one thing I was going to do myself.

Then, I realized something: I wasn't hooked up to R2D2 anymore. There was a small gauze bandage on my arm where the IV had been, but that was it. I was no longer connected.

I sat up and looked around. The light streaming in was

enough to allow me to see around the room. A shadow momentarily darkened the door as someone scurried past. I heard faint, distant laughter. In the bed on the other side of the drape, the old man snored softly.

And on the desk next to my bed: a dark, tiny disc. I picked it up.

My lucky black and white quarter. It had been in my pants. A nurse or doctor had probably come across it when they were taking off my clothes.

I returned the quarter to the desk, and noticed that my ATM card was there, too. I picked it up and fingered it, looking around for the remaining cash—thirteen dollars and some change—that had been in my pocket. Nothing. Maybe they put loose cash like that in a safe somewhere. I can't imagine someone from the hospital stealing thirteen bucks from a teenage patient. That kind of karma comes back to kick your ass big-time.

I sat up. Stretched. My head hurt a little bit, and my right arm and shoulder ached. But, all in all, I didn't feel too bad . . . considering I'd been in a serious car wreck that had killed one of my friends.

And I wondered where Eric, Lucas, and Shannon were. Eric was probably still in intensive care, as a collapsed lung is pretty serious shit. Lucas and Shannon? They'd been pretty lucky, too, apparently. I guess it was a good thing I'd been sleeping, after all. I hadn't been hurt badly, and I had no recollection whatsoever of the wreck.

o o o

I pulled the sheets away and slowly swung one leg off the bed. I was wearing a cotton hospital gown; nothing else. I wondered where my clothes were, and my bag. In the scheme of things, I guess they weren't all that important, but they were the only things I had besides my quarter.

After one more quick check to make sure I wasn't connected to anything that would go toppling over, I stood up. My left leg was sore, but other than my throbbing arm and shoulder and a very present ache in my head, I seemed pretty okay. I took slow, cautious steps to the foot of my bed. The bathroom was only a few feet to my right, near the door, and I didn't have any trouble reaching it. I clicked on the light, closing my eyes for a moment, then slowly opening them as they adjusted. I closed the door behind me and looked in the mirror. I looked like hell. My hair was messy, and I had a black eye. My face was chalk-white. I looked like I was prepped for a Marilyn Manson concert. But, again, all in all, I was in pretty good shape. I was alive. Score another one for the home team. Yeah.

After relieving myself, I crawled back into bed. I tried to go back to sleep, but too many buzzing thoughts kept my mind whirring and awake. *I'd lied to the doctor. What if he found out? He'd wonder why I lied. Worse: what if they figured out who I really was, and that I'd stolen Bruce's car? What if they made me go back home?* I didn't know if they could do that or not, but these were all things I thought of.

And the sooner I could get out of the hospital, the better. Funny thing was: I'd never been in a hospital before, except to visit someone else. I didn't know much about how they operated, or anything. For instance: in my case, who was going to pay my hospital bill? I didn't have any insurance and certainly no money.

I needed to get my bag with my clothing. It had to be *somewhere*. Problem was, it could be anywhere. It could still be in the van for all I knew, in some salvage yard, or wherever it was taken. There was nothing in the bag that would have identified me, nothing to say it belonged to me. For all anyone knew, it could have belonged to Eric, Lucas, Todd, Shannon, or myself. Maybe it had been taken for evidence, or something. I know it sounded crazy, but that's one of the things I thought, one of the things keeping me awake.

o o o

The door opened, and the light in the room grew brighter. Then, a shadow darkened the room, and the silhouette of a nurse appeared.

"Hi," I said quietly, and she flinched a little. She probably didn't know I was awake.

"Hello," she said. "How are you?"

"Fine," I replied. "I'd be better if I was out of here."

The nurse laughed. "I think everyone here would concur. Is there anything I can get you?"

Yeah, I thought. *Yeah, there is.*

"Well, I had a backpack with me, in the van," I said. "It's black. I was wondering where that was. It's got some of my clothes, and a book. That would be great to have. It's kind of boring here."

"I hear that one all the time," the nurse said. "I don't know anything about your bag, but I'll do some checking. You try to get some sleep. I'll see what I can do."

That said, she gave a quick check of the customer on the other side of the curtain, who was still softly sawing logs. Then she scurried off.

Some time later, I fell asleep.

When I awoke it was morning, and my backpack was sitting in the chair at the foot of my bed.

70

I'd discovered my backpack in the chair and was just about to get out of bed when I began picking up bits and pieces of a conversation just beyond the door. I heard words like 'false name,' 'no identification,' and 'Greg something or another.' Whatever they'd figured out, they knew I wasn't Matt Dunbar, and I knew it would probably be only a matter of time before they figured out who I really was. It was strange. I mean . . . I really hadn't done anything *wrong*, besides stealing my uncle's car. I'm sure lots of teenagers have done that. It wasn't like I'd broken into a house or robbed a bank or hurt anyone. Still, I felt like a criminal, like I had something to hide.

I heard movement, and I closed my eyes and feigned sleep. I recognized the big doctor's voice.

"I spoke with the Dunbars," he said quietly to someone else. "That was the number he gave me, anyway, when he said he was Matt Dunbar. Well, they have a son named Matt, but he was on their couch, watching television. They said our John Doe is probably Greg Chappell, one of Matt's friends who ran away a few days ago."

"Do you have contact information for his parents?" a

female voice asked softly.

"I've got a number and made a few calls, but there was no answer," the doctor replied. "No message machine, either. Call down to security and have them post someone at the door, just in case. He might be just a runaway, but it's better to be safe than sorry."

They walked away, and I didn't waste a second. After opening my eyes to make sure no one else was around, I snapped up and snatched my backpack and pawed through it. Good old Mrs. Hollister had washed and folded everything. It was a little disheveled in the pack, either from the accident, or perhaps someone rifling through it to look for some identification. But everything was there. I was hoping I might come across the cash that had been in my pocket. No such luck.

I quickly slipped into a new pair of underwear and new khaki shorts, pulled the hospital gown over my head and slipped into a T-shirt. I was vaguely aware of a few new aches and pains, but in light of the recent turn of events, they were hardly noticeable. Even my throbbing head didn't bother me. I wanted out of there, pronto.

I snapped up my black and white quarter and dropped it in the left front pocket of my shorts. I looked around for my shoes, but I didn't find them. No matter. I didn't have the time to look around. I found a pair of slippers under the chair; they would have to do. I stepped into them, zipped my backpack closed, and threw it over my shoulder. Then, I hustled into the bathroom for a quick check of my looks. My hair was tangled, but I turned on the faucet, wet my hand, and ran it over my head. For a moment I'd forgotten about the wound above my temple and winced as I bumped the injury. There was a black comb on the sink, and I pulled it through my hair. Actually, I was surprised at how much my appearance had improved just by combing my hair back. My right cheek was slightly swollen and bruised, and I still had a black eye, but least I didn't look as gaunt as I had earlier.

I had been able to find an elevator without arousing any suspicion. There were people all over the place: this was one busy hospital. But, for the most part, everyone seemed to have somewhere they were going, rushing here and there. No one seemed to pay any attention to the kid with the backpack, the black eye, and silly blue slippers.

o o o

In the elevator there were a few other people, but they weren't doctors or nurses. One lady was griping to her husband about how she was glad she was being discharged because the food they served here was *terrible*. I realized I was hungry, but food was going to have to wait.

From what I could gather, my room had been on the fourth floor. There were nine floors altogether, so I was in a pretty big hospital.

But where? I knew I must be in Florida, as I remembered crossing the state line in the van. What the hell city was I in? I had no idea, and it never occurred to me to ask the doctor or the nurse. And I sure as hell wasn't going to ask anyone on the elevator. They'd think I was crazy.

o o o

The elevator finally arrived at the first floor. The steel door slid open, and a security guard was waiting to get in. Those of us in the elevator exited, and I felt a huge surge of relief when the guard paid no attention to me. I didn't look back as he got on the elevator. I blended in with the husband and wife and the few others that had just emerged, and I walked with them as we headed for the front door. The husband and wife split away, as she must have had to check out at the front desk or something.

But I just kept walking in my blue booties, and in less than thirty seconds I was out the front doors and in the blazing Florida sunshine for the first time in my life.

o o o

The sunlight and warm air was invigorating. The hospital doors closed behind me, and I shot a nervous glance over my shoulder, expecting to see several men in white doctors' coats—or maybe cops, even—coming after me. There were none, and I quickened my stride as I walked away. My leg still hurt, but I knew I could run if I needed to. I was wearing those silly blue hospital booties . . . but I'd escaped. I'd worry about shoes when I had put some distance between me and the hospital.

As I put more and more distance between me and the hospital, I was feeling better. Confident, like I'd gotten away with something. And I had, too. If I'd waited any longer, I knew that security guard would have reached my room. Then I'd have been stuck. There was no way I'd be allowed to leave until they had some answers. And even after they got their answers, they *still* probably wouldn't let me leave. I was lucky to be able to make it out when I had, thanks to the nurse who had somehow located my bag of clothing. If it wasn't for her, I'd still be in the hospital room wearing that goofy-looking gown.

o o o

It wasn't long before the hospital was out of sight, tucked behind other large buildings. I still hadn't figured out what city I was in. I kept looking at street signs for clues, but they offered none. I looked into store windows, thinking for sure someone had to have a business with the city name built in, something like *Sunnydale Flowers* or something like that. Nope.

Not here, anyway. Maybe it was some city ordinance, or something. Maybe it was illegal to use the name of your city in conjunction with your business. Probably not, I know. But I'll be damned if I couldn't find one business that had a city name anywhere.

Finally, I had my answer. I found several newspaper machines under an awning near a street corner. One contained *USA Today,* and the other was filled with the *Palm Beach Post.*

Holy shit. I'm here. I made it to West Palm Beach.

71

A number of emotions whirled inside of me. Excitement, as I was now in the city I'd been trying to reach for days. Where Ellen was. It was October 9th; I'd made it in time. I felt confident and had a sense of achievement, as I'd been through a lot of shit. More shit than I'd ever been through in my life.

But I also felt sad. Guilty, maybe. Todd had been killed in the van wreck. I wondered if perhaps they'd let me sleep instead of taking my turn at the wheel. If someone had woke me up, I could have driven. Maybe the crash would have never happened.

I stood there on the street corner for a moment, wallowing in my guilt, until I realized it wasn't going to get me anywhere. I was in West Palm Beach, finally. I had to find out more about the *New World Peace Center*. I had to find out where it was.

First things first, though. I had to get out of the ridiculous blue booties and find a pair of shoes. Already, the hot cement was beginning to cook my feet. It felt like I was walking on coals. But the throbbing in my head had faded, and my minor aches and pains elsewhere didn't bother me much.

And I was hungry, too. I needed food. Shoes and food. Both of which cost money, and I had none. I had my twenty bucks in the bank; if I could find an ATM, I could take out five or ten dollars without closing my account. If worse came to worse, I supposed I could find a homeless shelter. It wasn't anything I wanted to do, but my options, at this point, were few.

I was starting to sweat, so I moved under the awning and into the shade. I sat against the building and unzipped my backpack. I pulled out *Galaxy Quest* and noticed I had only fifty or so pages to go before I was done. Not important, right now. Then, I found my phone card tucked in one of the pockets.

And that's when I got an idea.

72

The inside of the phone booth was hot and clammy. The windows were filmy, fogging the surroundings beyond. I picked up the receiver and dialed the number on the back of the card, tapped in the access code, then punched in Matt's number. Sure, it was doubtful anyone would answer. But the doctor at the hospital had gotten through. And apparently, the Dunbars figured out it was me in that hospital bed. I was hoping maybe they'd see the caller ID, and see that it was a Florida call. Maybe they'd think it was me, trying to get in touch with them.

The phone rang and rang . . . then Matt picked up.

"Hello?"

"Guess who?" I replied.

"You shithead!" Matt snapped. "What's going on? What in the hell are you doing? Are you all right?"

"Nice to hear from you, too," I said, and I laughed.

"Where *are* you?" he asked.

"I'm in West Palm Beach."

"Are you still at the hospital? Why'd ya tell them you were me?"

"No, I sorta checked myself out. Look, man, I can't go

into it right now. Have you talked to Lacy or Bruce?"

"Yeah. A couple of days ago, when I called looking for you. Bruce says you left him a note saying you were going camping, but he thought you ran away."

"I'm down here looking for Ellen."

"What?!?!" he exclaimed. "Ellen's there?"

"Yeah, somewhere," I replied. "She's at some place called the *New World Peace Center*. I'm supposed to meet her there tomorrow. I need some help. I need some cash. Not a lot. I can't explain it all now. Lots been happenin'. I don't have any shoes, and no cash at all. If I give you my bank account number, can you deposit, say, fifty bucks?"

"Fifty bucks?!?!"

"Or more, if you can bum some from others," I said. "Try Clay and Jim. And Tony Freemont. He just sold his Suzuki dirt bike a couple of weeks ago. Whatever you and anyone else can spare. Just tell everybody I'm really in a bind, and I need some help."

Matt softened a little. "Sure, man, sure, I can help." Then he lowered his voice. "Are you . . . are you in trouble?"

"No," I replied. "Nothing I can't handle. Really. I'm more worried about finding Ellen than anything. I just need some cash. You got a pen?"

"Hang on."

There was silence on the line for a moment, then Matt came back on. "Go for it."

I gave him my bank account number and my PIN and asked him to repeat it back to me, which he did.

"I'll go see what I can scrounge up," he said. "But even when I make the deposit, I think it takes a couple of hours before you'll be able to access it."

"That's fine," I said. "You don't know how much of a help this is. And tell anyone who donates I said, 'Thanks.'"

Donates. That was almost funny, like I was collecting money for the local animal shelter or something.

"Just be careful," he said. "You in your old man's car?"

"No," I replied. "It was stolen a couple of days ago. Look . . . I'll tell you everything when I get home, okay?"

"Everybody's wondering where you went," he replied. "I mean . . . you just disappeared, just like your sister."

"I know," I said. "But it was just one of those things. I promise . . . I'll tell you about it later."

"All right," Matt said. "Good luck."

"Thanks again," I said. I hung up, thankful it had been Matt who'd answered, thankful he was willing to help.

o o o

Now what to do?

I knew that, at the very least, I'd have a few hours to kill. There was even a chance I wouldn't be able to access the cash from an ATM until tomorrow, so I had to be prepared to spend the night somewhere. At least I wouldn't have to worry about cold weather.

When you're pretty much broke, you start thinking about things you can get for free. One thing that would be invaluable was a public library, being that they would have computers, which meant I could get on the Internet and check my mail. I didn't think I'd have much more luck finding out anything about the *New World Peace Center*; however, now that I was in West Palm Beach, maybe I could find someone who knew something about it. It sure seemed strange, though, being that I wasn't able to find anything about the place—good or bad—on the Web.

People were whisking by with purposeful, quick strides. I figured I might just go ahead and ask someone if they knew where the library was. An Asian man in a suit hustled past.

"Excuse, me, sir, but could you—" was all I was able to

303

get out before he was gone. He never once even looked at me. A man and a woman came by, and the result was the same. No one even acknowledged me. I couldn't blame them, I guess. Whenever anyone tried to get my attention in Bay City, I never looked at them. If you caught their eye, that was their first step before they pounced. They usually would want money or something, and I learned really quick to mind my own business. It was like that at the mall, too. There's a certain skill it takes to ignore the sales clerks at the kiosks that were selling everything from watches to jewelry to cell phones to sunglasses to remote-controlled helicopters. Calendars, candles, figurines, T-Shirts with cutesy sayings or pictures on them. It's an art to ignore these people when they go out of their way to make eye contact or get your attention. Otherwise, you'd spend all day telling everybody you're not interested, that you just want to go down to Sam Goody and check out the new CDs.

Well, I was on the other end of that, now. And I didn't even have anything to sell. I just wanted to know where a public library was. I figured there were probably a couple around, in a city the size of West Palm Beach. But no one was going to pay any attention to me. Everybody probably thought I was trying to bum some cash.

So, I'd get the next best thing: a phone book. Those things have everything from maps to zip codes, area codes . . . everything.

I walked back to the phone booth. My feet were starting to hurt. The hospital slippers not only looked stupid, but they didn't provide much cushion against the pavement. You don't really appreciate a good pair of shoes until you get a bad pair, or you have to wear something less adequate than shoes.

○ ○ ○

In the phone booth, a big, thick, yellow book dangled

from a strong, flexible wire. Its pages were warped and curled, well-aged from the elements. I picked it up. It was heavy and full in my hands, and the pages crinkled like rice paper, but they were readable, at least. I flipped to the yellow pages and found only four listings: the West Palm Beach Public Library, two Palm Beach County Libraries, and the Palm Beach Post Library. I was surprised, I guess. I figured there would be a bunch of libraries. Around Bay City, we have four or five, at least. I mean, it's not like Starbucks or anything. You don't see them on every street corner. But there are a few of them scattered around.

Next, I had to figure out where in the hell I was, so I could figure out the closest library. I kept my finger on the library page and flipped to the front of the book, looking for a map. When I found one, I tore it out and stuffed it into my backpack. Then, I flipped back to the library listings and tore that page out, too. All the while, the sun bore down, frying my skin like an egg. I'd heard about the Florida sun and how people who aren't used to it tend to overdo it and get burned really easily. I would do good to get out of it as soon as I could.

o o o

I looked around for a street sign, but I didn't see any. But I did see something else, and I don't know how I'd missed it. On the next block, there was a huge sign that read: Salvation Army.

It was like I'd struck gold. I'd located several libraries and now a store designed with my budget in mind. I was sure I'd be able to find a cheap pair of shoes at the Salvation Army. I didn't care if they were leather loafers or what. Anything would be better than what I was wearing.

The front of the Salvation Army listed its address as 3436 Banyan Blvd. I glanced down at the wrinkled, yellow map. Turns out, I was only nine or ten blocks from the West Palm

Beach Public Library. Still a hike, sure, but not bad. All of the others libraries were farther out of the city.

o o o

I dropped the phone book, leaving it to dangle on its taught, silver cord. Then, I got another idea, and I picked the book up again. I flipped through the business listings.

And I found it.

New World Peace Center.

It had a listing. A phone number.

I quickly slipped off my backpack and dug out my phone card. My hands were trembling as I dialed.

73

The call to the *New World Peace Center* had been disappointing. I didn't even reach a live person. All I got was a message stating that the Community Reception was October 10th from nine to six. Nothing was said about typing in an extension to reach a real person. I could leave a message after the tone, a voice said, and someone would get back to me.

Odd.

I started getting a really bad feeling about the *New World Peace Center*. I get hunches like that, and sometimes I'm wrong.

But sometimes, I'm *right*. That's what bothered me. And it turns out, this time, I *was* right.

o o o

The Salvation Army was huge, and there were a lot of people inside. Clothing was piled everywhere, like a ten-family garage sale. Dresses and slacks hung from racks, and there was an entire wall of shoes. I wouldn't have any problem finding a pair that fit. I found two pairs of comfortable sneakers: a white pair (a bit dirty and worn) and a blue/silver pair. I finally opted for the blue/silver pair, as they seemed to be a little less used, maybe a few less miles than the other pair. I also found a pair of used sunglasses. Not only would they block the sun's rays, but they'd hide my black eye, too. Bonus.

I left the shoes on my feet, donating my slippers. I doubted anyone would come along and buy them, but you never know. I had no use for the slippers anymore, so I just left them on the floor next to a pair of fake leather loafers. Of course, I had no money . . . except for my lucky black and white quarter. The shoes were a dollar, and the sunglasses were fifty cents.

There was no one in line at the register. The woman behind the desk smiled as I walked up. I raised my foot and pointed to the shoe and placed the glasses on the counter.

"The shoes are a dollar and the sunglasses are fifty cents," I said. "But I don't even have that." I dropped my backpack on the desk and zipped it open. "But I could trade you something. I have a shirt and a pair of shorts. Brand new."

"You don't have any money at all?" the woman said.

I shook my head. "It's a long story," I said, and I pointed to my black eye. "Car accident."

Yeah, I played the sympathy card. And it worked.

"Don't worry about it," the lady said with a wave. "Have a good day."

"Thank you so much," I said, elated. I picked up my backpack, put the sunglasses on, and walked off. In ten seconds, I was once again outdoors in the Florida sunshine.

o o o

I pulled the map from my pocket, unfolded it, and double-checked my route to the library. It looked like a straight shot up Banyan, all the way up to Clematis Street, and one block over. I re-folded the map and returned it to my pocket as I started walking. Florida was a lot different than Michigan. Up until now, I hadn't really paid much attention to trees and things. In Michigan, most of the trees are maples, oaks, pines, spruces. I didn't recognize many Florida trees except palms, and I'd never seen them before except in pictures and in the movies or on TV. I stopped next to one that was growing near the sidewalk, marveling at how different it looked, feeling the ruddy texture of its trunk, admiring the wispy, serrated leaves (Florida natives would call these 'fronds.' In Michigan, they're leaves). Other people walking by probably thought I was nuts or something. After all . . . palm trees to them were like oak trees to me: they grew everywhere.

o o o

I kept walking, and my thoughts turned to Ellen and the *New World Peace Center*. She told me to be there tomorrow, October 10th, but I'd already decided I wasn't going to wait. I knew I was going to find out where it was and go there. Today. I'd do my best to figure out what was going on, and figure a way to get her out if need be.

It was weird, as I didn't know anything about what kind of trouble she was in or what her problem was. But something told me she was being held against her will. It was just a hunch, but it was a feeling that was even stronger, now that I was here in Florida.

And maybe she'd e-mailed me again. That's what I was hoping, anyway. Maybe she'd managed to jot me another note. I hoped so. Either way, I'd know soon, as I was already halfway to the library.

74

There weren't many people in the library that particular morning, and only a couple of people on computers. I had no trouble locating an open one and helping myself. Within seconds, I had logged into my e-mail account.

Nothing from Ellen. All I got was the usual junk mail. Not even anything from Matt or any other friends in Bay City. I was a little bummed out, but I guess I should have expected it. No matter . . . I was in Florida. West Palm Beach. I'd finally made it here, despite all of the bullshit I had to put up with.

And I had an address. I scrolled down to my last e-mail from Ellen and opened it up.

4586 Montoya Dr., West Palm Beach, FL. 33480.

I typed an e-mail to Ellen.

El-

I'm in West Palm. It's October 9th. I'm going to try to find you. E-mail me when you can.

Love,

G

I sent the letter, realizing it was the first time I had ever added the word *love* to an e-mail to her. To *anyone,* for that matter.

○ ○ ○

I highlighted the address for the *New World Peace Center* and copied it to the clipboard. Then, I opened up another window and brought up a mapping site. I pasted the address in the query window. The map popped up just fine. After zooming in and out a few times, I was able to get a good idea where the center was in relation to where I was at the library. It was out of the city a ways, maybe four miles. I was also able to get a satellite picture. I couldn't zoom in really close, but I could make out two very large buildings in a green field, along with several cars in a parking lot. I printed a couple of maps, folded them, and put them in my backpack with my Yellow Pages map.

Plan of attack? An ATM machine. Check for cash. If Matt had come through, I'd withdraw as much as I could. I had a limit of two hundred dollars, but I knew there was no way he'd be able to scrounge up that much. Hell, if he could have deposited twenty bucks, I'd be thrilled. I could make twenty dollars go a long way.

○ ○ ○

I asked the librarian at the front desk where I'd find the closest ATM. Her brow knitted as she thought for a moment. Her hair was short, and she wore reading glasses.

"I would say your closest bet would be the Winn-Dixie on Manatee Street," she replied. "That's three blocks over," she pointed, "you can't miss it."

I thanked her and was just about to leave, when I hesitated.

"Is there anything else?" the woman asked.

"Yeah," I said. "Do you know anything about the *New*

World Peace Center?"

Again, her brow knotted as she thought. "Is it in West Palm?"

"Yes," I said. "On Montoya Drive. A few miles from here."

The woman thought for another moment. Then, she shook her head. "I can't say I've heard of it before. Have you searched on-line?"

I nodded. "Yeah, but I can't find anything."

"Is it new?"

"I don't know," I answered. "I found a listing for it in the phone book, but all I got was a message machine."

"Hold on a moment," she said, snapping up a phone from the desk. She pressed a single button and waited.

"Sharon? There is a gentleman here looking for information about—"

"New World Peace Center," I said.

"—the *New World Peace Center,"* she repeated into the phone. "Yes. Okay." She returned the phone to its cradle. "She'll be right out."

Now we're getting somewhere, I thought, and I stuffed my hands into my front pockets to wait for Sharon.

75

Sharon turned out to be a grandmotherly-like woman with white hair in a bun. She was stocky and solid and dressed in a salmon-colored dress. She had a look of importance and class.

And she was smiling. It was hard not to like her instantly.

"You're looking for information about the *New World Peace Center?*" she asked.

"Yes," I replied. "Have you heard of it?"

"Yes," she said with a nod. "I don't know too much about it, though. What is it you need to know?"

"Well, I don't know anything about it," I said, and it suddenly occurred to me that the lady was trying to find out *why* I wanted to know. Oh, she certainly didn't come right out and say it, but her body language translated perfectly. She seemed hesitant to volunteer any information . . . until she knew why I needed to know about the place.

And so, I told her. There was no need to lie, no need to make something up. Besides . . . if I told her the truth and she knew something about the place, maybe she could help me. I told her about how I'd received a call from my sister, telling me

I needed to be at the Center on October 10th. I told her I was worried about Ellen, and that something wasn't right. I even went as far as telling the woman I thought my sister was being held against her will.

"Have you gone to the police?" she asked me.

Here's where I had to dodge a couple of issues. I didn't want to fill the lady in *too* much, as I didn't want her to know about me stealing Bruce's car and all that. Nor did I want her to know Ellen was a runaway. I was really leery about getting the cops involved.

"Not yet," I replied truthfully. "I've been thinking about it, though."

"The *New World Peace Center* is some sort of spiritual retreat," she said. "I hear it's a very strict group that's separated themselves from the outside world."

That didn't sound like my sister at all. *How'd she get mixed up with a group like that?*, I wondered. Thoughts of David Koresh popped into my head. He was that nutcase in Waco, Texas, who thought he was God or Jesus or something. He and his followers built a huge compound and stocked it with all sorts of weapons. The government went to arrest him for something or another, but he barricaded himself and his followers inside. The siege ended a month later with most of the people inside being killed. About half of those were little kids.

Maybe my mind was just running off, but I'd had a bad, bad feeling about this whole thing . . . and it was getting worse. I felt like my hands were tied behind my back, and I was wading farther and farther out into a lake, the cold water creeping up over my waist, to my chest, neck . . . over my head.

"So, they're a cult," I said.

"I don't know," Sharon replied. "They've been in West Palm Beach for a couple of years. Last year, the leader of the group—Reverend Sloan, or something like that—was indicted on tax evasion charges, but the case was thrown out of court.

They've been in the news again, lately, because there have been reports of people not being allowed to leave. Some people have been able to get away, and they've gone to the police with their stories."

"What have the police done?" I asked.

"I guess they've been to the place," she said, "and apparently, they've found nothing wrong. They asked people if they wanted to leave, and they all said 'no.' There didn't seem to be any sort of abuse, nothing illegal going on. But there was a statement issued a few weeks ago by the group's leader. He said nothing is wrong at the center, that it's all just rumors. They're having an open house for anyone to attend. Sort of like a 'get acquainted' type thing, where people can come and find out more about the group. Tomorrow, I think."

"Yeah," I said. "October 10th. Tomorrow."

76

Once again, the searing sun caught me off guard, and I was glad I'd bought the sunglasses. It seemed even hotter than before, but maybe that was because the library had been air-conditioned. Now, I swore I could feel sweat seeping out of my pores. And, once again, I wondered what it would be like in the summer months. Hotter than hell, for sure.

Sharon hadn't known much else about the *New World Peace Center* . . . but she seemed worried for me. She asked a few questions about my sister and my parents. I finally did tell her that Ellen had run away, but I didn't say when she'd taken off. And I was evasive as to the whereabouts of my aunt and uncle, and she didn't press me for more information.

Good luck, she'd said. *I hope you find your sister.*

o o o

I felt a deeper sense of urgency now that my suspicions were confirmed. I had been fairly certain all along Ellen was somehow being held against her will. But why? What was going on? What were they doing with her . . . or *to* her?

Then I started getting really panicky, thinking I might already be too late. After all, she hadn't answered my recent e-mails. What if something had already happened to her? Sharon had said some people had already come forward, saying they were being held against their will. What if Ellen was one of those being held? It sounded like she was. I just had that hunch again, that notion that something was really, really wrong. Otherwise, Ellen wouldn't have called me in the first place.

I was walking fast and sweat was staining my clothing. Damn, it was hot. I hoped the ATM machine at Winn-Dixie was inside, as I was sure the store would be air-conditioned. Even if the machine *wasn't* inside, I decided I would walk through the aisles a couple of times to cool down. At the rate I was going, my clothing would be drenched in no time.

o o o

The parking lot of the Winn-Dixie was pretty full. Apparently, this was the day everyone decided to do their grocery shopping. Lots of people—older, mostly, dressed in light shorts and shirts or muu muus—pushed shopping carts loaded with white plastic bags to their vehicles. I didn't see an ATM machine outside, so I went inside and was immediately immersed in cool, crisp air. It felt like heaven.

Well, I found the ATM machine easily enough, but (just my luck) it was all torn apart. There was a guy working on it.

"Is it broken?" I asked, once again displaying my incredible sense of perception. Woo-hoo.

"Nothin' that we can't get taken care of pretty quick," the repair guy replied. He never even looked up from the machine. I imagine he probably went from location to location, all day long, fixing those damned things. He was probably pretty good at it, too, and he probably was used to the very same question I had posed. Probably heard it a thousand times a day, in fact. But, if he was annoyed, he didn't seem like it. He just kept working away, and I decided I wasn't going to make the second mistake of asking him how long it would be before it was repaired. He'd be done when he was done, and that was that.

o o o

I strolled down the aisles, which turned out to be the wrong thing to do. I hadn't realized how hungry I was, and now, seeing all of the food on the shelves in boxes and cans, my hunger roared like a lion.

After a few minutes, I made my way to the front of the store again. The guy was still working on the ATM machine, so I skirted past him. Near the front doors were several racks of brochures and flyers. Real estate literature. And there was a lot of it, too. It looked like just about every square inch of Florida was for sale.

And down by the other door, a guy in a blue uniform sat behind an old card table. A vet. He was an older guy, wearing a blue cap with some silver and gold buttons on it. A few strands of white hair poked out from beneath his hat, and his eyebrows were thick and gray. He was selling raffle tickets. I walked over to him.

"Chance to win a Honda *Gold Wing*, fella," he said, picking up a wad of tickets and holding them in the air. "One ticket for twenty, or six for a hundred."

"Sorry," I said, holding up my hands. "I'm outta cash. I don't ride a bike, either. Sorry."

"Hey, that's all right," he said, and he placed the tickets on the table. "Been a little slow today, anyway."

I looked around. "Really? With all these people?"

"Oh, not many folks are interested. A few, you know, they want to help out. All the money goes to help injured vets and their families. People try to help out, but hey . . . money don't grow on trees."

"I wish it did," I said.

The old guy laughed. "Reminds me of a time in 'Nam when we waz near this little village . . . ."

And that began an hour's worth of all kinds of war stories. I'll say this much: the guy was interesting to listen to. He really had some great stories, and he reminded me of Arnold, the guy who at first had hesitated, but finally gave me a ride. That guy could talk and talk, but this veteran selling tickets could sure give old Arnold a run for the money in the story department. He talked about being ambushed in the jungle, going for days without food, getting hooked on Vietnamese heroin (he spoke about this like he was talking about eating Twinkies or something), and he talked about being shot up a couple of times, once in the leg and once in the arm. He showed me the scar on his arm, too. Big one. He'd had a tattoo at one time, a dragon, he said, but the bullet wound had ripped it to hell. He rolled up his sleeve and showed me. The dragon wasn't a dragon anymore. It looked more like a first-grader had doodled on his arm with a dark blue ink pen.

He'd stop his story every few minutes when someone walked by. He'd hold up the raffle tickets and start his pitch. Not a single person paid attention to him except one other veteran. The two guys chatted in military language I didn't understand: regiments and tours of duty and platoons and brigades . . . things like that. The guy selling tickets looked pleased to talk with someone who was sort of a kindred spirit. A brother, so to speak. They even found out they knew some of the same people. The other vet bought twenty bucks worth of tickets and walked away.

Other than that, no one else came to his table. No one else bought raffle tickets. I felt bad for the guy, having to sit there all day and not have any customers. It wasn't until later that I got pissed off at the whole notion of him selling tickets in the first place. I mean, here's a guy that fought for his country—risked his life— and had been seriously wounded. Yet, this is what he has to do: try to raise money to help other wounded veterans like himself. That's a pretty shitty way to thank someone who did that for his country. It just didn't seem right.

77

While I was talking to the vet, I kept glancing over at the guy working on the ATM machine. He had it all back together, but he was still working on it, making sure it worked right. I wondered if anyone had actually been at an ATM machine to withdraw, say, twenty bucks . . . only to have the machine spit out a hundred or so. That would be great. Not for the bank, of course. But it sure would be somebody's lucky day.

Finally, Mr. Fixit was satisfied he got the thing working again. He loaded up all of his tools in a big, gray, heavy-duty chest. The manager of the store (she looked like she was probably the manager, anyway) came over to him. They chatted for a couple minutes, shook hands, and then the repair guy was on his way.

"Well, I gotta run," I told the vet.

"Nice chattin' with ya, fella," he said as I walked toward the ATM. Actually, it was *he* who'd done all the chattin'. I'd done all the listening.

o o o

I tapped in my password and PIN. My balance came up, and I about shit my pants.

Three hundred twenty six dollars and seventy-seven cents.

I couldn't believe it. For a minute, I thought there was some mistake, like I'd gotten into someone else's account by accident. Nearly impossible, sure . . . but seeing that amount of money in my account seemed impossible, too. At that moment, it wouldn't have mattered if there were three or four more zeros tacked on. I was as happy as that guy who won the Powerball lottery.

"Matt, you are awesome," I whispered, staring at the balance like I'd tapped into Bill Gates' checking account.

I withdrew seventy dollars, mindful of the fact that the more I carried around, the more I stood to lose. I'd already been relieved of the money Dawn had given me, thanks to four black dudes in Tennessee. If something like that happened again, I'd at least be able to get more from an ATM somewhere.

Then, I walked over to the vet.

"I'll take one," was all I said.

o o o

While I'd been hanging out and talking to the vet, I'd made some plans in my head. Things I was going to do, and in what order. First thing: I bought some food. Some jerky, a pint of milk, and a couple of sandwiches from the fridge. The sandwiches were two for three dollars, so I got a ham and cheese and a turkey on rye. I think I had the wrappers off before I even left the store.

o o o

Outside, I found a place in the shade beneath some palm trees. I dropped my backpack and sat in the grass, once again

322

marveling at the fact that I was in Florida. It was all strange and new. Even the air was different. Heavier, sweeter. Hotter, for sure. The few birds I saw were unfamiliar, and I got to thinking about how little I really knew about the United States. Most of what I'd known came from books, TV, or movies. I'd never really experienced anything outside of my own state. Now, I was getting a huge dose of experience in a very short period of time.

o o o

It didn't take me long to wolf down the sandwiches and polish off the milk. I saved the jerky and stuffed it into my pack, as it would keep well and make a good snack.

My next plan was to find the *New World Peace Center.* I know Ellen had told me not to come until October 10th, but that was the next day. If I couldn't get in until then, I was going to find out as much as I could beforehand. I still didn't know a lot about the place, but what I *did* know really bothered me. I had all sorts of thoughts bouncing around my head, everything from really extreme, bizarre stuff, like Ellen being kept a prisoner and used as a sex slave. I knew shit like that happened, because you hear about it in the news from time to time. But it always seemed so bizarre, so *outlandish,* I never thought something like that could involve anyone I knew . . . let alone my very own sister.

o o o

From what I could gather, I probably wasn't more than ten miles from the *New World Peace Center.* Now that I had a little bit of cash, I could afford a few small luxuries . . . like a taxi cab. The fare wouldn't be more than twenty or thirty bucks one way. Sure, I had to be careful with the money I did have, but I really wanted to at least scope out the *New World Peace Center* from the outside, at the very least. Maybe I could find Ellen. Sure, it was doubtful. They probably had that place tightened up like Alcatraz. They wouldn't want anyone getting out, and they probably didn't want any strangers getting in.

o o o

Finding a cab was easy enough. It seemed like every fifth or sixth car going by on the road in front of the Winn-Dixie was the old familiar yellow/orange. I flagged down the first one available.

The cabbie that emerged was probably one of the tallest, blackest men I have ever seen in my life. He was seven feet if he was an inch. He was thin, and his tightly curled hair was cropped close to his scalp. His shirt was colorful, foreign, and he wore khaki shorts and sandals.

"Hot again today, my young friend," he said with a disarming smile. I instantly liked him. Sure, you always have to be on your guard these days, but this guy just seemed so gentle and pleasant I was certain he didn't have a mean bone in his body. And his English was perfect.

"Hotter than hell," I said absently.

He opened the rear passenger door. "Where will it be?"

I tossed my back pack into the back seat. "I'm looking for the *New World Peace Center*. Have you heard of it?"

The tall black man cocked his head, scanning his mental map. He shook his head. "No, I cannot say I am familiar with such a place. Address?"

"4586 Montoya Drive," I replied, reciting from memory.

"Yes, Montoya," he said. "I know it very well." He gestured to the back seat, and I slipped into the coolness of the air-conditioned cab. For as tall as he was, he had no trouble slinking into the front seat, behind the wheel. There was an ID tag hanging from the mirror with a smiling picture of my driver.

Beneath it was the name Mohammed something-or-another that I wasn't even going to try to pronounce. The tag also indicated he was from Ethiopia.

I dug the printed map out of my backpack and handed it to him. He studied it for a moment before placing it on the seat. Then, he jotted something on a small clipboard fastened to the dash. Next to the clipboard was one of those portable GPS units. He tapped in the address, punched the meter, checked the mirrors, and pulled onto the road.

"Ethiopia, huh?" I said. I was in a talkative mood, but I think it was because I was more nervous than anything. Not about being in the cab. I think I was nervous—and anxious—about finally reaching the *New World Peace Center*. There had been times in the past few days when I thought I'd never make it here. I'd been through more shit in the past week than I'd been through in my life.

"Yes, Ethiopia is where I'm from," Mohammed said. Again, I was struck by his perfect enunciation and clear manner of speaking. "I have been in America for two years to study. That, unfortunately, might be changing. Visa trouble."

"What have you been studying?"

"Chemical engineering. But that may all be coming to an end, as I may be forced to return home."

"That sucks," I said.

"Yes, that is a good word for it," Mohammed replied. "I had not planned on returning until my studies are over. Now, I'm not sure what is going to happen. I love this country. America has been very good to me."

"Why might you have to leave?" I asked.

"My Visa will expire, and I have received notice that it will not be renewed. There are many new restrictions in security. Perhaps someone thinks that because I am studying chemical engineering, I am going to be a terrorist. I don't know."

"Where is your family?" I asked. This was a much better

topic, as Mohammed rattled on and on about his mother, father, brothers, and sisters. While he watched the road, he dug his wallet from his front pocket and flipped it open, holding it up over his shoulder to give me my own private slide show of his relatives. He named them off, gave simple details about each one. While he was explaining how his father was a farmer, and his father before that, he suddenly flipped his wallet closed. The cab slowed, and he glanced into his rearview mirror, then at the global positioning unit mounted to the dash next to the clipboard. "Here we are," he said. "4586 Montoya Drive."

78

Mohammad spun the cab around as I rubbernecked, trying to get a view of—

Of what?

There was nothing to see, really. There were several nice homes around on both sides of the street. There were a few flashy cars parked in the driveways: a few Mercedes-Benzes, BMWs, Lexus . . . cars like that. Tall palms reached skyward, their long, thin leaf blades still in the afternoon heat. But there was no sign designating a *New World Peace Center.* No huge, sprawling structure, nothing. I guess I wasn't sure what to expect, but I didn't expect to see . . . nothing.

"Are you sure you've got the right place?" I asked.

Mohammed picked up the map on the seat and studied it briefly. "It is correct," he said. "Here."

He slowed the cab and turned onto what I'd thought was a street. However, as we pulled onto it, I realized it wasn't a street at all . . . it was a driveway. It was long, and it turned and vanished several hundred yards ahead.

Mohammed cruised along at a steady but cautious pace. The houses thinned immediately, and soon, we were traveling beneath clusters of enormous palm trees. The lawn was green and tight. Neat, like a bed sheet. The houses and driveways vanished. My heart beat faster, and a lump formed in my throat. This is what I'd come for. I was here. Somewhere, not far away, my sister shared the same space.

Up ahead, a gate came into view. It was closed. On either side of the driveway, a tall fence extended. Coils of barbed wire barreled across the top in angry, wide loops.

Somebody doesn't want anyone to get out, or they want to keep people from getting in, I thought. The only time I'd seen that kind of security was at a prison. Again, I had that awful wading-in-the-water feeling. Up to my neck.

"Stop here," I told Mohammed. The cab slowed to a halt at the side of the road. "This is far enough," I said. "What do I owe you?"

The fare came to twenty four dollars. I handed him a twenty and a ten, opened the door, and got out. I picked up my bag from the seat.

"Thanks for the lift."

He glanced around, probably wondering where I was going. There were no houses in sight, only the closed gate ahead. "Would you like me to wait?"

I shook my head. "I don't know what I'm doing or where I'm going from here," I said. "I'm on my own from here on out."

Mohammed nodded, checked the side and rearview mirrors, turned around, and drove off.

o o o

I stood at the side of the road, taking everything in. A hundred yards in front of me, the fence stood as firm and secure as an iron belt. The gate remained closed, and I could make out some sort of small building on the other side, no doubt some sort of security checkpoint. My chances of getting inside were about as slim as rice paper.

Some kind of bird flew into a nearby tree. He was black with a gray head and a long, gray tail. He eyed me suspiciously for a moment before dipping off the branch and making a silent exit.

A movement in front of me caught my attention, and I turned. At first, I wasn't quite sure of what I was seeing. It seemed like a dream.

The gate was opening.

It seemed unbelievable, magical. Like I'd waved a magic wand or uttered the secret password. I was dumbfounded.

Ninety seconds later, I was on the grounds of the *New World Peace Center.*

79

Getting in had been ridiculously simple, and probably the most unbelievable stroke of luck I'd ever had. Talk about being in the right place at the right time.

o o o

A few seconds after I'd noticed the gate opening, I heard a vehicle approaching behind me. I turned to see two pickup trucks, their beds filled with dark skinned, dark haired immigrants. The first one passed. On the passenger door was a white magnetic sign with black letters that read *Hernandez Landscaping and Maintenance.* I looked at the faces of the men in the bed of the truck—all Mexicans or Cubans—their brown, sun-toughened faces expressionless, shiny with sweat.

When the second truck passed, I had an idea. I started running after it. It wasn't moving very fast, and as soon as the men in the bed saw me, they began shouting something. Just what they were saying, I didn't know. But they sounded like they were encouraging me. A couple of them laughed and waved their arms, urging me on. I had become sport. When I made it to the back of the truck, I tossed my backpack to one of the men. Two others reached out, took my hands, and hauled me up. One of them slapped me on the back and said something in Spanish. I had taken a year of Spanish in high school, but nothing really sank in beyond the basic *gracias* or *denada*. I knew some colors and a few other basic words, but certainly not enough to know what these guys were saying. A couple of them seemed to be asking me pointed questions, but all I could do was shrug. When I didn't respond, they just laughed. Seems they had accepted the new hire, regardless of whether I could speak their language.

o o o

The truck rolled on, through the open gate and past the small gray security building. There didn't seem to be anyone inside. Several cameras were mounted on the side of the building, and I figured there must be some remote monitoring system at another location. Regardless, I was now inside the perimeter, within the confines of the *New World Peace Center*.

The road wound around some larger trees. Soon, the foliage became dense and lush, jungle-like. The lawn vanished, and it seemed we were tunneling through a tropical rain forest, a corridor of palms under a balmy, blue sky. The truck slowed as we rounded sharp corners. Several of my new colleagues jabbered and laughed.

o o o

It wasn't long before the trees around the road thinned. Suddenly, the forest stopped altogether, and a sea of green, every bit as groomed and manicured as a golf course, lay before us. In the distance were several buildings. All were white, gleaming in the sun like polished alabaster. The largest of the

331

buildings, situated in the middle, was huge—a cathedral, it seemed—capped by a large, shining dome. To the left of the main building was a large garden with dozens of blooming flowers and plants. Several people walked among the flowers. A two-story building to the right of the cathedral had the structured look of a dormitory or a motel. Or a bunker. Another building in front of it had several garage doors and no windows . . . and that, apparently, was our destination. The two trucks pulled up in front of the building, in front of three closed garage doors, and two dozen men leapt from the vehicles like lemmings from a cliff. I took my cue and dropped to the ground. The men chatted in rapid-fire Spanish as they walked toward the building. I tried my best to fit in: just one of the guys, here to do the same job I do everyday. There were about two dozen of us in all. However, I was the only white guy, and I hoped I didn't stick out too much.

o o o

Garage doors opened. The inside of the building was filled with lawn maintenance tools and supplies, everything from large riding mowers, rakes, shovels, and electric trimmers. Engines fired up; men snapped up tools as if they'd done this a hundred times, like they each had their own specific duty. I felt immediately out of place and quickly slipped my backpack on and grabbed a rake. One of the men asked me something in Spanish, and I shrugged and pointed, as if indicating where I was heading to work. I sure hoped Hernandez, the owner, wasn't part of this crew, as he'd no doubt spot me as the imposter that I was and start asking a bunch of questions. Probably kick the white boy out.

I needn't have worried. The man who'd asked me the question waved me away. I turned and followed three men as they sauntered across the driveway, heading toward the garden, trying my best to belong.

Again, I looked around. The cathedral was quite a sight, all shiny and white. It had a majestic, yet official, appearance: part church, part governmental office. A place for kings and queens, knights and squires. I wouldn't say it was out of place, as there were no other buildings around it besides the dormitory-like structure. Although both buildings were different in size and shape, they were the same color and complemented each other.

o o o

A couple of people emerged from the main cathedral: a man and a woman. From where I was, they looked like bees leaving a hive. They were dressed in white robes, like the Hare Krishnas you see at the airport, only these people had hair and weren't carrying flowers. They paid no attention to us as they walked down the white steps and made their way to the dormitory. I wasn't sure, but I had a hunch that's where Ellen was. I don't know where the hunch came from . . . but there was only a fifty-percent chance of being wrong, as there weren't any other buildings around.

When we reached the garden, the three men immediately went to work, stroking their rakes among the plants. I fell into formation, trying to pay attention not only to what I was doing, but glancing around at my surroundings. There were four other people walking on the other side of the garden. Like the man and woman who'd emerged from the main cathedral, they were wearing white robes. Each seemed to be in their own little world as they strolled slowly among the plants. Although they weren't very close to where I was, it was easy to see none of them was Ellen. One was a man with thinning blond hair. Two women had dark hair. The other woman had blond hair similar to Ellen's, but it was stringy and she was much thinner than my sister. I wondered if any of them would talk to me. I'd have to be cautious, but maybe I could find out more about what the place was all about. Maybe one of them knew Ellen. But first things first.

o o o

I raked leisurely, whistling to myself as I made my way through the garden. The man glanced in my direction. I nodded, and he returned the gesture. I was about to head toward him, but he turned and walked off, heading for the cathedral.

The thin woman stopped and stared up into the sky, and I headed in her direction, raking and whistling. Somewhere, someone yelled something in Spanish. Several lawnmowers buzzed. My raking colleagues had spread out through the garden, busily tending to their duties. No one was paying any particular attention to me.

I kept raking gingerly, whistling Metallica's *Enter Sandman* softly as I worked. The thin woman was only a dozen feet from me, but she was kneeling on the ground. Her hair tossed lightly in the breeze.

I continued whistling, raking, glancing around. The woman paid no attention to me, and I realized she wasn't wearing a robe, but a nightgown. Her bones poked through the fabric, and I wondered if she was anorexic.

I was only five feet away when, out of the corner of my eye, I saw her turn toward me. I turned my head and froze. For the first time in a year, I was face-to-face with my sister.

80

I lowered my sunglasses and stared.

Ellen was impossibly—*impossibly*—thin. Her cheeks were sunken. Her lips, once full and pouty, were drained and colorless. Her skin was waxy and thin, nearly transparent. Her limbs were sticks and looked as if they would snap in the wind. Ellen's blond hair, once shiny and lustrous, was now dull and drab, like yellowed willow leaves in autumn.

It took a moment for her eyes to register who I was. Even then, there was no sudden burst of light, no surprise acknowledgment. She flinched in disbelief, but the gesture vanished instantly.

"Ellen . . . my God . . . what's wrong?" I said, taking a step toward her.

"They're watching," she said, and she turned away. "Keep raking, and don't look at me."

I did as she asked, but I kept wanting to go to her, to speak to her, to find out what in the hell was going on.

"You made it," she said. "I can't believe it. What happened to your eye?"

I ignored her question. A black eye was the least of my

concerns at the moment. "Ellen, what's wrong? What's going on here?"

"I'm sick, Greg."

I raked around a large plant with wide leaves.

"What's wrong?" I asked again, keeping my attention focused on the rake in my hands. My movements were stiff and unnatural, like a wax figure coming to life.

"I don't know," she said quietly. "But they won't let me leave. They keep telling me I'll get better, that it's just going to take some time. I used to believe them, but . . . ."

A million questions buzzed around my head like gnats. *Who is 'them'? Why are they watching? Why won't they let her leave? What was wrong with my sister?*

"Tomorrow is the 10th," I said. "What's going to happen?"

"It's Community Reception Day," Ellen replied. "Reverend Sloan is allowing people from outside to come in. I'm not sure, but it seems like some people from the outside have found out what's going on here. The Center is going to open up so people can see that nothing's wrong."

I kept working with the rake, trying to shake off my stiffness. When I spoke, I tried not to move my lips, like a ventriloquist. Hopefully, if anyone was watching, they wouldn't see me talking.

"But just *what* is wrong here?" I asked.

She lowered her head, and the nuggets of her spine bulged through the hollow, pale skin of her neck. Her skin was so translucent that her bones looked like grocery items bulging through a thin plastic bag.

"Everything," she replied without a hint of hope in her voice. "Everything's wrong."

My heart shattered.

81

The sun sank beneath the trees, and all I could think about was how gloriously wonderful it would be to finally move, to stand up and stretch. I'd been sitting cross-legged on my backpack in the bushes for hours, and every muscle in my legs burned like lava. My left leg below my knee had fallen asleep, and I could no longer feel it. Mosquitos buzzed my head, but I had to be careful as I swatted them away. I wasn't hidden all that well, and I didn't want anyone to see me.

Ellen hadn't been able to tell me much more. While I was raking and we were talking, several people emerged from the cathedral. One of them, a woman dressed in a gray business suit, approached us. She moved with purpose, very official-like. I moved a few feet away and continued raking. The woman said something to Ellen, and my sister asked for just a few more minutes, or something like that. I couldn't understand all of it. Apparently this was agreeable, because the woman strode off. I raked my way back to where she was seated.

"I've got to get you out of here," I said.

"Tomorrow, I hope," she said, looking the other way. "But there's a lot I've got to tell you."

"Then tell me."

"I can't. Not here, not now."

"I can ditch the work crew and hide. Over in the woods, over there." I did my best to manage a nod without making it look totally obvious to anyone who might be watching. "Can you meet me here tonight?"

"Tonight," Ellen replied. "After Evening Devotion. I might be able to get away. Only for a little while, though. They'll be looking for me in my room at light's out."

I raked in silence for a moment. In the distance, one of the Mexicans shouted something in speedy, staccato Spanish. I turned, just to make sure he wasn't yelling at me. He wasn't.

"How long have you been sick?" I asked.

"Later," Ellen said. "I have to go now. Are you really going to stay here? Are you going to hide in the woods?"

"I'll hide in the hedges on the other side of those flowers. I'll try and stay close to that big tree."

"Evening Devotion will start just after sunset. It'll last about half an hour. I'll have to go back to my room, but I think I'll be able to sneak back out for a while before final bed inspections."

She stood slowly, with the uncertain caution of an old crone. The girl before me couldn't be my sister. There had to be some mistake. Ellen was healthy, vibrant. The girl in front of me was nothing but a skeleton.

And I kept wondering just what was wrong. I kept thinking AIDS, but that didn't make sense. She couldn't have contracted the disease and be this sick within a year. And why wasn't she getting the treatment she needed? Why wouldn't they let her leave?

o o o

I continued raking while I watched her walk away out of

the corner of my eye. Gradually, I made my way around the garden and back to the big shed. One of the Mexicans barked something at me. I shrugged and he stormed off, shaking his head and muttering something in his native tongue.

There were various tools and gardening supplies on the walls and shelves: rakes, shovels, several leaf blowers, electrical cords. I looked for something that might come in handy, something I could conceal. When I found it, I tucked it in my jeans and beneath my shirt. Then, I walked to the garden and continued raking. I whistled another tune—*Breakdown,* by The Alan Parsons Project—while I worked. Every once in a while, I glanced up to see who was where. All the while, I kept moving toward the shrubbery on the far side of the garden. I raked around the bushes until I looked up to see if anyone was watching. Then, I slipped through the branches as effortlessly as a cat.

And waited.

82

It was getting dark quickly, and I saw movement near the dormitory. A few people trundled slowly, robotically, to the cathedral. Soon, there was a flood of people—men and women—heading across the lawn. They herded into the monstrous cathedral like drugged insects. When they were all inside, I stood. My left leg was still asleep, and I rubbed it while I tried to put weight on it. It was a good thing I didn't have to run anywhere.

Music came from the cathedral and rose into the darkening night sky. It wasn't churchy, organ music, more like a soft piano. Then I heard singing. I looked up and around and figured it was dark enough to chance a closer look.

I pulled a few branches away and surveyed the expanse of the lawn and the gardens. Where I was, concealed in the shadows, it was quite dark . . . but there were some large vapor lights that glowed from both the cathedral and the dormitory. The only way I'd be able to reach the cathedral without being in the light would be to follow the brush line around the flower garden. If I stayed close to the branches, I'd be hidden by shadows. I had no idea, of course, if there were any windows or doors on the other side of the cathedral, but it was worth a shot. I was dying to know just what in the hell was going on with this whole *New World Peace Center* deal.

o o o

I hustled along the wall of shadows, hunkering in close to the tall shrubs. At the edge of the garden, I stopped to make sure no one was outside the cathedral. I wasn't sure what sort of security system this place had, but I was pretty sure it was probably elaborate. You don't erect a ten-foot chain-link fence topped with deadly spirals of razor wire unless you want to keep people out—or in. And I hoped there weren't any of those motion sensors around, or lasers. That's just what I needed: set off an alarm louder than a Rob Zombie concert.

o o o

I didn't see anyone, so I started walking again, slinking along the shadows like a secret agent. As I neared the cathedral, the music and singing grew louder. I couldn't understand what was being sung; the words were muddled and dull as clay.

But I was in luck: there was a window near the back, glowing in the darkness like amber. I stopped, looked around cautiously, and sprinted across the grass to the building. Crouching low, I slowly crept toward the window. When I was beneath it, I stood, pressed against the building like a gecko, craning my neck to see inside. The window was closed, but the music was louder and more distinct, and I could pick out a few words here and there.

People were standing in rows. They had their hands raised up and some were swaying, just like you'd see on those Sunday morning church services on television. (I made a mental bet with myself: a thousand bucks says I won't see anyone pull live rattlesnakes from a box. Not in this place, no way. I don't know what these people were up to, but something told me they weren't snake charmers.) Some people moved dreamily, like tall blades of grass in a gentle wind. Most of them were looking up, eyes closed. All of them were wearing white robes. I looked for Ellen, but I didn't see her.

o o o

I ducked down and crept along the shadows to the back of the building, hoping to find another window or a door. No luck. Nothing but brick wall, solid and thick, cool and damp with the coming night. I continued around to the other side of the building where light burst forth like a mountain. A bright vapor light on an electric pole and another one attached below a dormer of the dormitory lit up the yard and part of the garden, bright as midday. New dew glazed the lawn, shining silver and aluminum in the sodium light. Several dormitory windows were lit up, yellow and lemony in the haunt of night. To the left of the dormitory was a parking lot with several cars. I recognized one of them immediately: a Bentley. I couldn't believe it. I'd seen these before in magazines like *DuPont Registry* and others that featured and sold high-end, expensive automobiles. But I'd never seen a Bentley up close and personal. Never been within a mile of one.

The expanse to the parking lot was cloaked in darkness, so I hunkered down and ran across the grass, down a low slope, and into the teeming shadows of vehicles. I counted twelve cars in all, including one big Cadillac Escalade that glowed pearl white. On the other side of it was the Bentley, with a vanity plate that read REVRND. I crept along the sleek sedan and peered through the window. The leather interior shined, reflecting the vapor light from the dormitory. There was nothing in the Bentley except a small notepad stuck to the dash with a suction cup. Several things were scribbled on the paper: *Miami - Delta 328 - Rio De Janeiro.* There was also a squiggly line, more like a doodle, and a phone number. To the left of the pad of paper was the ignition . . . where keys dangled.

Old Reverend Sloan must be doing pretty good, I thought. *Not many people leave the keys in their quarter of a million dollar car.*

But it was nice to know, just in case. If Ellen and I, for some reason, had to do the Bonnie and Clyde thing and blast our way out of here in a hot rod blaze of glory, I couldn't think of a sweeter ride than a Bentley. Talk about going out in style.

After doing a quick scan of the grounds to make sure no one was watching, I trucked through the shadows to the back of the cathedral. Inside, the music and singing stopped, replaced by the monotonous drone of crickets coming from the shrubbery. Far away a siren wailed, then fell silent. An small airplane buzzed high in the sky like an errant mosquito.

A voice boomed from somewhere in the cathedral, but it was bound tightly within the thick walls, and I couldn't tell what was being said, or whether it was male or female. It reminded me of the voice of the teacher in those old Charlie Brown cartoons, where you can't understand the words. Somehow, old Charlie did, but not the television viewer. It was too garbled.

I slunk back to the window on the other side of the cathedral. Inside, the people were seated, obediently facing the front. Not a head turned. No nose picking or ear scratching. These people were devout. Or devoutly programmed. Take your pick.

o o o

I leaned as close to the glass as I dared. I didn't want someone to turn and see me, a peeping Greg, watching and listening to their Evening Commotion or whatever the hell Ellen

343

had called it. Here, I could make out the voice a little better. It was a man, definitely. But I still couldn't hear what he was saying. Probably just typical churchy stuff.

I pressed close to the wall, a shadow within shadows, as I made my way to the front of the building. The expanse in front of the cathedral was brightly lit. White cement steps glowed like quartz. Part of the garden was visible, but the colors of the flowers weren't as vibrant, drained of their exuberance by the artificial light. The reds looked purple; the purples looked black. There was also a fountain I hadn't seen before at the foot of the garden. It was of a robed man, life-size. Smooth and white, like alabaster. His hands were out and up, reaching toward heaven, and his head was tilted back. Water fell from his hands into a slick black pool. Glints of the vapor light reflected in the rippling water. I wondered if the statue was of Reverend Sloan himself. Anyone that would leave the keys in a quarter of a million dollar automobile for anyone to swipe was probably the kind of guy who'd like to see his body set in stone for others to enjoy.

Other than that there was nothing to see, except for the front of the dormitory building. I considered sneaking over to it, maybe have a peek in some of the windows, but I decided against it. Even though I couldn't see anyone, I would be out in the open, exposed. I was taking a chance as it was, but I wanted to find out as much as I could about this place. My plan depended on it, in fact.

o o o

I went back to the window and peered inside the cathedral. The people remained as they had been: seated, eyes focused front. I thought I spotted my sister, but it turned out to be someone else. And so far, there didn't seem to be anything unusual about the gathering. I hadn't had much time to talk to

Ellen, so she couldn't explain what the whole group was about. But it seemed like any other church group.

Normal church groups don't keep people from medical attention, I thought. *That's reserved for the weirdo cults.* A while back, there was this big thing going on in New York about some kid that had some sort of disease that was threatening his life. Doctors said he had an eighty-percent chance of living if he had a blood transfusion, but his parents wouldn't allow it, saying it was against their religion. Doctors said if he didn't get the transfusion, he would die. And this kid was something like ten years old or so. There was some huge legal battle, and it went all the way to the state Supreme Court, who sided with the parents: citing their religious beliefs, the state couldn't interfere and force the kid to have a transfusion. Even the kid himself didn't want the transfusion. He died a week later. I couldn't help but wonder: didn't the kid and his parents ever think that all this great technology might have been given by God, so doctors could save people like him with life-threatening diseases? I'm not going to speak for The Man, but I think God probably frowns on parents who let their kids die when they have a good chance of living if they just bend their beliefs a little bit and use some common sense.

○ ○ ○

Inside the cathedral, the congregation stood. I heard the piano again, and the group began singing. A few people slowly began filing out from the pews, walking reverently toward the back of the cathedral. I figured the service was over, and I couldn't risk hanging around where I might be discovered.

I darted across the lawn and made it to the safety of the shadows, stole my way past the garden, and found the place where I'd been hiding most of the day. I had a fairly clear view of the front of the cathedral, and I watched as people filed out and returned to the dormitory. It didn't appear anyone was speaking to one another. There were dozens of them, both men and women. I watched them file obediently into the dormitory like human cattle herded by an invisible hand.

And a really odd feeling came over me. Things seemed too manufactured, too uniform, too regimented. I knew nothing about these people or the group, but I still sensed an air of unease. Ellen was being held against her will. How many others? All of them? Hard to know.

But tonight, both of us would be gone. If everything went as I planned it, we'd be ditching this place and leaving it behind. I hadn't thought too much about where we would go once we got out, but I figured the first place would be a hospital. Sure, we had no way to pay. But Ellen was really sick. I doubted they would turn her away because we didn't have any money or insurance. At least, I hoped they wouldn't.

o o o

I sat in the bushes, a black knot among the branches knitted around me. Concealed in the dark flower of night, I was a little more comfortable than I'd been during the afternoon. I could shift and move, certain that no one could see me. I found my jerky in my backpack and ate it. Soon, I saw a thin silhouette appear, drifting across the grass like a limp ghost, coming toward me.

83

Ellen's silhouette vanished as the shadows scooped her up. She was nearby, but I couldn't see her. I hissed as loud as I dared.

"Ellen! Over here!"

Suddenly, she was only a few feet in front of me. I put my hands on her shoulders, and she fell into my arms and began to cry.

"It's all right," I said. "We're getting out of here. Tonight."

She drew back. "How?" she asked. Two pinpricks of light—reflections of the vapor light in the distance—shined in her wet eyes. I held her shoulders as tight as I dared, afraid her collarbones would snap.

"I swiped some garden shears from the garage over there," I said. "I'm going to cut a hole in the fence. We're getting out of here. Now."

I hustled back to the bushes and retrieved my backpack, slipping it over my shoulder. Then, I picked up the garden shears I'd swiped earlier in the afternoon from the maintenance garage. I returned to Ellen and found her hand in the darkness. "Are you all right?" I asked.

"I'm just really weak," she said.

"You can do it," I said, taking her hand. "We're going to get out of here and get you to the hospital. Come on."

I led Ellen to the edge of the shrubbery until it met with the road. If a car came, we'd have to duck into the brush and hide.

"How are you doing?" I asked as we made our way along the road.

"Okay," Ellen said, but she sounded tired.

Finally, a light appeared in the distance. I could make out the gate and the fence ahead. The security booth was lit both inside and out, and I didn't dare venture any closer.

"This way," I said, skirting into the grass and heading away from the gate. We kept our distance from the security building and its glowing lights

Finally, we reached the fence. I let go of Ellen's hand and held the shears out. Just before I cut the fence, I had another thought. I drew the shears back.

"This thing isn't electrified, is it?" I asked.

"I don't think so, no," Ellen replied.

I went to work. The shears weren't designed for cutting metal, but with a little extra mustard, they did the trick. Soon, I'd created a slice big enough to slip through. I dropped the shears and carefully pulled at the fence, bending it back, expanding our exit.

"Go ahead," I said. "Careful . . . the metal is sharp."

Ellen bent down and ducked through the fence. Her robe caught on one of the protruding points and it ripped a small hole, but she kept going. When she was completely on the other side, I slipped through.

"Now where?" she asked.

"Let's find a ride and get you to a hospital."

o o o

We started walking. In the distance, I could make out a few streetlights and houses. They were a few hundred yards away, on the other side of the huge lawn speckled with dozens of trees.

"What in the hell *is* that place?" I asked as we walked.

"They're really weird," Ellen replied. "They weren't at first. When I first met a few of them, they were really nice. I didn't have any money, and Dave had—"

"Who's Dave?"

"He's a guy I met down here. We were going out, for a while. When Susan . . . Susan Spencer—"

"Is that who you ran away with?" I asked. I knew Susan Spencer. She went to our high school. Kind of ditzy, but nice. Not a chick you'd want to run away with, though.

"Yeah," Ellen said. "But she moved in with her boyfriend. I didn't have the money to pay the rent on my own, so I asked Dave to move in and help out. That was when he broke up with me."

"But how did you get mixed up with those people back there?" I asked.

"I was walking to work—I was waitressing at a restaurant—and I stopped to catch a bus. A man and a woman just started talking to me. They said I looked sad and wanted to know if they could help. I started talking to them. We talked on the bus, and I told them all about running away, about Dave, about not having enough money to pay the rent, that I was going to have to move out or go back home. They listened, Greg. I don't know why I told them everything. I guess I just felt comfortable with them. They told me all about that place—the *New World Peace Center*—and said it was some sort of 'safe haven.' They told me I could stay there for a while, until I got back on my feet. They gave me a telephone number and told me to call anytime, day or night.

"At first, I just blew them off. But a week later when the rent was due and I still didn't have enough money, I thought about it. I didn't know much about the people I'd met or the place they were talking about, but it seemed like a good idea. You know . . . just to be able to live somewhere until things got better."

We made it to the street. Being a residential area, there weren't many cars going by. No matter.

Ellen spoke. "God . . . I've been in that place for six months. This is the first time I've been outside the Center." There was a sense of wonder, of hopefulness in her voice. For the first time that day, Ellen sounded positive about something.

I led her up to the front door of the closest house and rang the doorbell. Inside, I heard footsteps approach the door. There was silence for a moment as the person, I was sure, was inspecting us through the tiny peephole buried in the door like a glass eye. I felt like a bug beneath a magnifying glass.

"What do you want?" came a gruff voice on the other side.

"We need to get to a hospital," I said.

"This ain't a hospital," the voice replied.

No shit, Sherlock.

"All we need is a ride," I said.

"Get outta here, you druggies, or I'm gonna call the cops."

Which might not be a bad idea, I thought. They would take Ellen to the hospital, I was sure. But then we'd both be in more trouble. Two teenage runaways, one of them wanted for grand theft auto, the other—well, they'd probably think Ellen was strung out on heroin or something. And the way she looked, I wouldn't blame them.

"Go on, get out of here," the man snarled. He never opened the door.

We backed away, turned, and left.

"Everybody's too worried about getting robbed or killed," I said.

o o o

We walked to the street, and my eyes followed the sidewalk. I thought about trying the house next door, but I figured we'd probably get the same reaction. Ellen was pencil thin beneath her white robe/nightgown; I probably didn't look a whole lot better.

Several blocks away, cars and trucks were passing through a moderately busy intersection.

"There," I said, pointing. "Let's go."

While we walked, I quizzed my sister more about the *New World Peace Center.*

"When I first got there, it was great," she said. "I felt like I was part of this huge family."

"What religion are they?" I asked.

Ellen paused. "You know," she said, "they really aren't any particular religion. I mean, I never heard them talk about it. Reverend Sloan says God speaks to him through dreams."

Here we go, I thought.

"Anyway," Ellen continued, "everything was great at first. Reverend Sloan was great. He was like a grandfather. Others, too, were like that. Like parents, or brothers and sisters. After a couple of weeks, I didn't want to leave. I ate for free, I had a place to sleep. It wasn't until a while later that I found out I couldn't leave if I wanted."

I could hear the traffic as we drew closer to the intersection. A horn honked. Tires whined on pavement. High above, a jet threaded the stars with its red-orange lights, so deep in the heavens that it barely made a whisper. Crickets competed with the monotonous drone of traffic.

Then, Ellen began to cry.

"Don't," I said, slipping my arm over her shoulders and pulling her close. I couldn't believe how bony and brittle she felt. "You don't have to tell me anymore. You're out of there. You're safe."

At the intersection, it took less than thirty seconds to find a cab. I flagged it down. The driver was Mexican who spoke very little, if any, English. Somehow, I managed to convey that we needed to go to the hospital. When he finally figured it out, we took off. Ellen and I rode in silence. I held her hand the whole time. The cab driver was listening to a Spanish radio station. He tapped the steering wheel and said nothing.

84

Standing in front of one of the pay phones in the hospital waiting room, I held the phone to my ear and listened to it ring.

Once.

Twice.

The Mexican cab driver had taken us to a hospital only a few miles from the *New World Peace Center*. I was thankful it wasn't the same hospital I'd fled earlier in the day.

The decision to call Lacy and Bruce had been something completely out of left field. If I had taken another moment to think about it, I probably wouldn't have done it. I sure as hell didn't want to, but it seemed only right. Regardless of how much I hated them or how little I cared, something inside me told me to make the call. At the very least, I wanted them to know that Ellen was sick. No, worse than that. Ellen wasn't just sick . . . but that was a thought I wouldn't allow into the perimeter of my rational thought. That thought stood just beyond the window, staring at me like some malevolent demon, but I wouldn't look at it, I wouldn't listen. Ellen was going to get better, I told myself, and I ignored the dark figure on the other side of the window.

Ring....

o o o

Earlier, when we'd arrived at the emergency room, we weren't given too much trouble. Ellen gave her real name, but I told the lady my name was Greg Miller, that I was a friend and not her brother. Ellen gave me a glance of mild surprise, but she seemed to understand.

She asked my sister all sorts of questions, had her fill out papers, the usual bit. She listed Lacy and Bruce as legal guardians and gave their address. Maybe that's what prompted me to make the phone call. The hospital would probably be calling Lacy and Bruce anyway, as Ellen wasn't eighteen. They would probably need permission to treat her.

Ring....

o o o

After Ellen had filled out the paperwork, we sat in the lobby and waited for about an hour. Ellen filled me in more about her time at the *New World Peace Center*. From what I could gather, they were more of a cult than a religious group. No surprise there. Really strict eating habits: no meat, only organic vegetables and fruit. Nothing really wrong with that, I guess, but there were other things that were more disturbing. Seems old Reverend Sloan demanded that he have his say and his way in every matter. Typical cult shit, like Jim Jones, that guy that murdered hundreds of his followers in Guyana back in the seventies. Or David Koresh, the nutcase from Waco.

How many of these fucked-up groups are out there, right now? I wondered. *How many wacked-out cults are out there, waiting for the end of the world? How many madmen are demanding this or that, having convinced his followers that God talks to him or her?*

354

I thought again about how the government tried to intervene with that David Koresh guy in Waco. Sure, I was only seven or eight years old at the time, but it was on the news. I was old enough to understand some guy and all his followers were in some big camp of some sort and wouldn't come out. So, the government tried to make them. Most of them got cooked when a fire started.

Ring . . . .

o o o

Seems to me, when it comes right down to it, all those looney-tunes want is power. They want to control people. If you can make someone afraid of something and offer a solution to their fears, man, you've got 'em. I can't say that for all religions. I mean, I don't believe every church or religion is some sort of cult. Although that church in the woods with the hissing rattlers was pretty damned close, I was sure.

The emergency room doors burst open, and a stretcher was hustled in by three white-clothed paramedics. Orders were barked, people scurried about like rats in an alley. Those in the waiting room looked on with vapid stares, then looked away as the stretcher vanished down the hall. They had their own shit to deal with.

Ring . . . .

o o o

I was going to give the phone a few more seconds before hanging up. A Doctor Waldren was paged over unseen speakers. Shoes scuffed the tile floor. A nurse was on the phone behind a desk, saying something about some free flu vaccine clinic coming up. A little kid sat on the floor next to a couch, pushing a toy train. Next to him, his very pregnant mother thumbed through the current issue of *Star*.

Ring . . . .

o o o

I hung up as footsteps approached. I turned to see a woman with a light green sweater and beige slacks. A stethoscope hung from her neck and dangled between her breasts. She had a small red ribbon about the size of a half-dollar pinned to her shoulder.

"Greg Miller?" she asked. She smiled, but it was strained. She looked as if she knew something I didn't. And, as a matter of fact, she did. This was Ellen's doctor.

"Is she all right?" I asked.

"She's resting," the doctor said. "She's dehydrated and malnourished. We've got to run some tests. She's going to be here for a few days."

"Can I see her?"

"Yes, for a few minutes. But she needs to sleep. She's going to need a lot of rest. I'll take you to her room."

She turned. I picked up my backpack and followed her down a sterile hallway and into a bland gray elevator. A woman in a wheelchair rolled off, and we got on. The doctor pressed the '5' button, and the doors closed. We were alone as the elevator began to climb.

"She's very weak," she said. "You can only spend a few minutes with her. Tell me: does your sister have any allergies, anything you know of that might be the cause of her condition?"

"No," I said, shaking my head. "No allergies. She's always been really healthy."

The elevator stopped, and the doors swept open. I made a move to get off, but the doctor grabbed me by the arm. Not hard, but enough to stop me. I looked at her, and her eyes bore into mine.

"Greg," she said, "whatever you're hiding, whatever you're keeping to yourself, it's not going to help Ellen. Your sister is in serious condition. You're not being straight with me."

I blinked. She knew. The doctor knew.

"How did you know she's my sister?"

"You just told me."

o o o

The light clicked in my head. *Jesus. How dumb can I be.*

I looked down, and the doctor gave my arm a squeeze. "If there's anything you can tell me about her medical history, anything at all, I need to know it. I've tried calling your parents, but there's no answer."

"They're not my parents. They're my aunt and uncle. My parents have been dead for a long time."

"I'm sorry," the woman said. "Is there another way I can reach your aunt or uncle?"

"Try calling the bar at *Strikes,*" I said.

The doctor looked at me with quizzing eyes. *"Strikes?"*

"Happy hour goes until midnight."

85

The doctor led me to Ellen's room.

"Ten minutes," she said, and she whisked away.

I walked through the door. Ellen was in bed, wearing a powder-blue gown. The covers were pulled up to her waist. An IV was attached to an anorexic arm. Her blond hair fell over the front of her shoulders and splayed onto her chest.

"How's the newest customer?" I said with a grin.

Ellen smiled thinly. "I forgot I used to say that," she said. "Customers."

"How are you feeling?"

"Tired. Exhausted. Glad to be out of that place, though."

"The doctor says you're going to have to stay here for a couple of days."

"I know. Tests and rest. She told me."

"Have you told them anything else?" I asked. "Have you told them about where you were and what happened to you?"

Ellen looked at the wall. "I can't," she said. "Not yet, at least."

"I tried to call Lacy and Bruce."

Ellen looked at me. She didn't say anything.

"No answer," I said. "Sooner or later, they're going to find out you're here. I think the hospital needs permission to treat you."

"So?" Ellen said. "What are Lacy and Bruce going to do?"

"I don't know," I said.

"Did they even look for me after I left?" she asked.

It was a tough spot to be in. Should I tell her the truth? Should I tell her that after a couple of weeks they just gave up on her? That might just make things worse. Or, should I lie and tell her Lacy and Bruce did whatever they could to find out where she was?

"They . . . they were really worried," I said. "I was, too."

There was a long silence. Then, tears welled up in her eyes and spilled onto her cheeks. "I'm scared, Greg. I'm really, really scared."

o o o

I sat on the bed. She rose up, and I took her in my arms. It was strange: I'd done this very same thing a year ago, at home, when she'd told me she was running away. Only now, there seemed to be only a shell of what she once was. Her full and growing body had become a friable, shrunken sheath, as if she'd cast off a layer of beauty like a snake sheds its skin. I held her carefully, afraid I would crush her in my arms.

And I was worried, too.

o o o

I drew back and held her shoulders. "What *happened* to you?" I asked. "When did you start to get sick?"

"A few months ago. I was really weak, and I couldn't

keep anything down. I thought it was the flu. I slept a lot."

"Didn't anyone take you to a doctor?" I asked.

"No one is allowed off the grounds of the Center anymore," Ellen said. "Besides, Reverend Sloan says all illnesses are caused from not living and thinking right. They said I needed to pray and not eat any food at all. That was the only way I would get better. At first, I thought they might be right. But I just kept feeling worse and worse. The worse I got, the weirder they acted toward me. It was like they treated me like I had some sort of curse. Finally, after a week of not eating, I was still sick. They let me start eating again. We all ate together in a lower level in the cathedral. Usually, I ate with the others. Then, they started avoiding me. Soon, hardly anyone was talking to me. I overheard someone saying that Reverend Sloan said I brought this sickness upon myself, and once I was right with God, He would heal me."

"What's going on with the open house tomorrow?" I asked.

Ellen nodded and lay back in bed. "Word somehow got out that some people are being held in the Center against their will. And they're right. There are a few people who want to leave, but can't. No one is allowed to leave. Not anymore. Not after—"

Ellen looked away, and I took her hand.

"There are some men," she continued. "The elders. They . . . they *expect* . . . certain things. Reverend Sloan, too."

Tears formed in her eyes again, and she looked at me. I squeezed her hand.

"I was . . . I was only doing what I was told," she said, sobbing.

And that's when I started to cry.

86

I still had a lot of questions, but I knew Ellen needed to rest. The most important thing was that she was away from that place. Now, she could get the help she needed. I said good-bye, gave her a hug and a kiss on the cheek, and told her I'd be back in the morning.

In the lobby, I tried Lacy and Bruce again. No answer. I hung up and took a seat. There was a television set hanging from the ceiling. The news was on. There was a near collision of two jets on the runway at Miami International Airport, some drug smugglers had been arrested with a thousand pounds of cocaine in their van, a couple of murders, a robbery at a jewelry store—the usual shit. Before I knew it, I was asleep.

87

I didn't sleep all that well. I kept waking up, shifting to try and get more comfortable. At times, I sprawled out across two chairs. The sounds of footsteps on the floor and pages over the intercom kept me from ever really reaching a point of deep sleep, and I don't know if I ever really slept for any amount of time. And I wasn't the only one, either. There were three or four people who were also in the waiting room, curled up, trying to get some shut-eye.

Around five-thirty in the morning, I got up, stretched, and suddenly realized how hungry I was. It was strange: it came on like a sudden rain shower. One minute I was standing with my arms outstretched, yawning, and the next minute I was so hungry that I knew if I didn't eat something quickly I was going to pass out.

I walked over to a couple of vending machines, and my mouth watered just looking at the contents. One machine had chilled sandwiches, and another had candy bars, gum, cupcakes, and chips. Still another machine had Coke products and water.

I dug into my pocket and pulled out a small wad of bills. I mentally thanked Matt for coming to my rescue as I slipped a five into the sandwich machine. I selected a ham and cheese sandwich. A metal coil turned, and the wrapped sandwich dropped to the bottom of the machine. I reached into the bottom tray and pulled it out as the vending machine spit back my change.

The sandwich was bland and chewy, but I didn't care. I hadn't eaten in nearly twenty-four hours, and the flavorless little sandwich was gone in two minutes. I bought a Hershey bar and a bottle of water, then returned to my seat in the waiting room.

○ ○ ○

Sitting there, watching others in the room, the few nurses behind the desk, the hustle of orderlies back and forth and up and down the halls, I thought about how my life had changed. In a span of about a week, my life was turned completely upside down. I went over the events from the time I ripped off Bruce's car, to the present. It seemed like a year had gone by. So much had happened that it seemed there was no way it all could have come down in a matter of days. And I felt a certain pride, too. I'd done what I'd set out to do: find my sister. Not only did I find her, but I was able to get her out of a serious situation. Of course, she still had another problem, but at least she now was somewhere where she would be able to get the help she needed. Hooray. Big brother saves the day.

I curled up in the chair, closed my eyes, and listened to the sounds of the hospital, trying to fall back to sleep. I succeeded to a point and was able to ignore much of the noise around me and tune it out. I had some weird dreams, but they slipped away, and I had no recollection of them when I finally did wake up a few hours later.

○ ○ ○

It was the ballooning sound of the television that caused me to open my eyes. Several people were standing, watching the TV. One of them, a man, held the remote in his hand, pointing it at the screen. There was murmuring and several loud gasps. I rubbed my eyes and sat back in the chair, but when I heard the words *New World Peace Center* I was suddenly wide awake.

I looked at the television, and I couldn't believe what I saw. A television reporter was standing at the gate of the compound. The gate was open, but two police cars, lights pumping like a dance club, blocked the entrance. Two uniformed officers stood by the vehicles. One was chatting on his radio. The television reporter, a black-haired woman, was speaking and gesturing behind her.

". . . came in shortly after nine this morning. When officers arrived, they found the gate open, and that's when they made their grisly discovery."

I stood. My skin felt cool and clammy in my clothing, and I felt an odd buzzing in my head. I listened and watched.

"Police say many of the members of what has been described as a 'new-age cult' are dead. Today was the day the Center was supposed to have opened their doors to the public as a show of receptiveness, as there have been several reports over the past year of people being held within the compound against their will. Details are still coming in, and we'll have more to bring you as this story continues to develop. Once again: there's apparently been a gruesome mass murder at the New World Peace Center *here in West Palm Beach. Initial reports are that dozens of people are dead. Lauren MacLellan, Channel Four Eyewitness News."*

o o o

The few people watching televison chatted among themselves, but I didn't hear what they were saying. The buzzing at my temples had turned into a roar, and I took off down the hall, swinging my backpack, nearly running. The elevator doors were just closing, but I managed to squeak through and join two nurses and a doctor. I hit the '5' button and leaned against the wall. The elevator stopped on the fourth floor and the two nurses got out. It seemed to take forever to make it to the fifth floor.

o o o

I stopped in the doorway.

Ellen was awake. She was sitting up in bed, watching the television. When she turned and saw me, her expression was lifeless and blank, like a somber marionette. She looked drained.

o o o

On television, the news channel was continuing their coverage of the massacre at *New World Peace Center*. I entered Ellen's room slowly, and she returned her attention to the TV. The images now showed the outside of the cathedral, tall and glorious with a backdrop of a robust, blue sky. Police crawled the grounds like scurrying ants. Stretchers with black body bags wheeled past. A police officer could be heard, ordering the television news crew to back up, back up, keep a distance. The news reporter wasn't saying much, but letting the scene speak for itself. Sirens could be heard as more ambulances and police cars arrived.

"Did you know something like this was going to happen?" I asked.

Ellen blinked. "No." Her lips barely moved. She sounded drugged. "I . . . I knew something . . . something was going on. It was like I could feel it. That's why I called you at home. That's why I wanted out. But I never imagined something like this would happen."

o o o

On television, the image now showed the fence. In particular, the hole I'd made the night before with the garden shears.

"Holy shit," I breathed. "Holy shit."

o o o

There was too much going on at the moment for the reporter to speak. People were shouting, cops were barking orders. The reporter was just letting the cameras roll, and the scenes flashed from the cathedral to the dormitory and to the garden. The fountain with the man with his arms outstretched continued to flow. It was impossible to believe I had been at that very spot less than twelve hours ago.

"There's hope for everyone," Ellen said, still sounding stoned.

"What?"

"There's hope for everyone," she repeated. "That's what they kept telling me, over and over, when I first got there. Reverend Sloan ended all his talks and sermons by saying that. When they came around for bed checks, that's what they said. There's hope for everyone. It was like a catch-phrase."

I glanced up at the television. I didn't know how many people belonged to the cult, but it didn't look too hopeful for any of them. Not anymore.

88

I stayed with Ellen for a couple of hours, not saying much. We were too fixated on the television, watching the story of the massacre unfold. Ellen cried a lot. I sat next to her bed and held her hand.

It was theorized the elders went around that night with guns and shot everyone execution-style in the head while they slept. Silencers on the barrels of the weapons apparently kept everyone from waking up. Then, the men turned their guns on themselves, but not before one of them called the police, saying everyone at the Center was now finally at peace, and there was 'hope for everyone.' He shot himself while he still had the phone to his ear.

The whole thing was surreal. Shit like this didn't happen in real life. This was shit for the movies, not something people actually *experience*. I mean . . . come on. After everything I went through to get here, to find Ellen and the *New World Peace Center,* what were the chances of arriving on the eve of what had been a carefully planned mass murder? What were the odds of being at the gate at the exact time the migrant workers came along? And seeing Ellen in the garden? Finding the garden shears?

Suddenly, it seemed to me that everything had been planned carefully from day one, from the moment of Ellen's phone call. Regardless of what had happened or how it happened, it had all occurred for a reason, like someone had orchestrated each and every instance, right down to every detail. If one thing had been changed, if one thing had been different, the outcome would have differed dramatically. I might have arrived in West Palm too early . . . or too late. All those cosmic boomerangs had had their purpose, each and every one of them. And as I sat with Ellen, I remembered the conversation I'd had with Martin Khul in seventh grade, and how he didn't believe in God. He made some good points, but I really wondered how all of this had happened without careful design from an outside force. Somewhere, there had to be a briefcase containing blueprints, detailing a master plan. Maybe it all was coincidence; maybe it wasn't. But, if there was a God, and He was responsible, I thanked Him for His help right then and there. I didn't say anything out loud, as I figured anyone that powerful would have to be able to read my mind. I'm sure He heard me.

o o o

A nurse came in with breakfast: scrambled eggs, sausage, and a fruit cup. Ellen devoured the eggs and sausage, but she didn't want the fruit.

"I've had enough of that for the rest of my life," she said. "You want it?"

I said I did.

o o o

We continued to watch the television. The massacre at *New World Peace Center* pre-empted all other programming. I clicked around to different channels, not surprised in the least to see the bigger networks carrying the story live. Fox News had some cult expert, and he was saying that Alexander Sloan had been on their 'watch' list for years, as he'd been the leader of some cult in Nebraska before he and several of his followers had been arrested on various charges, including kidnapping and rape. He got off due to lack of evidence, and he moved to Florida in 2003 where he re-formed his group under a new name. There had been a few complaints over the years, mostly from members who'd left the cult, but there was never enough evidence to bring charges. Recently, the group had been in the news again. Someone had managed to get out—one of the elders—and went to the police, telling them about people being held against their will. The police investigated, but they never found anything. In fact, the open house was supposed to be Sloan's effort to show everyone that there wasn't anything illegal going on, and no one was being held against their will. However, based on what the escaped elder had told police, the prosecutor had enough evidence to arrest him on various charges. They'd hoped to do it on the day of the open house, when they'd have free access to the facility.

"But, if the police were there over the past year, how come they didn't know people weren't allowed to leave?"

"There is a basement beneath the dormitory," Ellen said. "We—about thirty of us—were put there for prayer sessions. Mostly the younger ones, but there were several adults. What we came to realize was that the only ones in the basement prayer sessions were the ones who talked about leaving the Center. They put us there whenever the police or someone showed up with questions. We had no idea the police or anyone was there, until after. Only afterwards did I hear anything about it, but most people in the group didn't say much. If you weren't an elder, you were pretty much kept in the dark about everything. No televisions were allowed, and no newspapers. The only things we had to read were books Reverend Sloan approved.

And his own writings."

"But what about the open house today?" I asked. "You knew about it?"

Ellen nodded. "We all did. But we also knew we wouldn't be a part of it. There was another prayer session scheduled for today, and we were told it would be all day, and no one would be allowed to leave the basement."

"Were there others like you who wanted to leave?"

"A few. Mostly, we were too afraid to talk about it. A few months ago, a girl named Julie tried to leave. She tried to dig a hole under the fence using a plate from the kitchen."

"What happened to her?"

Ellen shook her head. "I don't know. She disappeared. But I heard she didn't escape, and that she was getting 'treatment.' That was right about the time I decided I didn't want to be there anymore. But I didn't know what to do. Finally, I was able to sneak into one of the offices in the main building and call you. I almost got caught. That's why I had to hang up so fast. And I was able to use a computer, but only when no one was around. And that wasn't very often. No one was allowed to use the computers except the elders. And Reverend Sloan, of course."

I sat on Ellen's bed and held her hand, and we continued to watch the news. Apparently, there were no survivors at *New World Peace Center*. Everyone was dead; however, the body of Alexander Sloan hadn't been found, and it was speculated he had slipped away.

o o o

The nurse came in periodically. Then, the doctor came in and told me I'd have to leave. I stood, squeezed Ellen's hand, then let go.

"I love you, Greg," she said.

That caught me by surprise, and for a moment I couldn't say anything. I just stood there, letting the words register. I guess I wasn't surprised she loved me . . . just the simple fact that she said it out loud. The phrase seemed oddly foreign, even though she was my sister.

"I love you, too," I said, and I left before she could see the tears in my eyes.

89

With my backpack over my shoulder, I took the elevator back to the lobby and walked outside. The sun was a fiery lemon drop, and I thought about what it would be like in Michigan. It would be cold and crisp, with most of the leaves brown and falling from the trees. The ground would be glazed with frost in the morning, and there might even be a few snow flurries.

Here, however, the weather was warm and glorious. The sun was a warm cloak on my skin, and for the first time in a couple of weeks, I didn't feel restless. Sure, there still were a lot of things to think about. Ellen, number one. She was sick, but at least she was now getting help. But there were other things to think about, too. Where was I going to sleep? I couldn't continue to sleep in the hospital. In fact, I was in pretty bad need of a shower. A motel? That could get expensive, really quick. Homeless shelter? I'd never considered it before, and I didn't want to consider it now. But you gotta do what you gotta do.

And—

Lacy and Bruce.

Sooner or later, they would find out about Ellen in the

hospital. The doctor had said she tried to call; maybe she'd already tried to reach them this morning. Maybe she *had* reached them. What would their reaction be? Would they be too far gone to even care? It was crazy that, here I was, sixteen years old, and I couldn't predict what their reaction would be.

o o o

Cars and trucks buzzed by on the street. I continued up several blocks until I found a bank. There was an ATM machine in the anteroom, so I plugged in my name and password to check my balance. Matt had scrounged up a bit more money, and there was now over five hundred dollars in the account. I felt rich, like I had when Dawn had left me the stack of twenties in the Bible at the hotel.

I left the bank thinking about Dawn, wondering if she'd made it home all right, if she and her mom had made up. She really was a good person. I mean, when you think of prostitutes, you think of sleazy chicks whoring themselves out to any guy that comes along. I guess Dawn might have been like that, as she had perceived the whole venture as a business: a business designed to earn money. She was able to detach herself from her work, and I hoped she had also been able to detach herself from her mask. In fact, I hoped she threw the damned thing away.

o o o

I walked a little farther until I came to a YMCA. I was familiar with the Y in Bay City, as I used to go there to swim years ago. That was always a lot of fun. But the YMCA had something else: showers. And usually, a day pass was pretty cheap. Pretty cheap was right in my budget. Some of them even have rooms where you can stay. A room at the Y was bound to be cheaper than a hotel room any day of the week.

I walked in and found that this particular Y didn't have rooms. It was a nice place, though. Clean. I got a day pass for five bucks and headed straight for the shower. I wished I had a fresh pair of clothing to get into, but I'd worry about that later. Later, I could find another thrift store and pick up some more clothes.

o o o

The shower was just what I needed. I was already feeling pretty good and hot water on my skin put me over the top. Somehow, everything was going to work out. I'd stolen Bruce's car and had it stolen from me, I got robbed and decked by four black guys, nearly bitten by rattlesnakes, and survived a car crash. I found Ellen in the nick of time. If I would have been any later, she'd be dead right now. My whole life had taken on a sort of surreal, movie-like quality. And, like in the movies, things were turning out okay.

I left the YMCA and headed back toward the hospital. Behind me, someone from inside a restaurant shouted something. I paid no attention until the shout came again, louder, from someone who had just emerged from the building.

Someone called out my name. First and last.

90

I stopped and spun around. A tall black man was standing just outside the entrance of the restaurant. A big sign hung from above. *Tiempo's* was painted in blue cursive letters with a thin stroke of red. The black man beneath the sign was wearing shiny black shoes, black pants, and a white shirt with a bow tie. His hair was cropped short, his facial features were strong and angular. I seemed to recognize him, but I couldn't place him. A ghost of a distant memory.

"Greg Chappell, right?"

I stood my ground, still trying to place the stranger standing a few yards away. "Yeah," I said, reaching up and taking my sunglasses off.

The man flashed a big, gleaming smile and pointed to his chest with his index finger. "Tyrone! Tyrone Whiting! From Bay City!"

That damned boomerang just about knocked me over. I couldn't believe it. When he said his name, the realization was instant. The ghost vanished and a friend appeared. His cheeks were chubbier when he was little, and he was twice the size I last remembered him. But that smile, that light in his eyes? That was all Tyrone.

I walked up to him and extended my hand. He took it, but he also took a step toward me and gave me a big hug, which I reciprocated.

"I can't believe it!" I said. "I haven't seen you since elementary school!"

"I've been here for eight years," he said. "After Mom died, Dad took a job down here. This is where I work." He hiked his thumb toward the restaurant. "I'm assistant manager. What are you doing down here?"

I wasn't even going to begin to recap the chain of events that brought me to West Palm, not here, not yet. I summed it all up in two words.

"Family emergency," I said.

A look of concern fell over Tyrone's face. "Everything okay? You got a nice shiner goin' there."

I looked away, then looked back. "I hope so," I said. "I think the worst of it is over."

Which, of course, wasn't even close to the truth. Just because I'd hoped it, didn't make it so. Not by a long shot.

91

Tyrone invited me in, explaining that *Tiempo's* wouldn't open until noon. He motioned for me to sit at a table and offered coffee.

"Nah," I said.

"Coke?"

"That'd be great."

Tyrone whisked away and returned. He sat.

"Man," he said, shaking his head and grinning. His teeth were perfect: porcelain-white. "I still can't believe it. I was standing there, staring out the window, and you walk by. Funny thing was: I knew it was you the moment I saw you. You look the same. 'Cept, you're a lot bigger."

"You look great," I said. "How's your dad?"

He sipped his coffee. "Doing great. Got remarried. He's gonna retire in a couple of years. My sister went into the Air Force. She's in Germany. She loves it. I graduated high school early."

"No shit?"

"Yeah. Now I'm taking some college courses. I've been here at the restaurant for a year. Started out as a server, got bumped up to assistant manager after six months. I'm still a server, but now I got benefits, and I help manage the staff. But what's going on with you? What's the emergency?"

I smiled and shook my head. "You don't have the time."

Tyrone looked at his watch. "It's ten o'clock," he said. "I got 'till noon."

o o o

I laid it all out for him. Everything, from Ellen running away to me stealing Bruce's car. I skimmed over a few things—the Dawn episode, in particular—but I told him everything else. He about came out of his seat when I told him about the hillbilly church and the buzzing rattlesnakes. I told him about finding Ellen and getting her out of the *New World Peace Center* and taking her to the hospital. Tyrone sat listening the whole time, his eyes glued to mine. The only time he looked away was to pick up his coffee.

o o o

When I finished my story, I took a final sip from my glass and swirled the ice around.

"You're lucky to be alive," he said.

I nodded. "Ellen, too."

"I saw something about that on the news this morning, but I was getting ready for work and didn't have time to pay much attention."

"It's insane," I said. "Everybody's dead."

"So, now what?" Tyrone said.

I shrugged. "Not sure," I said. "Main thing is Ellen has to get better. She's not going anywhere for a couple days."

"Where are you staying?"

I shook my head. "Not a clue. Haven't thought that far

ahead." I pointed to the backpack on the seat next to me. "You're looking at everything I own. Remember Matt Dunbar?"

Tyrone nodded.

"He scared up some cash for me and put it into my bank account, so I've got about five hundred bucks. That's gonna go in a hurry, though."

"Stay at my place," Tyrone said. "You can stay there long as you want. Ellen can stay, too, when she gets out of the hospital. I can probably get you a job here, if you don't mind busing tables and doing dishes."

I was stunned. In five seconds, Tyrone had the answer to my second and third biggest problems: shelter and money.

"Are you sure?" I asked. "I mean, that would be great. Only for a while, though, I promise."

Tyrone waved it off with a sweep of his arm and a shake of his head. "Stay as long as you need. We just had a busboy quit yesterday. I can get you in at *Tiempo's* no problem. Pay's not very great—"

"I don't care," I said, shaking my head. "I'll take it."

Tyrone reached into his pocket and pulled out a business card. He turned it over, blank side up, and wrote his home address and phone number.

"My place is easy to find. Four blocks over. You can start work tomorrow. I'll give you the employment app to fill out. Drop it by later today. Cool?"

I told him it was so cool that he didn't know how cool it was. "I can't thank you enough for this," I said.

Again, Tyrone waved it off. "We're friends, man. Always have been. And my mom? Boy, she sure loved you."

"I know she did," I said, recalling the way she would hug me and pinch my cheeks, remembering the cookies and the lemonade. "I know."

92

Back at the hospital, I tried calling Lacy and Bruce again. Still no answer. I spent the rest of the afternoon with Ellen in her room. As much as the nurses would let me, anyway. The doctor appeared now and then to ask Ellen some questions. She told us she'd been trying to get in touch with Lacy and Bruce, but she had no luck.

I told Ellen about Tyrone. She remembered him, vaguely. She hadn't hung out much with him. I told her I was going to stay with him for a while, that he got me a job at the restaurant he worked at. And I told her Tyrone offered to let her stay at his apartment, too, when she got out of the hospital. She thought that was really nice.

"And what about Lacy and Bruce?" she asked. "Once they know where we are, will they want us to come home? Can they make us?"

"You sound like you don't want to go home," I said.

Ellen looked out the window. "I would," she said. "I mean . . . I . . . I might, if things were different." She looked at me. "But things aren't different, are they?"

I answered by shaking my head, and added: "Not the last

time I checked."

o o o

Ellen threw up a couple of times during the day, but I was able to help her to the bathroom before she lost her cookies everywhere. She was still weak and seemed to be getting weaker. Even with her gown on, it was easy to see how much weight she'd lost, and when I slipped my arm around her waist, it was like holding a child. Later in the day, she developed a fever. The nurse said I had to go, that Ellen needed rest. She told me to come back tomorrow. I kissed Ellen on the cheek, told her I loved her, and left.

o o o

Tyrone's restaurant was really cranking when I stopped in just after five o'clock. There wasn't a vacant table in the room. He had just enough time to take my application and introduce me to the manager. He tossed me the key to his apartment and told me he'd be home around nine. That was still a few hours away, so I made the most of the time. I needed to find some work clothes.

I found a thrift store several blocks over and was able to find a couple pairs of shorts and even a pair of black pants and shoes that weren't half-bad. I found a white dress shirt that was a little worn, but not too much. They didn't have used socks, but they had a bunch of new ones on sale. A buck for three pairs, so I bought some black ones to go with my pants and shoes and three pairs of white cotton ones. But I couldn't find a bow tie. I did, however, find a black silk tie for a dollar, so I'd look reasonably presentable for the first day on the job. My entire bill came to less than twenty bucks.

381

o o o

Tyrone's apartment was small, but it was neat and orderly. There was a stack of textbooks on the kitchen table. I imagined his days were pretty hectic, being that he was a full-time assistant manager *and* taking college courses.

There was a small living room and a single bedroom off to the right; no long hallways here. A cream couch was the only furnishing in the living room, except for a television on a stand. I turned it on and hunted through the channels until I saw the unmistakable cathedral at the *New World Peace Center*. The channel was CNN, and they were televising a live news conference with the West Palm Beach chief of police. There hadn't been too many developments over the day except for an accurate count of all who'd been killed: ninety-four. And the good Reverend Sloan wasn't among them. He was missing, along with his Bentley. They flashed a picture of him, smiling and smarmy, with aluminum-silver hair forming a sharp widow's peak, and dazzling blue eyes. He looked phony: too flashy and perfect. A sleazy aristocrat. Anyone who knew of his whereabouts was asked to call the West Palm Beach police.

This time, I saw the boomerang coming and was able to duck before it clocked me at full force.

o o o

I hurried to the phone perched on the kitchen counter and dialed the number on the television screen. A woman answered after one ring.

"West Palm Beach Police, Officer Mendoza."

"Yeah . . . um . . . that guy on television you're looking for. Sloan?"

"Yes?"

I paused and closed my eyes, making sure I remembered

correctly.

"Sir?" Mendoza said.

"Yeah, sorry. That guy. Sloan. Try Delta flight 328 out of Miami. He's headed for Rio De Janeiro."

I hung up. Let's see Sloan duck *that* boomerang.

93

Tyrone came home just after nine. He was in great spirits.

"This whole thing still blows me away," he said as he changed out of his work clothing and into a pair of jeans.

"What's that?" I asked. I was seated on the couch, glancing at the images on the muted television.

"The whole thing!" he said, emerging from his room. "You coming down here and everything. Seeing you on the street. Too much of a coincidence to be a coincidence."

"Maybe so," I said. "I can't thank you enough for your help."

I showed him the clothes I'd bought; he said they'd be fine. *Tiempo's* didn't necessarily have a dress code, but staff was expected to dress the theme: upscale. He said my new ensemble would be fine, I'd fit right in. And, being a busboy/dishwasher/gopher, I'd be wearing an apron, anyway.

o o o

We talked well into the night. Tyrone wanted to know about all his old friends, and I was able to let him know who was doing what, who'd moved, whatever. We talked about him graduating early and taking college courses. Here he was, barely eighteen, living on his own with an assistant managing job, rocking down the education superhighway like a Ferrari. Tyrone was going places fast, and I couldn't be happier for him.

o o o

My first day of work at *Tiempo's* went okay. I'd never done the busing/dishwashing thing before, but after I learned what to do and where things went, it was a piece of cake. It was simple work, but it was nutso-fast paced, especially during the lunch and dinner hours. There was no way I could move fast enough, and Ed Franke, Tyrone's boss, let me know it. He was cool, but he told me several times to move faster. So, I did. By the end of the day, I'd gotten the hang of it, and I figured I was going to do okay. Tyrone even said so.

After work, I hoofed it on over to the hospital to see Ellen. When I got to her room, she was sleeping. I tiptoed to the bed, not wanting to wake her, but she heard me and opened her eyes. Smiled a tired, weak smile.

"Hi," she said.

"How are you feeling?" I asked, taking her hand. Her skin felt hot.

"Like hell," she said. "I'm burning up. And I feel achy all over. Exhausted."

"Anything from the doctor?"

Ellen shook her head a tiny bit. "Nothing yet. She says they're still running some tests. I can't keep any food down, and she says if I can't get any food to stay down, they're going to have to feed me through a tube."

"At least you won't have to taste it," I said, trying to make light of it all. "I hear hospital food sucks."

Suddenly, her eyes widened, and I thought something

was really wrong, like she was going to have a seizure or something. But she pulled her hand from mine and pointed to the television set. The volume was down, and she pawed for the remote control on the bed, picked it up and pointed it at the television.

o o o

On the screen: the face of Alexander Sloan. Except this one was different than the photo they'd showed earlier. This picture showed a much more harried, distraught person. His silver hair was in shambles, and there were drooping red bags beneath his eyes. He no longer fit the part of the perfect, smarmy cult leader. The announcer told the story.

"... *arrested by Brazilian authorities as he got off a plane in Rio De Janeiro. An anonymous tip phoned in late yesterday provided police with the flight number and destination of the fugitive. Sloan will remain in Brazilian custody until authorities from this country arrive to extradite him back to the United States. Sloan was combative and* . . . ."

Ellen turned the volume down. "Good," she said. "I hope he gets what he deserves. And I hope whoever called in the tip gets the reward of a lifetime."

"I hope so, too," I said.

I never told Ellen—or anyone—it was me that called. I was alive, and so was Ellen. That seemed enough of a reward.

o o o

I visited with her for a little while. She said the doctor told her she still hadn't had any luck contacting Lacy and Bruce, but she shouldn't worry about that. Being that she was sick, the hospital had the authority to perform any necessary treatment. Right now, however, they needed to find out what was wrong with her. Ellen was hopeful, and she was sure her condition was brought about by her treatment at the *New World Peace Center*.

I was thinking something else entirely, however.

"Do you think they were poisoning you?" I asked.

Ellen thought about this. "I don't think so," she said. "I don't see why they would. Nobody else was sick like I was."

"Well, I don't see why the elders would kill everyone and then commit suicide," I replied. "That's just plain insane."

Still, Ellen thought the idea of being poisoned wasn't all that plausible. She seemed convinced her illness had to do with not enough food for too long a period of time.

Turns out, we were both wrong.

94

The next day was Friday. It was my second day of work, and Tyrone warned me it would be brutal, as I'd be working a double. Friday meant big business at *Tiempo's*. I wasn't worried about hacking it, as I thought I'd do okay. I was just disappointed that I wouldn't be able to see Ellen. I did call her during my afternoon break. She sounded sleepy; I'd woken her up. We chatted for only a few minutes. Still no test results, the doctor had told her. Maybe after the weekend. I told her I'd drop by in the morning, and hung up.

And Tyrone was right: *Tiempo's* was a rocking place on Friday, especially after the dinner hour. People kept pouring in, and there was a thirty-minute wait at the door. I worked furiously every minute of the day (except during my few and far between ten minute breaks) and I never thought I'd get caught up. I mean, I was *cranking*. Mr. Franke said I was doing well, that I was hustling, so that was cool. And I got a free meal for dinner, anything off the menu I wanted. One bite and it was easy to see why the place was so popular. I had pecan encrusted whitefish, and it was out of this world. Best fish I've ever tasted—even if I had only ten minutes to eat.

So, the job was going to work out okay . . . as long as I could put up with people. I'd never had a job where I had to deal with the public in such an in-your-face way. I had a job at a convenience store two summers ago in Bay City, but that was pretty simple. Keep the shelves stocked, keep the restrooms clean. Once in a while, I'd have to deal with someone nasty. But at *Tiempo's?* It seemed like *everyone* was nasty. People were demanding to get a table *now,* and they complained about everything. They were like a bunch of whiny first-graders. No matter what you do, there are just some people you'll never be able to satisfy. And me, being the low man on the totem pole didn't help any. People asked me to refill their waters, check on their food, shit like that. Oh, I did whatever I could. With a smile, even. But I sure encountered a lot of ungrateful people.

And the messes some people left at their table? Jesus . . . do they do that at home, or do they feel that since they're paying for their meal they have an *obligation* to be pigs? I couldn't believe the shit I had to clean up.

But, like I said: the day went well, other than the bitchy people. By the time Tyrone and I got to his apartment, I was so exhausted I fell asleep on the couch without taking my clothes off.

o o o

I didn't have to go to work until noon the next day, so after I got up and showered, I went to see Ellen with Tyrone in tow. He had remembered Ellen, even if he didn't know her very well all those years ago.

Tyrone didn't have a car; he said he was saving his money, so we set out for the hospital on foot, which was only seven or eight blocks away. He said it was easy enough to get around town with the bus, and not having a vehicle didn't really hinder him. I asked why he wasn't living with his dad if he wanted to save money.

"Dad got remarried a couple of years ago," he said. "His new wife and I don't really see eye-to-eye. Oh, she's fine and all that. But I don't think she wants to share her new man all that much. It's just as well. I like being on my own. And I get along great with both of them now."

He was shocked when I told him Lacy and Bruce weren't my parents. We didn't go into the particulars of the relationship I had with them. I'd given him a few details; not much more was necessary. I think he had a pretty good idea what Ellen and I had been dealing with growing up.

"Does anyone know she's the only survivor of the *New World Peace Center?*" Tyrone asked as we strode into the hospital.

"No," I replied. "I think we're going to keep it that way, at least for now. She's pretty wiped out, and the whole thing has really gotten to her. Besides . . . I don't think she'd be able to handle it. The media would want to interview her, not to mention the cops. She's not ready for that. Maybe when she gets better."

"Yeah, that's probably best, if she's sick and all that."

o o o

We took the elevator to the fifth floor. Ellen wasn't in her room, and I had to track down a nurse who said they'd taken my sister to another floor for tests. We waited around for about half an hour, watching the television in her room. The *New World Peace Center* massacre was still big news, and it seemed every channel had interviews with former members of cults, cult specialists, and even a few former members of the Center in West Palm, ones who'd managed to get away in past months or years. They provided more clues about what went on behind the scenes. There was a lot of sexual activity, mostly involving the younger females and elders. Some of the guests were pretty graphic about it, and I couldn't help but cringe as they spoke about what they'd experienced. But no one—none of them—could have predicted the horrific mass murder.

Ellen never did return, and we were running short of time. I jotted her a short note and told her I'd try to stop by in the evening after work. I closed the note with a silly smiley-face, and told her I loved her.

o o o

Tiempo's was every bit as busy on Saturday as it had been on Friday. The good thing, though, was I didn't have to work a double and was out of there by eight. I went straight from the restaurant to the hospital, where I found Ellen in her bed, eyes closed. She was so still and motionless I began to worry that something really *was* wrong. I leaned closer and could see the gentle heave of her chest, and I backed away.

Ellen opened her eyes.

"Hey, sleepyhead," I said as I pulled up a chair and sat next to the bed. "How are you?"

"Terrible. I've never felt this bad before, not ever."

"Any news?"

"The doctor says I might have some kind of viral infection. I don't know what all that means, but she said I need more tests. I hope they figure out something quick, because I can't stand feeling this way."

"Tyrone came to the hospital earlier today," I said. "He said to tell you hello, and he hopes you get well soon."

Ellen managed a smile. Her lips were thin and dry. "That was nice of him," she said and closed her eyes.

o o o

The rest of the conversation was light. Ellen talked

about Florida and how she liked it, how she decided she was never going back to Michigan, not ever, no matter what Lacy and Bruce said. I laughed. I felt a little like that, too. I was enjoying the warm weather and looking forward to not having to wear a coat or go out in the snow during the winter months. Tyrone had told me the weather stayed pretty nice all season long, but he had warned me about the summers, saying that it got hotter than the devil's furnace.

"He's right about that," Ellen said. "But it's great. Sunshine every day. The beach is great, and there are lots of people. I'd like to get a job waitressing at a restaurant near the water," she said. "That would be awesome. Maybe down in the Keys."

It was good to hear her talking about the future, talking about doing things and having fun again. Sure, she was fifteen, and there still was that whole runaway issue. By law, Lacy and Bruce were still her legal guardians, no matter what Ellen said. And fifteen is a little young to be on your own, especially for a girl, especially in Florida. Ellen had already found that out; I didn't need to explain it to her.

Still, the upbeat conversation seemed to do her good, and she managed to give me a tired hug as I gave her a kiss good-night on the cheek.

"I'll stop back in the morning," I said. "Is there anything you want?"

Her grin grew, and for a moment, I was hit with an optical illusion: Ellen was eight years old again, following me around the yard like a happy puppy. When she was little, she would follow me everywhere. Back then, a smile was tattooed on her face.

"Yes," she said.

"Anything."

"A Snickers bar. I know I'm not supposed—"

I silenced her by pressing my index finger to her lips.

"You got it. I'll smuggle it in tomorrow. Mum's the word."

She giggled, and I left.

o o o

The elevator doors slid open on the first floor, and I nearly ran into Ellen's doctor. She looked just as surprised to see me as I was to see her.

"Greg," she said, and her eyes darted over mine.

"Hi," I said as I stepped out of the elevator and into the hall. She didn't get into the elevator; in fact, she backed away, still facing me.

"I'd like to speak with you, if I could, in the morning."

I searched her eyes; there was nothing I could see that could give me any indication of what she wanted to talk to me about. Ellen, of course. But what?

"Sure," I said. "I work at noon, though."

"Can you be here at ten?"

I nodded and said I could.

"I'll find you in the lobby," she said. "See you in the morning." Then, she stepped into the elevator and pressed a button. I looked at her, but her eyes didn't meet mine. I had a bad feeling that damned boomerang was on its way back around again.

95

When I returned to the hospital lobby at 9:55 the following morning, the doctor was already there. She was standing off to the side of the reception desk, carrying a manilla folder. There was a man with her. He was wearing a suit, and I knew in an instant he was a cop. Had to be. The jig was up, as they say. I wondered what they knew. The doctor, no doubt, had been able to reach Lacy and Bruce. No doubt she now knew about the stolen car and whatever else they told her.

And I'll admit it: I had a quick notion inside me to turn and split, to get the hell out of there while I could. If Bruce was going to press charges against me for swiping his car (and I knew he would), the cop was probably going to haul my ass off to jail right then and there.

But I didn't. I was tired of running. Whatever I had to face, I would face. At least Ellen was okay. We were both okay, in that big picture scheme of things.

So, I strode across the lobby . . . and the doctor did an odd thing. She extended her hand in greeting, and I took it. Not that the gesture was strange. It was just that she seemed warmer, more pleasant. Less doctor, more friend.

"Greg," she said, "I don't think we've been properly introduced. I apologize. Things get a little crazy sometimes. I'm Dr. Donna Weir."

I nodded and mumbled something to the effect of it being nice to meet her.

"This is Robert Clayton."

I shook hands with the cop, and he nodded. "Hi, Greg."

"Let's go to my office," Dr. Weir said. She and Clayton turned, and I followed them silently down the hall, to the left, to a door that had a brass nameplate on the wall next to it: Dr. Donna Weir, M.D. We went inside. Dr. Weir closed the door.

"Please, have a seat," she said, motioning to a plush leather chair. I sat, and the chair gave off that air-squeezing-through-seams sigh. Dr. Weir took a seat behind her desk and placed the folder on a stack of papers. The only other chair in the room was a plastic desk chair, and Clayton the Cop sat in it.

Dr. Weir looked at me for a moment before she spoke.

"Greg, I've been trying to reach your aunt and uncle for a few days now," she began. "As you know, your sister is very sick."

I nodded. Clayton the Cop cleared his throat.

"I'd been unsuccessful in reaching anyone at your home. That is, until yesterday."

Here it comes. She was about to tell me how things were going to work, now that the cat was out of the bag. Two teenage runaways in Florida. One sick, the other, a car thief. We're shipping you back to Michigan to face charges.

"And what did dear old Bruce have to say?" I said. I didn't mean it sarcastically, but that's the way it came out.

Dr. Weir looked down, then she looked at Clayton. Then back to me. She sighed.

"The person who answered the phone wasn't your aunt or uncle," she said. "It was another relative. Another uncle, actually. Phil."

Which wouldn't be all that unusual, I thought. *Uncle Phil spends a lot of time with Lacy and Bruce. Probably more so, now with the two brats out of the house. When the cats are away, the mice will get toasted.*

"Greg, your uncle had some bad news. Your aunt and uncle—Lacy and Bruce—passed away. Two nights ago."

The boomerang hit, all right, but it was one of those delayed reaction things. I couldn't believe I'd just heard those words.

Your aunt and uncle—Lacy and Bruce—passed away. Two nights ago.

"It was at your house," Dr. Weir continued. "There was a gas leak. They think from a faulty furnace. They died in their sleep. I'm so very, very sorry to have to bring you this news."

And I believed her. She probably had to deliver news like this all the time, and you'd think she'd get used to it. But I actually think I saw tears welling up in her eyes.

"Your uncle—Phil—happened to be at the house to find some paperwork the authorities needed. That's when I called, and he answered. I told him about you and your sister."

"What did he say?"

"He said Ellen ran away last year, and you ran away last week. He said you stole your uncle's car."

I said nothing. Here I thought I was going to be hauled off to jail. Instead, the doctor is telling me that my aunt and uncle are dead.

"This is very difficult, Greg. For all of us." She looked at Clayton the Cop, who was looking at me. His gaze was comforting and disarming, and somehow I knew he wasn't there to cart me off to jail.

"Have you told Ellen?" I asked.

Dr. Weir swallowed. Hard. She looked down; then she looked at me.

"Greg, Ellen has leukemia. She is in the final stages. At

this point—" She swallowed again. Looked away. Looked back at me. This time, I *did* see tears in her eyes. "—there's nothing we can do, Greg. Your sister is dying."

96

I know that most people, upon hearing all this bullshit, would have crumbled. They would have cried like a baby and turned into blabbering idiots. I didn't do that. But hang on. In looking back, it's certainly not because I didn't care. It's not because I'm so tough and macho that I could handle it; hardly. But think about it: you get hit with the unexpected death of your aunt and uncle, and then you find out your only sister is dying of cancer. I was too shocked to cry. This wasn't happening. Couldn't be happening, shouldn't.

There's nothing we can do, Greg. Your sister is dying.

Half my family was gone. What was left was on its way—

Your sister is dying.

—out.

"There's noth . . . nothing you can do?" I stammered.

Dr. Weir shook her head. "We've done test after test. I've consulted with our specialists in this hospital, as well as others. If we could have caught this a few months ago . . . well, we might have had a chance. She has a very aggressive form of cancer. Greg . . . do you know how long she's been sick? When her symptoms started?"

"I'm not sure," I said. "Maybe four months ago."

"And this is the first time she's sought treatment?"

I nodded and contemplated telling Dr. Weir the whole thing about the *New World Peace Center,* but I realized that was the absolute *last* thing Ellen needed: here she was, dying, and the media hounds would be all over her. Oh sure, she'd be protected somewhat in the hospital. But the cops and investigators would want to talk to her, interview her. Me, too. I couldn't do that to Ellen. Especially not now. Not ever.

"I . . . I don't . . . yes," I managed to say. "This is the first time she's been in to see about this."

"Greg, I can't tell you how sorry I am. I've been a doctor for twenty years, and this kind of news is always hard. But your situation is unique, and believe me when I say it's been one of the most difficult situations I've ever dealt with as a doctor."

"How . . . how long does she have?"

Dr. Weir sighed again. "Hard to say. But I will say this: her condition is deteriorating, and rather quickly. She might have two weeks; she might have a month or two at the most."

Tears burst and rolled down my cheek. "And there's nothing you can do? Nothing at all?"

Dr. Weir's tears, which she had been holding back, fell. "If there was, we'd be doing it. We're doing the best we can. If there was something we could do, we'd do it, Greg. We'd send her anywhere, do anything. In fact, in situations such as this, I always look to others." She tapped the manilla folder. "I spoke with three independent specialists. Unfortunately, they've all reached the same conclusion. Your sister's leukemia has spread like a wildfire. Cancer is a vicious animal. It devours everything. It's gone into her bones, into her lymph nodes. There's nothing we can do to destroy it without destroying her. Anything we tried would only increase the pain and probably not even prolong the inevitable."

I hated that word, then, and I still do to this very day. I don't like hearing it. I don't like reading it.

Inevitable.

It's just too final.

Inevitable.

Lacy and Bruce were dead, my sister was dying. In fact, if I hadn't run away, I would be dead, too. For the very first time ever, I felt wholly, completely, and totally alone.

And scared out of my mind.

97

Turns out: Clayton the Cop wasn't a cop, after all. He was Clayton the Volunteer Counselor. I'd pegged him all wrong by a mile.

The rest of our meeting was a blur. In recollection, even the sound in my head seems muddled, and the scene moves in slow motion. Dr. Weir tells me what to expect regarding Ellen's condition, Robert Clayton tells me he's going to help in any way he can. What I do remember very clearly is when I ask a pointed question.

"Does Ellen know this yet?"

Dr. Weir shook her head. "No," she said. "I knew her condition was serious, but I wanted to wait until I contacted your aunt and uncle. I thought they should be here when we told her."

"So, how do we tell her, now?"

"Like I said," Dr. Weir replied, "it's usually best if family is with her. I can explain the details, and the family is there for support. I think now, in light of—"

"I'll do it," I interrupted. "I'll tell her."

Dr. Weir paused for a moment. She looked at Clayton,

and he spoke.

"It might be better if we—"

"No," I said, shaking my head. I wiped a tear from my cheek. "I'll do it. I'll do it myself. Alone."

There was no further opposition from Dr. Weir or Robert Clayton.

o o o

The elevator ride to the fifth floor seemed to take only a split second; the walk to Ellen's room seemed to take even less. I guess I was dreading what I was going to have to do so much that I just wanted time to stop, to slow down, to freeze. Anything to prolong giving the news to Ellen. But I also knew this was something I had to do, something that wasn't going away. It was—

Inevitable.

o o o

Ellen's door was partially closed, and I pushed it open slowly. She was sleeping. The television was on, but the sound was muted.

I stole quietly inside and pulled the chair to her bedside and sat. I stayed there like that, just watching her. It seemed she was barely breathing. And, I had to admit, she looked worse now than when she'd first arrived. Despite getting her to the hospital, despite all the technology in the world, despite everything: my sister was going to die. She was being eaten alive by a monster inside her body.

While she slept, while I watched her, while I listened to the subtle, monotonous beeping and blipping of machines I knew nothing about, all I could do was think about our lives growing up. Despite our home life, despite Lacy's and Bruce's crippling alcoholism, we'd had it pretty good. Most of my memories were happy, and Ellen was always smiling, except for the few minor childhood tragedies: falling off her bike, getting stung by a bee, skinning her knee. Ellen was a happy kid, always.

Her eyes flickered open, and her smile was strained, like she barely had the strength to move her lips.

I took her hand in mine, and drew a breath.

"You're dying," I said softly. I didn't know any other way of putting it, other than the way Dr. Weir had put it to me. No beating around the bush, here. Not with something like this.

She blinked once, twice.

"I know," she said. Her eyes never left mine. There was no shock in them, no huge rush of emotion. She squeezed my hand with what little strength she had. "I know," she repeated. "I can feel it."

o o o

Nothing more was said for a long time. It might have been ten minutes, it might have been an hour. Ellen closed her eyes, but she didn't fall asleep. I knew this because she kept giving my hand gentle squeezes. Finally, when she did open her eyes again, she spoke.

"You came," she said. "You were my only hope, and you came."

I didn't know what to say, so I said nothing.

"I had a feeling something was really wrong, something really serious," Ellen continued in a voice that was barely a whisper. "I don't know why. On the first day here at the hospital, I started having dreams about growing up. So many things, so many memories. When I woke up, I felt really good inside. I can't really explain it. I knew I was really, really sick, but I felt calm. And this morning, I knew for sure. I knew I was dying. I just woke up, and it was all so clear. I don't know how or why."

She closed her eyes again, and my mind tossed around Lacy and Bruce, and how I should tell Ellen about what happened to them. Sooner or later, she'd ask about them. She'd wonder if they knew, if they were coming to Florida.

Then, without thinking anything more about it, I stood. I pushed back the chair with my leg and let go of Ellen's hand. She opened her eyes. Very gently, I pulled back the covers and slipped one arm beneath her brittle legs and one behind her back. I lifted her just enough to move her over. Then, I carefully climbed into bed, slipped my arm around her and pulled her close.

"Lacy and Bruce died two nights ago," I whispered. "At home."

A wet tear hit my Adam's Apple. A sob choked through Ellen's body. She cried into my neck for nearly a minute. Then, she placed her hand on my chest and fell asleep.

98

Ellen died on Halloween. She was buried in Florida, at Beechwood Cemetery in West Palm Beach, four days later.

o o o

The last few weeks of her life had been, at the very least, comfortable for her. There were moments where she was in a lot of pain, but thanks to an IV of morphine, the pain was, for the most part, tolerable for her. I'd heard stories about people who'd suffered horrible pain for months before they passed away, and I was thankful Ellen didn't.

Turns out Robert Clayton the volunteer counselor was also the pastor of a small church nearby and, after explaining to the congregation about Ellen's situation (and my situation as well), they took up a collection. I mean, they really helped out. Not only did they raise a couple thousand dollars, but one of the members of the congregation had a rental house—just a simple mobile home— he offered, free of charge. We moved Ellen from the hospital to the mobile home, which was in a quiet, if busy, residential area. It was actually Clayton's idea to get her out of the hospital to somewhere private, somewhere more personal, if at all possible. The hospital had done all they could do.

Having the extra money allowed me to quit my job at *Tiempo's* so I could be with Ellen full-time. My boss was very understanding and offered to hire me back, any time. I'd only worked there a couple of days and I hardly knew anyone, but the staff took up a collection from their tips and gave it to me. Someone from Hospice named Laura (I never knew her last name) came by once a day to check in with us and make sure Ellen had everything she needed, made sure she was comfortable. Once in a while Laura brought a dog or a cat, which Ellen loved. One time, she brought a black lab puppy named Elmo. Ellen, although quite ravaged by the effects of the spreading cancer, actually became quite giddy as the little guy scampered all over her bed. Laura left Elmo with us for the day, and he fell asleep on Ellen's chest while she scratched his ears and held him. After a while, Ellen also fell asleep. I sat there watching them, balling my eyes out.

o o o

On occasion, someone from Clayton's church would stop by. They didn't ask to come in or see Ellen. They'd bring by baked goods, sandwiches, things like that. They asked if there was anything we needed. Mostly, there wasn't. But I was glad they came.

To spruce up the trailer a little, I went to Kmart (which, conveniently, was within walking distance) and bought a bunch of Halloween decorations. I hung cats and bats and pumpkins and witches all over the walls and windows. Nothing spooky or scary: just fun stuff. I also bought a few strings of orange pumpkin lights and draped them from the walls. The little pumpkins were about the size of a quarter and some of them didn't work. No matter. It wasn't much, but it gave the room a little color and livened the place up a little bit. And Ellen seemed to like it.

o o o

Around noon on Halloween, Ellen started having trouble breathing. I called Laura, and she came right over. Ellen could barely speak. By now, she'd lost even more weight. If she'd looked emaciated when I saw her in the garden of the *New World Peace Center,* it was nothing compared to the coathanger-thin frame beneath the sheets. In the kitchen, Laura told me that Ellen's death was quickly approaching, and that she probably wouldn't make it through the day. She asked if I wanted her to stay. I told her no.

o o o

The rest of the day I sat next to Ellen, holding her hand, listening to her struggled breathing. She slipped in and out of consciousness most of the afternoon. Finally, in the evening as it grew dark, I knew she couldn't hang on much longer. Just after six o'clock, Ellen opened her eyes and looked at me.

"Everything is going to be okay," I whispered. I held her hand. "It's all right."

"I know," Ellen breathed. I felt her try to squeeze my hand. Her eyes flickered a couple of times. "I love you," she said.

She closed her eyes. Her chest stopped moving. The muscles in her hand loosened.

Ellen was gone.

99

I was really amazed by the outpouring of support I got from Clayton's church. They'd raised enough money to pay for all the funeral arrangements, the burial, a headstone—everything. Clayton himself conducted the eulogy, and most of the members of the congregation attended. Every single one of them expressed their sympathy to me, and there was no doubt it came straight from the heart. Many were crying. Tyrone was there, too, along with his dad and stepmother. After all the shit I'd been through, it really helped. I ached inside. I mean—I *really* ached. It was like a physical pain, like someone placing a hot iron to my intestines. But I didn't feel so all alone.

o o o

After everyone had left, Clayton put his arm around my shoulders.

"So, what's next?" he asked.

"I guess I've got to go home," I said. "There are things to take care of with my aunt and uncle's house. I guess I'm supposed to get it. Lacy and Bruce had no will drawn, so I hear it's going to be a big mess. I have a friend—Jason Stien—whose dad is a lawyer, and he's going to help me out with everything."

I stared down at the casket in the open grave, tears still falling down my cheeks. A trickle of sand spilled over, and the grains bounced off the casket. Clayton released my shoulders. Took a breath. Sighed. By this time, I'd come to think of him as more of a big brother than an adult. He was probably in his forties, but our relationship had grown closer in the past weeks. He was never overbearing; he didn't call me all the time to see how I was, to check on Ellen. He was just—*there.*

"You know," he said. He looked up at the sky, the trees. "I don't know why things happen the way they do. I don't know why God allows some of us to be heaped with the most devastating circumstances and events. Others, so it seems, lead a life of bliss with little or no problems. I've always wanted answers, I've always wanted to know. I grew up thinking that everything was cut and dried. I used to think that if you did bad things, bad things happened to you. If you did good things, good things happened to you." He paused and looked at the ground. Then he looked up again. "But it's not that way. Not at all. And it's hard not to lose hope in the world and lose faith in humanity. It's important to keep sight of what's right, despite whatever comes your way. And you've had a lot come your way. Stay focused on the good, no matter how much bad you have to deal with. Let the good expand and grow in your life, no matter what you're hit with. Somehow, there's a plan and a purpose in everything."

He fell silent, and we listened to the wind rustle the palm leaves and the light hum of the distant traffic.

"Chet says you're welcome to stay in the mobile home until you decide what to do," Clayton continued. "If you need anything else—anything at all—just call. We're here for you."

He placed his hand on my shoulder. "I'm going to leave you alone. Take all the time you need. I'll be in the car, and I'll give you a lift back to your place when you're ready."

He walked away. All I could do was stare down at the casket and think: *That's my sister in there. My sister is in that box, and she's not coming out.*

A burst of wind shook the palm leaves. A car honked. Somewhere, a dog barked. My tears fell into the grass at my feet. The only sound they made was in my head, where each droplet crashed like thunder.

100

For the record: November in Florida beats the hell out of Michigan.

Two days after Ellen's funeral, I sat on the little porch of the mobile home. It was noon, and the sun was shining. The temperature was seventy-nine. I knew from good experience that in Michigan, the temperature was probably in the low thirties. There might even be snow on the ground. Yet, here I was, in shorts and a tank top, no shoes, soaking up the Florida rays. I'd even managed to negotiate more than a hint of a suntan.

Still, I knew it wouldn't last. I had to head back north, at least for a while. The whole deal with Lacy and Bruce's house needed to get settled. Jason Stien's dad assured me that the house would ultimately wind up in my hands, but because Lacy and Bruce had no will, things were going to be dicey and take some time. I had no idea what I would do: stay there, sell it and move, or rent it out. I've never owned a house before, and I had no clue how to take care of one, not in the sense that a house needed to be cared for. I could easily see Matt Dunbar wanting to move in with me and turning it into a party house, which I wasn't going to let happen.

But I wasn't all too worried about it. In fact, there really wasn't a lot I was all that concerned about. Thanks to the generosity of people I didn't know, I was able to stay afloat. The bad days were all in the past. Of course, I didn't really believe that, as I'd certainly learned one valuable lesson: things are never so bad that they can't somehow get worse.

o o o

So, I took it easy for a couple of days. I called Robert Clayton and told him of my plans. He said the church could make arrangements to pay for a bus fare back to Michigan. I really appreciated the offer, but he and the church had done enough. I had over five hundred dollars in the bank; that was enough to keep me on my feet until I got back to Bay City. Jason's dad, the attorney, said a mortgage payment of six hundred dollars was due in a few weeks, but he told me not to worry, he'd contact the bank and get something worked out, some sort of extension, considering the circumstances. He asked if my aunt and uncle had any life insurance; I told him I highly doubted it. What money Lacy and Bruce had wasn't spent on insurance or investments.

o o o

Two days later, I packed up everything and put it in a big duffle bag I'd bought at Kmart. I even bought some new clothes and tossed out the ones I'd bought at the thrift store. I wanted to buy a winter coat, but they didn't have any. In fact, when I asked one of the Kmart employees where the winter coats were, she gave me a strange look and pointed to a rack of wind breakers and sweatshirts.

"Nothing heavier?" I asked.

She shook her head. "Why?"

It took me a moment to realize people in West Palm Beach wouldn't have any use for a nice, thick, goose-down coat.

No problem. I had a couple of winter coats at home. I wouldn't freeze, and it was one less thing I had to carry with me.

The last thing I did before I set out was make a couple of phone calls. I called Robert Clayton at the church and thanked him for all his help. I told him I wanted to thank every single person at his church who'd helped me, but I'd never be able to get up in front of everyone and give some sort of speech. I'd crumple. So, I asked him if I wrote a letter, could he read it to the congregation? He said of course he would. He asked if I needed a ride to the bus station; I told him no.

o o o

I called Dr. Weir at the hospital and got her voice mail, but I left her a message thanking her for everything she did. I also called Laura, the lady from Hospice, and told her how grateful I was for her help during Ellen's last days. She wished me the best. Lastly, I called Tyrone Whiting and thanked him. He said if I needed his place ever again, I was always welcome. He reminded me that my job was waiting if I ever needed it; I told him to tell his boss thanks, but I didn't know if I would be coming back this way.

"Take care, man," Tyrone said.

I hung up. My doors in Florida were closed.

101

One more note for the record: a bus is no way to travel.

Oh, it's not that bad if you're someone like me: a little low on bread and willing to accept some minor inconveniences. My seat didn't recline very far back, and it was hard to sleep. On the other side of the aisle there was some snot-nose kid, about eight years old, who created a nonstop fuss. His mother had headphones jammed in her ears and was clueless. Someone around me smelled like stale beer and cigarettes, and it was nauseous. The ride was scheduled to take three days; I didn't know if I could take three hours of that shit.

But hey . . . as the slogan goes: I left the driving to them. And somewhere in the hills of Tennessee, I finally finished reading *Galaxy Quest*. Turns out Lora 447 got captured by the Drioleans and, being she was an android-type-female, they programmed her to kill Robert 342. He was able to capture her, but he didn't kill her because, by this time, he'd fallen in love with her. So he de-programmed her and re-programmed her back to her normal self. They used a nuclear warhead to blow the Driolean planet to space pebbles. Then, they had a little part-android baby they called Joe 548, and everything was cool.

The end. All in all, the book was pretty good, even without a cover.

But life just isn't like that. Sometimes, maybe more often than not, the endings aren't so happy.

o o o

The weather had been good until we hit the Ohio/Michigan border early in the third day of the trip. This was about three in the morning, and we were expected to make it to Bay City by six. However, the farther north we traveled, the worse the weather got. Snow—tons of it—had been falling for hours, leaving I-75 slick and slushy. The road in front of us was blanketed, the snow in the headlights whipping like a swarm of angry white bees. Cars and trucks littered the ditch like discarded cans. One particular accident involved a mini van that had hit a guard rail. The rail itself was bent like a mad roller coaster; the vehicle's entire front end had been pulled back like the lid of a soup can. But our driver was either fearless or stupid, maybe a little of both. He plowed on through at seventy miles an hour, the posted speed limit. He slowed a little when we passed an accident, but he kept the speed up as long as he could. Finally, right around Flint, traffic backed up to a standstill. The windswept snow was relentless, and the bus shook during some of the heavier gusts. When we finally did make it to the bus terminal in Bay City, it was just past eight in the morning. The snow kept falling and drifts had formed on city streets, as the snow plows couldn't keep up with it. Plumes of snow whipped off the tops of buildings like fire in the wind, creating dripping overhangs of thick, white putty. It was seven degrees—and I'd just arrived from West Palm Beach, where the temperature had been seventy-seven. I had no coat, no hat, no gloves, no warm boots. Yet, somehow, I didn't mind all that much.

o o o

  I took a cab home. I had no key to get inside; with any luck, the spare key Bruce kept behind the garage beneath a rock would be there. He kept moving it because he was sure that sometime, someone was going to find it and get into the house. I hoped he hadn't moved it since I'd taken off.

  I had to dig through two feet of snow. My teeth chattered and my exposed skin turned pink, particularly my bare arms and hands, which were wet and red and stiff. The wind whipped at my face, and the snowflakes melted as they hit my cheeks. But I kept digging, pawing through the snow like a fox after a mouse. Lo and behold, the key was there, and I let myself into the home that I never thought I'd see again.

102

I felt a rush of warm air the moment I opened the door. A blast of snow whirled in, and I flicked on the living room light and closed the door. I dropped my duffle bag on the floor and looked around. All in all, not much had changed. The place looked a little neater than usual; maybe Uncle Phil had tidied things up a bit. I walked into the kitchen and opened a few cupboards. There were some canned vegetables, Campbell's soup, Bush's baked beans, and a few boxes of Kraft macaroni and cheese. I hadn't eaten since the previous evening, and I could feel my hunger beginning to chew at my belly.

The fridge was empty, except for a few cans of Budweiser. I turned and walked down the hall, visiting my bedroom first. It looked pretty much the same as I'd left it. There didn't seem to be any disturbance to much of anything. One of my drawers was left hanging open and my socks and underwear were shuffled around. That was about it. *If I hadn't run away, I would have died here,* I thought. I'd always been aware of that fact, but now, being in the very room where I slept, where I would have died, really creeped me out.

I continued down the hall and pushed Ellen's door

open.

Empty.

All the furniture, everything she owned—gone. Somewhere along the line, between the day I left and the day they died, Lacy and Bruce decided to get rid of her stuff or maybe move it out into the garage. Somewhere along the line, they decided Ellen was never coming back.

And they had been right.

o o o

Moving down the hall, I came to Lacy and Bruce's room. It looked the same, but the bed was made. I stood there for a long time, thinking: *This was the spot. Only a few weeks ago, they had been alive. They died in that very bed, right there, the victim of a silent, invisible killer.* Everything seemed very strange and alien, but I'd gone over this moment in my mind a dozen times in the past week: coming home to an empty house, what I would do, what I would see, how I would react. Truthfully, I reacted just as I thought: the house was empty, I was empty. I knew things couldn't be changed, and I knew the worst was over. I was sure about it, and, for once, I was right.

But it didn't make any of it any easier.

Part Three: Things Past

I summon up remembrance of things past.

-*Shakespeare*

103

Two years went by.

Shortly after I'd returned from Florida, I got a job at Burger King and another job at a Marathon gas station/convenience store. It made for long weeks, but it kept me busy, and I was able to keep up with the house payment. I even bought a used car. It was a fairly nice one, too: a 2005 Nissan Sentra with only forty thousand miles. The whole house issue got settled after about a year thanks to some tough legal fighting by Mr. Stien. He put a lot of work into my case, and when it was all said and done, he never charged me a dime. He said he had a brother who'd recently died of pancreatic cancer. He said he knew what I was going through. I didn't doubt him for a second.

o o o

The house was put solely in my name, and Phil couldn't have been more pissed off. I stayed there for about a year, then sold it and moved into an apartment. I just couldn't keep from thinking of Ellen and Lacy and Bruce every time I was there, so

I dumped the place. After the bank mortgage was paid off, I had just under forty thousand dollars left over. I put it all in my savings account. I was still working two jobs, so I didn't need to dip into the money in the bank. Oh, sure, I thought about doing something cool, like buying a nice Trans Am or Corvette. I must say I was tempted. But I decided to wait a while. Cars like that are expensive, not including insurance. I didn't want to have to work just to pay for a vehicle. The way I figured it, I was doing pretty well, what with my two jobs and all. If I was smart, I could sock away some serious cash in addition to the forty grand in the bank.

o o o

Matt Dunbar got picked up on possession of pot. Not a little possession, either. Two pounds. I bailed him out, did whatever I could. I never forgot what he'd done for me when I was in Florida. Turns out he'd gone to everyone in school, asking for money, saying a friend needed help. That's how he was able to get the five hundred-plus dollars to sink into my bank account. In fact, after I made it back to Bay City, I still had just under four hundred dollars. I wanted to give it back to Matt, so he could give it back to the ones who'd chipped in; he told me to keep it. After he got busted, he wound up with a conviction and spent six months in the county pokey . . . which was light, considering the amount of hooch he was nabbed with. I visited him in jail when I could, but man . . . I really didn't have a lot of time. We talked about music and bands and things like that—nothing very heavy. When he got out, he needed money. I gave him five hundred dollars. It was a gift, not a loan.

o o o

Two of my former classmates were killed in a drunk driving

accident. I hadn't known them very well, but I went to their funerals. It was sad.

I contemplated going to night school to get my diploma, but I hadn't done anything about it yet. My group of friends thinned. I didn't have the time, and, quite honestly, wasn't very interested in the party scene. I didn't get home until midnight six days a week, and by that time, I was pretty whipped and just wanted to hit the sack.

o o o

Then, this past October, almost two years after Ellen died, I decided to visit her grave on Halloween, the anniversary of her death. It was an impulse decision, but there was another factor that I'll soon get to. It was getting colder, and I remembered how gloriously warm the Florida sunshine is that time of year. I remembered the sun on my skin, the smell of the air.

Yep. A return trip to Florida was in order.

But there was something else altogether that prompted my journey . . . I just hadn't admitted it to myself yet.

104

My boss at Burger King was sympathetic. She said I could take whatever time I needed and keep my job. At the Marathon station, my boss wasn't so kind. (He was an asshole, actually.) In essence, he said if I left, I wouldn't be coming back. So, I gave him two week's notice. He got all pissed off and told me not to bother coming in anymore. Screw him. The job was okay, but he'd always been a jerk to me, anyway.

o o o

I locked up my apartment and asked Mrs. Cutwieller, my neighbor in the apartment next door, to keep an eye on things. Mrs. Cutwieller was about a thousand years old if she was ten, but she got around like a teenager. She has thick hair, as shiny and white as a swan. She was always baking me cookies and pies and things like that, saying she had 'leftovers.' In truth, I don't think that was the case. I think she just liked to bake; I happened to be the lucky recipient of her efforts. I think I became an adopted grandson, of sorts, and I didn't mind one bit. I kind of felt the same about her, and I made it a point to pop in once a day if I could just to check in on her and say hello. She seemed to like that.

o o o

I set out for Florida on a Saturday morning. The weather was sunny and bright, and the temperature was surprisingly warm: a balmy fifty-five degrees. I had the same duffle bag I'd bought at Kmart in West Palm Beach. I turned the radio on and tapped the wheel to the beat as I retraced the path I'd taken two years before.

In Ohio, the rest area where I'd first met Dawn was just as packed with semi trucks as it had been on my first trip through. Even in the middle of the morning, they were lined up like giant iron caterpillars with their little orange and red beads glowing like a string of Christmas lights, each one a chrome and metal chrysalis with a dormant occupant inside. It wouldn't be long before said occupant would be emerging to take a leak and then haul his cocoon to Kansas or Arkansas or California or wherever.

And yes, I took a cruise through, but I didn't stop. I was looking, but I knew I wouldn't see her.

The miles rolled on. I found it disturbingly ironic I was headed to Florida for the same reason I had two years ago: to find my sister. My trip, although a somber one, was a little more pleasant this time around. I had about eight hundred dollars in cash and a VISA card. I didn't have to be so frugal as I had two years ago. I stopped at an Applebee's in Findlay, Ohio, had a burger for lunch, then kept going. I was hoping to make it to Knoxville by nightfall, where I could find a motel. The next day I'd make it to Atlanta and stay the night there, unless I was feeling really good and decided to hoof it the rest of the way to West Palm Beach.

The road spun beneath the car as I sped through rural

Ohio. The sun remained my friend; there were only a few clouds in the sky. Many of the trees had morphed into their fall colors: brilliant reds, yellows, and oranges. The freeway was relatively uncluttered, barring a few big rigs and recreational vehicles. It was a great day for a drive—until a single alarm bell went off. I checked my gauges.

Low on gas.

No problem. I had just passed through Cincinnati and crossed the Ohio/Kentucky border. Ten miles up was a sign for gas and an exit; I took it. Not until I saw the rundown shack of a gas station did I realize I'd broken my vow of never returning to Doorville, Kentucky.

o o o

I stopped at the freeway off-ramp, staring at the old station. It looked just as it had two years ago: worn, run down, ancient. A fleeting deja-vu came over me, and I glanced at the passenger seat, half expecting to see Dawn slumbering, as she had been on our previous stop to Doorville. Then it passed.

I was about to get back onto the freeway and head for the next station, but one glance at my gas gauge changed my mind. The little orange finger was touching 'E.' I had no idea how far the next gas station was.

So, I crawled across the overpass and turned into the gravel parking lot, sneaking up to one of the pumps like a thief. Again, it seemed like not a moment had passed. It was impossible to believe two years had gone by. MP3 players had dropped in price by fifty percent, the stock market was soaring at over 13,000 points, text-messaging had burst onto the scene. Yet, in tiny Doorville, Kentucky, someone had pulled the plug on the Progress Clock.

And that same old hillbilly dude came out of the store in what appeared to be the same clothing he'd worn two years ago.

At least, I *thought* it was him. He had the same build, the same look. Hell, it could've been the same old raggedy flannel shirt, for that fact. However, as he came closer, I could tell it was a different guy. He was a little heavier and had a bigger nose. And there was a touch of gray—just a smattering of scattered aluminum—in his beard and mustache. He lumbered on over to my car, and I rolled the window down.

"Fill 'er up," I said. The hillbilly dude grunted some sort of hillbilly-speak, pulled the nozzle from the pump, and began to fill 'er up, as I'd asked.

I was bored, and I hadn't spoken with anyone except the waitress at Applebee's. So I poked my head out the window.

"I came through a couple of years ago," I said, "and there was another guy here."

"Tha'd be Ray, ya-huh," the hillbilly said. "S'mah bruther." And that's just what he sounded like, too. "Jew know'um?"

"No, no," I said.

"Hay do'n work here no mo," he said. His voice was so full of the hills it was hard to understand him. "Wun thu lot-er-ee, shor did. Fahve meeyon bucks. Took off on outta here. Been gone since."

"No shit?" I said.

The hillbilly attendant looked at me and said nothing.

I couldn't help it: I laughed out loud. It just struck me so damned funny, so ironic. I immediately started to think of what the lucky bum would be buying with his lottery winnings.

The gas nozzle clunked off. By now, the hillbilly attendant was glaring at me.

"Whasso funny?" he asked.

"Nothing," I said, shaking my head. "Five million dollars? Couldn't have happened to a nicer guy."

And I meant it.

105

Doorville was in my rearview mirror, but not for long. I jumped back onto the expressway with a full tank of gas and a grin engraved on my face. I couldn't help thinking about that hillbilly gas station attendant (or owner, part-owner, or whatever he had been) winning the lottery and where he took off to. It's nice to see the old cosmic boomerang come back in a good way for people, no matter who they were.

I-75 was getting busier; it was getting on in the day, and people were heading out and about. Traffic was flying along pretty well, though, and I had the cruise control set at seventy-nine. Still, cars flew past me.

o o o

By the time I made it to Knoxville, I was tired. I'd had thoughts of driving farther, continuing on into Tennessee, but I decided not to push it. Instead, I found the very same Days Inn—the one Dawn and I stayed at—two years ago. And man, did I get lucky. I never thought about the fact that, being it was Saturday, there might be a lot of people looking for a motel.

And there were, too. I had to stand in line at the front desk. There was an elderly couple being checked in, and a younger couple in line ahead of me. When they reached the front desk, they told the lady behind the counter they didn't have a reservation, but were looking for a room. The lady shook her head and said all rooms were booked. Frustrated, they left. The phone rang and the lady picked it up, motioning to me with a single finger. I waited patiently, but I knew there was a Fairfield Inn down the street and was already making plans to head there. Chances were, however, they'd be booked, too.

In listening to her conversation, I heard her take a room cancellation. When she hung up, I spoke.

"Was that a cancellation for tonight?" I asked.

She nodded.

"I'll take that room if I can," I said.

The lady said that was fine . . . and I had a room for the night. While she took my credit card and processed the reservation, I parked the Nissan and came back in with my duffle bag. The lady behind the counter handed back my credit card and the plastic room key.

"You're in room 255," she said with a smile that could sink a ship. She was cute. "Elevator to your left, your room will be down the hall on your right. Anything else?"

I told her thanks, there wasn't.

It wasn't until about three o'clock in the morning that I realized something: I was in room 255—the very same room, the very same bed in which Joe had made his worldwide Internet bondage debut. I grinned and fell back asleep, wondering where he was and what he was doing now.

o o o

The remainder of the trip to West Palm Beach was uneventful. I got up early Sunday and drove straight through to West Palm, arriving just after seven in the evening. In a display of brilliant genius, I actually called ahead and made a reservation at a Red Roof Inn, which was only two miles from the cemetery where Ellen was buried. When I arrived the temperature was a pleasant seventy-eight degrees; I'd driven with the window down all the way from Valdosta, Georgia, which is just north of the Florida state line. I heard on the news that Michigan was getting an early snowfall: up to eight inches was expected in Bay City. I laughed out loud.

I was awash with a peculiar mix of emotions as I rode the elevator to the third floor and carried my bag to my room. I was excited to again be in Florida; however, the reason for my trip kept me in a somber mood. Although two years had passed, it still hurt to think about Ellen and what she'd gone through. There were times I thought it was all a dream, that Ellen couldn't *really* be gone. Lacy and Bruce couldn't *really* be gone. Shit like that happened to other people and their families, not mine. In the first few weeks after Ellen's death, it was all I thought about. Gradually, I would think of her less and less, but she was always there. Lacy and Bruce, too, I guess.

o o o

A thunderstorm passed through Monday morning, but by eight or so there was no trace of it, except for a few latent puddles in the motel parking lot, which were on their way to quickly drying up under the rising sun. When I strode outside, I was hit by a wall of thick, moist, warm air and the musky odor of wet wood and punky soil. I jumped over a puddle and thought about everyone back home in Michigan all bundled up in winter coats, shoveling their driveways, and driving on the slippery, snow-covered roads. I even thought about maybe hooking back up with Tyrone and spending the winter in Florida, but I knew I wouldn't. Tomorrow morning, I would be heading north again . . . but I wouldn't be heading home.

o o o

I fired up the Nissan and headed for the cemetery, but there was one stop I needed to make. I pulled into a Piggly Wiggly's, went inside, made a very minor purchase, and came back out. Five minutes later, I was pulling into Beechwood Cemetery.

106

I'd never really done anything like this before.

Oh, sure, I'd been to cemeteries before. But I can't remember ever visiting the grave of anyone I knew—let alone a close relative. It felt really weird. There was no one at the cemetery, but I still felt like a hundred eyes were upon me. I felt sullen, maybe a little nervous. I wondered how I would feel when I reached Ellen's grave.

It was easy enough to find; two years hadn't faded my memory one bit. I walked right up to it without any hesitation whatsoever. Now, of course, there was no longer a hole in the ground as I remembered. That had been my last recollection of Ellen's grave: her casket, resting on black nylon straps, ready to be lowered the rest of the way into the ground. The grass had long grown over and a single, marble headstone read:

> Ellen Jane Chappell
> June 14, 1992 - October 31, 2007
> We Miss You

o o o

I pulled out the Snickers bar I'd bought at Piggly Wiggly's and placed it on the headstone.

"I promised I'd smuggle this to you," I said. "I didn't want you to think I forgot."

A breeze came, cooling the tears on my cheeks.

107

After visiting Ellen's grave, I drove across town to *Tiempo's*. Tyrone saw me coming across the street and burst outside, running up to me. He gave me a huge hug, and I realized his genuine kindness and exuberance were genetic traits handed down through his family. His mom had hugged me like that.

"Man, how are you doin'?" he asked, squeezing my shoulders. "Where you been?"

"Up in Bay City," I replied. "Just making a short trip to take care of a few things."

He searched my eyes, but he never asked what sort of 'things' I had to take care of. I knew he knew.

o o o

"Come on in," he said. "Have you had any lunch yet?"

We spent the next hour yakking. I told him I'd sold the house up north and was working two jobs. He said he was now the manager and part owner of the restaurant. He'd finally gotten his degree in business management; he and a couple of partners planned to open several more *Tiempo's* around south

Florida. And he again offered me a job and a place to stay if needed. He said he was in the process of buying a home and was engaged to be married. I congratulated him and said I was happy for him. And I really was, but I couldn't help feeling a little envious. Not jealous, because I really and truly was excited for him. It had been two years since I'd seen him, and he was working hard to make a good life. I hadn't done much of anything except work. True, I'd been able to stash away a fair amount of cash for someone who was still a teenager. But I hadn't really thought about the future all that much. The only thing I'd thought seriously about was something I couldn't do anything about.

Or could I?

o o o

When it got right down to it, that was my reason for hitting the road. It wasn't something in the back of my mind; it was something I thought of every single day. Over the past couple of years I had dated a couple of girls, but it was nothing serious. Part of me didn't want to get tied down. The rest of me—all of me—continued to wonder what in the hell had ever happened to Dawn. I thought about her every single day. She was the smile of every girl I saw, she was the spark in every girl's eye. I couldn't look at another girl and not think of her. I loved her, and I'd known it for two years, ever since she left me in the motel room. Not a day went by without thinking about her, about what she was doing. I dreamed of being with her. I couldn't get her out of my head. Hell, I never even tried. Memories are like strange vapors, emotional mirages. It's like you can see them, but not really, not in a sense like you see other things. But they're there, all right. They're real. My memories of Dawn were more than that, though. The memories I had of her weren't so transparent, like so many others. There were times when I swore I could feel her skin pressed to mine. I could smell her hair and taste her lips. Sometimes, I would wake up at night and close my eyes and think about that night in the hotel room.

And I would wonder. I would dream.

All of this was running through my head while I was talking to Tyrone. He was going on and on about his new girl, about how great she was. I know I was being impolite, but I wasn't really paying much attention. I looked at him, smiled, nodded in the right places. But my thoughts were on the real reason I had made this trip. I hadn't admitted it to myself, but I wanted to find Dawn. I had spent too long telling myself I couldn't have her, that she was out of my life forever, no matter how much I thought of her or how much I dreamed. I had no idea where she was now or what she was doing. Maybe she was living with her mom in Ohio. Maybe they'd patched things up. Maybe she'd gone back to hooking, after all.

Highly unlikely.

○ ○ ○

Tyrone was still jabbering away, but I wanted to leave right then. I wanted to drive to Ohio and find Dawn. I didn't even want to finish lunch. If I left at that moment, I could make it to Ohio by the next day.

Crazy, I know. But I really wanted to see her again. I had tricked myself, like the time I had scoured the parking lot of the truck stop looking for Dawn. I had told myself I wasn't looking for her . . . just like I'd told myself the reason for this trip had nothing to do with her. Sure, I wanted to visit Ellen's grave. But in hindsight, I realized it was just a mental ploy to get me moving, get me on the road.

And it was crazy that I'd *waited* this long. It was a waste of time to have dated other girls. I knew who I *really* wanted, who I *really* loved. Now that I admitted it to myself, now that I really and truly made up my mind, I couldn't leave Florida fast enough.

○ ○ ○

After having lunch with Tyrone, I told him I was heading back. Everything was still up in the air, but I said I'd give him a call if I decided to come back to Florida. I didn't tell him my plans to find Dawn; that would be for another time.

Twenty minutes later I was on the road, headed north. It's funny how it happened so fast. Sitting there, having lunch and talking with Tyrone had sparked something. I'm not sure exactly why or what it was. In talking with him, I felt his drive, his energy, his purpose. He was a man with a plan; I wasn't. I realized my plan was being held hostage by my failure to act. I had to do something, and as soon as I made the decision I was overcome with a sense of urgency, of now, now, now. I wondered why I'd waited so long. As I drove, I had a hard time keeping within the speed limit. The only thing I could think of was finding Dawn in Ohio. Seeing her again, talking to her. Maybe there was something there. Maybe she felt the same way I did.

Georgia was a blur. I sped through Macon and Atlanta, stopping only for gas, food, and restroom breaks. It was smooth sailing, all the way . . . until I stopped to help a broken down motorist just north of Dalton.

108

I saw the red flashing hazard lights blinking in the distance like the eyes of some infernal, giant bug. As I passed, I caught sight of a man standing behind the open trunk. He was just standing there, perplexed. I slowed, pulled to the shoulder of I-75, turned on my emergency flashers, and backed up until my car was only a few feet away. I got out. The air smelled of hot rubber, dry meadow, and punky grass.

I walked to the back of the car. The man was alone; there was no one else in the vehicle.

"Everything all right?" I asked.

The man's silhouette appeared from the back of his car.

"I've got a flat, and my spare's flat, too," he replied in a mild southern drawl.

"There's a station a couple miles back," I said as I walked toward the back of his car. "I can give you a lift down there."

In the murky light glowing from within the trunk, we sized each other up for a moment. No doubt both of us were wondering the same things: Lunatic? Serial killer? Queer? Or just a good Samaritan?

He must have decided upon the latter, because he didn't hesitate too long.

"That'd be great," he said

○ ○ ○

He picked up a tire, and I picked up the other. We loaded them into the trunk of my Nissan, then got in the car. I got a better look at him in the yellow glow of the dome light, and I'll be damned if he didn't look oddly familiar. But there was no way I could have ever seen him before. I thought about the time two years ago when Tyrone spotted me and came bursting out of *Tiempo's*. It took a moment to recognize who he was. Now I wondered if I could have possibly met the guy in the passenger seat on my first time through. If I had, it would have only been something trivial. Maybe he was a clerk at a convenience store. Maybe I saw him at one of the hotels we stayed at. I tried hard, but I couldn't place him.

"Thanks for the help," he said.

"No problem," I replied, and I felt good that I'd stopped. I was glad to be able to help him out.

"Where ya from?" he asked.

"Michigan," I replied.

"Long ways from home."

I checked the mirror, then pulled onto the freeway.

"Yeah," was all I said.

"Headed back home?"

"Sooner or later," I said. "No rush. Not this time of year, with winter coming."

"I hear ya," the man said.

"You from around here?" I asked. I was still trying hard to place him, but I couldn't. And I couldn't place his voice, either.

"Originally," the man said. "I moved away a few years

ago. Just moved back." He stuck his hand out. "Name's Isaiah," he said, and the moment I clasped his hand the boomerang zapped me upside the head. All I could do was smile.

"Greg," I said, shaking his hand across the seat. "Greg Chappell."

109

I made an illegal turn in one of those 'authorized vehicle only' places and drove to a service station a few miles back. The night attendant (an oak tree of a man who had a map of horrible, ruddy pockmarks on his cheeks) said he'd probably be able to fix both tires, just give him ten minutes. Isaiah and I sat in the greasy waiting room on a greasy plastic couch surrounded by greasy magazines, a greasy calendar on a greasy wall, and greasy windows. The air was greasy, and I wondered if it would wind up greasing my lungs.

I never let on that I met Isaiah's family and spent the night in his room two years ago. I just asked him about New York, and listened.

"I moved out there a few years back," Isaiah said. "New York, that is. That place was something else! Bein' that I was raised in the hills, I'd never seen anything like it. So many huge buildings, so many people. I learned to like it. It was so different, so much more industrial and modern from what I was used to. Movies, theaters, concerts. There's a strong heartbeat in New York. When people say it's the capitol of the world, they're not kidding."

"So, why 'dja leave?"

Isaiah shrugged. "Got old after a while. I never thought I'd ever say that, but it happened. I'd come home to visit the family, and I realized how much I missed the simple peace and quiet of the country." He laughed. "You know, for my first year, whenever I thought about home, I couldn't understand why anyone would want to live such a life. New York—and most big cities, for that fact—offer everything and anything you could possibly want. During my first year, I knew I'd never go home, except to visit family. It's funny. After a while, the city just started to eat away at me. I know it might be different if I'd grown up there. It might be in my blood, like the country is. Just took me a while to realize that."

I listened intently, but I couldn't help but think about the life he was going back to. He left New York City to live in the backwoods where there really aren't many modern conveniences. Sure, New York might have its own rattlesnakes . . . but I'd take my chances there before I took my chances again with a dude who pulls them out of a box with his bare hands.

o o o

The oak tree mechanic emerged from the garage rolling a tire. "Good as almost new," he said to Isaiah. "'Cept, you might think about replacing this one in another few thousand miles. Gettin' some wear n' tear on her."

Isaiah and I stood. The mechanic went back into the garage.

"I'll take this one out to the car," I said, and I wheeled the tire out the door and into the parking lot lit by large mercury vapor lights.

When I returned, Isaiah was leaning on the counter. He had a look of mild panic. The oak tree had his upper limbs on his hips.

"My wallet's in my car," he said. "I don't have any cash on me."

"Whaddya need?" I asked, digging my hand into my front right pocket.

"Fifteen," Oak Tree said as he tapped the cash register. I dug a small wad of bills from my pocket and handed him a twenty.

"Man, thanks a lot," Isaiah said. "I can pay you back when we get to my car."

The mechanic handed me a five, and I put it in my pocket.

Isaiah rolled the remaining tire to the door, and I followed. We loaded it into the trunk.

"We'll have you on the road in ten minutes," I said.

And I was true to my word. In no time at all, we had the spare back in the trunk of his car and the repaired tire replaced. Isaiah lowered the jack, broke it down, and packed it back into the trunk.

"Thanks," he said, and we shook hands. "Let me get that fifteen bucks for ya."

I shook my head. "You know what? Don't worry about it."

"No, really," he said, and he moved toward his car.

"I won't take it," I said. "I really won't. A couple of years ago, someone gave me fifteen bucks when I really needed it. I've been waiting for a chance to do the same for someone else."

He stopped and looked at me. Stuck his hand out. I took it.

"I can't thank you enough," he said.

"I hope you re-adjust to country life," I said.

"Oh, I don't think that'll be a problem," he said. "I guess I needed to walk in a different pair of shoes for a while. I think we all need to do that, now and then."

"Yeah, we do," I replied.

I smiled and got into my car. As I drove off, I couldn't help but think of the strange irony that I had walked in his shoes—in a very literal sense—two years ago.

110

I found an Econo Lodge in Chattanooga, just ten miles up the road. Slept, got up the next morning, and should have been in London sometime in the afternoon. I was delayed by a massive traffic backup on I-75, the result of a bad accident involving several cars and a tractor trailer. Police had to route traffic off the freeway and through a small town. All in all, it was about a ten mile detour that put me (and a couple thousand other motorists) behind by about four hours. I wound up not getting into London until just after dark.

And I was dying to see Dawn again. To talk to her, to see her smile, hear her laugh. All day long, that's all I thought about. I cautioned myself not to get my hopes up too far. But I did. I remembered the first time her mask had slipped and I'd gotten a glimpse of the *real* Dawn. It killed me to think about the time when she'd come back into the motel room after a night of 'working.' I laughed out loud when I thought of Joe tied to the bed with the webcam streaming. And I remembered the moment I awoke to find her standing next to my bed in the darkness. I remembered her clothes tumbling to the floor, her warm, soft skin against mine. So, so many wonderful memories.

111

There weren't any motels in London. It only took me a couple of minutes to drive through town. I saw a sign for a big bed and breakfast, but that wasn't my style. However, I'd spotted a Holiday Inn Express when I got off the freeway a few miles back, so I headed back there and got a room (thankfully) with no problem. There was a Ruby Tuesday's just across the street, so I walked there and had a bite to eat. By then, it was nearing ten o'clock, so I returned to the motel and hit the sack.

I woke up just after eight the next morning. I didn't sleep very well. I had been pretty tired the night before, but I had too many thoughts running through my head. Mainly, I wondered how I was going to find Dawn, if she was still in London. I wondered if she'd made it back here, after all. I had no last name to go on, I didn't know the name of her mother, nothing. And I couldn't just start walking around the city asking people if they knew a former hooker named Dawn. I had no picture to show and could only remember her face by memory.

Those were the thoughts that went through my head all night long. I don't think I slept for more than twenty minutes at a time.

But I did have one piece of information, and I hoped it might help. Dawn said her mom had worked at a furniture store. She also had worked cleaning houses, as a housekeeper of sorts. That had been two years ago, but it was all I had.

A quick check of the yellow pages revealed three furniture stores in London. I took the phone book with me and traveled across town.

The first furniture store was closed down. It looked like it had gone out of business some time ago. The building was completely empty, and there was a FOR SALE/LEASE sign hanging in the window.

The second furniture store, only a few blocks away, was open. And that's where things got interesting.

112

I was greeted by a woman the moment I walked through the door.

"Good morning," she said. "Can I help you find anything in particular?"

"Yeah," I said with a smile. "I'm actually looking for a person. I'm wondering if her mom works here."

"What's her name?" the woman asked.

"Well, I don't know the name of the woman who might have worked here, but her daughter's name is Dawn."

"No last name?"

"I never got that."

The woman thought about it for a moment. "Seems to me there was a woman who had a daughter with that name," she said. "Her name was Donna. In fact, I think her daughter used to come and pick her up after work. Seems to me I remember her saying something like 'There's Dawn, right now. See you tomorrow.' She quit, though."

My mind was buzzing. "How long ago?" I asked.

The woman looked up, deep in thought. Her brow furrowed, and the right corner of here mouth cocked up.

"About a year. I had just been hired, so I didn't know her very well."

"The daughter . . . how old was she?"

The woman glanced up. "Oh, early twenties, maybe. Dark brown hair. Pretty."

My pulse accelerated.

"Do you know where she lives?" I asked.

The woman shook her head. "No, and I don't think we'd be able to give you that information, even if I did. Sorry."

I thought really hard to come up with another question that might give me more information. But I couldn't. I knew the woman couldn't dig through the files and find out what her address had been. Sure, I wanted to ask her to, but I didn't.

"Well, thanks," I said, and I turned to leave. Just as I reached the door, the woman spoke again.

"Carlton," she said in sudden recollection. "The woman who worked here was Donna Carlton."

I couldn't get to the car fast enough. I leapt into the driver's seat and flipped open the phone book I'd borrowed from my motel room.

Carlton, D. 344 Countryside Lane. 555-7967.

I flipped open my cell phone and dialed. It rang and rang. No answer, no answering machine.

Then, I flipped through the phone book again until I found a map of London. Countryside Lane was on the outskirts of town, maybe a mile or so to the east. I closed the phone book, dropped it on the passenger's seat, and fired up the Nissan.

My mind was spinning, my heart was thrashing.

Has to be the place, I thought. *That has to be it.*

Still, I cautioned myself that it could be another dead end. Donna Carlton (if she was Dawn's mom) might have moved. Dawn might have moved.

I'd know soon enough.

o o o

The house was easy to find, and I didn't try to be inconspicuous in the least. I pulled right into the driveway. The house was medium-sized, modest and clean. Sharp, even. Nice neighborhood. There weren't any cars around, except for the few that sat in the driveways of other homes. A couple of cars were parked on the street.

I got out of the car, and walked to the porch. My heart was hammering away, bruising my rib cage.

This is the place, I told myself. *I know it is.*

I rang the doorbell. Once. Twice. Again.

Nobody home. From what I could gather, though, the home was lived-in. The curtains were drawn, but there was no evidence the house had been vacated.

Well, I'll just wait.

I went back to my car got inside, and backed out of the driveway. I drove down the street, turned around, and parked on the side of the road. I had a clear view of the Carlton home and driveway.

And I waited.

113

I skipped lunch, not wanting to leave and take a chance of missing Dawn or her mom. I sat in the car for hours. Each time a car drove by, my heart cranked up a notch. *Is that her? Nope.* I was hoping that five o'clock—quitting time for many—would be more prosperous.

Throughout the day, I received a few suspcious looks from people who drove by. Countryside Lane was a sparsely populated neighborhood with nice homes. I'm sure someone had spotted the strange guy in the car, sitting there all day. I was actually surprised nobody called the cops. I wasn't doing anything illegal, but *I* would be suspicious of anyone sitting in a car all day long without getting out. Especially if the plates on the car were from another state.

But I didn't have any problems. No one came up to my car and asked what I was doing, no cop car appeared in my rearview mirror. My only trouble that day was boredom—until five thirty, when a car pulled into the Carlton driveway.

o o o

It was a blue Chrysler minivan. From what I could see, there were two people in it. If my heart had beaten fast earlier in the day, it was pile driving now.

The passenger door opened, and a person stepped out. A woman.

Dawn.

o o o

She was wearing a heavy, gray knit sweater and beige slacks. Her hair was longer. And her *face*. It was the face I remembered so very well. It was the face I'd seen when she dropped her mask. Only now, somehow, her face was different. It shined. She was radiant, just standing in the driveway next to the van. And when she smiled, it was the essence of happiness.

I placed my hand on the door handle.

Mom Carlton (I assumed) came around from the other side as Dawn slid open the panel door. Inside were a couple of grocery bags.

I pulled the door handle, and the door clicked open a tiny bit. Another car was coming up from behind, and I waited for it to pass before I opened the door and stepped out. The car—a silver BMW—went by, slowed, and pulled into the driveway behind the minivan.

A man got out. Slick, perfect hair. A long leather coat. Gloves. He looked like a banker or a stock broker. Young, maybe mid-twenties.

Dawn smiled. Glowed, actually. The man approached, the two embraced, kissed. I caught site of the gold flash on Dawn's left hand—and everything came crashing down around me. A vice clamped around my heart and squeezed. I watched as the man opened up the rear door of the BMW, then went to the minivan where he picked up a sack of groceries and placed them in the back seat of his car. He closed the door and returned to the minivan. I could hear them speaking. The man was offering to carry the last bag of groceries inside; Dawn's mom was waving it off, she could get it, she was fine. The man hugged Dawn's mom, gave her a kiss on the cheek. Then, Dawn hugged her mom and said something.

There was a moment when I almost—*almost*—threw the door open, intent on . . . *what?* I wasn't sure. Have a face-off with her man? Duke it out like in the movies? A western duel? I didn't know what I was about to do, but I almost did it. Something stopped me.

I gently closed the car door.

Dawn and the man got into the BMW. The car backed out and started coming toward me.

I turned my head down and to the side. I didn't want to be seen. I wanted to be two inches tall.

After the car passed, I looked into the rearview mirror. I saw the silhouette of Dawn. She was leaning toward the middle of the car, like she had turned around and was looking out the back window. Then, the car rounded the corner and was gone.

114

There's nothing like a long drive to put things into perspective.

Let the good expand and grow in your life, no matter what you're hit with. Somehow, there's a plan and a purpose in everything.

Those had been the words of Robert Clayton, two years ago, as he and I stood next to Ellen's open grave.

Somehow, there's a plan and a purpose in everything.

o o o

After Dawn vanished with her husband (or fiancee, or whatever) I just sat in the car, thinking. What had I expected? I knew all along that if I found her, things had probably changed, for better or worse. For her, obviously, it had been for the better. Still, I couldn't have her, and I never would. Oh, sure . . . I could have followed her home or wherever she went. I could have gotten out of the car and talked to her in the driveway. What would she have done? Thrown her arms around me? Ditch her guy for me? In my own fairy tale, sure. But I knew that wouldn't have happened. She had closed her door on her old life, including me. I know the letter she wrote two years ago had been heartfelt, but there had been no invitation in her words, nothing that told me to hunt her down, that she was waiting for me. She had told me the truth: she wanted to get her life straightened out . . . and she had. In a big way. She'd reconciled with her mom, most obviously. Ditched the mask. Found someone to love, someone to love her back. Despite the fact I was crushed that things were never going to be what I'd hoped for the two of us, she seemed incredibly happy. So happy. And that's what mattered most.

o o o

As I pulled away and turned the car around, I began to think about my trip from Bay City to West Palm Beach two years ago. I thought about Dawn, Joe, Arnold. I thought about Rucker the Trucker, and his lost boomerang, and how, when he'd finally found it, he decided to give it up. It was more important to someone else. I could almost hear his voice in my head.

Sometimes, things are only s'posed to be yours for a short time.

Maybe that's what stopped me from getting out of the car and making a fool of myself in front of Dawn and her significant other. Maybe Rucker the Trucker was right: things don't really belong to us—people included—and we're only meant to share a small amount of time with them. Sure, it hurts, sure it might seem unfair. Maybe that's just the way it is.

And I remembered the book I'd found in the dumpster, *Galaxy Quest*. It was a good book, and everything ended well. But books aren't real life. Sometimes, things just don't work out. Bad things happen, things don't go as planned. The hero doesn't always save the day, doesn't always get the girl.

But my book—my story—wasn't over. As I looked back at my life up to that point, I tried to look at it not as the ending, but the beginning. Maybe this was only the first couple chapters of the Life of Greg Chappell. I hoped so. Maybe the first few chapters were a little dismal, and things would get better. Hopefully, there were a lot of great things to come.

o o o

By the time I made it back to my apartment, I had put my thoughts in order. I had let Dawn go. That didn't mean it didn't hurt, and it didn't mean that I hadn't shed a few tears. But I was truly happy for her. Her life was good, and if there was anyone who deserved peace and happiness, it was her. Somehow, I had been a part of helping her realize something about herself: something that made her decide to leave me at the hotel room and go fix some things, get her own house in order. And yes, I'll admit it: I felt proud. She had told me in her note two years ago she thought I'd saved her life. Personally, I wouldn't go that far . . . but it made me feel good that I had a hand, in some small way, in helping her.

Somehow, there's a plan and a purpose in everything.

o o o

Mrs. Cutwieller was happy to see me and loaded me up with a tray of cookies and an entire apple pie.

"Is everything all right?" she asked, studying my face. Her eyes were ice-gray. All knowing, all seeing.

I smiled. "Everything's perfect," I said. Not only did I say it: I *meant* it.

"I can tell," she said, still studying my face. "You look lighter. Happier."

"I think I am," I said. "Thanks for the cookies and the pie."

o o o

Later that evening as dusk fell, I bundled up and took a walk down to the Saginaw River. The wind blew crisp and cold. Turns out, the snowstorm that was supposed to dump eight inches of snow all over Michigan earlier in the week had fizzled out. It dumped about three inches; most of it was melted by the time I got home. There were patches of it piled in parking lots and driveways. A few wilted, crusty snowmen had been erected by eager children. But winter was on its way, there was no doubt about that. Soon, a blanket of white would cover the city. The air would be frothy and arctic. The skies would be cloudy and gray.

Gray.

That had been a word Dawn had used in her letter to me two years ago.

Maybe there's too much gray, and you don't always see what's black and what's white.

It had been so simple when I was younger. Finding that silly quarter, so many years ago, and equating it to different points in life. Black and white. Right and wrong.

Dawn was right. Things aren't always like that. Some things just aren't black and white. Like the winter sky, some things are a mixture of both. Black and white makes gray, and sometimes it's hard—maybe even impossible—to separate the two.

I dug into my left pocket and found my quarter. I couldn't believe I'd managed to keep it for so long. For years, I'd carried it with me. I hadn't lost it, not once. Oh, I'd misplaced it from time to time. But I always found it.

It all seemed so childish now. The whole notion that everything is in perfect order, making perfect sense, just seemed so ludicrous. And that a black and white quarter could actually bring you luck.

Somehow, there's a plan and a purpose in everything.

And maybe that was it. Maybe nothing really makes sense in this world. Maybe it's our job to try and make sense of things, and try our best to understand them. But it sure makes things hard to comprehend or tolerate when you go around judging books by their covers. When I first met Dawn, I hadn't understood her behavior. Actually, I had been repulsed by her. But like my quarter, there were two sides of Dawn. Black and white.

While I never understood why four guys would rob and beat up someone else, I knew their motive was clear: they wanted money. That was black and white, for sure. Picking up live rattlesnakes? Black and white, right there. No gray area when it comes to pissing off poisonous reptiles.

I flipped the coin over in my hand, then cupped it in my palm. I drew my arm back and chucked it as hard as I could. It landed far out in the river, but I closed my eyes and never saw it hit the water.

THE END

About The Author

Christopher Knight is the author of 6 adult novels, and hundreds of short stories and magazine articles. Under his pen name (Johnathan Rand), he's written over 50 books for children and young adults, with over 3 million copies in print. Series include **AMERICAN CHILLERS, MICHIGAN CHILLERS, FREDDIE FERNORTNER, FEARLESS FIRST GRADER** and **THE ADVENTURE CLUB**. When not traveling, Knight lives in northern Michigan with his wife and two dogs. He is also the only author in the world to own a store that sells only his works: **CHILLERMANIA!** is located in Indian River, Michigan, and receives thousands of visitors each year. More at:

www.americanchillers.com

www.audiocraftpublishing.com